Magic *and* Loss

JOHN DAVID WELLS

iUniverse LLC
Bloomington

Magic and Loss

iUniverse books may be ordered through booksellers or by contacting:

iUniverse
1663 Liberty Drive
Bloomington, IN 47403
www.iuniverse.com
1-800-Authors (1-800-288-4677)

Because of the dynamic nature of the Internet, any web addresses or links contained in this book may have changed since publication and may no longer be valid. The views expressed in this work are solely those of the author and do not necessarily reflect the views of the publisher, and the publisher hereby disclaims any responsibility for them.

Any people depicted in stock imagery provided by Thinkstock are models, and such images are being used for illustrative purposes only. Certain stock imagery © Thinkstock.

ISBN: 978-1-4917-1480-5 (sc)
ISBN: 978-1-4917-1481-2 (e)

Library of Congress Control Number: 2013920217

Printed in the United States of America.

iUniverse rev. date: 11/13/2013

PART ONE

He stood at the window of the empty café and watched the activities in the square and he said that it was good that God kept the truths of life from the young as they were starting out or else they'd have no heart to start at all.

—Cormac McCarthy, *All the Pretty Horses*

1

Norton, Virginia
1950

J ACKIE RIDDICK PEERED OUT FROM his hiding place below a patterned wingback chair, wondering why his father was sleeping in a glass-covered wooden box in the middle of their living room. His father was wearing his dark blue double-breasted suit and printed tie, as if he was relaxing for a few minutes before going to church. Jackie rolled out from underneath the chair, scrambled across the room, and leaped into his mother's lap, clutching her so firmly she almost toppled over backward. Gripping her tightly with both hands, he buried his face into her chest, confused and afraid someone was going to grab him and stuff him into that scary, airless container. His mother stared straight ahead, her eyes glistening as she stroked Jackie's forehead, smoothing his dirty-blond hair away from his face. Grownups all around were crying out like the ones he heard a few months ago when Billy Joe was hit by a car in front of their house.

Unable to ignore the tension in the room, Jackie turned and opened one eye, peeking at the faces of his relatives and the grownups. Solemn, hollowed-eyed men in brown or black suits stood stiffly around the perimeter of the room like soldiers at attention, their hands cupped together in front of them, staring granite-faced at the casket. Pale, forlorn women in long black dresses were sitting on the sofa and chairs, weeping and crying, nervously wringing their hands together, bowing their heads, or sobbing fitfully into wrinkled tissues wet from tears. All of a sudden, Aunt Inez rushed toward Jackie's father, collapsing on top of the glass dome, her arms splaying out as if she was nailed to a cross. She pounded on the glass, lifting her head toward the heavens, unspeakable anguish spreading across her face, pleading—or demanding—that God change his mind and bring Emmitt back into this world.

In the mountainous region of southwest Virginia in the late 1940s, it was common practice to conduct open-casket viewings of the deceased in the living room. It was cheaper than a funeral home. At four years old, Jackie didn't know the difference between sleeping and death. He didn't understand why people were so upset, but he knew something was terribly wrong. So he began to cry too, pretending to realize his father was dead.

On a raw, blustery winter day shortly after the viewing, Jackie was trudging up a steep hill, struggling against a howling wind that swirled around him. He was following Donna and Danny, his older sister and brother, stumbling and crawling, desperately trying to keep up with the funeral procession in front of him. It was a long, torturous mountain climb.

Years later, when Jackie went back to his father's grave, he was amazed to discover that his father had been buried on a simple plot of earth atop a grassy knoll. The steep hill had been nothing more or less than a product of his mind and body trying to confront the reality of losing his father and the road he'd have to walk from then on. It was a strange experience, like going back to an elementary school as an adult and seeing just how small those drinking fountains really were. The procession finally reached the burial ground. Jackie spotted the same wooden box from the viewing suspended over a big hole in the ground, held up by a metal contraption and thick, coarse ropes. The glass covering was gone. Jackie couldn't remember any prayers or a funeral service of any kind. His only recollection was watching two strange men in gray overalls methodically lowering the casket into a bottomless black pit. There was no denying what it meant. Nobody had to tell him he was never going to see his father again.

The Riddicks lived in Norton, Virginia, a hardscrabble wreck of a hillbilly town with one main street that wound through the valley like a river flowing between two mountain ranges. This was the heart of the coal mining region of the South, a land and people hidden from view like an unwanted step-child, thoroughly forsaken by the rest of the country for more than two centuries. It was a town supported by hardworking, burned-out coal miners who, in the wintertime, literally did not see the light of day. There were low salaries, long hours, extreme heat and cold, no job security, no safety codes, no pensions, no health benefits, no unemployment insurance, and not the least bit of sympathy for the working man. Jackie's uncle Joe worked in the mines for twenty-five years before developing black lung and coughing himself to death. He once told Jackie that the boss man at one of the mines ordered him to carry a flashlight and toolbox into a collapsed, dust-filled, potentially combustible coal mine. Joe asked him, "Why don't you send in a mule for the job?" The boss man replied that he could always get another worker, but mules were expensive and harder to replace.

For a man, success in life was measured by a simple accomplishment: work above ground. If you did that, you were considered intelligent, crafty, ambitious, or just plain lucky. Jackie's father owned a small grocery store in town. Emmitt Riddick looked like a Hollywood leading man with his jet-black hair, deep-set hazel eyes, high cheekbones, and lady-killer smile. He died at thirty-three because he had rheumatic fever as a child and it damaged his heart. The doctor told him to stop drinking or it would kill him. One week before he died, Jackie's mother, Betty, found a half-empty bottle of raw whiskey hidden under the bed. Like a lot of men back then, he drank himself to death.

The men in Jackie's hometown were strong, athletic, rowdy, boisterous, rude, and spent a lot of time outdoors. They hunted, fished, camped, drank rotgut whiskey till they were bat-shit crazy, drove drunk and reckless down winding mountain roads, ran foot races, ran moonshine, and ran from the law. Southern men did everything in the extreme—working hard, drinking, fighting, cursing, bragging, hell-raising, chasing women, cheating, lying, and holy-rolling. Somehow these hard-living men who were secluded and forgotten in the flesh, blood, and bone marrow of Appalachia were held together by peculiar combinations of love, honor, brotherhood, respect, family loyalty—and the fear of burning in hell forever.

The women left home and school early because they knew they were just another hardship on the family, another mouth to feed. Betty's family was so poor that she had to go foraging for berries and ate bark off the trees. Single women got married, bore children, and grew wrinkled and old very quickly, and by the time they were forty, all of them had developed the same drawn, world-weary expression on their faces. In old family photos displayed on mantles, the women stare out of gray, faded pictures with cavernous black holes for eyes.

The women worked hard in the home, raised their children, went to pray at the Mt. Holiness Baptist Church on Sunday, formed sewing circles, baked delicious apple pies, and gossiped across backyard fences while hanging clothes on the line. On Saturdays, nearly identical women in plain cotton dresses and blue bonnets paraded downtown to the Piggly Wiggly. A big treat was buying everybody's favorite lunch: processed bologna sealed in plastic, a jar of French's mustard, and a loaf of Wonder Bread.

The land is about as beautiful as any on earth, filled with spectacular colors, proliferating foliage, breathtaking flowers in bloom. The woods are full of ferns, flowering plants, fire azalea, and seas of mustard carpeting entire meadows with bright flashes of yellow. The beauty of trees like white pine, red cedar, Fraser fir, cottonwood, and black birch are stunning scenery for hunters, hikers, and campers. The woods are full of sonorous birdcalls and wildlife is plentiful, with deer, bears, coyotes, foxes, box turtles, wild geese, and majestic eagles soaring over the tops of trees. The midnight-blue lakes are cool and placid, and clear cold streams rush down the mountainside. On most days, a pale blue haze shrouds the valley in the morning. The haze will linger on until the rising of the morning sun. Then it slowly burns away, thin wisps of smoke dispersing in the wind.

Nowhere on earth have I heard a more haunting cry of sorrow than the hunting hounds moaning in the night from the bowels of hell, booming nightmare cries echoing down the desolate, lonesome valley. My mother told me the hounds and owls lived together in peace in a place called Hoot Owl Hollow. She said the owls were hooting and the hounds were baying to remind everyone of all the pain inflicted on our people for so many years.

Two years after Emmitt died, Betty married Roy Shifflette after knowing him for only three months. Betty was in high spirits, because she thought she had found someone who was kind and willing to support a widower with three little kids. No one ever did figure out what Betty saw in Roy Shifflette. To everyone in Norton, Roy was a slack-jawed congenital idiot with a lazy eye and bad teeth. But Roy put on a good act in the beginning, keeping his life before Norton a secret, especially the two years he served in jail for savagely beating up Mildred, his ex-wife's mother. Roy told Betty that Tillie, his ex-wife, was a low-down whore who ran off with the town sheriff. Tillie had not exactly run off but had divorced Roy while he was in jail. He had quit school when he was fifteen and moved to a cabin in the woods to drink whiskey, hunt coons, and distill moonshine. He never caught a coon or sold an ounce of moonshine, but he did manage to drink himself into oblivion every night.

2

Baltimore, Maryland
1957

R OY MOVED THE FAMILY TO Baltimore, and they settled into a brick row house he bought with Emmitt's insurance money. The house was located in the middle of the black section of the city, and the Shifflettes were the only white occupants on the block. Things may have worked out, except Roy was a narrow-minded, bony-headed psychopath who hated black people. It did not take long for Betty to realize she had made a terrible mistake.

Roy landed a job at the Bethlehem Steel plant in Sparrows Point. He told everybody he was a "structural steel detailer," but in reality, he was a spot welder in a small machine shop adjacent to the main industrial complex. Roy hated the job and all his coworkers. "Too many goddamn Yankees and ball busters," was the way he described them. The feelings were mutual. Roy's fellow employees considered him one of the biggest assholes on the planet. They never called him by his first name; he was always "that Shifflette asshole" or "the Twerp."

The Civil War was still very much on Roy's mind, because he traced his ancestry back to John Brown, the fanatical abolitionist. Roy claimed John Brown was his great-great-grandfather. This was not true, although his mother did own John Brown's sword and rifle, stolen by a ne'er-do-well distant uncle at Brown's hanging in Harpers Ferry, West Virginia. Roy prided himself on his Rebel heritage, still carrying a grudge for having lost the war to the "fuckin' Federals." Roy had heard stories about John Brown's malevolent, demonic personality. He was doing his best to continue the family tradition. Roy attributed his sudden, sadistic rages to his infamous bloodline and in drunken, screaming monologues would bellow blustery exclamations like, "John Brown's body may be molding in his grave, but I'm alive and ready to kick some ass!" Unfortunately, the ones who got their asses kicked were his wife and three stepkids.

Three months after arriving in Baltimore, Roy had his first drunken, brutal outburst. On that day, it was all about the peas.

Donna never liked eating her peas. Just the thought of putting those slimy little green morsels in her mouth made her stomach recoil as if she had swallowed a big gulp of sour buttermilk. Donna said they tasted like rotten garbage, staining your teeth the color of a sick frog. On this particular night, she was determined to avoid ingesting those tiny little bastards, but at the moment there were not many options available to her; Roy was sitting across from her at the dinner table. He always insisted that the children eat everything on their plates. His logic was never entirely clear, but it usually involved comparing the kids' lucky lives to emaciated people starving in third-world countries, surviving on bugs and tree bark while suffering droughts, typhoons, and other terrible calamities.

Donna thought she had a terrific idea. Instead of eating her peas, she leveled the mound of peas on her plate, forming single rows, trying to give Roy the impression there were not enough peas to form a whole pile. Donna appeared confident her ploy would work on Roy since he was already blind drunk, slobbering over his own pile of peas. Betty was slumped in her chair, staring into space.

"So," said Roy. "What did you do at school today?"

The three kids glanced furtively at each other, not sure who he was asking. Donna, being the oldest, offered an answer.

"Oh, nothing much. We had a contest to see who could name all the capitals of the United States."

"Is that it?" demanded Roy, suddenly more alert, his elbows propped on the table, a knife in one hand, a fork in the other.

"What about dinner etiquette? They teach you how to behave at the dinner table in that fancy school?"

"Now, Roy," said Betty patiently, "let's not start something."

Roy delicately placed the knife and fork on the table in a pathetic attempt to appear refined and dignified, as if he was a Southern gentleman about to excuse himself in an upscale restaurant. He audibly sighed, shaking his head, indicating his disappointment with this sneaky little stepdaughter.

Suddenly, Roy leaped over the table like a bloodthirsty wolverine, grabbing Donna by the neck with both hands. He hauled her up, slapping her face back and forth like a rag doll, and then slammed her back in the chair. As she hit the chair, it collapsed beneath her, sending her sprawling on the floor clutching her face with both hands.

Quickly, Roy took a few steps in Donna's direction. He stood over her, thrusting his fists into the air like a triumphant boxer. Donna lay on the floor coiled in a fetal position, crying and shaking.

"You stupid little bitch! You think I'm stupid? I saw what you did! Now here's the rest of your peas! Eat them!"

Roy hurled a bowl of peas in Donna's face, covering her with a mass of green, wet slop. Danny and Jackie rushed to her defense, but Roy pushed them aside, whacking Danny in the head and shoving Jackie into a corner. Jackie hit the floor and banged his head against the wall. A steak knife was lying just inches away from him. He was about to reach for it, but Roy glared at him, screaming, "Jackie, go to your room!"

"Me? What did I—?"

Roy reached down, grabbed Jackie by the shirt collar, and slapped him in the face repeatedly.

"Roy!" Betty cried. "Are you out of your mind?"

She ran up to him, kicking his legs, thumping her fists on his chest. Roy looked at her. An evil grin spread across his face before hit her over the head with the empty bowl of peas. Betty crashed into the table like a sack of potatoes and rolled over, landing on the floor as food and tableware flew all over the kitchen.

"You're all a bunch of fuckin' idiots, ya hear! You think I don't know what's going on around here? You're all making fun of me behind my back, mocking me like a retard! Well, I'm not going to stand for it! Not in my house!"

Roy stormed over to the refrigerator, grabbed a beer, marched into the living room. He turned on the TV and sank into his easy chair to watch his favorite western, *Have Gun, Will Travel.* The kitchen resembled a war zone. Betty and the kids gathered themselves, surveyed the wreckage, and checked their physical condition. Luckily, no one was seriously hurt. Betty had an ugly bruise forming on her forehead. Donna's face and neck were still flushing red. No one said a word as they began putting the disheveled kitchen back together.

Donna finally spoke, uttering in a low, determined voice, "I don't care. I still hate peas."

THE NEXT MAJOR INCIDENT OCCURRED on a Saturday morning. Roy decided it was time to clean out the rats from the basement of the house. He stormed into the boys' room and shook Danny and Jackie awake, immediately ordering them to pick up the empty beer cans in the living room.

"After you knuckleheads finish, we're taking care of those rats in the cellar."

Danny and Jackie were still rubbing the sleep from their eyes. Danny was sitting on the bed, searching for some pants to put on. Jackie rolled over and covered his head with a blanket.

"What do you mean ... about those rats?" asked Danny.

"We gotta clear 'em out. You don't want rats running into your room at night, do you?"

As usual, Roy made the boys' lives miserable by giving them two choices they hated. It was impossible for Danny, who was fourteen years old, to stand up against Roy. Jackie had just turned twelve, but he was already planning on how he was going to kill Roy. Jackie rolled over and uncovered his head, asking, "How we going to do that?"

"Leave that up to me. Just get dressed meet me outside—and don't forget the beer cans."

The boys got dressed, walked into the kitchen, got a couple plastic trash bags, and collected the crushed National Bohemian beer cans strewn all over the floor. They went outside and dumped the trash bags in a large plastic container. Danny and Jackie didn't see their stepfather until he yelled from the base of the building.

"Hey, you two! Over here!"

They looked in the direction of the cellar and saw Roy swinging a huge sledgehammer into the brick foundation, smashing the age-old bricks into pieces, dust and debris exploding in the air. Quickly, Roy created a four-foot hole and tossed the remaining bricks into a growing pyramid next to the opening.

"Okay, guys. Come over here."

Roy had never served in the military, but he always imagined himself as a brave Marine overtaking a German stronghold. He saw the rats as pesky little German rodents to be taken out of their machine gun bulkhead.

"Okay, you knuckleheads. Grab a couple bricks. Now, I'm going in with this hammer and chase these mothers out of their happy little home. When they come out, smash 'em with your bricks—and don't miss, 'cause these are big suckers and I don't want them gettin' away."

The boys stared at one another, dumbfounded. Having no choice, Danny and Jackie grabbed two bricks apiece and reluctantly shuffled over to the pile. Jackie still had one thing on his mind: how to kill Roy.

"Wait a minute," said Roy. "Danny, come over here and look at this."

Danny dropped his bricks, cautiously creeping to the entrance. Roy leaned halfway into the cellar, the hammer still in his hand.

"Look at those creatures, will ya?"

Danny peered into the blackness of the hole. He couldn't see anything, but then a splinter of light shining through a floorboard revealed a nest of baby rats huddling together, squirming like tiny pink piglets. They actually looked cute to Danny. Suddenly, Roy swung his hammer, crushing the litter of rat pups, blasting a shower of baby rat flesh in their faces. Danny staggered backward nearly fifteen feet, slammed into the neighbor's fence, and slumped down the side, his legs collapsing underneath him as he hit the ground. He rolled over and wiped his face with his sleeve. Then he threw up. Jackie ran over to him.

"Are you all right?"

Danny's glassy eyes rolled around like he was punch drunk.

Roy hollered across the yard, "Come on, you little punks! Get your bricks! I'm going in! Get ready for these bastards!"

Jackie helped his brother off the ground. Danny wiped his mouth again while Jackie slapped bits of pulverized baby rats off his shirt. Jackie glared at Roy, thinking about a phrase he had heard from his mother: "If looks could kill." For a few seconds, Jackie tried to kill Roy by staring him down. It didn't take long to realize Roy was not going to die from his death stare. So he made a solemn vow to use a greater force some day.

"I said come on, punks!" screamed Roy.

The two youngsters shambled back to the entrance, obediently picked up their bricks, and waited sheepishly outside the gaping hole.

Roy squeezed his body through the opening, started waling away with a shovel. Without warning, a dozen nasty, angry rats stormed out of the hole, scurrying over the ground like the basement was on fire.

"You're missing them! You're missing them!" yelled Roy. "You little pissants! Hit the fuckers!"

Jackie tried to hit one of the rats but missed badly. Then he grabbed another brick and missed again, backtracking the whole time, hoping he wouldn't hit any of them. He glanced over at Danny. He had turned into a frozen lawn statue, his arms outstretched, gripping the bricks like they were seared into his hands. He wasn't going to throw anything anywhere.

"Goddamn it! You punks are worthless! You didn't hit one of them! Danny, you little shithead! What are you? A fuckin' mummy? Christ almighty, get back in the house! Pieces of shit ... pieces of shit ..."

SEVERAL MONTHS WENT BY WITHOUT an unprovoked outburst from Roy. "The Twerp" came home from the machine shop, ate dinner, and retired to his easy chair to drink National Bohemian beer and watch television. He wasn't into any sports except boxing. One time Jackie came home terribly excited that he had a chance to meet Gus Triandos and Willie Miranda, two prominent Baltimore Oriole baseball players. Roy was not impressed, calling baseball a "sissy game for fags." Betty would sit across from him on the couch, occasionally trying to engage Roy in conversation, but for the most part she kept quiet, taking cold comfort in the fact that at least no one in the house was getting beat up.

Roy forgot all about the incident with the rats. He ignored the gaping hole, which had taken on the appearance of a grotesque, screaming monster mouth. A few bricks were piled in front, but Roy was too lazy to rebuild the wall, so he just threw up some random bricks in a pitiful attempt to cover the opening. Mr. Harrison, the next-door neighbor, told everyone it looked like a wild boar with crooked bottom teeth mocking the neighborhood.

It was a quiet Saturday afternoon. The kids were playing stickball in the alley facing the back of an abandoned warehouse. Donna had already blasted three homers off the roof of the building. Danny was batting. Donna threw him a pitch that he fouled wide left over a fence.

"I'll get it!" Jackie yelled.

Jackie tried to climb over the fence. He managed to get one leg over; then his foot got caught between the white pickets. He didn't have enough strength to hoist himself over onto the sidewalk, and his leg was stretched too far to lift it back into the playing field. Donna came over to help. She tried to get his foot unstuck, but it was too far extended in the air. She decided it would be easier to lift his body over the fence onto the sidewalk.

"God, what a klutz," muttered Donna. "You look like you're stuck on a high-jump bar. No Olympic glory for you."

"Very funny. Get me off here."

"Okay, pal," said Donna. "Let's go."

As Donna was lifting Jackie off the fence to the other side, Roy came out the back door to get someone to buy him a pack of cigarettes just in time to see Donna lifting her brother over the other side of the fence. Roy's demented brain fired into warp speed, quickly assuming the wrong thing, as usual.

"What the hell are you doing? What the—?"

Roy ran toward Donna before anyone had a chance to explain. Danny thought he was mad because he had hit a foul ball out of territory. Donna knew from the crazed look on Roy's face that inexplicable violence was about to occur. She saw his beady eyes bulging out of their sockets, his skinny arms flailing wildly, his mouth twisting into a petrified grimace. Donna closed her eyes, her body stiffening, bracing herself for the onslaught.

Roy grabbed her by the shirt collar and punched her in the face, sending her sprawling to the ground, unconscious by the time she hit the dirt. Then Roy plucked Jackie off the fence and set him on the ground, brushing dirt off his clothes.

"Are you okay, Jackie?" he asked, ignoring Danny, who was kneeling beside Donna, shaking her into consciousness.

"Are you crazy?" screamed Danny. "Donna's hurt!"

"Donna's hurt? Who cares? She tried to kill Jackie!"

Jackie was going to explain that Donna was trying to help him when his mother emerged from the house running madly toward Donna, who was now sitting up and showing mild signs of recovery.

"Roy! What have you done? What's going on? Did you hit Donna?"

"Damn right I did, the murdering little bitch! Trying to kill her own brother! She deserves to go to reform school!"

"Kill Jackie? Are you nuts?" Betty raced over to Donna and bent down, examining a huge red welt forming under her right eye.

Donna kicked dirt in Roy's direction.

"He hit me! The son of a bitch hit me—for nothing!"

"Roy," said Betty, "this is the last straw."

She lunged at Roy, trying to yank her son out of his grasp. He was too strong and shoved her on the ground. Roy picked Jackie up and sprinted toward the Studebaker parked in the driveway, Betty, Donna, and Danny quickly giving chase. Roy got to the car, jerked the door open, and shoved Jackie in. Before anybody could do anything, Roy locked the door, cranked the engine, and slammed the car in reverse. He spun the sedan around and jammed the car in drive, squealing out of the alley, dirt and dust spewing from the back of the tires.

"Get back here, you bastard!" cried Betty.

Her frantic, pleading voice was ignored as the car disappeared down the alley. Betty turned around, looked at Donna and Danny, and dropped her head into her open palms, closing her eyes.

ROY DROVE JACKIE TO A cheesy, rundown motel and made him watch his favorite television shows. Before too long, Jackie was lonely, bored, and nauseated by the constant fetid smells of stale beer and leftover hamburgers from the White Tower. Betty called the police, but they informed her that Roy had broken no laws. They were reluctant to get involved in a domestic dispute. One young officer asked, "How can a man kidnap his own son?" Betty realized it was impossible to describe the intimidation and abuse of someone like Roy Shifflette, especially to policemen who didn't care too much in the first place.

After three days, Roy and Jackie pulled into the driveway and walked into the house, Roy acting like they had just gone out for some ice cream. As soon as he saw his brother and sister, Jackie ran and hugged them, jumping up and down with joy. Roy marched over to the television set and turned it on, promptly retiring to his easy chair. Soon *The Guiding Light*, a soap opera, appeared on the screen. After making sure Jackie was okay, Betty entered the living room looking drawn but determined.

"Where the hell have you been, you son of a bitch?"

"Fuck you."

"You had no right to take Jackie. Donna didn't do *anything* wrong. You're a monster—a complete and total monster!"

Roy bounded from his chair and clenched his fists, standing over Betty growling like a ferocious beast.

"You two-bit whore! Who do you think you're talking to? Monster? You and these rotten kids are the monsters! I work all day and night trying to provide for your thankless ass—and these worthless brats! I took them in, you hear! *Nobody* wanted these kids! *Nobody!* And by the way, nobody wanted *your* ass either! You're lucky I'm still around to keep you all from starving in the streets! Monster, my ass!"

Roy swung viciously at Betty's face, but she managed to blunt the severity of the blow with her hand and his fist grazed the side of her head, knocking her sideways on the couch. Roy continued beating her until he was exhausted. Betty never uttered a cry or made a sound. Roy had finally beaten everything out of her, including fear.

IT WAS THREE O'CLOCK ON a bitter cold February morning when Betty woke the kids up. She shushed them with her index finger to keep them quiet. She had packed the barest necessities for a new life. The bags were placed next to the front door. Betty could hear the soft shuffling of feet on bare floors as they were getting ready. Donna, Danny, and Jackie moved like clever little kittens around the house, getting dressed and gathering their things, and met Betty at the door. They snuck out of the house, breathing the brisk early morning air, waiting for Uncle Willie to arrive and make their escape.

Roy woke up early with a raging, hair-burning hangover. He looked at the clock and began cursing his rotten life, especially his lousy job at the steel plant. At first, he didn't notice anything unusual. Betty was not in bed, so he figured she must be making coffee. He went to the bathroom and then walked toward the kitchen. Betty was not there either. *Maybe she's in Donna's room,* he thought. Roy had been in her room before in the middle of the night, but Donna was too terrified to tell my mother about the visits. He peeked into Donna's room and saw an empty bed. For the first time, Roy became concerned. He bolted back to the other bedroom, looking for the boys. Now it was clear: the bastards had deserted him.

The first thing he destroyed was the couch in the living room. He retrieved a butcher knife from the kitchen and then ripped the couch to shreds, pausing only to throw one of his shoes through the television set. He began crushing all the furniture, slamming his foot through several pictures, breaking very mirror in the house. He shoved the refrigerator over on its side, spilling all the contents on the floor. Finally, Roy slumped on the floor exhausted, wondering where the hell those sneaky bastards were and already plotting what he was going to do to them after he found them.

Roy didn't know it, but the family was moving swiftly away from him. They were all riding comfortably in Uncle Willie's brand-new 1957 blue Chevrolet Bel Air along Highway 95 North, thankful to be free at last and anxious to begin a new life in Palmyra, New Jersey.

As she gazed out the passenger window at the open fields, meadows, and farmlands along the highway, Betty felt a welcome surge of relief and optimism. Things were finally going to get better. Life without Roy would be safer, more enjoyable, and her children's future would be happy and secure. It would turn out to be a fleeting moment of hope. Unknown to Betty, Donna was four weeks pregnant. Roy had raped her repeatedly.

Donna was looking impassively out the car window at the huge expanse of the Delaware Memorial Bridge, staring at black plumes of smoke billowing from the grimy smokestacks at the DuPont chemical factories. She also felt a rare moment of peace and tranquility, but this too would be fleeting. Donna didn't know she was pregnant either.

Danny was sleeping contentedly. Jackie was quiet in the backseat, thinking about how pleased he was to get away from his stepfather. He thought about Roy's violent fit of anger over a small portion of peas and how close he had been to that kitchen knife. *Just a few more inches and I could have sliced that bastard's guts open.* The thought of seeing Roy lying on the kitchen floor bleeding to death made him feel strangely serene. As Uncle Willie drove across the bridge into the flatlands of New Jersey, Jackie continued to enjoy thinking about the day he would return to Baltimore and plunge a knife into that worthless piece of shit.

3

Palmyra, New Jersey
Spring 1958

T HE MID-MARCH WINDS WERE BLOWING briskly as two lively, high-spirited boys ran about twenty yards apart in the far corner of the baseball park playing a vigorous game of catch. Suddenly, one of the boys, who was wearing a Baltimore Orioles cap, took off sprinting as fast as he could while the other boy heaved a high fly ball over his head, forcing the kid with the Orioles cap to race it down at full speed. The boy caught up to the ball, lunged out, and grabbed it with his glove, then instantly spun around, his hat flying off his head, and fired a soaring moon shot back in the direction of his companion.

On an adjacent field, Coach Osa Martin was finishing up the second practice of the new season, telling the kids to grab all the equipment and sit on the bench for a few last-minute instructions. He looked down the third baseline and spotted a neglected baseball lying in short left field.

"Hey, Louie!" he cried. "Don't forget the one out there!"

Out of the corner of his eye, Osa spotted a figure moving swiftly along the grass a couple hundred feet away. He gazed into the distance, detecting a youngster with a glove dashing across the field, desperately trying to run down a fly ball. Osa had been around a long time and knew instinctively that there was no way the kid was going to catch up to the ball. Still, somewhat bemused by the youngster's effort, he continued to stare long enough to see the boy unexpectedly accelerate with breathtaking speed, tracking down the ball and making an outstanding over-the-shoulder catch in the webbing of his mitt.

"Does anybody know those boys out there?" asked Osa, pointing and turning to his squad, who were now clowning around on the bench, restless and waiting to go home.

The boys on the team turned toward left field, peering into the green expanse of the outer reaches of the park. A few shook their heads. A couple players muttered no. Apparently, none of the players had seen the extraordinary catch.

Osa found it hard to believe that none of his players knew about two other kids their age that could play baseball in this small town. He decided to forego last-minute instructions.

"Okay, fellas, that's it for today. See you all next Saturday. Louie, would you mind putting the equipment in the car? I'll be right back."

"Sure, Coach," said Louie.

Osa left his team and walked slowly toward the two young men, who were still tossing the ball back and forth, seemingly unaware that other kids were playing on any of the three diamonds at Palmyra Memorial Park. Osa approached the taller youth, who was clutching his knees and gasping for breath like an Olympic sprinter moments after reaching the finishing line. The other boy, the one who had displayed his remarkable speed, was about ten feet away lying face-up in the grass, arms and legs splayed out in angel-in-the-snow position.

"Excuse me, son," said Osa, "are you two boys from around here?"

"Yes, sir," the boy replied politely. "Me and my brother here, we just moved to town."

"Well, I'm Osa Martin. Glad to meet you. Where do you boys live?"

"Over on Broad Street," said the youth, pointing beyond the other side of the field.

Osa glanced in the direction the boy indicated. He knew Broad Street very well. It was in the black section of town where there were only a few white residents. The two young men lived only a few blocks from Osa's house.

"Are you boys on a team this year?"

"What team?" asked the taller one.

"We have a Little League here in Palmyra."

"We don't know anything about that," said the taller boy.

The shorter boy was listening to the conversation and stood up, shaking off bits of grass from his pants and shirt. He looked up at the towering, neatly dressed black man, who looked a lot like his idol, Willie Mays.

"You have teams?"

"Yes, we do," replied Osa. "Six teams, ages ten through twelve. How old are you guys?"

"I'm twelve," said the shorter boy.

"I'm fourteen," said the taller one.

"And neither of you guys are signed up for a team right now?"

"No, sir," said the taller boy. "Are you some kind of coach ... or something?"

"Yes, I coach the Kiwanis Tigers. We just finished practicing over on number two field. What are your names?"

"I'm Danny Riddick," said the tall one. "This is my brother Jackie. We just came from Baltimore."

Osa looked over at Jackie, who was absentmindedly tossing a ball into his glove.

"Well, Danny, I'm afraid you're too old for my team, but you are eligible for our Babe Ruth League. The ages there are thirteen to fifteen. Jackie, you can play in our Little League. You say you're not on a team yet?"

"No, sir. I don't know anything about any league or anything. We just got here. We played a lot of sandlot ball around Baltimore before we moved to the city."

"Would you guys like to play some real baseball this year?" asked Osa.

"Yes, sir!" cried Danny.

"Me too!" yelled Jackie.

"That's great, fellas. Danny, I'm going to put in your name to be picked for the William's Fuel team in the Babe Ruth League. Harry White is the coach. He's a friend of mine and a very good coach. Jackie, I am going to sign you up for my team. Is that okay?"

"Sure," said Jackie.

"That means you can't sign up for anyone else, right?"

"Right."

"Okay," continued Osa, "my team is practicing next Saturday right over at field number two—that one over there—where I just came from. You fellas be there at ten o'clock. Danny, Mr. White will be here and give you all the information about his club. Is that okay with you guys?"

The boys nodded.

"Now, don't forget," said Osa, turning to leave. "Don't sign up for another team. Got that?"

"Yes, sir!" the boys yelled in unison.

Osa left the two brothers and began walking toward his station wagon. He suddenly turned around and hollered back to the boys, "Hey! Danny! Jackie! What did you say your last names were?"

"Riddick!" cried Danny. "We're the Riddick brothers!"

Danny and Jackie slumped down in the grass, watching the dominating figure of Osa Martin striding across the abandoned field, the sun gleaming down on his broad shoulders.

"He seemed real nice," said Danny.

"He sure did," said Jackie. "Damn, he looks like a black John Wayne. All he needs is a horse."

"Yeah, I bet he was some athlete in his day," said Danny. He was thinking about cowboy movies where the hero rides off into the sunset.

"I can't wait for next Saturday," said Jackie. "I wonder if we're good enough to play."

"Of course we are! We're gonna be all-stars!"

"I hope so," muttered Jackie. "I'll be happy to make the team."

"They can't be much better than those kids in Arbutus. We played some tough competition."

"I guess you're right," said Jackie. "We're gonna be awesome all-stars!"

Danny rolled over on his side, grabbing his mitt. "That's the spirit! Hey, let's go down to the record store!"

"No, you go on ahead. I'm going to check out that luncheonette place across the tracks."

"Suit yourself. I'll see you back at the house."

LINCOLN'S LUNCHEONETTE WAS A TINY, gray, bullet-shaped diner on Main Street wedged between two nearly identical brown Cape Cod houses. Jackie had heard it was the place where all the cool kids went after school to hang out with their friends, smoke cigarettes, drop nickels in the jukebox, and gobble up submarine sandwiches, sodas, and ice cream sundaes. As he opened the door, he was startled by the sudden ringing of high-pitched bells clanging above him. Jackie quickly turned around, placing his hands on his head and bracing himself as if someone was going to hit him. He looked up at the bells and relaxed as the door slowly closed behind him, leaving him alone in the diner.

He turned back around and noticed a row of six red-topped swivel stools placed in front of a slick chrome countertop. There was a large fire-engine-red Coca-Cola dispenser stationed next to stacks of sundae dishes, soda glasses, and aluminum napkin containers. Behind the counter, colorful commercial signs advertised Pepsi Cola, Chesterfield cigarettes, and Lady Borden's ice cream. To the left, there were five red-and-white checkered booths lined along the wall near a shiny rainbow-striped Seaburg Select-O-Matic jukebox. Jackie didn't see any customers or employees. Then a pretty raven-haired girl wearing a pair of black pedal pushers and a tight, short-sleeved pink sweater materialized from a blue curtain hanging next to a cigarette machine. Her surprising appearance reminded him of a beautiful actress pulling back the curtain, making a dramatic entrance onto the stage.

"Can I help you?" she asked.

Jackie said nothing, staring at her, wondering how someone who looked his age could be working in a luncheonette.

"I don't know," he finally stammered. "What do you have?"

The girl smiled and then pointed to the wall behind the counter. "Well, there's the menu. We have mostly hamburgers, sandwiches, and ice cream sundaes—and sodas, of course."

Jackie looked up at the menu. Items and prices were listed on both sides of a Royal Crown Cola clock. A hand-printed sign next to the menu read, Hot Fudge Sundaes: Twenty Cents. The girl slipped under a break in the counter and stood behind a bulky white cash register.

"I guess I'll have a hamburger, french fries, and a Coke."

"Okay," she responded cheerfully. "Comin' right up!"

She grabbed a glass from the counter, dipped it in a bin of crushed ice, and poured a Coke from the dispenser.

"Here you go," she said, placing the Coke on the counter.

"Thanks."

Jackie hopped up on one of the stools, placing his glove on the stool beside him. He glanced down and spotted a row of metallic plungers for syrup toppings above a storage bin displaying cartons of ice cream flavors.

"Were you playing baseball?" she asked, putting on a white apron. She retrieved a patty from the refrigerator and tossed it on a blackened, grease-stained grill.

Jackie glanced at his glove, feeling anxious, as if he had done something wrong.

"Yes, me and my brother were having a catch."

"Are you new in town?"

"We just moved here from Baltimore."

"Hence the cap."

"What?"

"Did you forget you had it on?"

"Oh, right," Jackie muttered, taking it off and putting it on top of his glove.

The girl gave Jackie an engaging smile. "It's okay to wear your hat in here. This isn't church, you know."

Jackie shrugged, not sure if she was making fun of him. Beads of sweat were forming on his forehead, tiny droplets already beginning to drip into his eyes.

She returned to grilling the burger but momentarily turned halfway around, speaking over her shoulder.

"Baltimore? That's a long way off."

"I know. We came here because my uncle lives here. He sells used cars."

She flipped the burger a couple times. "Do you know what school you're going to?"

"I'm not sure. My mother is checking that out."

"What grade are you in?"

"Sixth."

"Oh," she said, "you'll be going to Charles Street School. We're in the same grade."

She turned away from the grill, clutching a silver spatula. "My name is Vera Lincoln. What's yours?"

"Jackie Riddick."

"Nice to meet you. You'll like Palmyra. There's lots of fun stuff to do."

"I guess your parents own the place, huh?"

"That's right. We live in the back. I'm just filling in for my dad."

Jackie pulled his shirt out and wiped his forehead with the bottom of his T-shirt. He kept staring at Vera. She was the most beautiful girl he had ever seen. She was a slim, petite girl with a smooth complexion and delicate features, already possessing head-turning beauty with gleaming violet eyes, long eye lashes, full red lips, shoulder-length black wavy hair. Jackie thought she looked remarkably like Elizabeth Taylor in *National Velvet*.

"How do you like it?" she asked.

Jackie shook his head slightly like he was trying to remember his own telephone number. "What?"

"Your hamburger. How do you like it? Medium? Well done?"

"Oh, medium's fine. Just ketchup. No mustard."

Jackie took a sip of his Coke and swiveled around on the stool, pretending he was on an amusement park ride, clutching the sides, kicking his legs back and forth. All of a sudden, he was jolted by the bells ringing above the door. He stopped instantly, bracing his left foot against the floor railing. He grabbed his Coke, trying to look cool and nonchalant. He turned around, spotting an older youth with a protruding hawk's nose wearing Wrangler dungarees and a plain white T-shirt, walking impassively toward him. As he neared, Jackie almost fainted from the oily aroma of Vitalis Hair Tonic coating his slicked-back, greasy pompadour.

"Enjoy the ride?" he asked, unraveling a pack of Lucky Strikes from his rolled-up sleeve.

"I was just fooling around," said Jackie, wondering if the guy was going to beat him up.

"Hey, don't worry about it. They're, you know, *swivel* stools. What the hell are you *supposed* to do in them? Want a cigarette?"

"No, I don't smoke."

"Oh, a ballplayer," he said, looking down at the hat and glove. "You like the Orioles?"

"Yes."

The older boy smacked the pack of cigarettes down on his right-hand index knuckle, extracted a cigarette, dangled it from his lips. He grabbed a Zippo lighter from his hip pocket and held it out in front of him, like he was inspecting a rare coin. He paused dramatically, then flipped the lid, sparking an instant flame with one quick, single snap of his fingers. Jackie was impressed; he had tried but could never do that trick. To Jackie, it put the older boy in a class with Houdini.

"I don't know why you like those pathetic Orioles," he asserted, blowing smoke in Jackie's face. "They suck."

"I know."

"Triandos is a pretty good catcher. That new guy on third base …"

"Brooks Robinson."

"Yeah, he might make it." Unexpectedly, he reached out his hand. "I'm Bumpy Bowers. Who are you?"

"I'm Jackie Riddick."

Jackie shook his hand, relieved that apparently he wasn't going to get beat up after all.

Bumpy ignored Jackie, ambled over to the jukebox, and started looking over the selections. Vera finished up Jackie's order, placing the hamburger and fries on the counter.

"Here you go. Anything else?"

"No … no thanks."

Vera cried out, "Bumpy, can I get you anything?"

"Just a Cherry Coke, Vera. Thanks."

"Hey!" yelled Bumpy. "When are you going to get some new tunes in this place? Some of these records are from the forties, for crying out loud."

Vera smiled at Bumpy. "Come on. You know Dad likes that old stuff. The record guy is coming in next week. I'll tell him to put in some new ones."

"I can't believe you don't have any Little Richard."

Bumpy slipped a nickel in the jukebox. Seconds later, the wailing, electric-guitar sound of Chuck Berry's "School Days" exploded from the jukebox. Vera brought a Cherry Coke to Bumpy, who was lighting another cigarette with the tip of the old one, tapping his feet, snapping his fingers to the beat.

"Thanks, Vera. I love that line—'even the teacher don't know how mean she looks.' Boy, did I have some mean-looking teachers. You know Mrs. Bointner?"

"Yes, I've heard of her."

"Mean as a snake ... but I think she kinda liked me. I remember the day I quit school. I went in to hand her my books, and she asked me if I was sure I wanted to quit—being just sixteen and all. I told her school wasn't for me, and she said that was probably true, and wished me luck. You know what the last thing she said to me was?"

"No, what?"

"Happy birthday, Bumpy. In front of the whole class. It was pretty funny, really. Me quitting on my sixteenth birthday. Didn't stay one day too long."

Vera gave Bumpy a thin smile and then went back to the counter and began washing a few dishes. Jackie ate his food in silence, listening to the music. He was trying to think of something else to say to Vera. Meanwhile, Bumpy played "Don't You Just Know It" by Huey Smith and the Clowns. Jackie was forced to shout above a rocking piano, "Oh, Vera! Can I ask you something?"

Vera flung a dishrag in the sink and approached Jackie.

"Sure, Jackie. What do you want to know?"

"That fun stuff ... the fun stuff you mentioned. You know—things to do in Palmyra. What are some of them? You know ... I'm kinda new here ..."

"Well, there's lots of sports, as you can imagine. We go ice skating at Strawbridge Lake in the winter—and sledding down Highland Avenue. In the summer, there are boat races you can watch down by the Riverton Yacht Club. There's a glee club, a jazz band that plays in the park on Wednesday nights. Lots of community-type stuff, mostly for old folks. Things like card clubs, bowling leagues, garden clubs, and church groups—things like that. Oh, yes! The best thing is the dance at the community center every two weeks. They have a cool deejay that plays great records! Just like on *American Bandstand!* My friends and I go to every one. You should come to the next one on Friday night."

"I'd like to."

"Do you like rock 'n' roll?"

"Sure."

"Do you like to dance?"

"Well … I'm afraid I'm not too … ah … musical."

"That's okay. Maybe I can teach you."

"Really?"

"Sure. Let me write down the address. It's easy to find. It's right across from Mac's."

"Mac's?"

"That's the soda fountain downtown where everybody goes after school—if they don't come here. It's in the middle of town, right up the street about a mile. You can't miss it."

"Do they sell records?"

"Yes, they have a pretty good selection."

"I think my brother is there right now. What time do the dances start?"

"Around eight o'clock—until eleven."

Vera wrote the address on a napkin and handed it to Jackie.

He took the napkin, finished off the last of his fries, and then got up to leave.

"How much do I owe you?"

"Sixty cents."

He reached in his pocket, dropped three quarters on the counter. "Keep the change."

"You sure?"

"No problem. Call me Mr. Money Bags."

"Oh, are you a rich kid?"

"Hardly. I deliver papers in the afternoon—the *Philadelphia Bulletin.*"

"Well, Mr. Money Bags. Come again."

"It was nice meeting you, Vera."

Vera smiled broadly at Jackie. "Yes, it was nice meeting you too."

"I hope to see you again real soon."

"We'll see," said Vera. "We'll see."

Jackie grabbed his hat and glove and turned to leave. Bumpy was still smoking, gyrating to the music. As he was leaving, Bumpy called out to him, "Hey, kid! You sure you don't want a cigarette?"

JACKIE LEFT LINCOLN'S AND HEADED for home, walking quickly another half-mile down Main Street before he turned left onto Broad Street. In a few minutes, he arrived at the apartment Betty had recently rented. It was a tiny two-bedroom apartment on the second floor of a faded-green, neglected colonial home in desperate need of basic repairs. The washed-out paint was chipping, peeling from all sides, and several exterior boards were dry rotted. The tiny lawn was a sad mixture of dirt and gravel, patches of water-starved grass, and overgrown weeds split in the middle by a cracked, buckled cement walkway leading to the front porch. The owner, Mrs. Antonioni, lived by herself downstairs. She had never bothered with any improvements on the house since her husband died ten years ago. Jackie went over to the side of the house and bounded up the rickety set of rusted metal stairs leading to the apartment. He opened the door to the living room and immediately saw his sister Donna dancing frenetically to a rock 'n' roll song using the bedroom doorknob for a partner.

He shouted above the raunchy sound of "Betty Lou Got a New Pair of Shoes," "Hey, Donna! What are you doing?"

Donna twisted her body around, still clutching the doorknob. "I'm dancing, silly! Come here. I want to show you some new dance steps!"

The record was spinning inside a lunchbox-sized RCA red-and-white portable record player placed on the end of the coffee table. A dirty penny was Scotch-taped on top of the arm of the needle to keep the record from skipping. Scattered records with multicolored labels were spread out over the floor like tossed playing cards. Donna continued dancing with the doorknob. Jackie walked over and slumped on the couch, watching his sister swinging her hips and legs like she was squashing a hoard of fire ants. Her long, wheat-colored ponytail flew out of control, smacking her cheeks, her head bobbing up and down to the crazy beat. She was the very essence of teenaged kinetic energy, an electric jitterbug.

The song ended, but Donna kept jumping in the air, waving her arms as if the song was still playing. She rushed over to Jackie and flopped on the couch, breathless.

"Is that a *hot* record, or what!"

"Yeah, it's great. Where'd you hear that one?"

"South Street in Philly," said Donna, rummaging through her record collection like she was missing one.

"There's a *really* hip record store over there. They played it Friday night at Hy Lit's dance party, and everybody went nuts over it. Are you gonna learn to dance, or what?"

"Well, that's funny. You're the second person today who has offered to teach me to dance."

"Oh, yeah? Who's the other one?" asked Donna, picking up a record and staring at the label.

"A girl I met at the luncheonette."

"Lincoln's?"

"Yeah."

"Oh, right. Hey, there *is* a cute girl working there. She's your age too, buddy."

"I don't know … dancing seems kinda—"

"Kinda what?"

"For sissies."

Donna rolled her eyes toward the ceiling, addressing an unseen deity. "Jesus, how on earth did I get such a dork for a brother?" She placed a record on the spindle and paused, sighing. "Listen, Jackie, let me ask you something."

"What?"

"Do you want to be a virgin all your life?"

"Of course not."

"Well, you better learn how to dance—and learn how to dress while you're at it."

"You think you can teach me—to dance?"

"Of course! All we have to do is watch *American Bandstand* every day and copy all their moves. As for dressing your skinny ass, leave that up to me."

"We don't have any money for clothes."

"Look, Romeo. You don't need a lot of money—just style. For starters, don't wear white socks."

"But these are for baseball!"

"I don't mean while you're playing sports, goofus. When you go out—to the dances, school, the snack shop—don't wear white socks, okay? White socks spell d-o-r-k! I can't have a brother of mine with a hint of uncoolness. You seen *Rebel Without a Cause*, right?"

"Yeah."

"Well, learn to walk and talk like James Dean. Mumble a lot. Look confused. Act like you don't give a shit about anything. Walk like you're stuck in molasses ... This girl, what's her name?"

"Vera."

"Why did she offer to teach you to dance?"

"There's dances every other Friday night at the Community Center. She sort of asked me to go."

"Sort of?"

"Yeah."

"Look, my pathetic little bird-brain brother. Girls don't sort of *anything*. Girls know exactly what they are doing. Got it? Boys know nothing. Boys are stupid—just like you. Girls are always ten steps ahead of you boys—so get used to it. If she mentioned teaching you to dance, she likes you. Period."

"Really?"

"Yes, really. So you better watch *American Bandstand* with me on a regular basis. Maybe there *is* hope for you ... but, I believe to my soul, it's too early to tell. By the way, dorky, I'm going to try and get into *American Bandstand* as soon as I can. I'm taking the bus over to Philly."

"By yourself?"

"Sure. Why not? It's in the middle of the afternoon."

"Well, be careful. I don't know about those Philly guys."

"Well, that makes us even, because I sure don't know about you either, dear brother."

"Where's Danny?"

"In the bedroom. I think he's sleeping."

"Did he get any records?"

"I don't know. I didn't see any. So do you want your first dancing lesson? It's Saturday. *Bandstand*'s not on."

"I'm kinda beat. I think I'll take a nap."

"Suit yourself, kiddo. The doorknob's working just fine."

Donna reached over, slid the record down the spindle, and switched it on. The next sound was the earth-shattering shout of Little Richard screaming "Good Golly Miss Molly!" Donna pranced over to the doorknob once again, dancing with reckless abandon, oblivious to her surroundings.

A MONTH LATER, ON A warm April afternoon, Jackie was walking home from a baseball game. It was a beautiful, cloudless Saturday afternoon. Many residents were outside lounging on their front porches, doing chores, washing cars, mowing lawns, or playing street games. Some of the men were busy doing odd jobs while others were socializing, drinking, and gambling. Strange music resounded from open windows and cars, speakers blasting electric guitar riffs blending seamlessly with soulful vocals: "You got me doing what you want me, baby, what you want me to do" … "I'm gonna get up in the mornin', I believe I'll dust my broom" … "The eagle flies on Friday, and Saturday I go out to play" … "I'm like a one-eyed cat peeping in a seafood store, one look at you, I see you ain't no child no more" … "At last, my love has come along" …

He cruised past a crowd of mostly older black kids playing a chaotic game of dodgeball in the street, zigzagging to and fro like a dozen skittering pinballs careening wildly off rubber bumpers. The game looked similar to the one he had played in Baltimore. He heard one of the kids scream, "You're out!" as he walked by without anyone acknowledging his presence.

On one porch, he spotted tight-lipped, accusatory grandmothers in cotton dresses and broad floppy hats rocking back and forth, fanning themselves, observing the men drinking and gambling while nodding to each other, casting aspersions on these poor, lost souls who had somehow strayed from the path of holy righteousness.

In one backyard, Jackie spotted an attractive young black woman wearing tan short shorts and a blue blouse trying to cope with two little toddlers running underfoot as she was hanging clothes on a line.

While her youngsters were giggling, tugging on her shorts, begging for attention, she calmly clutched two clothespins in her left hand, two in her mouth, and withdrew a damp shirt from a straw basket before clipping it firmly to the line. Then she playfully chased the kids around the yard, their squeals of laughter growing louder.

Farther up the street, three spirited skinny girls were playing on a cement driveway, swinging Hula-Hoops wildly around their waists in earnest competition to see who could outlast the others. He waved to a skinny girl in pigtails jumping rope double-dutch style in the middle of her two friends, who twirled the ropes in speedy, looping windmills. The girls were laughing raucously, singing a silly nursery rhyme at the top of their lungs:

> *Strawberry shortcake, cream on top,*
> *Keep on goin' till we can't stop.*
> *Look out Corrina, you're gonna drop!*

The girls smiled at Jackie, waving their hands energetically for him to come over and join them.

"Come on!" yelled the one in pigtails. "Get in the middle! I bet you can't last ten seconds!"

He laughed, shrugging his shoulders and holding up the palms of both hands, a sign of complete helplessness.

"Sorry, but you're right! I couldn't last *five* seconds!"

Jackie was cutting across Market Street when he spotted a gray-haired black man sitting in a broken lawn chair beneath one of the maple trees. The old man was dressed in faded denim overalls, a stained red T-shirt, and a battered brown fedora full of holes pulled down tightly over his face. He was bending forward, arms folded together, resting his hands on a carved wooden cane. A half-empty quart of Pabst Blue Ribbon beer was leaning against the lawn chair in the shade. Jackie wondered if he was homeless. As he was passing by, the old man looked up, peering at him with drowsy, half-opened eyes. Jackie figured he must be homeless and drunk.

"Where you goin', young man?" the old man asked, tipping his hat backward.

Jackie wasn't going to stop, but the old guy seemed harmless enough. And the stranger aroused his curiosity. He reminded Jackie of the old men who used to sit outside his father's grocery store in Norton, telling him funny stories.

"I'm going home," he said, pointing in the distance. "Over there—on Broad Street."

"What's your name, son?"

"Jackie Riddick."

"Well, I'm Rufus Johnson. Nice to meet you."

"It's nice to meet you too."

"You a baseball player?"

"Yes, I play for the Kiwanis Tigers."

"Oh, yeah? Who's your coach?"

"Coach Martin."

"Did you say Martin?"

"Yes, Coach Osa Martin."

The feeble old man squeezed his eyes closed as if a puff of dust had blown in his face. He reached down awkwardly, steadying his frail body with his cane, grabbed his bottle, and slowly took a sip of warm malt liquor. "Osa? Did you say Osa?"

Now Jackie was convinced the old codger was drunk. He turned to leave.

"You mean *Mighty Man* Martin, son!"

Jackie turned around and faced the old man. "I've never heard him called that."

"I know'd Osa Martin is his given name, but in the day, he was the Mighty Man."

"I don't understand."

"Don't you know, young man? You is being coached by one of the greatest players in the Negro Leagues. Where you been?"

"I ain't been nowhere," Jackie muttered, wondering why he was still listening to this babbling old fool.

Rufus paused, shaking his head. "Well, you is certainly right there, young man. You *ain't* been nowhere. Don't *know* nothin', neither."

"Who did he play for?"

The old man suddenly rose up, waving his arms around his head like he was warding off a swarm of angry bees.

"Why, the best damn team there ever was! The Pittsburgh Crawfords! Won the championship back in thirty-five. Ole Mighty Man Martin played with the best of 'em. Satchel, Cool Papa Bell, Josh Gibson—all of 'em. Better believe it, son. Craws best baseball team ever! White, black, green—don't matter."

Jackie had never heard of the Pittsburgh Crawfords or any of the players the man named. He thought he was not only drunk but crazy too.

"How come I never heard about this before?"

Rufus drooped his head, shaking it slowly from side to side, as if pondering the very quintessence of man's fate in the universe.

"'Cause it's a cruel world, son. A cruel world. Don't nobody stand a chance, especially us black folks."

Jackie turned to leave.

"Hey, boy!" cried Rufus, shaking his finger at Jackie like a parent scolding a naughty child. "Look it up! Go on! Look it up, if you don't believe ole Rufus—but don't go tellin' Osa you heard it from me, okays?"

"Sure," Jackie said, shrugging his shoulders. "Whatever you say. I won't say a word."

He left the old man sitting in his chair. Glancing back one more time to see the man reaching for another sip of his Colt 45, Jackie continued walking home.

JACKIE ARRIVED BACK AT THE apartment and noticed the landlady, Mrs. Antonioni, sitting quietly on her porch, her eyes fixed on the abandoned field across the street. The field was virtually empty except for an old rusted-out bicycle; a couple of dry-rotted tires; and some empty, torn-up cardboard boxes. Jackie always tried to make a point of saying hello to Mrs. Antonioni, but in the few months he had lived here, she had never spoken to him. Betty said the woman didn't speak to her either and insisted that she simply put the rent check in her mailbox every month. Today was no exception. Jackie walked along the side of the house, glancing over at the elderly woman who, as usual, remained silent, staring straight ahead.

"Good afternoon, Mrs. Antonioni!" Jackie exclaimed, trying his best to sound upbeat and friendly.

Mrs. Antonioni continued staring at nothing but a patch of weeds and discarded trash. Jackie shrugged his shoulders and trotted up the stairs to the second-story apartment. His mother told him Mrs. Antonioni was sad because her husband had died ten years ago. Jackie didn't know much about life and death and grown-up behavior, but it seemed to him that ten years was a long time to be grieving over a lost loved one. He also had another thought: maybe she was just unfriendly.

He entered the apartment, dropped his glove on the couch, and went over to the refrigerator to get something to eat. He opened the refrigerator door, but there was not much in there except for a quart of milk, three carrots, a bowl of leftover tuna fish, and a can of Cheez Whiz. He walked to the cabinet where the canned goods were stored and found a small tin can of potted meat and a can of Spam. Jackie grabbed the can of potted meat and a plastic roll of Ritz Crackers, pried open the can, took a case knife from the drawer, and went into the living room to watch *American Bandstand.* He turned on the Philco television, adjusted the rabbit ears for better reception, and relaxed on the couch. At the moment, the song "Tequila" was playing. The kids were jitterbugging like crazy to a rowdy chorus of raunchy saxophones and deafening drums, swishing their hips manically side to side, moving their legs with astonishing speed and rhythm. Jackie tried to imitate some of these dance moves, but the kids were just too good. He saw one skinny kid wearing a thin tie and dark pants lift his partner by the shoulders and, in one silky smooth motion, hoist her high above his head, suspending her in midair. As she was spinning around, he pulled her down swiftly through his legs, brought her back up, and let her go, but not before completing the move with a full split, shifting his body left and right, and touching the floor with his fingertips before bouncing up and grabbing her hand once again.

The song ended. The camera shifted to Dick Clark, who was holding a microphone and standing behind a podium. Jackie liked Dick Clark. He was young and boyish-looking and neatly dressed and possessed a very soft, soothing voice. With his easygoing manner, he made all the kids feel comfortable, like he was just one of their friends chatting in their living room. Teenagers were getting a bad rap all over the country in movies like *I Was a Teenage Werewolf* and *Teenage Rebel,* and there were TV stories about "kids gone bad" doing shocking things like playing hooky from school, riding in fast cars, making out at drive-in theatres, carrying switchblades in their hip pockets, and smoking cigarettes. But Dick Clark had the ability to put parents' minds at ease. They could watch *American Bandstand* and feel secure that there was some hope for the future. These kids didn't look or act bad. Dick Clark treated kids with respect. He seemed like an older, wiser brother. Jackie tried desperately to convince his mother that rock 'n' roll and dancing were great fun and not the terrible worldly activities condemned by the Jehovah's Witnesses. But Betty refused to listen. She followed the strict teachings of the church, and no argument from Jackie could change her belief that this music and wild dancing were harmful and would lead a young person away from the true teachings of the Jehovah's Witnesses.

Dick Clark was about to announce the Rate-A-Record segment of the show. He went over to a plain chalkboard hung on the wall. The board contained three columns marked one, two, and three. Each contestant was going to rate three new records. Jackie was scarcely paying attention to the introductions of the kids. The first two gave their names, ages, and where they went to school.

Suddenly, he bounded off the couch, running toward the TV and pressing my face against the screen. Donna came into the picture! She was standing next to Dick, quietly asserting, "I'm Donna Wells, sixteen—from Palmyra High." Jackie was so excited he forgot nobody was home.

"It's Donna! Donna's on TV! *American Bandstand!*"

He was jumping and shouting in the living room, glued to the television set. Dick Clark played three records, and Donna gave them all good reviews. Her favorite song was "I've Had It" by Dickie Do and the Don'ts. Jackie noticed that Donna carefully avoided saying, "It's got a good beat, and it's easy to dance to." She always made fun of the kids who used that tired cliché. When Dick Clark asked her about "I've Had It," Donna said she liked the lyrics because she understood why guys would get irritated with a girl being late all the time.

Jackie continued watching the show, hoping to get another glimpse of Donna. He thought he saw her one time in the back of the studio, but he wasn't sure. The producers of the show made sure that the viewing audience saw their much-adored regulars as much as possible. They were the ones spotlighted by the camera. He felt like the luckiest kid in the world. How many other twelve-year-old boys could come home and watch their sisters on TV?

Jackie thought he had the coolest sister in the world.

ON THURSDAY, MAY 24, DONNA was standing by herself in a long line of teenagers at 4548 Market Street in Philadelphia, sweating uncomfortably in the heat while waiting to get into the *American Bandstand* show. She had been waiting for more than an hour. Gradually, the line in front of her moved up near the back door entrance, and at 2:30 p.m., a fat, bald man wearing a wrinkled brown suit escorted her with a group of ten other teenagers to join the other kids already chosen. Donna had never been so excited in her life, feeling like she was entering the Emerald City. She was so wound up she almost peed herself. The teenagers picked for the show were bunched together in the back as bored-looking technicians moved bulky, hard-to- maneuver cameras into strategic positions. Black, metal cylinder spotlights hung from the rafters, blazing down on the bare concrete floor, turning the tiny studio into a sweltering minifurnace. Thick electric cables coiled around the floor. As the stagehands were putting the set together, Donna, along with other members of the audience, was directed toward the aluminum bleachers to the left, where Donna climbed up to row ten, took a seat, and waited for the show to begin.

Donna didn't care about the heat, the hard floor, the burning lights, or the surprising ordinariness of the studio. She was on *American Bandstand,* and therefore she was in heaven. As she looked around, she spotted some of the regulars on the show like Pat Molittieri and Kenny Rossi sitting together in the front row. She had seen them many times dancing on the show, tried to copy their dances moves, spent hours reading about their personal lives in *Teen Magazine.* These regulars were the envy of thousands of teenagers watching the show every day and were becoming celebrities in their own right.

As she was waiting, she glanced around to see what the kids were wearing. Many of the girls sported brightly colored ankle-length pleated dresses or below-the-knee plain or plaid skirts with matching blouses. The girls from West Catholic High School wore sweaters over their school uniforms, little white collars flipped over the sweaters showing around their necks. Their shoes were mostly black-and-white saddle shoes or brown penny loafers. She couldn't help noticing the enormous attention they paid to their hairdos. The girls were mostly adorned with big, hair-spray induced beehives spiraling above their heads or medium-length cuts precurled with large, flowing waves. The boys were all required to wear suits and ties in order to avoid the blue-jean-T-shirt-motorcycle look of a juvenile delinquent like Marlon Brando in *The Wild One*. The boys did look very sharp in their sharkskin suits, tweed jackets, button-down shirts, and thin black or designed ties. The guys from South Philly tended to wear their hair shiny and slicked back, swept up in a high pompadour, while the boys from North Philly or South Jersey preferred their hair short, dry, and combed to the side like the suave detective Peter Gunn on TV.

The girls were giddy with excitement, nervously chattering in small groups, checking out the stylish boys, fixing their hair, earnestly discussing their favorite songs and dances. The boys tried to look cool, distant, and tough, like they were hanging out on one of South Philly's notorious street corners smoking cigarettes, flirting with the girls, and participating in nonstop neighborhood trash talk.

The stagehands were in the process of building the set for the show. Donna couldn't believe how cheesy the stage looked. The backdrop was a simple piece of painted plywood resembling a vintage record shop from the forties with pictures of old, clunky 78 rpms stacked on shelves. Dick Clark's bandstand was only a small, four-foot-high podium with a black 45 rpm record painted on the front with a plain white label in the middle. The word *band* was written on top of the label, and *stand* was printed beneath the circle.

A cute, dark-haired girl wearing a blue cardigan sweater buttoned in the back was sitting next to Donna. She leaned over and spoke to her.

"Hey, do you know who the special guest is today?"

"Oh, no," responded Donna. "I haven't heard."

A short kid with a big nose and beady dark eyes overheard the girls talking. "It's Danny and the Juniors!" he cried out. "They're gonna sing 'At the Hop!'"

"Oh wow!" exclaimed the girl.

"They're really boss!" yelled Donna.

Without warning, Dick Clark bolted from a back door behind the podium, sprinting energetically to the crowd smiling and waving his hands.

"Hello, everybody! Are you ready for *American Bandstand?*"

The kids in the bleachers instantly sprang to their feet, clapping their hands, whooping and hollering like their home team had just scored a winning touchdown.

"Yes!"

"We're ready!"

"All right!"

"Let's go!"

Dick stood in front of the teenagers with his face beaming, clapping his hands, still exhorting his exuberant fans.

"Okay, folks!" cried Dick, calming the kids by pushing his hands down in front of him. "We're going to start the show real soon, but we need three people for the Rate-A-Record portion of the show. Would anybody like to volunteer?"

More than half the crowd jumped up and down, pumping their arms wildly in Dick's direction. Donna leaped up, waving her arms, trying to get Dick's attention. He swung his arm around the audience, picked out two kids, and then looked and pointed directly at Donna.

"You!" he hollered. "The girl in the blue skirt with the brown hair!"

"Me?" asked Donna, looking around to see if there was another girl in a blue skirt with brown hair.

"Yes, you!" exclaimed Dick. "Now come on out to the dance floor, and let's get rockin' 'n' rollin'! Don't forget, couples only!"

Immediately, the throaty, fast-paced do-wop voices of the Silhouettes blurted loudly from the studio's speakers: "Shan a na na, sha na na na na ... ! Get a job ... !"

Donna was so excited she leaped from her seat and started moving down the row of steps. The dark-haired girl in the cardigan sweater yelled out to her, "Hey, blue skirt! He said couples only!"

Donna turned around, stared at the girl, and quickly put her hand to her wide-open mouth, her eyes rolling toward the ceiling.

"Oh, my God! I'm so stupid!"

All the kids laughed good-naturedly as Donna sheepishly returned to her seat.

"Hey, don't worry," said the dark-haired girl. "Somebody will ask you to dance."

Within a half-hour, Donna was stunned when a broad-shouldered, handsome teenager asked her to dance. She had seen him earlier slow-dancing with Carman DeCarlo and noticed the way he moved smoothly across the floor clutching Carman close to him during the song "To Know Him Is to Love Him." Now he was holding her in his arms, her head resting on the lapel of his tailor-made black suit as he glided her effortlessly among the throng of other dancers. They were playing "Two Silhouettes on the Shade" by the Rays: "Took a walk and passed your house … late last night. All the shades were pulled and drawn … way down tight."

Donna was almost too nervous to breathe looking up at Joey, staring into his deep midnight-blue, dreamy eyes. She was waiting and hoping he would say something to her; she had lost the ability to speak. When he finally spoke to her, she almost forgot the answer to his question.

"What's your name?" he asked.

"Donna."

"You from Philly?"

"No, South Jersey—Palmyra."

"You're a good dancer. I don't have any trouble leading you."

"Oh, I practice a lot—I make my brothers dance with me, so I can learn how to follow and not step on anybody's toes."

"You haven't stepped on mine."

Donna blushed, knowing she was acting like a preteen swooning over a picture of James Dean. "You're a terrific dancer—easy to follow."

"What are you doing tonight? Are you busy?"

Donna was shocked by the question. She had never even been on a car date. She had completely forgotten that guys his age could own cars.

"Uh … no," she stammered. "I was just going to go home on the bus."

"Why don't you come with me to the Chez Vous ballroom? Jerry

Blavet is the deejay tonight. It should be a lot of fun. We could go to the Upper Darby car hop, get a bite to eat, and then we can dance some more."

"That would be great! Let's go!"

DONNA WAS RIDING ALONG IN Joey Korkinian's 1956 diamond blue Ford Sunliner convertible with teardrop skirts, rolled and pleated interior, and a continental kit on the back. Joey was an eighteen-year-old amateur boxer who was known in boxing circles by his ring name, "Kid Kory." He was also well-known as "The Prince of South Philly." Without a doubt, he was considered one of the hippest, most popular kids in Philadelphia. As they rode along, Donna's long, sandy-blonde hair blew wild and free in the night-time breeze, and she glanced over at Joey, the very essence of modern cool, a Pall Mall cigarette dangling from his lips, his right arm slouched across the steering wheel. They were cruising along Marvine Avenue in Upper Darby, Pennsylvania, on their way to the Chez Vous ballroom. Donna flashed a wide smile and threw up her hands, shouting, "Whoopee!" as if she was a little kid again screaming down a wild roller coaster. Donna could not get over how good-looking he was. She figured he must be Italian because of his dark complexion and coal-black wavy hair and the classy way he dressed in a tight-fitting black suit and a thin maroon silk tie.

When they arrived at Chez Vous, Joey pulled into the parking lot and parked the car, and the couple walked into the elegant art deco ballroom. Donna had heard about Jerry Blavat, but she was not prepared for the dynamic ball of energy and excitement that Jerry brought to these dances. As they approached the dance floor, Joey whispered in Donna's ear, "You're gonna love this guy. He's lightning in a bottle." Donna looked up and saw a skinny, clean-cut young man on stage with slick black hair combed to the side, his high-collar white shirt already drenched in sweat. He seemed to be having a fit of bodily spasms as he began rocking his wiry frame back and forth, belting out a nonstop staccato stream of yowls, groans, gurgles, and roll-on nonsensical syllables like a Sunday-morning holy-roller preacher:

"Come on, South Philly! Come on, South Jersey! Come on, you yon teenagers! Once again, yours truly, the geater with the heater! The big boss with the hot sauce! Tick-tock rockin' swinging with the big tower of power—Chez Vous! Come on, now—here we go—

"Sixty seconds make one minute! Sixty minutes make one hour! Twenty-four hours make one day! And out of *that* twenty-four hours— *two and a half hours* are dedicated to the yon teenagers at the hippest club in the whole wide rockin' world! And yes! The hottest show on the radio! So without further ado, let's carry on through now!

"Five! Four! Three! Two! One! *Blastoff!*

"Once again, let's kick it off with that openin' Buddha that's bound to boot—fifteen million bootin' ... Buddha-scuddhas!

"This is the geater with the heater, yours truly! The boss with the hot sauce! Havin' my say, makin' it on my merry way—with the big boss sound of my main group—the group of all groups—comin' right out the bottle for you yon teenagers! *The Genies!*"

Joey and Donna raced onto the dance floor in the midst of a feverish crowd of delirious teenagers, jitterbugging to the pounding beat of the ear-splitting music:

> Who's that knocking on my door?
> All last night and the night before
> Boom, boom, boom, bang, bang, bang
> I can't stand this awful thing
> Who's that knocking on my door?

A crazed Jerry Blavet continued playing an astonishing collection of great rock 'n' roll and do-wop songs while exhorting his frantic fans with a barrage of spontaneous be-bop, motor-mouth monologues. Joey and Donna danced to every one of them, literally dancing the night away. Finally, it was after midnight before the show ended. Joey took her home, kissed her goodnight, and dropped her off at the apartment on Broad Street. It was one o'clock in the morning.

BETTY HAD BEEN SITTING IN her favorite chair all night worrying about Donna. She was sitting in the dark, trying to read her Bible but unable to relax and fall asleep. She knew Donna was becoming more uncontrollable, and if there was a lively, rowdy bunch of teenagers out on the town, Donna would surely find them. Her thoughts drifted to the painful decision to have Donna get an abortion. As a Jehovah's Witness, the very idea of ending a life, even a life created by a monster like Roy, was against her religious beliefs. When Donna told her she thought she was pregnant, Betty had been horrified, feeling guilty for not realizing what seemed so obvious now. She had no idea what to do. Donna had told her mother that if she had to have this baby, she'd kill herself. Betty had believed her. Donna had mocked her mother, pointing out all the different ways she would commit suicide if she didn't get an abortion. She had threatened gruesome things: "I'm going to slit my wrists all the way up to my elbow." "You know those railroad tracks downtown? I'm going to stand in front of a train and let it squash me to pieces."

Finally, Betty went to Uncle Willie for help. Uncle Willie was a successful car salesman and had lived in Palmyra for a long time. Willie told Betty that Palmyra was too small of a town to get something like this done. "Too many nosy people," was the way he put it. He arranged for a doctor in Philadelphia to perform the operation and offered to pay for it. Betty found out later it cost a thousand dollars. Throughout the whole ordeal, it was Betty, not Donna, who was more anxious about the decision and the possible complications. Donna was totally composed and flippant when she entered the back room of the doctor's office. She joked with him, needling him: "Do you think you will go to hell for being a baby killer? ... What are you going to do with it? Flush it down the toilet? ... Can I get a discount on the next one?"

When it was over, Donna left the operating room acting nonchalant, as if she had just gotten her teeth cleaned. Betty was tortured by the obvious physical and mental damage inflicted by Roy. She wondered how much irreparable psychological trauma her daughter had suffered. Betty was beginning to notice that Donna was different from most sixteen-year-old girls. She found it practically impossible to get up in the morning and complained of horrible nightmares. She had some peculiar habits, like washing her hands three times and removing all her jewelry every time she sat down to eat. She wouldn't wear the color black on Wednesdays. She would occasionally talk to herself when she was alone. Betty learned later that she was talking to imaginary friends.

She had strange phobias like being deathly afraid of dogs, lawnmowers, Asian people, cigarette lighters, ketchup, elevators, and umbrellas.

Suddenly, Donna flung open the apartment door, still scatty with excitement, tossed her pocketbook on the couch, and twirled around the room like a tipsy ballerina, singing, "To know, know, know him, is to love, love, love him ... and I do!" She didn't even notice her mother slumped in her chair. In her dizzy, boy-crazy enthusiasm, Donna had completely forgotten to call her mother and tell her where she was going and who she was going with. Donna stopped spinning around and looked into the corner of the room, glimpsing a faint outline of her mother.

"Oh my God, mother! I forgot to call! I'm so sorry!"

"Where were you? I was about to call the police. You scared me to death."

"I'm sorry! I went to *American Bandstand,* and this boy—a real nice boy—asked me to this dance outside of Philly. I just—"

"Why didn't you call me?"

"I forgot! I swear—"

"Don't say, 'I swear,' Donna. It's inappropriate language. How could you forget to call me? It's inexcusable."

"I was so excited! I saw Dick Clark and this boy—Kory—asked me to dance, and he ... then we went right from there to this fantastic dance hall, and—"

"Enough! I don't want to hear about your fancy dance hall. In other words, you have no excuse. You're just irresponsible."

"No, I'm not! I promise it will *never* happen again! Promise!"

"Donna, you could have been kidnapped, or worse. Don't *ever* do that again."

"I won't! You have my word of honor!"

"All right. I'm too tired to deal with anything right now. I'm going to bed."

"Wait!"

Donna walked over to her mother, lifted the Bible from her lap, and held it in front of her, placing her right hand on top of it.

"Mother, I swea—I mean, I *promise* on my oath and this Bible, I will never again stay out late without calling you—promise!"

"All right … all right. Goodnight, Donna."

Betty stood up wearily and walked slowly to her bedroom, leaving Donna standing in the middle of the room holding the Bible.

Neither Betty nor Donna knew it then, but this incident was only the first of many, many nights when Betty sat waiting and worrying late into the evening with frazzled nerves for her selfish, party-girl daughter to come home.

Part Two

You see you spend a good piece of your life gripping a baseball,
and in the end it turns out that it was the other way around.

—Jim Bouton, *Ball Four*

4

Palmyra Memorial Park
Fourth of July, 1958

I T WAS A PERFECT DAY for a baseball game.

The blazing sun was rising steadily over a row of tall poplar trees lining the back of the left-field bleachers at Palmyra Memorial Park. The entire Little League field was rapidly transforming into a dazzling, sun-drenched coliseum reminiscent of the glory days of ancient Rome. Shimmering rivulets of red, white, and blue reflected off the patriotic flags, posters, sparklers, decorations, ribbons, and brightly dressed fans pouring into the park. From high above the rolling cumulus clouds, the dazzling colors bursting from the field appeared to be sparkling sunbeams glittering off a lake of precious stones.

In the stands, tiny, pig-tailed tots were already giddy with excitement, jumping up and down in their seats, frantically waving their miniature flags in the air. The kids were desperately trying to get the attention of George Palmer, one of the school board members, who was wearing a flashy, sequined Uncle Sam costume and wobbling along the sidelines high atop a pair of rickety wooden stilts. It appeared as if he was going to lose his balance any second, but George somehow managed to toss handfuls of candy to the youngsters without toppling to the ground.

In the middle of the bleachers, a flirtatious young woman in blue short shorts and a low-cut red V-neck blouse was leaning back in her seat, showing off her curvaceous figure and slender legs. With her wavy platinum blonde hair and ruby-red lips, she looked like Marilyn Monroe playing a scene in a movie as she inhaled a deep drag off a cigarette and blew out a gusty plume of smoke with dramatic flair, leaving a sticky red smudge on the tip of her cigarette. Marty Casey, the designated town drunk, couldn't help but notice the eye-catching woman in the stands. He was leaning on the chain-link backstop wearing a silly Statue of Liberty hat, drinking whiskey from a plastic cup. Marty, hoping to grab her attention, suddenly belted out an incoherent, drunken version of "God Bless America."

A few curious fans in the bleachers looked down at Marty, wondering why this pathetic buffoon was even allowed to attend the game. But unfortunately Marty's lively vocal performance was wasted on the vivacious lady with the sexy legs. She never even noticed Marty; she was too busy staring at George Palmer, with whom she was currently having an affair.

On the sidelines, a cute, red-headed majorette in a skimpy scarlet uniform and matching boots tossed her silver baton high into the air. She turned around full circle, waved enthusiastically to the crowd, and then extended her hand and let the airborne baton land perfectly in her waiting fingertips.

Occasional clusters of snapping firecrackers and exploding cherry bombs blasted off in the distance while the pounding drums and brassy horns of the high-school marching band clanged and boomed like a thundering cavalry charge. Beyond right field, on a side street, nonstop dueling horns blared from a collection of antique cars, trucks, and fire engines. A blue and white Good Humor ice cream truck pulled up next to the curb rattling its tinkling bell, creating an army of riotous kids pleading to their parents for a dime followed within seconds by a screaming mob of youngsters rushing to the curb as if the Good Humor man was the Pied Piper in a starched white uniform.

The short-sleeved, neatly dressed crowd was settling into their seats, sipping Cokes, chomping down on hot dogs, munching peanuts and Cracker Jacks, lapping up ice cream cones, pulling tufts of cotton candy off sticks, or chattering away while fanning themselves with the program for today's game. Wholesome-looking, Norman Rockwell families gathered together on the corrugated aluminum benches, watching the pregame action on the field, soaking in the myriad sights and sounds of Independence Day in small-town America. The sights and sounds blended seamlessly into the baseball smells ascending from the grass, dirt, dust, and sweat on the field. In the stands, pungent aromas from pipes, cigars, and cigarette smoke floated in the breeze, merging with the smells of hotdogs, hamburgers, ketchup, and mustard wafting from the makeshift booths of the Palmyra Lion's Club. In the dugout, two youngsters were adjusting the rawhide laces of their Spalding gloves while sniffing the grimy leather, which still reeked from a slathering of Neatsfoot oil over the winter. One of the players, trying to get a better grip, nervously rubbed handfuls of dirt into the handles of his white ash Louisville Slugger.

Jackie Riddick and several other City League All-Stars were in the outfield catching lazy fly balls off of Osa Martin's fungo bat. Jackie surveyed the growing crowd filling up the bleachers, wondering if his mother had made it to the game. She disapproved of baseball almost as much as *American Bandstand,* because she felt it occupied far too much of Jackie's time "in the world." But Jackie had begged his mother to attend, telling her that Danny would come with her and help her feel at ease. Betty was uncomfortable in large crowds.

Suddenly, Coach Martin hit a high fly ball over Jackie's head. Jackie quickly turned around and chased the ball almost to the fence before snaring it over his shoulder. Before throwing the ball back, he took a few steps toward the bleachers, hoping to catch sight of Vera Lincoln. He spanned the entire outfield from right field to left and was about to give up when he recognized Vera and her mother sitting together near the left-field scoreboard. Jackie waved to them, tipped his cap in their direction, and was rewarded with a waving hand and glowing smile from Vera. Jackie ran back to shallow centerfield, his heart pounding even faster than it had been five minutes ago.

In the stands, fathers of all ages sat together with their sons or grandsons, pencils in hand, quietly explaining the rules for scoring the game with their red, faded, dog-eared scorebooks, preserving the history of ball games played on other fields in other hallowed, mythical eras. More than a few of the scorebooks were considered nearly as holy as the family Bible, and the father-son scorebook ritual was considered a truly special occasion, almost as sacred as attending church on Sunday.

The hometown crowd loved every glorious moment of this annual holiday combining the celebration of America's Independence with the great national pastime. Perhaps no two other social events better signified the glory and triumph of a country that had managed in less than two hundred years to create a stable democracy, win two World Wars, and establish the highest standard of living in the world. Baseball just *seemed* like a patriotic sport, an integral part of a distinctly American culture creating its own mythology with legendary gods to worship like Ruth, Williams, Mantle, Mays, and DiMaggio.

At the moment, the carefree fans in the park felt very good about themselves. Any suggestion of an undercurrent of impending social disturbance or psychic discontent stirring among a few of the townspeople would have brought only derision and disbelief. This was, after all, the golden land of opportunity, the great melting pot of American assimilation. If the majority of people in the stands had cared to look, they would have noticed different minorities congregating in the park segregated into isolated clusters with friends and family. But if they weren't on the field or managing, they may as well have been on the dark side of the moon.

And if they chose to look even closer, some patrons in the crowd might have noticed that one of the City League teams was named the Indians. Of course, there were no Native Americans in the ballpark that day. The only visible image of those vanished inhabitants was a cartoon of a goofy Indian with a big-toothed grin plastered on the front of a couple baseball caps.

As more fans entered the park, Louie Foreman, the catcher for the Kiwanis Tigers, was squatting on the sidelines warming up Nate Green, the starting pitcher. Without warning, Nate reared back, hurling a sizzling fastball from his high-arching right hand, scorching Louie's mitt and spraying glove dust in his eyes. Louie wiped the dirt from his burning eyes, wincing in pain from the throbbing in his left hand. He grabbed the ball out of his mitt, shaking his glove like it was on fire.

"Hey, Nate!" screamed Louie. "Ease up! Save some heat for the game, okay?"

Nate gave his catcher a quizzical look, seemingly unaware of his own strength. Feeling a slight breeze on the back of his neck, Louie instinctively checked out the tallest American flag waving in the distance. It was positioned directly behind the centerfield fence, blowing straight out toward Strawbridge Lake and the Palmyra Country Club. *Maybe Ritchie will hit one out today,* he thought as a sweeping curve came slicing in from the big right-hander.

On the other side of the diamond, Bob Jennings had just finished warming up his pitcher, Mike Barnes. The two players were members of the Sacred Heart Yankees in the Catholic League who had challenged the best players from the City League for the past four years. The Sacred Heart team had won every game. As the two young men huddled together at the end of the dugout, Bob gazed warily in the direction of Nate Green.

"Jesus, that guy throws hard," said Bob, wiping his sweaty face with the sleeve of his shirt.

"Did you ever bat against him?" asked Mike.

"No," said Bob, "but Dale Headman faced him last year before he came to play with us. Dale swore he never even *saw* the ball."

Mike looked across the infield. "Did Dale give any advice on how to hit this guy?"

"Yeah. He said to get to him early—don't let him settle in. He also said he's got control problems, so take as many pitches as you can."

"You tell Coach O'Toole?"

"Yeah. He's gonna include that in his pregame speech."

Mike reached down, picked up a fist-full of dirt, and tossed it toward the third baseline. "Shit, do we have to listen to that same old pregame rah-rah speech?"

Bob shrugged, glanced at Mike. "Only if you want to pitch in this game."

Mike audibly sighed and began rubbing the baseball with both hands, smoothing out the seams with his thumbs. "I guess that's the price you pay. Anyway, we're not going to lose to these jokers. We haven't lost yet, right?"

Bob leaned forward, resting his forearms on his knees. "Yeah, we've won every year, but I don't know … they look a lot better this year."

"Are you kidding?"

"No, I hear this new guy Jackie Riddick came out of nowhere, and that lousy Kiwanis team hasn't lost a game since they got him."

Mike stared at the baseball in his hand like it was a crystal ball. "Waddaya mean he came out of nowhere?"

"He's new in town; that's all I know. Coach Martin found out he could play and grabbed him up."

"No surprise there," said Mike, flipping the ball to Bob. "Coach Martin knows his stuff. He could out-coach O'Toole blindfolded."

Mike stood up from the bench and stretched his arms out wide, staring into centerfield just as Jackie was running down a weakly hit flair. Sprinting rapidly and closing fast, he kicked in his blazing afterburner speed, took a flying leap into the air, and caught the dying quail in his glove seconds before it hit the ground.

Mike thoughtfully rubbed his chin.

"That, I guess, would be Jackie Riddick."

"I'm afraid so," said Bob.

THE OVERFLOWING CROWD WAS ANXIOUS for the game to begin. The constant chatter among the local fans was mostly about how evenly matched the teams were this year. The supporters for the City League All-Stars were eager to end the four-year losing streak and felt the team could beat the Catholic squad with their improved pitching, defense, and hitting. In addition to Jackie, the clean-up hitter Ritchie Edwards was a new member of the team. He had just moved to the area from South Carolina. Ritchie was a tall, muscular black player with superlative skills who played left field. He was also notorious for hitting monstrous, tape-measure home runs.

Ritchie had already contributed to local folklore. That summer he had become the first Little Leaguer to hit a home run over the center-field fence clear out of the park, the ball splashing somewhere in the middle of Strawbridge Lake. The only witness to see the ball hit the water was fifteen-year-old Harry Greenfield, who was fishing in the lake at the time. Harry said he heard the roar of the fans inside the ballpark and looked up to see a baseball rising like a mortar over the centerfield flagpole.

According to Harry, he followed the flight of the ball until it came crashing down on the head of an unsuspecting mallard duck paddling in the middle of the lake. Harry swore the stunned duck made a futile attempt to fly but collapsed dead in the water, rapidly sinking to the bottom. The story may or may not have been true, but it was colorful enough for county residents to forever afterward refer to the home run as the "duck-pond shot" without any need to mention who hit the ball.

The rest of the starting team was a collection of solid players, especially the slick-fielding double-play combination of Jimmie Harlow at shortstop and Billy "Archie" Steele at second. Kurt Cummings, anchoring third base, possessed sure hands and a strong, accurate throwing arm. First baseman Phil DeMarco, although clumsy and slow, provided additional power, having slugged eight home runs so far in the season. The weakest player was Dave Carmichael in right field, who wasn't much of a hitter but played a steady right field. The savviest player on the team was catcher Louie Foreman. Louie was the unofficial team leader and was known for boosting morale, soothing fragile egos, and encouraging players who made errors or struck out in crucial situations. Nothing ever seemed to rattle Louie. He was mature beyond his years. All his teammates called him "Captain Lou."

The coach of the City League All-Stars was Max Dunberry, a chain-smoking, square-jawed veteran of the Korean War who had led his Rotary Cardinals to a first-place finish the previous year. Dunberry was considered an excellent coach, noted for his fiery brand of leadership, aggressive style, and determination to make his own decisions. As he often noted, "I don't play by the book—I coach." Dunberry was only forty-eight years old but looked much older. He was a short, stout man with heavy lines on his face; deep-set charcoal-gray eyes; a pale, sallow complexion; and a slight beer belly protruding from his tight-fitting Rotary T-shirt. He sported a close-cropped crew-cut already a shade of gray-white. His attire was simple and constant. Few people ever remembered him wearing any other outfit than his Rotary Cardinal T-shirt, black cotton slacks, baseball cap, and US Keds sneakers.

The assistant coach of the All-Stars was Osa Martin, a forty-five-year-old black man who had been coaching the Kiwanis team for five years. Coach Martin commanded a great deal of respect in the community and had been picked for the job of assistant coach because he was considered the most knowledgeable baseball man in town. He was six feet two inches tall, powerfully built, an imposing figure with broad shoulders, a muscular upper body, and a trim waist. It was often said that he looked in good enough shape to play in the major leagues. Osa's social presence was enhanced by his large, intense, dark eyes, high forehead, and prominent nose. His short hair was just beginning to show traces of gray at the temples. He was a sharp dresser, always wearing neatly pressed khakis, colorful sports shirts, and black, low-cut Converse sneakers. Osa Martin was a solemn, taciturn man, but when he spoke in his deep, full-throated voice, it seldom left any doubt about what he meant to say.

At the moment, Coach Martin was still hitting fly balls to the outfielders while Dunberry was delivering infield practice. Martin was distracted from hitting fungoes, because he was concerned about Nate Green. He kept looking over at Nate and Louie warming up on the sidelines, trying to see if Nate was getting the ball over the plate. He turned again just as one of Nate's pitches bounced in the dirt in front of Louie. Osa waved his outfielders in from the field and trotted over to Nate and Louie. In their meeting before the game, Osa had suggested to Dunberry that Jackie should start the game, pointing out his superior control and the advantages of starting a left-handed pitcher. Since Dunberry was the designated coach of the team, he had seniority over Assistant-Coach Martin. Dunberry had overruled Martin. He had told Osa he was confident the Sacred Heart kids would never get around on Nate Green's blistering fastball. Osa had taken the decision with quiet consternation, figuring that Dunberry was probably right—to a point. If Nate Green was on his game, the All-Stars would be hard to beat. Osa reached the sidelines beyond first base and stood next to Louie.

"How's he look?" asked Osa.

"Not bad," said Louie. "His fastball is ripping my glove off, and the curve looks okay—if he can get it over the plate. I'm gonna start them off with the heat and see if they can catch up with it. Maybe he won't need the curve too much."

"He's getting the fastball over?" asked Osa, glancing in Nate's direction.

"Most of the time."

Louie looked up at Coach Martin, and when their eyes met, they expressed the same gnawing concern.

"He better get it over," said Osa.

"And if he doesn't?"

Osa paused. "Well, Louie, let's just say it might be a long day." Osa waved his hand toward Nate, indicating that warm-ups were over.

As COACH DUNBERRY WAS FINISHING up infield practice, he surveyed the playing field. The grounds crew had worked all week getting the field ready for the big game. The infield was an all-dirt surface smoothed out by a large heavy roller, bits of debris and pebbles carefully removed, creating a glass-like, level infield. A landscaping crew had been brought in to spruce up the outfield grass, transforming the normally dry, clumpy playing area into a lush green outfield. The groundskeepers had also limed the field to perfection, straight white lines extending outward from home plate to the left- and right-field foul poles.

The diamond itself was flanked on both sides by two sections of bleachers with fifteen rows of benches extending twenty yards past the first and third baselines. From left to right, the outfield bleachers started at the 215-foot foul pole in left field, crescent-mooned around the outfield grass, angled to the 235-foot sign in centerfield, and then tapered off at the 210-foot foul pole down the right-field line. The outfield fence was a uniform, eight-foot chain-link fence plastered with a series of multicolored four-by-six plywood billboards advertising local businesses. A large red and blue wooden scoreboard donated by Howard's Delicatessen was located in foul territory adjacent to the left-field foul pole. Eddie Dunberry, Coach Dunberry's eight-year-old son, hand-operated the scoreboard from his seat perched beside the foul pole.

Dunberry always ended infield practice by driving a hot grounder to the infielders and making them fire the ball to Freddie Canton, the backup catcher, as they were rushing toward him. Freddie would glove the ball and then toss a slow roller to the incoming player. The player would grab the ball barehanded and toss it back to Freddie before sprinting into the dugout. Dunberry ran the drill without any infielder missing a grounder or flubbing a toss from Freddie. When the last player on the field threw the ball home, Dunberry walked toward his anxious players sitting in the dugout. He saw them huddled together on the bench making nervous small talk, tossing balls up in the air, compulsively adjusting their uniforms, hats, and gloves.

The coach stood next to Martin at the end of the bench. He took out one of his Chesterfield cigarettes, lit it, and took a deep drag before pulling the lineup card out of his back pocket. He stared down at the row of boys, who became instantly silent, knowing it was time for the lineup announcement.

"All right, guys, listen up. This is the way we're gonna start. Remember, everybody gets to play, so don't worry if you're not out there right away."

Most of the players already knew who was going to start the game based on the way practice had been held, with certain players getting more batting and fielding than others. The only thing they didn't know was the exact batting order.

"I want Jimmie Harlow at short, leading off," announced Dunberry. "Jimmie, make sure you take as many pitches as you can. This kid Barnes is really tough, especially on right-handers, so we need base runners any way we can get them.

"Archie, you're on second, batting number two."

Billy "Archie" Steele, as usual, was sitting next to Jimmie Harlow, his best friend since first grade and half of the slickest double-play combination the county had ever seen. Billy was nicknamed "Archie" for a good reason. Everyone in town said he was the spitting image of the comic book character because of his light skin, freckled face, burnt-orange wavy hair, and beaming smile. Some of the kids also called him "Elvis," because he loved to sing rock 'n' roll songs in the dugout and always had a transistor radio glued to his ear so he could listen to the latest hits on station WIBG across the river in Philadelphia. Archie told everyone that he was going to be the first combination major-league baseball player and rock star in American history.

"Jackie," continued Coach Dunberry, "you're in center field in the three hole. Remember to be patient. He's not going to want to give you anything good to look at.

"Ritchie, you're clean-up. Don't be too anxious and overswing. Barnes will try to throw you off with off-speed junk. Remember, this guy has three good pitches, so don't guess unless you're ahead in the count. If you get your pitch, hit it out—and don't be afraid to hit the duck pond!"

All the kids cracked up. Peals of laughter rolled down the dugout, loosening up a nervous bunch of young ballplayers.

Kurt Cummings, the designated class clown of the team, howled over the laughter of his teammates, "Oh, please don't hit a poor little ducky, you mean old man!"

Dunberry waited a moment for the kids to settle down. "Louie, you're behind the plate, number five. Kurt, you're at third, hitting sixth. Now be patient up there. Don't swing at any bad pitches."

"Don't worry, Coach!" exclaimed Kurt. "I've got my lucky charm!" Kurt reached in his back pocket and pulled out a dried-up dead spider tied to a string. Holding on to the string, Kurt dropped it between his knees, the spider swinging like a hypnotist's talisman.

"Jesus," said Coach Dunberry. "*That's* your lucky charm?"

"His name is Fred," said Kurt without further explanation.

Nobody was surprised at Kurt's odd selection of a lucky charm. He was the team prankster, and they were used to Kurt's off-beat antics. The most famous one was pulling down his pants and lighting farts with a cigarette lighter.

Dunberry continued reading the lineup card. "Phil, I want you at first base, in the seven slot. I want you and Kurt to play in real close to the first two hitters. Dave, you're in right field, number eight. Watch that fence out there. There's not much of a warning track, so don't go banging into the fence."

"Why not?" yelled Kurt. "It might knock some sense into him!"

Again the whole team exploded with shouts and laughter, a few players throwing their gloves in Dave's direction.

"Nate will pitch and bat ninth," said Dunberry, sticking the lineup card in his back pocket and motioning Osa to his side. "Okay, guys. Let's huddle up."

Immediately, the kids jumped up, forming a wide circle around the two coaches.

"Mr. Martin will be coaching first base, and I'll be giving the signals at third. Any questions about the signals? Remember, on my team if a player misses a signal he has to run five laps around the field after the game. So pay attention! Don't forget to check with Coach Martin before you go trying to stretch a single into a double. Also, be alert when you're on first base. If there's a passed ball, don't steal unless you know you can make it. Keep an eye on Mr. Martin and me for the signals. Got it?"

The players nodded seriously, their faces tightening, stomachs churning.

"Okay," said Dunberry. "Let's come together for a 'Go team!'"

The players crowded together, extending their hands into the middle of the circle, and on the count of three, they all screamed a spirited "*Go team!*" Then they ran to the bench while the coaches walked toward home plate to meet the umpires and the coaches of the Sacred Heart team.

Joe McGuire, the public address announcer for the game, was sitting in a booth above the field drinking a Coke and eating a bag of peanuts waiting for the game to start. His official scorebook, information about the players, relevant statistics, and personal notes were strategically placed on the table before him. Joe was perched high above the chain-link backstop cramped in a small room at the top of a tall concrete building. The aging structure contained restrooms, a tiny locker room, storage facilities, and a PA system consisting of a single microphone, amplifier, and two speakers facing the field on both sides of the cubicle. Joe had a perfect seat to watch the game. He was admiring the beautiful scenery in front of him, checking out the grassy outfield and smooth dirt infield, the throng of fans still arriving at the ballpark, and the fresh faces of the young ballplayers waiting anxiously in the dugout. Joe glanced down at the two opposing benches. He could not help but notice the sharp contrast in uniforms. Both teams wore itchy, baggy wool uniforms, but that was where the similarity ended. The Sacred Heart squad looked resplendent dressed in their brand-new white pinstripe uniforms with *Yankees* scrolled across the front in solid black lettering, numbers printed on the back. The white initials *SH* stitched into their black starched hats matched their heavy cotton black stirrups worn over white socks. Every team member wore identical, freshly polished black spikes.

On the other side of the diamond, the City League All-Stars were clearly not as stylish as their opponents. The players for the City League squad were selected from different teams in the league, each player wearing the uniform of his own team. The City Leaguers were outfitted in used, worn gray uniforms ripped and torn from numerous games. Their caps were discolored and flattened; a few were missing the team logo on the front. The players were not provided new spikes, so they wore their own, and these were not in perfect condition or the same color. All of them could have used a good polishing.

Joe concluded that if it was a fashion show, the Yankees would win hands-down. But this was baseball, not *Vanity Fair*. He saw no indication on the faces of the All-Stars that they were the least bit intimidated by the sartorial splendor of the Yankees. But then again, the faces on the Sacred Heart players appeared deadly serious, showing no signs they were taking this team lightly no matter what they were wearing.

After a few minutes, Joe saw the coaches and umpires shake hands all around; then they assumed their respective positions. This was Joe's cue to switch on the microphone. He waited until the coaches reached their dugouts before addressing the overflowing crowd. He held the microphone close to his mouth, and Joe McGuire's deep, baritone voice resonated loudly throughout the ballpark: "Ladies and gentlemen and children of all ages, happy Fourth of July! Greetings to everyone on this glorious holiday to celebrate the founding of our great nation and a chance to enjoy an exciting baseball game! I want to welcome each and every one of you to the fifth annual All-Star game between the Sacred Heart Yankees and the City League All-Stars! Please rise for the singing of our national anthem."

The fans immediately stood up, taking off their hats and placing their right arms across their hearts, staring solemnly toward the American flag in center field. The familiar sound of Kate Smith's recorded voice singing, "O say can you see, by the dawn's early light ..." came ringing out. For the next few minutes, the robust matriarch best known for "God Bless America" stirred the souls of all in attendance like the Reverend Billy Graham delivering one of his fiery sermons.

Following the national anthem, home plate umpire Wilson Collier dusted off the plate, put his mask on, and bellowed out to the hometown fans, "Puh-lay ball!"

5

First Inning

T HE CITY LEAGUE ALL-STARS STORMED out of the dugout screaming
and hollering, gloves in hand, racing for their positions on the field.
Nate calmly walked to the mound. He was the picture of confidence as
he approached the rubber and began his warm-up tosses to Louie. First
baseman Phil DeMarco threw practice ground balls to the other infielders
while Jackie, Ritchie, and Dave tossed lazy fly balls to each other. The
sun was directly above the field, further intensifying the heat of the day.
The flag in center field waved lightly, unfurling in graceful pleated rolls
as a temperate breeze continued blowing steadily beyond the center-field
bleachers. Louie caught one of Nate's warm-up pitches and glanced up
at the flag in the distance. Once again, he hoped the breeze would help
Ritchie hit one out of the park. Then Louie fired the ball down to Archie
at second, who swiped an imaginary runner and started their routine of
tossing the ball around the horn: Steele, Harlow, DeMarco, Cummings.
After Kurt got the ball from Phil, he took a few steps and flipped the ball
to Nate.

"Let's get 'em!" urged Kurt as Frankie Doyle, the leadoff hitter for
the Yankees, came strolling to the plate.

Frankie was a diminutive second baseman, a dead pull-hitter with
a quick bat and good bunting skills. Kurt moved in at third base. The

outfield swung over to left, Ritchie guarding the line. Nate's first pitch was a fastball, high and tight. Frankie took it for ball one. Louie set his mitt a little lower, called for another fastball. Nate reared back and hurled another heater high and outside.

"Ball two!" bellowed umpire Collier.

Louie motioned for Nate to go lower with his catcher's mitt, pushing his hands into the dirt like he was pressing down on a large plunger.

Nate nodded, kicked some dirt on the mound. The next pitch was a fastball right down the middle. Frankie let it go.

"Strike one!" shouted Collier.

With the count 2-1, Louie called for another fastball, not wanting to go 3-1 on the first batter. Again Nate fired a blistering fastball up and away for ball three. Louie thought, *He's got to get these pitches down. If he doesn't, they won't swing at anything and just wait for a cheap walk.* Frankie was taking the pitch all the way as Nate's 3-1 offering soared far outside the strike zone, not even close. Frankie trotted down to first base.

The next batter was Joey McCall, the left fielder. He dug his cleats into the batter's box and arched his bat high above his head, waiting for Nate's first delivery. It was a belt-high fastball on the outer edge of the plate. Joey swung mightily but a fraction late, fouling it sharply down the third baseline. Kurt instinctively moved back, closer to the line. Louie signaled for the first curve ball. Nate nodded, wound up with a high kick, and threw a roundhouse curve that started out wide right and then broke directly into Joey's hitting zone. Joey swung and connected, sending a blistering ground ball past Nate's outstretched glove. Jimmie Harlow dashed to his left and dove for the ball, but it skidded past him into center field. Jackie raced in, fielded the ball cleanly, and heaved a low-flying line drive to third base, trying to nail Frankie Doyle running full speed toward the bag. Kurt took the throw on one hop and slapped the tag on Frankie as he slid hard into the bag.

"Safe!" yelled Homer Anderson, the third-base umpire.

Dunberry immediately bounded out of the dugout and ran toward third base swinging his arms in windmill fashion, his face contorting into spasms of wrinkled pain. "Are you out of your mind?" he screamed, charging up to the umpire, jutting the bill of his cap into Homer's face.

"He made the tag! He made the tag! You didn't see that? He made the tag! Are you blind?"

Homer Anderson had witnessed Dunberry's antics before and stood impassively with his arms folded, staring into the distance, patiently waiting for him to finish his predictable rant.

"Sorry, Max," said Homer after Dunberry had burnt off enough steam. "He slid *under* the tag. He's safe."

Dunberry clenched his fists, making a frustrated motion like he was squeezing an accordion. He stomped back to the dugout, kicking dirt and cursing Homer under his breath. Then yelling back to him, "Okay, Homer! You better not miss another one!"

With runners on second and third and nobody out, Bob Jennings, the catcher for the Yankees, stood in the batter's box. Bob was a powerfully built twelve-year-old who looked much older and was known to hit home runs as far as Ritchie. Louie wanted to mix up the pitches to Jennings, but he knew if Nate threw another hanging curve they might never see the ball again. He called for a fastball. Nate leaned back and sent a bullet streaking down the center of the plate. Bob saw the ball all the way but was overanxious. He swung hard but missed the center of the bat by a fraction of an inch. The ball skied straight up in the air, a pop-up to third base, where Kurt barely moved and settled under it for the first out.

The next batter, Jamey Bradshaw, was the Yankees' best hitter and fielder. He also played center field. Jamey stood erect in the batter's box, his bat held high and back over his shoulder, his right foot planted far back in the box, left leg stretched out stiff and straight toward the pitcher. Standing that way, it was no accident that Jamey looked exactly like a young Joe DiMaggio. He had seen a picture of the famous Yankee's stance in a magazine and practiced it in front of a mirror.

Louie called for an inside fastball, hoping to jam him into a weak grounder or pop-up. As the pitch sailed in, Louie knew at once they were in trouble. The pitch was too much over the plate. Jamey rapped a clean line drive over Archie's head into right center field. Jackie ran the ball down and fired to second base, holding Jamey to a single as two runs easily crossed the plate. The Yankees fans leaped to their feet, clapping their hands, cheering loudly, waving flags and banners. A few of the

Yankees fans looked knowingly at each other, already convinced that it was going to be five in a row for the Catholic squad.

Martin gave Dunberry an uneasy look; he didn't have to say anything. Louie glanced into the dugout, getting Osa's attention. Osa calmly nodded, gestured for him to go out and talk to Nate. Louie called time-out, took off his catcher's mask, and walked up to his struggling pitcher.

"Hey, Nate! You're trying too hard. Relax. These guys aren't the *real* Yankees, you know?"

Nate dropped his head, smiling ruefully. "Of course not. I know that."

"How do you feel?"

"I feel fine. I'm all right—just a little nervous, I guess. But hey, the butterflies are gone. Let's get these guys out."

"Listen, you're getting the ball up way too high. Take a longer stretch before you let go of the ball. Just like practice, right?"

"Right."

"And don't groove another fastball, okay?"

"Okay."

Louie returned to his catching position as first baseman Butch Skinner came to the plate. Louie signaled for a low outside fastball, hoping to induce a double play. Nate fired a perfect pitch, low and away. Butch swung late, hitting a ground ball up the middle. Jimmie Harlow ranged quickly to his left, fielded the ball cleanly, and underhanded it to Archie Steele, who tagged second base and spun around in the air, throwing a strike to Phil at first base. Phil caught the ball a split second before a lumbering Butch Skinner touched the bag. Double play!

The All-Stars ran like lunatics into the dugout, slamming their gloves down hard on the bench, slapping each other on the back, whooping and cheering while every player came running to Jimmie and Archie, smacking them with high-fives. Coach Dunberry ran the length of the dugout pumping his fists, shouting, "All right! Now let's get those bats going!"

The All-Stars were down by two runs, but they knew it could have been a lot worse.

LEADOFF HITTER JIMMIE HARLOW APPROACHED home plate, eyeing the third baseman to see if he could lay down a bunt. But "Scrappy" Cartwright had been warned by Coach O'Toole that Harlow liked to bunt for base hits, so he edged closer to home. Jimmie stood in the batter's box waiting for the first pitch from Mike Barnes, the tall, lean, hard-throwing right-hander for the Yankees. Barnes' first pitch was a fastball on the inside part of the plate. Harlow swung late and missed it. The next pitch was a sharp-breaking curve that caught the inside corner.

"Strike two!" yelled Collier.

Jimmie dug his spikes into the batter's box, shoving dirt back with his feet like a racehorse in a starting gate. Barnes fired the next pitch at Jimmie's head, sending him sprawling backward to the ground. A few of the All-Star fans booed. Jimmie got up and dusted himself off. He settled back in the box, gritting his teeth, awaiting the next delivery. It was another fastball, but Jimmie was ready for it and slammed a deep fly ball to left centerfield. Jamey Bradshaw got a great jump, sprinting for the ball like he had been jettisoned from a cannon. The ball looked like it might clear the fence, but at the last moment Jamey leaped in the air and grabbed it before slamming into the Merrifield's Landscaping billboard. He banged into the sign at full speed and bounced off, landing hard on his stomach. The stunned crowd gasped as Jamey lay motionless on his side. But within seconds he rolled over, bounced up, brushed his pants, and nonchalantly threw the ball back into the infield. The crowd cheered as the fleet-footed outfielder trotted gingerly back to his position.

After the crowd settled down, Archie Steele came striding toward the plate. Mike Barnes started Archie off with a vicious fastball low and away. Archie took it for ball one. The next pitch was a sharp-breaking curve that nipped the inside corner for a called strike. Archie guessed the next pitch was going to be a fastball, but instead Barnes threw a much slower curve tailing off the plate. Archie, fooled, swung feebly, lurching way out in front of the pitch. Mike had the reputation of a crafty, cocky, tough competitor who loved to fool hitters and was not afraid to brush them back with a little chin music. With the count 1–2, Barnes wound up and threw a letter-high fastball. Archie saw the ball coming all the way and took a healthy cut but tipped it into Bob Jennings' mitt. Archie slammed his bat into the dirt and turned to the dugout in disgust, knowing he had missed a pitch he should have hammered. Two outs.

As Jackie came to the plate, Coach O'Toole motioned for his outfielders to take a few steps back. The third baseman yelled to his teammates, "Good wheels! He's got good wheels!" Jackie had never faced Mike before, but he had heard plenty of talk about his pitching skills and defiant unpredictability both on and off the mound. There was a legendary story that he once had walked three guys on purpose just to strike out and humiliate another player who had called him a pussy. Jackie went up looking for a pitch he could drive. Mike hurled a belt-high fastball down the middle of the plate. Jackie turned on the pitch, lashing a streaking line drive deep into right center field. Motoring quickly to first base, he saw Coach Martin swinging his arms, giving him the go sign, and dashed for second base without missing a step. Jamey came up with the ball and fired it into shortstop Frankie Doyle, but by the time the ball arrived, Jackie was standing on second base with a double.

And Ritchie Edwards was coming to the plate.

Ritchie Edwards was the biggest, most powerful kid on either team and looked a lot older than his twelve years. He was temperamental and emotional off the field but carried himself with uncanny poise and confidence on it. As he strolled to the plate, an eerie silence descended on the ballpark. The fans knew a great matchup when they saw one. The right-handed clean-up hitter stood in, his bat cocked, his right elbow pumping as if to juice up more muscle power in his swing. Mike was not the least bit intimidated by Ritchie Edwards or anybody else. He actually enjoyed these kinds of matchups, knowing in his baseball bones that there was no better pitcher in the state of New Jersey.

The first pitch was a wayward curve that sailed low and outside. Ritchie mistook it for a fastball. It badly destroyed his timing, causing him to swing much too early. Strike one. He backed out of the box, took a few practice swings, and settled back into his stance, glaring at Barnes. Mike had a mild sneer on his face. He moved off the rubber and picked up and squeezed the rosin bag, pretending to dry off his sweaty pitching hand. He savored the moment, making Ritchie wait at the plate. Mike's next delivery was a high and inside fastball. Ritchie took it for ball one. With the count 1–1, Mike threw a slow, looping roundhouse curve that started far out of the zone but, at the last second, curled at Ritchie's knees, just nipping the inside corner.

"Strike two!" yelled Collier.

Ritchie cursed beneath his breath. Bob signaled for another curve, but Mike shook him off, waiting for Bob to give him the fastball sign. Bob thought Mike was out of his mind for challenging the great Ritchie Edwards, a notorious fastball hitter. Undaunted, Mike leaned back and hurled a nasty heater on the outer edge of the plate. Ritchie took a mammoth swing at the pitch but swung his powerful bat right through it, hitting nothing but air. The ball smacked Bob's mitt for the third out, leaving Jackie stranded on second base.

At the end of the first inning, it was Yankees 2, All-Stars 0.

Second Inning

MIKE BARNES, THE NUMBER SIX hitter for the Yankees, was leading off the second inning. He was tall and lanky but could hit the ball with power and rarely struck out. Mike stepped into the box and arched his bat, waiting for Nate's first delivery. Nate wound up and threw a wild pitch so far out of the strike zone that it sailed over the heads of Louie and Collier, rattling the chain-link backstop. The ball also rattled Marty Casey, the town drunk, who was slumped on the fence in an alcoholic stupor. When the ball slammed into the fence, Marty jolted from his slumber, shaking his body and quickly raising both his hands, thinking that he was being arrested. The crowd roared with laughter.

The next three pitches got closer to the plate, but none of them crossed it. Mike jogged to first base after Collier called ball four. Louie grimaced, knowing that if Nate had shown any control at all, he might have gotten the call. He motioned for a time-out and went out to the mound to settle down his pitcher. The message was simple: throw strikes. He also told him to relax and not to aim the ball but just to let it flow naturally. As he handed the ball to Nate, Louie joked to his pitcher, "Hey, I never thought I'd say this, Nate—but, you're thinking too much!"

Nate forced a thin smile and then kicked some dirt off the rubber, gripping the baseball tightly in his right hand.

The next hitter was shortstop Itchy McDermott, a switch-hitter who could spray the ball to all fields and showed occasional power. Itchy knew he was going to get the take sign. The whole Yankee team knew that the obvious strategy was to make Nate throw strikes. If he was going to walk batters around the diamond, it was okay with them. Itchy stood in the box and watched a perfect belt-high strike sail right past him for strike one. He looked down at O'Toole and didn't see the take sign. Itchy knew the next pitch would be a fastball, and he didn't miss it. He turned quickly on the ball, pulling a scorching line drive over the head of Kurt at third base. Ritchie raced in from left field, gloved the ball, and fired a bullet to third base, holding Mike at second. First and second, nobody out.

Osa glanced warily in Max's direction. They were both thinking the same thing: *How long should we stick with Nate Green?* Osa had already made up his mind. In his view, it was simply not Nate's day. If it had been up to him, he would have pulled the kid right then. Osa thought the Yankee hitters were seeing baseballs the size of soccer balls coming across the plate.

Dunberry remained sitting at the end of the dugout nearest home plate. Osa figured he was going to the mound to remove his starting pitcher. Instead, he shouted words of encouragement and told him to relax and settle down. Nate nodded to Max, giving the coach a confident look that seemed to say, "No problem. Everything's under control."

Osa knew that if Nate continued to struggle, he would have to talk to Dunberry about bringing in another pitcher. He was a patient coach, but he was afraid Nate was only a couple of pitches away from putting the game out of reach. Meanwhile, Nate paced around the mound, looking down at the dirt as if command of his pitches could be found under a pebble somewhere.

The next batter was Bobby "Scrappy" Cartwright, the small-framed third baseman nicknamed "Scrappy" for the way he played the game. Before the game, Kurt, in characteristic fashion, had mocked the two Yankee players by asking his teammates, "You mean we can't beat a team that has players named Itchy and Scrappy?" Kurt's sarcasm had fallen flat, because the other players knew better than to underestimate the Yankees, no matter how silly their names might be.

Louie knew the Yankees were sitting on the fastball and felt he had nothing to lose by calling for a curve. Nate nodded agreement and then tossed a beautiful curve that started far inside before sweeping in the middle of the strike zone.

"Strike one!" hollered Collier.

Louie breathed a sigh of relief, called for a fastball. Nate heaved a letter-high heater that completely overmatched Scrappy. He swung late and underneath the pitch. With the count 0–2, Louie called for a changeup. Nate took an exaggerated windup and lofted a marshmallow toward the plate. Scrappy was thrown totally off guard, swinging way out in front, missing badly. One out.

Nate seemed to be regaining his confidence. Dunberry leaned back against the dugout wall. *Maybe,* he thought, *we'll see the real Nate Green from now on.*

The weakest hitter on the team, right fielder Denny Smith, stood in the box waiting for the first pitch. Nate fired a fastball at his knees. Denny barely saw it.

"Strike one!"

Denny dug his spikes into the dirt, choking up on the bat, determined to get some wood on the ball. Another fastball came swizzing in on the outside corner. Denny swung late, but made contact, chopping a one-hopper to Phil at first base. Phil blocked the ball with his chest, grabbed it, and raced to the bag a split-second ahead of Denny. Meanwhile, Barnes and McDermott, running on the pitch, were now standing on second and third.

Two outs.

Denny had turned the batting order over. Frankie Doyle was coming to the plate for his second shot at Nate. Louie signaled for a fastball. Nate delivered a pitch, just missing the inside corner. Frankie was a patient hitter; he was looking for a fastball over the plate. On the next pitch, he got his wish. Louie put his mitt on the outside corner, but the pitch got too much of the plate. Frankie hammered a towering fly ball into right center field. At first, the ball looked like it was going to clear the fence, but it landed a few feet short, ricocheting off the fence and luckily bouncing into Dave's glove. Dave fired the ball to Billy, the cutoff man, who whirled and threw a strike to Kurt as Frankie steamrolled into third base. The ball was on target but a little high. Frankie slid under the tag for a triple. Barnes and McDermott scored easily, giving the Yankees a four-run lead.

With the All-Stars down by four runs, Osa figured Max would surely make the move to replace Nate. As the Yankee fans were cheering loudly in the stands, Max stood up and headed for the mound. Louie took off his mask and joined the coach and Nate.

"Nate," said Dunberry, "tell me the truth. How do you feel? Are you tired? Is the heat getting to you?"

Nate looked up at his coach. "I'm okay coach. I'm not tired, really. I just got that one pitch up too high. My arm feels great."

Dunberry eyed Nate with suspicion. Of course the kid was not going to admit he was tired. They never did.

"Louie, how's he look?"

Louie was in a tough spot. Part of him wanted to scream, "Get him the hell out of there! He's toast!" But another part of him knew Nate had not expended all his energy and should have plenty of gas left in the tank—if he could command his pitches.

"He looks okay," said Louie. "He just needs to get ahead of some hitters so they don't sit on the fastball."

"Okay, Nate. Let's see you mix up those pitches. Throw some curves and changeups—and don't worry about walking anybody. That's when you get in trouble—when you're afraid of failing. Got it?"

"Sure, Coach," said Nate. "No problem."

Dunberry walked back to the dugout, carefully avoiding the glaring eyes of Osa Martin.

With Doyle on third, Joey McCall sauntered to the plate exuding a quiet air of confidence. Nate started Joey off with a curveball breaking low and away. Joey almost went for it but held up at the last second. The ball floated out of the strike zone for ball one. The next pitch was a fastball, high and tight and out of the zone, but Joey took a vicious cut, tomahawking it to deep left field. Ritchie got a bead on the ball as he scrambled back toward the fence.

When it was first hit, everyone in the ballpark thought the soaring fly ball was a sure home run, but at the last second it lost momentum, falling harmlessly within a foot of the wall. Ritchie was waiting at the fence and settled under it for the third out.

WITH THE TEAM DOWN 4–0, many fans in the park had already concluded the game was out of reach, especially with Barnes looking in complete control. But as Louie strode to the plate, he knew if they could get to Mike and knock him out, the team could mount a comeback. Louie stepped into the box and stared intently at Mike, expecting a fastball. But an off-speed curve caught him by surprise. He let the pitch drift slowly past him for strike one. Louie was aware he looked confused by the pitch and figured Mike would try to mix it up and slip a fastball by him. He guessed fastball, steadied his bat—and then a smoking heater came right down the middle. Louie jumped on the pitch, pulling it sharply down the third baseline. Scrappy dove quickly to his right, but the ball bounded over the bag into left field. Joey alertly ran it down and threw the ball to Itchy at second, holding Louie to a single.

Kurt Cummings stepped into the box, cocked his bat, readied himself for the first pitch. Mike came in with a high fastball. Kurt ripped it savagely, fouling it straight back to the backstop. Bob was surprised that Louie and Kurt were getting around on Mike's fastball, so he called for a slider, placing his glove low and away. Kurt saw the ball coming in but mistook it for a fastball, swinging too early as the ball veered far outside the plate. With the count 0–2, Bob called for a changeup waste pitch out of the zone, but Mike shook him off. Bob knew his pitcher. He knew Mike wanted to reestablish his dominance and nail Kurt on three pitches by blowing him away with a smoking fastball. Bob signaled fastball. Mike leaned far back on the mound, turned his head skyward, and hurled a strike right down the center of the plate. Kurt saw the pitch clearly and took a healthy cut but a fraction too late. He whiffed right through it for the first out.

Phil DeMarco came to the plate with one thing on his mind. He wanted to throw Barnes off his rhythm. Barnes looked just too damn comfortable on the mound. Phil wanted to distract him any way he could. He entered the batter's box. Then, just before the first pitch, he called timeout. He walked methodically out of the box and dropped his bat, reaching down to retie shoelaces that did not need retying. He glanced up at the scoreboard, pretending to see what the score was. He grabbed his bat, hiked up his pants, and then stepped back into the batting box. Just before Barnes delivered his pitch, Phil unexpectedly pulled the bat off his shoulders and wiggled it around, jerking it up and down and inside and out like he was trying to hit twenty balls at once.

The normally composed Barnes fired a ball high and inside, almost hitting Phil. On the next pitch, Phil did the same thing, and again Mike seemed rattled, the ball running even closer to Phil's head. Bob motioned Mike to settle down by pumping his hands up and down. Bob knew Phil had no intention of swinging at the ball, so he called for a fastball. This time Mike delivered a perfect strike past the bat-wiggling DeMarco. Phil decided to continue his antics until he got two strikes. The next pitch was another inside fastball below the knees for ball three. Phil geared up his gyrations to the point where he looked like he was being attacked by a hoard of hungry red ants. Barnes almost laughed at the silly-looking All-Star goofing around the batter's box, waving his bat back and forth. Phil's attempt at distracting Barnes seemed to be working. With the count 3–1, Phil was taking it all the way. Mike wound up and threw a pitch streaking across Phil's letters.

"Strike two!"

Phil stopped jerking the bat and whirled around. He glared at Collier, giving him a disgusted look.

"Come on, ump," cried Phil. "Get 'em down!"

As Phil was berating the umpire with his head turned, Mike was already in his windup. Realizing he was still in the batter's box, Phil spun around to face Barnes, but the ball was already in the air. Phil froze in place as the ball came zooming in directly over the plate.

"Strike three!"

Phil pounded his bat into the dirt, gave the umpire another dirty look, and stomped over to the dugout, flinging his bat on the bat rack.

There were two outs and a runner on first with Dave Carmichael coming to the plate. Mike got two quick strikes on Dave. Dave knew he was terribly overmatched and had very little chance of catching up to Mike's fastball. He decided to pick a spot in the strike zone and swing at that exact spot when the ball was delivered. As soon as Dave saw Mike's arm release the ball, he swung with all his might into the middle of the plate.

No one was more surprised than Dave when he connected on the fat part of the bat, sending a hard grounder between first and second. Louie took off, rounded second, and headed for third as Denny Smith fielded the ball and threw it back to Itchy McDermott. The stunned All-Star fans cheered wildly, their faint hopes suddenly renewed.

After Dave's miracle hit, Nate Green came to the plate with runners on first and third with two outs.

Mike started off Nate with a slow curve that didn't break, almost hitting him. The next pitch was an inside fastball, knee high. Nate swung from his heels, but he hit it on the end of the bat, and the ball flared into right center for a base hit. Louie held up at third until the ball dropped, then easily scored the first All-Star run. Dave was still standing on second base with leadoff hitter Jimmie Harlow coming to the plate.

No one had to tell Jimmie this was a critical moment in the game. He needed to keep this fragile rally going and get a hit. Barnes was pitching a solid game, but the All-Stars knew a couple hitters had gotten good wood on the ball.

Neither Mike nor Bob was terribly concerned at this point in the game. They knew Dave's hit was pure luck, and giving up a hit to Nate Green was no cause for alarm. Mike started Jimmie off with a curve that didn't curve. The pitch came in sweet as a batting practice fastball with nothing on it. Jimmie uncorked a tremendous high-arcing shot to the flagpole in center field. Jamey Bradshaw turned around, flying toward the 235-feet sign in dead center field. With his back turned to the infield, Jamey wasn't even looking at the ball but sprinting as fast as he could toward the fence. He was about twenty feet from the warning track when he glanced back over his shoulder and spotted the ball sailing away from him to his left. He turned on a dime and tracked the ball, diving head-first, his feet propelling him airborne. With his body suspended above the ground, Jamey stretched out his glove, snared the ball in the top of his webbing, and then landed with a heavy thud on the warning track. Jamey never hesitated. From his prone position, he smiled broadly, holding up his glove like a trophy, half of a little white ball perched securely on top of his mitt.

The ecstatic Yankee fans roared their approval, cheering Jamey all the way as he ran into the dugout.

At the end of the second inning, it was Yankees 4, All-Stars 1.

Third Inning

The sun continued to gleam brightly in the afternoon sky, bearing down on the sweltering fans in Palmyra Park. Despite temperatures approaching ninety-five degrees, the local supporters of Little League baseball were still in a lively, festive mood. The men sitting in the bleachers were now sweating profusely, taking off their straw hats and baseball caps, wiping their red faces with handkerchiefs. The women hid their pale faces under the shade of large floppy hats, fanning themselves with programs of the game. The kids in the bleachers jumped up and down, screamed and hollered, begged for more ice cream, and chased one another, oblivious to the heat and humidity.

Not all the fans in the ballpark were particularly joyful. The early lead by the Sacred Heart team had taken its toll on some of the die-hard supporters of the All-Stars. The unrelenting sun only served to intensify their anxiety and taunt feelings created by the three-run deficit. Disgruntled murmurs drifted among the crowd: "Oh no, here we go again." "Not five years in a row!" "Same thing every year." "How long they gonna stick with Nate Green?"

In sharp contrast, the Yankee faithful in the stands were much more comfortable and relaxed, basking in the glow of the sun and the warmth of unbridled optimism. Mike Barnes looked sharp, and they were getting around on Nate Green's fastball much better than anticipated. Victory seemed well within their grasp.

Although down by three runs and aware a few malcontents in the crowd were getting restless, Max sent Nate Green out to start the third inning. As Nate was taking his warm-up tosses, Coach Martin was pacing up and down in the dugout, encouraging his players, reminding them they were only down by three runs and it was still early in the game. Osa was acutely aware of the tension in the air but appeared relaxed and confident that the team could overcome the Yankee lead.

But Osa Martin was far from relaxed. He was very concerned that if the Sacred Heart team scored any more runs, the mountain would be too high to climb. His instincts told him Nate Green was off his game; he just didn't look comfortable on the mound. Nate had not beaten his Kiwanis team during the regular season, but not because Nate hadn't pitched well. Both games had been low-scoring pitchers' duels between Nate and Jackie. Osa was very aware of Nate's prodigious skills as a pitcher. But not this day; he looked shaken and out of sync. As Nate was finishing his warm-up pitches, Osa called out to him, "Come on, son! You can do it! Give 'em your best stuff!"

Then Bob Jennings, the sturdy catcher for the Yankees, stepped into the batter's box, opening the third inning. With the count 2–1, Louie signaled for a curve, hoping to throw Jennings off stride. The looping curve came in wide right and then broke directly into Bob's hitting zone. But the pitch did not have any snap to it and hung over the middle of the plate for a split second. Bob swung mightily, sending a sharp grounder down to Kurt at third base. The ball rocketed so fast that Kurt had no time react. He dropped to his knees, blocking the ball with his chest, but the ball skidded away from him along the third baseline. By the time he retrieved it, Bob was standing on first base.

The next batter was Jamey Bradshaw. Louie called timeout and went out to the mound, telling Nate to nibble at the corners and not give Jamey anything good to hit. Nate followed Louie's instructions, promptly walking him on four pitches, all of them at least six inches off the plate.

As Butch Skinner stepped in to hit, Dunberry signaled for his players to look for a ground ball they could turn into a double play. Jimmie Harlow moved in a few feet at short, and Archie Steele inched toward second base, setting up ideal positions for a double-play combination.

When Nate had two strikes on Butch, Louie called for a curve. It broke sharply into Butch's hitting zone, and Butch wailed away at it but struck nothing but air.

One out.

Mike Barnes came striding to the plate with runners on first and second. Nate reared back and threw a letter-high fastball that Mike swung late on, lifting a harmless fly ball to right field. Dave came drifting under the ball, raised his glove—and dropped it. Bob raced to third; Jamey took off for second. Dave hurriedly reached down, grabbed the ball, and threw it to Jimmie at second. The speedy Bradshaw slid hard into the bag just underneath Jimmie's quick tag.

The bases were loaded, still one out.

Osa Martin moved closer to Dunberry at the end of the dugout. "I think he's done, don't you, Max?"

Dunberry glanced in Osa's direction, took off his cap, brushed back the short hairs of his crew cut, and thoughtfully rubbed his chin. His sunburned face had the seamed and weathered look of a man who had spent years in the military.

"I'm not so sure," muttered Dunberry. "He's got a strikeout, and that last fly ball was a sure out."

"Why don't we give Jackie a chance?" Osa suggested, raising his voice a fraction higher. "The next hitter is a left-handed batter—should be a good matchup for him. This kid got a hit off Nate last time."

Dunberry stared toward the infield, owl-like, a deep furrow forming between his dark brown eyebrows. "Let's give him one more batter," said Dunberry. "If this kid gets a hit, we'll pull him."

"Max, I think you're wrong," asserted Osa. "Nate just doesn't have it today. Give Jackie a chance."

Dunberry turned directly toward Osa and looked intently at him as if coming out of a fog and noticing him for the first time. "Sorry, Osa. It's my decision."

With the bases jammed, Itchy McDermott, the shortstop for the Yankees, stood in the batter's box, anticipating a fastball right down the middle. Everyone in the park knew the All-Stars could not afford to walk in another run. Louie placed his mitt in the center of the plate, hoping for the best. Nate wasted no time and hurled a fastball over the heart of the plate. Itchy uncoiled a solid swing at the ball but was a fraction too low, fouling it straight back. The next pitch was in the same spot only a little lower. Itchy was trying to hit the ball in the air for a sacrifice fly, but he got under the pitch too much and sent a weak flair to short right field.

Archie Steele immediately turned completely around and dashed for the ball. Dave was playing deep in right and also charged for the ball, but it seemed destined to drop into no-man's-land. With the ball falling rapidly, Archie kept running, not even looking behind him to find it. With his back still to the ball, Archie instinctively lunged forward, glancing over his shoulder just as the ball was about to hit the outfield grass. His body was parallel to the ground, suspended in space, his glove hand desperately stretching out into empty air. Archie's glove landed on the grass a split second before the ball smacked into his mitt. Then, as if sprung from a jack-in-the-box, the ball popped out, bouncing three feet away. Archie was still on his knees and dove for the ball, miraculously recatching the ball in the webbing of his glove. He instantly turned around, firing the ball back to Jimmie at second.

Bob Jennings was on third base watching the weak fly ball Archie was trying to catch, knowing he could score if Archie caught the ball or if it dropped in for a hit. When Archie made his amazing catch, Bob easily tagged up from third while Jamey scampered from second to third. Mike was still on first base, unable to advance. Jimmie ran the ball toward the mound, making sure nobody else was going to score.

Top of the third. Runners on first and third, two outs.

Once again, Osa looked at Dunberry, expecting him to trot out to the mound and remove Nate. And again Dunberry stood motionless.

"Okay, fellas, one more out! One more out, then it's our turn! Come on, Nate! just one more!"

Osa tried not to look disappointed. He didn't want the players on the bench to notice any disagreement between them. He glanced down the dugout, peering into the faces of the little guys. The body language of the players wasn't too difficult to read. Heads were slumped down, eyes staring into the dirt. They looked forlorn and gloomy, nervously shuffling their feet back and forth. Osa noticed their hands were clenched together almost as if they were praying. Osa turned around, looked at his players a second time, thinking, *Maybe they are praying. We are certainly going to need divine help from somewhere.*

As Scrappy Cartwright stepped into the box, Louie gave the curveball sign. The pitch started out wide right and broke over the plate but hung squarely in the middle of the hitting zone. Scrappy crushed a line drive that soared over Kurt's head at third. The ball rose quickly toward the bleachers. But it was hit so hard it didn't have time to clear the fence and slammed into the right field wall. Ritchie was waiting for the ball to rebound, but it hit a fence pole, ricocheting crazily back into the playing field. The ball whizzed past Ritchie. Jackie chased it down, picked it up, and threw a strike to Kurt. Scrappy was rounding second, halfway to third base. Kurt wheeled and threw to Louie waiting at home plate. Scrappy never broke stride, barreling straight for home as the ball came sailing in nearly a foot over Louie's head. Louie reached up, grabbed the ball, and applied a hard tag to Scrappy sliding underneath him.

"Safe!"

Scrappy leaped in the air, arms waving frenetically. His teammates rushing from the dugout and swarmed over him until Scrappy lost his balance and collapsed beneath a cloud of dust, buried by delirious teammates piling on top of him. Scrappy had just rounded the bases for a rare inside-the-park home run, creating an almost insurmountable lead for the Yankees.

There was such a raucous celebration at home plate and in the stands that the fans did not pay much attention to Coach Dunberry, who was quietly on his way to the mound to take out Nate Green.

After reaching the mound, Coach Dunberry took the ball from Nate and waved Jackie in from center field. Nate lowered his head, kicked some dirt off the rubber, and slowly walked off the mound toward the dugout like a family member leaving a funeral. As Jackie trotted in from the outfield, Dunberry motioned to the bench for Allie Reynolds to take center field.

When Jackie reached the mound, Dunberry handed him the ball. "Just throw strikes, Jackie. Get us out of this inning."

As Dunberry walked back to the dugout, Jackie began his warm-up tosses. After a few throws, he motioned for Louie to fire the ball to second base. Jimmy caught the ball a foot above the bag and whipped it around the horn until Kurt tossed it back to Jackie. Louie turned to the umpire, called timeout, and hustled out to the mound.

"Okay," said Louie, "let's just put out this fire and get in the dugout and start hitting. We're going mostly with fastballs. You got the signals, right?"

Jackie nodded.

"Maybe a lefty will throw them off. Hey! This game's not over yet, buddy!"

"It sure isn't."

Denny Smith approached home plate, made a sign of the cross with his right hand, and then gazed toward the heavens, praying for a hit. He stepped into the batter's box.

Louie flashed the fastball signal. Jackie leaned forward, took the sign, and began his windup, swinging his arms back and forth, rearing back on his left foot with his left arm extended, practically touching the ground. He hurled a sizzling heater that came in knee-high and across the plate. Denny had trouble picking up the flight of the ball, and before he had time to react, the ball smacked Louie's mitt.

"Strike one!" yelled Collier.

Denny dug his cleats into the dirt, choked up on the bat, moved back in the box. Louie signaled for another fastball. Jackie wound up and fired another fastball in the same location. Denny picked it up this time, but a fraction too late, lifting a harmless pop fly to Phil at first base.

Two outs.

Frankie Doyle strolled to the plate exuding the kind of rarefied confidence that is bestowed on any member of a team leading by seven runs. Jackie wasted no time with Frankie, launching a fastball down the middle. Frankie took a powerful swing but came up empty, his spinning torso corkscrewing until he lost his balance and fell awkwardly on the ground. Frankie helped himself up using his bat for a crutch, dusted himself off, stepped back into the box. The next pitch was another fastball up and out of the strike zone, but Frankie couldn't lay off and whiffed underneath it for strike two. Louie decided it was time for the Yankees to see Jackie's curve ball. He flashed two fingers. The ball started out like a medium fastball far outside the zone, hung in midair for a split second before breaking sharply over the heart of the plate. Collier was about to say, "Ball one!" but he was taken by surprise, hesitated, and then screamed, "Strike three!"

The Yankees half of the inning was finally over. It was cold comfort, but at least Jackie had stopped the bleeding.

At the end of the third inning, the Yankees were up 8–1.

COACH DUNBERRY TOLD THE TEAM he needed a smoke break and sent Louie out to coach third base. He took a seat next to the water cooler at the end of the dugout.

The first batter, Archie Steele, had just popped out to shortstop when Osa Martin realized Louie was coaching third base. Osa called out to backup second baseman Mike Dugan to coach first base and walked down the length of the dugout to talk to Dunberry. He sat down next to him but remained silent. It was Dunberry who spoke first.

"Thanks for coming over. We can pretend we're having a strategy session. Hell, I guess you were right. Just not Nate's day."

Osa leaned forward, rested his elbows on his knees, and watched the action on the field. "Nate pitched pretty well. His control was off, that's all. You can't predict that sort of thing."

Dunberry managed a tight smile. "You did."

"It was just a hunch. We all play hunches. That's what coaching is all about. You don't go by the book—you know that."

Dunberry took a deep drag, sending a thin spiral of smoke toward the first baseline. "What is this shit about going by the book? Who the hell wrote this book? Where is it? Is it some kind of ancient scroll that everyone talks about but nobody ever sees? How the hell are you supposed to coach a team going by—or not going by—a book nobody's ever fuckin' seen? If it's such a great book, why can't I buy it at the bookstore?"

"I don't know," said Osa, shrugging his shoulders. "I guess it's like some kind of baseball wisdom passed down through generations. Who knows?"

"Exactly. Who the fuck knows? Who knew Nate was going to forget how to throw the fuckin' ball across the plate?"

Osa was still staring straight ahead watching the game. Jackie had just crushed a hard liner but right at Itchy McDermott, the shortstop for the Yankees.

"Like I said," continued Osa, "you did the best you could. There's no way of knowing. If he pitches well, you look like a genius—"

"And if he doesn't?"

Osa grinned for the first time, glancing at Dunberry. "Well … if you're in the pros, you start looking for another job."

"I really wanted this game."

"We can still win it. We've got five innings to go."

Just as Osa spoke, Ritchie Edwards sent a towering fly ball to left field, but it was hauled in a few feet from the fence by Joey McCall for the third out.

Dunberry's head slumped to the ground. "You mean four innings to go."

Osa started to get up and see if Robbie Patterson felt okay to pitch if Jackie got in trouble.

"Wait a minute," said Dunberry, pulling on Osa's pants. "I need to tell you something."

Osa sat back down.

"The truth is, I knew Nate needed to be taken out exactly when you told me to. I didn't do it because I wanted to prove you wrong—even though I knew you were right. Does that make sense?"

"Yes, it does."

"And I didn't do it because you are a Negro—"

"I know that. Max."

"No, listen. I know a bad coaching move when I see one. I didn't do it for the good of the team—I did it so I would look better than you and let you know I was in charge. It was stupid."

Osa patted Dunberry gently on the back, giving him a commiserating look like he was comforting a teammate who had just made an error. "We haven't lost yet, remember?"

"Hey, that's another good sign of a great coach—never give up, right?"

"Right. Now, let's figure out how we're going to make this major comeback."

Dunberry looked directly into Osa's eyes, his voice softening. "Osa, can I ask you a personal question?"

"Sure."

"Someone told me you were in the Negro Leagues but quit playing after a couple years. Did you get hurt?"

"No, I didn't get hurt."

"You just lost desire for the game?"

"Well," said Osa, standing up and glancing down at Dunberry, "let's just say I was in the wrong place at the wrong time."

Dunberry nodded. Then he flipped his cigarette on the ground, rubbing it out with his shoe. "I'm going to see if George Beauchamp's knee is okay. I'm going to put him in right field. He's a little faster than Dave."

"Hey, Coach," said Osa, smiling. "*Everybody's* a little faster than Dave Carmichael."

Fourth and Fifth Innings

The Yankees–City League All-Star game had settled into a slow-moving groove. It was not as bad as an eight-hour airport delay, but it seemed as if the game had been placed on quiet autopilot. In the fourth and fifth innings, Mike and Jackie pitched nearly flawless baseball. Mike gave up two weak singles, and Jackie gave up a double to Jamey Bradshaw and walked a man. The game had evolved into a slow-motion, uneventful event with most of the crowd barely paying attention. Some disappointed fans left the park muttering, "Get 'em next year," while other patrons went down to the street to grab a hot dog. They talked idly about the fireworks display planned for the evening, how hot it was, or how great the parade had been this year. They knew the rhythms of the game. They knew this slow-motion, uneventful part of the game might change with another rally by either team. But if a camera had panned the City League fans still sitting silently in their seats, it would have easily captured the look of stoic resignation on their faces.

Sometimes, highly anticipated baseball games end with an enervating, dying whimper, a result nobody really wants: a blowout.

Bottom of the Sixth Inning

Coach Dunberry replaced Nate Green, Dave Carmichael, Kurt Cummings, and Phil Demarco with substitutes but kept his best players in the game, hoping for a miracle. As the Yankees took the field in the bottom of the sixth, Mike Barnes was sitting on the bench. Another pitcher, lefty Eddie Derringer, was heading to the mound. Everybody was shocked to see O'Toole take out Mike, who was pitching a nearly perfect game. In the dugout, Mike angrily slammed his glove into the dirt while giving O'Toole a nasty look. Mike kicked the dirt, threw his hat to the ground, and then picked up his glove and hurled it halfway down the length of the dugout. O'Toole ignored Mike's antics, quietly sipping a drink of water from the cooler at the other end of the dugout. O'Toole, like Dunberry, had replaced four of his starters but also kept the heart of the lineup in the game.

The first batter to face Eddie Derringer was center fielder Allie Reynolds, who took one pitch high and away, then grounded weakly to Frankie Doyle at second base. Jimmie Harlow came to the plate, watched two pitches bounce in the dirt, and then promptly rapped a clean single up the middle for a base hit. Eddie Derringer was a good pitcher but not in the same class as Mike Barnes. He wasn't nearly as fast or crafty and occasionally had trouble finding the strike zone. As Archie Steele walked calmly toward the plate, he was greeted with excitable words of encouragement from his teammates. "Come on, Archie, you can do it!" "Get a hit!" "Pick out a good one!" Archie stood defiantly in the batter's box, glaring at Eddie Derringer as if Eddie was the devil himself. Eddie quickly got ahead of the count 0–2, nipping the outside of the plate for called strikes. On the third pitch Archie uncorked his bat, smashing a blistering line drive to the left side of the infield. Scrappy Cartwright lunged to his left and speared the ball in his outstretched glove, landing hard on the infield dirt. He jumped up, fired a bullet to first base, hoping to double up Jimmie, who was scrambling back to the bag. Jimmie's hand touched the bag just as the throw came in—a split second before Butch Skinner slapped him with the tag.

With two outs and a runner on first, Jackie took a couple practice swings and then stepped into the box. He decided to guess fastball and concentrated on Eddie's windup and arm motion. The ball came in quickly from the southpaw belt-high on the inside part of the plate. He swung into the pitch, pulling it sharply between first and second. The substitute right fielder, Georgie Salvino, chased down the ball but mishandled it, allowing Jackie to race toward second base. Salvino quickly recovered, but his throw was off as Jackie slid safely into second base. Dunberry raised up both hands, giving Jimmie the stop sign at third.

Eddie Derringer had never faced Ritchie Edwards but knew his cocky reputation and was determined to wipe that smirk off his face. Derringer had never wanted to strike out a batter more in his life. Ritchie was swinging two bats around his head so they made swooshing sounds from slicing through the air. After taking a couple practice swings and tossing the other bat to the side, Ritchie stepped into the box and tapped the end of the bat on the plate, staring into the beady eyes of Eddie Derringer. Bob Jennings called for a fastball and set up on the outside corner. Eddie wound up and through a wicked fastball that zipped over the edge of the plate, catching the corner.

"Strike one!"

Ritchie's demeanor didn't change, nor did he seem particularly concerned about anything, maintaining an implacable image of self-assurance. He stepped out of the box, shaking his head at Eddie as if to say, "Is that all you got?"

Eddie cursed under his breath, "You son of a bitch. This one's coming at your head."

Ritchie moved into the box, cocked his bat high back over his shoulder, waited for Eddie's next delivery. It was a fastball flying directly toward his head. Ritchie instinctively ducked down, stumbling backward into the dirt. He got up quickly, smiled sarcastically, and once again looked at Eddie with mild contempt. Bob signaled for another fastball on the outside corner. Eddie nodded, wound up, and threw a fastball that didn't go far enough outside the zone.

There is a seldom-heard sound in baseball that is like no other sound on the planet. It's not just the sound of a hard-hit line drive, or someone pointing out the crack of the bat, or even the sound of a typical home run. It only happens on those rare occasions when all the elements of physics and athleticism are in perfect tune, with all the right combinations of hand-eye coordination, balance, strength, agility, timing, and awesome unleashed power coming together in one brilliant moment on a baseball field. It is the earth-shattering crack and brutal collision of the sweet spot of a white ash bat pounding a leather sphere with such force that it shakes the foundations of the stadium and paralyzes the fans like God himself striking a thunderbolt. It's a sound that every fan knows, and it means only one thing: this ball is going a *long* way.

And so the ball came off the bat of Ritchie Edwards like it had been jettisoned from an ICBM. It rose majestically into the air straight toward the sun, arching like a rainbow over the center-field flagpole, traveling farther and farther until it finally landed with a splash on the far side of Strawbridge Lake. Ritchie Edwards admired the shot for a second and then rounded the bases. By the time Eddie Derringer threw his glove to the ground in disgust, O'Toole was already on his way to the mound to take him out. In the dugout, Mike Barnes buried his head in his hands, letting out a slow, moan of despair.

O'TOOLE SENT IN RIGHT-HANDER BARRY Emmons to replace Eddie Derringer, who was still fuming over giving up the titanic homerun to Ritchie. Barry was a short, stocky, muscular kid with short-cropped black hair and bushy eyebrows and wore a pair of thick horn-rimmed glasses. He looked more like a nerdy wrestler than a baseball player, but he had a lively fastball and a slow curve that routinely threw batters off stride.

After a few warm-up tosses, Louie Foreman came to the plate hoping to keep the rally alive. Louie could feel the presence of the crowd, which was finally calming down after the massive home run by Ritchie. The fans gathered at Palmyra Park were suddenly back in the game, still amazed at the unexpected turn of events, wondering whether this might turn out to be a close game after all. Louie could hear the City League fans yelling out encouraging words from the bleachers.

Louie stepped into the box, arched his bat, waited for Barry's first pitch. It was a high fastball that Bob Jennings had to reach up quickly and grab. Bob motioned with his hands for Barry to get the ball down. On the next pitch, Barry threw a one-hopper to Bob, who blocked it with his chest protector. Louie figured Barry would try to aim the next pitch instead of throw it, and maybe take something off it in order to find the strike zone. Barry wound up and threw a medium fastball over the heart of the plate. Louie swung with all his might, driving it deep into left center field. Joey McCall and Jamey Bradshaw hustled after the line drive as it took a couple bounces and rolled to the fence. Louie rounded first and headed for second as Joey McCall fired the ball back to Itchy McDermott, the cut-off man. In his hurry to throw out Louie, Itchy dropped the ball on the ground and then panicked, picking it up and throwing wildly over the head of third baseman Scrappy Cartwright just as Louie was approaching third base. As the ball flew into the stands, Louie trotted home easily for the fifth run.

The next batter was Bobby Graves, the replacement for Kurt

Cummings at third. Bobby was known more for his fine fielding than his hitting, but he was currently hitting a solid .285 for the Fire House Braves. Barry started him off with a fastball high and tight for ball one. On the second pitch, Bobby looked at a fastball right down the middle. With the count 1–1, Barry threw his slow curve, which caught Bobby completely off guard. He watched the ball drift toward his left shoulder before sinking to the middle of the zone. Bobby couldn't believe the pitch was that slow and broke that much. Down in the count, Bobby choked up on the bat and moved up in the box, hoping to catch that curve before it broke. Bob Jennings saw Bobby move up in the box and called for a fastball. Barry leaned back and hurled a heater, just catching the outside corner.

"Strike three!" hollered Collier.

The inning was over. The All-Stars were still down 8–5, but most of the players were thinking that with one inning to go, anything was possible.

Seventh Inning

As JACKIE TOOK THE MOUND for the start of the seventh inning there was renewed hope among the City League fans. The usually reliable bullpen for the Sacred Heart club had been surprisingly ineffective. Mike Barnes was still sitting alone on the far end of the bench, not even speaking to his best friend and catcher, Bob Jennings.

Louie Foreman fired the ball down to Archie at second. Archie whipped it around the horn until it landed in the mitt of Bobby Graves, Kurt Cummings's replacement at third base. Bobby tossed the ball to Jackie

"Come on, Jackie," Bobby pleaded. "Just three more outs!"

Joey came to the plate. Louie called for a fastball low and away. Jackie hurled a bullet down the middle of the plate. Joey McCall unleashed a smooth, powerful swing as he timed the pitch perfectly, driving it to the deepest part of the park. Allie Reynolds, the backup center fielder, tore after the ball, but it kept rising in the air as if lost in the clouds. Allie was running full speed toward the fence in left center but chasing a fly ball that seemed destined to leave the ballpark.

But throughout the afternoon, the wind had shifted slightly, blowing more toward the first baseline. The ball lost some of its momentum as it neared the flagpole. Allie backed up to the fence and, at the last second, leaped in the air, grabbing the ball just inches from the wall. The City League fans roared their approval, giving Allie well-deserved cheers and applause.

The next hitter was Jamey Bradshaw. Louie figured the only way to get Jamey out was by throwing him something just outside the strike zone. The idea was to get him to swing at a pitch he couldn't get the meat of his bat on. Louie called for a fastball, high and tight. Jackie wound up and threw a letter-high fastball. Jamey's whole body sprung to life, spiraling forward as he shifted his front foot slightly forward like his idol DiMaggio. The bat made solid contact, sending a deep fly ball to the left-field corner. The ball sailed toward the left-field foul pole with plenty of distance to spare. The fans rose in their seats, straining their necks to see if it was going to be a fair or foul. Ritchie was hustling toward the scoreboard near the foul pole, but by the time he arrived he could only watch and pray as the ball sailed over the scoreboard—foul by two feet! The Sacred Heart fans groaned their disappointment while the City League fans breathed a huge sigh of relief.

Louie knew Jamey would be looking for a curveball after that shot, so he called for another fastball and raised up his glove, signaling for another pitch just like the last one, only higher and out of the zone. Jackie took the sign and threw a heater that flew up and out of the zone for ball one. Jackie's next two pitches also missed the strike zone. With the count 3–1, Louie ordered a fastball low and away. Jackie reared back and lasered a fastball right down the middle. Jamey turned quickly on the pitch, blasting a rocket down the third baseline. The blistering line drive was smashed directly at Bobby Graves. It took one hop, caroming off Bobby's chest, and flew beyond the bleachers, clearing the chain-link fence. Bobby collapsed in the dirt, grabbing his chest and rolling over screaming at the top of his lungs. The entire infield, O'Toole, Dunberry, and Martin immediately rushed to Bobby, who was still curled in a fetal position, writhing in pain,

"Ohhh … my shoulder!" screamed Bobby as O'Toole tried to lift him up and examine the wound. O'Toole opened Bobby's shirt and was horrified to see a huge reddish-purple welt already forming just below his right shoulder.

"Just relax, son," said O'Toole. "Let me have a look at this."

Bobby slowly uncurled his stiff body and managed to sit up, his eyes trying to focus like he was a knockout victim. He was surrounded by a host of ballplayers from both sides. He sucked in a couple deep breaths, twisted his head around like he had a crick in his neck, and rubbed his chest with both hands.

"Jesus," he said, almost laughing. "What the hell happened?"

"Are you okay?" asked Jimmie Harlow, who had never seen a ball hit any harder—or a *player* hit any harder.

"Yeah," muttered Bobby, trying to regain his focus. "I'll be all right. I think I got the wind knocked out of me."

Dunberry and Martin were squatting next to O'Toole watching Bobby intently.

"You're gonna have quite a bruise there, young man. You sure you're okay?" asked Dunberry.

"I'll be all right," said Bobby. "Hey, it's only a flesh wound. Let the battle go on."

Bobby staggered to his feet, looking around for his glove while the fans gave him a hearty round of applause. Bobby tipped his hat to the fans, smiling painfully and suddenly feeling a little more important.

"Are you okay to stay in the game?" asked Osa.

"Sure," said Bobby. "You mean they can't hit 'em any harder than that?"

The players and coaches chuckled at Bobby's gallows humor, knowing the kid was still in extreme pain. Dunberry decided to keep him in the game, letting him throw some practice throws over to first base to make sure he was not seriously injured.

The umpire had ruled Jamey's hit a double, and he was standing on second base. He yelled over to Bobby, "Way to hang in there, buddy!"

"Thanks," said Bobby, shaking his head like a boxer recovering from a shot to the jaw.

Bobby looked at third-base umpire Homer Anderson. "Where is the ball?"

"It's over there," said Homer, pointing his finger at the Babe Ruth field adjacent to the park.

"It bounced *over* the stands?" asked Bobby incredulously.

"'Fraid so," said Homer.

After the players returned to their positions and the coaches were assured Bobby was fit to play, umpire Collier let Bobby take a few warm-up pitches.

Gary Malloy, the backup first baseman, approached the plate, stuffing another stick of Juicy Fruit chewing gum in his mouth, glaring at Jackie, chomping on wads of chewing gum and gnashing his teeth at the same time. Louie planned to set him up for an off-speed pitch. Jackie threw two fastballs for strikes. The third pitch came drifting over the plate like a floating badminton shuttlecock. Gary was anxious and committed himself too early in the swing, his stocky body totally off-stride, trying desperately to adjust to the speed of the ball in midswing. Falling awkwardly forward out of the box, Gary hit the ball about half-speed, lofting a harmless fly ball to Jimmie at second.

Two outs.

The next hitter was Barry Emmons, the pitcher. With his black crew cut, bushy eyebrows, and horn-rimmed glasses, he looked like anything but a dangerous hitter. Louie decided to go right after him and called for a fastball. Jackie promptly hurled a sizzling heater that nailed Louie's target on the outside corner. The next pitch was another fastball down the heart of the plate. Barry followed the pitch the whole way until it smacked Louie's glove.

"Strike two!"

Wasting no time, Jackie quickly wound up and threw a fastball in the same location, quickly dispensing with Barry. He never got the bat off his shoulders.

The All-Stars rushed to the dugout in a chaotic frenzy, still losing 8–5 and still full of hope even though they were down to their last three outs. All the team members were jumping up and down, shouting, cheering, and encouraging the hitters to get on base any way they could.

THE BOTTOM OF THE ORDER was due up. In practical terms, the remaining fans knew the City Leaguers had little chance to win the game. Osa glanced at Dunberry and then surveyed the dugout to see if any good hitters were left on the bench. Dunberry, true to his word, had put every available player into the game. There was no one left to pinch hit. Osa looked at Dunberry, who shrugged his shoulders, giving him a rueful smile. They would have to go with what they had.

Mark Greenberg, a light-hitting utility player who replaced Phil DeMarco at first base, strode to the plate, head bent, looking down at the dirt. He looked like a kid totally unprepared to hit a baseball. He held the bat weakly to his side, took a few mild practice swings, and then stepped in against Barry Emmons. Barry started him off with a curveball that sliced right into the middle of the plate. Mark took a late swing, fouling it at his feet. The next pitch was another curve, completely fooling Mark. He missed it by two feet. Bob Jennings signaled for a fastball. Barry threw a pitch that whizzed past Mark, a perfect example of the term *overmatched*.

The next hitter was George Beauchamp, who had taken over in right field for Dave Carmichael. George was a small, skinny kid but played with high energy and might have gotten the nickname "Scrappy" if it hadn't already been taken. George figured Barry would try to get ahead of him with a fastball and stepped into the plate with one thing on his mind: *Get a hit.*

The first pitch was a rising fastball that George got around on but fouled straight back to the backstop. On the next pitch, Barry swung late on another fastball but connected just enough to loft a short fly over the outstretched glove of Gary Malloy at first. George reached safety at first base, clapping his hands, yelling to his teammates, "Come on! We can do it!"

Osa reminded George that there was one out and not to get doubled up by a line drive. He also told him to steal the base on a wild pitch but only if the ball rolled all the way to the backstop. "Don't run us out of this inning," instructed Osa.

Allie Reynolds, the speedy center fielder batting in Nate Green's slot, came to the plate appearing befuddled and insecure. But Allie was jittery on purpose, because he wanted the opportunity to glance down the third baseline without anyone noticing if Scrappy was looking for a surprise bunt. Osa had given Allie the idea before he stepped into the on-deck circle. Scrappy stayed at his normal position, and when the first pitch came in, the little lefty laid down a perfect drag bunt down the third baseline. Barry Emmons rushed toward the ball, but by the time he grabbed it and threw to first base, Allie was crossing the bag, George cruising into second. O'Toole cursed himself for not moving his third baseman in to protect against the bunt. Now the bunt in that situation seemed like an obvious strategy he should have foreseen.

Jimmie Harlow was completely relaxed and walked confidently to the plate, sensing a momentum swing in the All-Stars' direction. He was hoping the pressure would cause Barry to tighten up on his delivery and groove one down the middle. Barry seemed unaffected by the growing tension in the game and calmly waited for Jimmie to enter the box. Barry started Jimmie off with a painfully slow curve, just nipping the outside corner for strike one. Jimmie thought, *He's going to throw the heater. That pitch was just a setup.* Bob Jennings flashed one finger, indicating a fastball on the outside of the plate. But Barry uncorked a straight pitch, running inside Jimmie's wheelhouse. Jimmie turned quickly on the pitch, slamming a screaming two-hopper down to Scrappy at third base. The ball bounced wickedly off Scrappy's chest but luckily popped straight up in the air. Scrappy quickly recovered and grabbed the ball in midair, diving toward the bag with his outstretched glove. George steamrolled into the base, executing a perfect slide as Scrappy lunged at him, nipping his right shoulder.

"Safe!" yelled Homer Anderson. Scrappy immediately jumped up and ran up to Homer holding the ball in his hand like it was a foreign object Homer had never seen.

"I tagged him! See! I tagged him! On the shoulder! See!"

O'Toole flew out of the dugout, screeching like a wounded hyena. "He made the tag! He got there ahead of him! Come on, Homer!"

Homer Anderson behaved exactly as he had with Dunberry. He calmly stood his ground and folded his arms, staring impassively into the blue sky above him. "The kid got in there," said Homer. "Play ball."

O'Toole clenched his fists and stomped on the ground, kicking loose dirt in Homer's direction. Still boiling with rage, O'Toole swiped his cap off and slammed it at Homer's feet, hysterically jumping up and down on his own baseball cap.

Homer looked at him as if he was ready for a straightjacket.

O'Toole finally ran out of steam, picked his dirty hat off the ground, and started slapping it against his leg like a jockey lashing a whip to a racehorse. He marched back to the dugout, punched the water cooler, and plopped down on the bench, glaring evil death rays at Homer.

All of a sudden, the carefree, calm atmosphere in Palmyra Memorial Park changed had dramatically, as if the jovial passengers on a cruise ship suddenly heard ominous, unexpected storm clouds rumbling in the distance. A palpable tautness coursed through the crowd, creating an eerie midafternoon silence. What had once been a taken-for-granted blowout by the invincible Yankees now seemed in serious doubt. With the bases loaded and one out, anything could happen—and O'Toole knew it.

O'Toole had one more pitcher on the bench, Tracy McDowell, a hard-throwing but erratic left-hander. He hollered for Bob Jennings to go to the mound to calm down Barry Emmons and stall for time. O'Toole walked down the end of the bench. Tracy, like every other player on the bench, had a concerned look on his face. He was sitting next to Mike Barnes. Unlike the rest of the players, Mike Barnes seemed to be enjoying the recent turn of events. The smug I-told-you-so expression on his face made O'Toole want to punch out the kid. He asked Tracy how he was feeling.

"I feel great, Coach," replied Tracy.

"Well, go warm up. We might need you."

Tracy grabbed his glove, asked reserve catcher Pat Shea to help him get loose, and then walked over to the bullpen area and began tossing a few pitches. O'Toole went back out to the mound, where Barry and Bob were deciding how to pitch to Archie Steele.

"How do you feel, son?" asked O'Toole.

"I feel fine, Coach. Let me finish. I'll get these guys out."

O'Toole looked skeptical. "Bob, what do you think? How's he throwing?"

"He looks okay. He just got that last pitch up a little."

"All right, let's go. This kid Steele likes to pull the ball, so pitch him outside—try to get him to ground out."

Barry nodded. Bob walked back to the plate, putting his mask back on. O'Toole strolled back to the dugout.

As Archie approached home plate, he glanced down at third to see where Scrappy was positioned. This time the third baseman had moved in about eight feet, clearly on the lookout for a bunt. Archie stepped into the box. Bob flashed the fastball sign. Barry wound up and threw a perfect strike on the outside corner.

Archie shook his head as if to ward off a bothersome fly, dug his cleats into the dirt, raised his bat even farther behind his back. The next pitch was a slicing curve that appeared to be over the plate. Archie took a mighty cut, but the ball faded away from him. Strike two. With the count 0–2, Archie told himself that he wasn't going to go down looking and was determined to swing at the next pitch. Bob called for a waste pitch that was supposed to be several inches off the plate. As soon as the ball left Barry's hand, Bob knew they were in trouble. The pitch was a made-to-order average fastball—and Archie didn't miss it. He uncoiled his taut body, connecting solidly on the sweet part of the bat. The ball exploded on contact, a scorching line drive zooming up the middle. Shortstop Itchy McDermott, acting solely on instinct, dove for the speeding projectile heading directly into center field. Itchy leaped parallel to the ground almost like Superman without a cape, flying through the air with his left arm extended just beyond second base. It happened so quickly that some of the fans thought the ball disappeared when it made a brutal smacking sound in the mitt of Itchy, who bounced hard on the ground, scraping his chin on the dirt. Itchy recovered quickly, hoping to double up George, who was halfway to home plate. Itchy fired to Scrappy, but the throw was off, and George barely managed to scramble back to the bag. The crowd roared their approval, and even the City League fans had to admit they had witnessed something very special, a catch for the ages.

The City League All-Stars were down to their last out with Jackie waiting in the on-deck circle. He was about to move toward the batter's box, but O'Toole jumped from the bench, calling timeout. O'Toole did not like the way Steele had crushed that ball and knew it should have been a sure base hit, driving in at least two runs. As he walked to the mound, Bob Jennings joined him for the decision. To Bob's surprise, O'Toole wasted no time. He asked Barry for the ball. Barry reluctantly handed the ball over, and O'Toole signaled for Tracy McDowell to come in and finish the game. O'Toole figured he was better off with the lefty-lefty matchup, and if McDowell could control his stuff, he was sure Jackie would be overmatched. Tracy came lumbering to the mound. O'Toole gave him the ball, looking down at the young man who literally held the game in his hands. "Try to stay away from the middle of the plate, Tracy—and don't give him anything inside, okay?"

Tracy nodded. O'Toole went back to the dugout. Bob Jennings returned to home plate. After several warm-up pitches, Collier yelled, "Play ball!"

Jackie stepped into the batter's box, twisting his back foot into the dirt, getting better traction. There was scarcely a sound to be heard in the park. Anxious fans were twitching eyes, gnawing fingernails, biting lips, wiping sweaty brows, rubbing pants, clenching fists, crossing fingers for luck, placing hands in prayer position amid the constant lighting and relighting of cigarettes, pipes, and cigars.

Bob Jennings called for an outside fastball, not wanting his pitcher to go anywhere near Jackie's power zone. Tracy took a full windup and sent a wild, out-of-control pitch at Jackie's chin. Jackie jerked his head back, stumbling backward, knees buckling, his legs almost giving out on him. The pitch wasn't even close to where Bob wanted it. He angrily threw his glove hand toward third base, indicating he wanted the pitch *outside*—not at Jackie Riddick's head. Tracy nodded, concentrated on clipping the outside corner. He wound up and heaved the ball with all his might toward Bob's glove. But the pitch started out wide right of the plate, and by the time it arrived, it was hovering over the inside corner. Jackie saw the pitch all the way, liked it, raised his bat, cocked his wrists, smoothly shifted his body forward—then viciously attacked the ball. He struck it dead-on, crushing the sweet part of the bat.

The ball exploded off Jackie's bat, heading swiftly toward the right-field bleachers. It kept soaring up and up, not like a rainbow but a low, streaming line drive that kept rising steadily into the air. The stunned crowd rose to their feet, standing on their toes, straining their necks to see how far it would go. The ball kept sailing until it cleared the fence, disappearing beyond the row of vehicles parked on the street.

Jackie rounded the bases, clapping his hands, jumping up and down, arriving at home plate greeted by his ecstatic teammates, who were beside themselves with joy, whooping and hollering, slapping Jackie on the back, giving him high fives and rowdy cheers before he was buried under an avalanche of twelve-year-old kids.

Jackie emerged from the dusty pyramid of scrambling, sweaty bodies in wool uniforms, dusted himself off, and waved to everybody in the stands. The fans were cheering so loudly he could hardly hear his teammates congratulate him. He ran to Coach Martin and jumped into his arms.

"I did it!" he screamed. "We won!"

Osa smiled expansively. "You sure did, son. I knew you could do it."

Suddenly, his brother Danny ran up to Jackie, giving him a big hug and mock punching him in the stomach. "Hey, bro! I told you you'd be an all-star! Now you're a hero!"

"Thanks, Danny. This is the best moment of my life! Do you believe our comeback?"

"Truly magnificent, Mr. Clutch. What a homer!"

"Say, did Mom come?"

"Well, why don't you look over there?" Danny pointed toward the backstop.

Betty was alone standing next to the end of the bleachers. Jackie looked over and gave his mother a big wave of his hand, grinning widely. Betty, appearing shy and uncomfortable, nevertheless waved vigorously at Jackie, giving him a beaming smile and then clapping her hands and doing her best to jump up and down like a cheerleader.

"Wow," said Jackie. "I can't believe she came!"

"Well, there was a little kicking and screaming, but I got her here. She really enjoyed the game and watching you play."

"Enough to change her mind about baseball and religion?"

"Sorry, bro. Jehovah's Witnesses always come first."

"That's okay. I'm glad she had a good time," said Jackie. Then he gazed into the stands hoping to get a glimpse of Vera. He surveyed the bleachers and the fans streaming out of the park, but he didn't spot her. Turning toward his brother with a wide grin spreading across his face, Jackie shouted, "Now let's go down to Lincoln's! There's somebody I really want to see!"

"Got it," said Danny.

"I'll see you in a few minutes."

The ovations and pandemonium were gradually slowing down, the players and fans finally returning to their senses. Jackie got in line as the two teams, showing good sportsmanship, marched single-file across the field, forming two lines that met in the middle, where the players shook hands as they passed one another. As Jackie approached Mike Barnes, Mike stopped him, placing his hand on his shoulder. Then he gave Jackie a warm hug, whispering in his ear, "See you in Yankee Stadium, slugger."

After shaking all the Sacred Heart players' hands, Jackie headed for the dugout. Jimmie Harlow ran up to Jackie, wrapped his arms around him, and lifted him high in the air, shouting, "You played a perfect game!"

Jackie's face was beaming. "Put me down, you dummy!" cried Jackie.

Jimmie set Jackie on the ground, gave him another big hug, jabbed a few mock punches to his stomach, and then ran off toward Archie Steele.

Jackie stood near home plate looking upward to the skies, thinking, *No, I didn't play a perfect game, but boy, this is a perfect day.*

PART THREE

And it was a time of relentless, compulsive attempts to wear a bland cloak of normality, with everyone going around pretending they lived lives like Ozzie and Harriet, and other perfect families on television. But in reality, no sane adult could possibly live such a well-ordered, boring, and uneventful existence—not even Ozzie and Harriet.

—Robert Metraux, *Sundown in Williamsburg*

6

Palmyra, New Jersey
August 1958

THE COMMUNITY CENTER IN PALMYRA was an imposing gray sandstone mansion that looked more like a European medieval monastery than a venue for the town's numerous social activities. Located directly across the railroad tracks in midtown, the building housed a basketball court, gymnasium, pool tables, ping-pong tables, and a weight room. It towered three stories high, each floor containing several small, brown paneled rooms and larger areas for classrooms and group exercises. The townspeople used the Center, as it was called, for a variety of social gatherings, town committee meetings, weekly card games, women's clubs, and political discussions. Built in 1910, the colossal structure was originally the summer home of a millionaire industrialist, but he lost all his money in the stock market crash of 1929. It was neglected for years until the city council decided to completely renovate it in 1951.

On this hot August night just before school started, Jackie walked up the cement stairs leading to the dance floor of the Center. He was wearing a pair of slim-fitting tan Chino slacks held up by a thin silver belt with the buckle angled to the side, and a short-sleeved, dark green polo shirt. He was also wearing a new pair of shoes, and his sandy hair, which normally fell loosely in his face, was slicked down on both sides by a solid dabbing of Brylcreem. This was the first time he had been able to attend a dance, because his mother strictly forbade him to fraternize with "worldly people" and was terrified this devil-inspired rock 'n' roll music would ruin his moral principles, turn him into an oversexed degenerate and a juvenile delinquent. After telling his mother he was going to a sports banquet, his sister Donna dressed him in his bedroom, and he skulked out of the house like a thief in the night. He hated lying to his mother, but Jackie just couldn't accept being an outsider and a loner practicing a strange religion nobody understood. He knew he was just postponing a huge argument with his mother, but for now, sneaking around seemed like a better idea than confronting his mother and totally disavowing the church.

Jackie opened the door and entered a wide reception area supported by a pointed cathedral ceiling flanked on both sides by two large, elaborate stained-glass windows. For a second, he thought he was entering a church. To his left, Jackie noticed an older woman in a yellow cotton dress standing behind a plain white counter displaying an assortment of footwear.

"Good evening, son," she called out to him. "You need to check your shoes here."

"Okay," he said, approaching the lady.

"I'm Mrs. Thomas. Is this your first time at the dance?"

"Yes, ma'am. I'm Jackie Riddick."

"Glad to meet you, Jackie. Do you understand why we need to check your shoes?"

Jackie shrugged. "I guess it's so we don't scuff up the floor, right?"

"That's right. The dance floor is also the basketball court, so we can't allow any hard-soled shoes."

Jackie slipped off his white bucks, revealing the black socks Donna had insisted that he wear. "It's okay by me. I'm glad I didn't wear the socks with the holes in them."

Mrs. Thomas laughed good-naturedly, unaware that Jackie wasn't kidding.

Jackie was disappointed that he had to relinquish his new shoes, because he wanted to show off his new white bucks that Donna had picked out for him. She said even though Pat Boone wore them, they were still cool.

Jackie handed his shoes over to Mrs. Thomas and walked through the wide-open double doors of the basketball court. Immediately, he noticed a bunch of boys and girls on the floor jitterbugging to a raucous rock 'n' roll song. At the far end of the court, a pudgy older guy was dancing by himself on stage wearing a colorful Hawaiian shirt, gripping a microphone near a brown record player with two speakers. He was playing "That'll Be the Day" by Buddy Holly, one of Jackie's favorite songs. Buddy Holly, Ritchie Valens, and the Big Bopper would all be killed in a plane crash within a few months. After the tragedy, Donna said losing Buddy Holly was like losing an older brother. Donna also mourned the loss of Ritchie Valens for a different reason. His big hit at the time of his death was "Oh Donna," a gorgeous, aching, romantic ballad played by deejays at the end of the evening to grant starry-eyed sweethearts one last chance to hold each other closely on the dance floor.

Jackie surveyed the expansive court to see if there was anyone he knew, hoping to spot one of his teammates on Kiwanis or some of the guys from the All-Star team. Near the bleachers, he caught sight of Kurt Cummings and Phil Demarco talking to a guy he didn't know. Phil looked up and saw Jackie coming toward him.

"Hey, Jackie! Come on over!"

Jackie walked over to the other side of the floor, realizing for the first time that the boys were hanging out on one side of the gym and the girls on the other. The girls huddled together in small groups, sitting on the bleachers or drinking punch at a nearby table. A few of the girls were on the dance floor dancing with each other. As he crossed the gymnasium, Jackie tried not to stare at the girls, but he really wanted to find Vera Lincoln.

As he neared Phil, he bumped into Jimmie Harlow, who was dancing up a storm with a pretty blonde in a ponytail wearing bright red lipstick.

"Hey, Jackie! Great to see you!" cried Jimmie, turning around while swinging the girl under his arm and grabbing her by the waist.

"Hey, Jimmie!" Jackie yelled above the music. "You can play baseball *and* dance?"

"This is nothing, buddy!" screamed Jimmie. "I can do all kinds of shit you don't know about!"

"I bet you can!"

Jimmie swung the girl around, and they disappeared into the crowd. Jackie kept moving, bumping into people, and finally came up to Kurt, Phil, and another kid he didn't recognize.

"Hey, sweet swingin' Jackie!" cried Phil. "Good to see you! This is Tommy Waters."

Jackie shook his hand.

"I hear you're quite a baseball player," said Tommy.

"Well, I should be," Jackie said. "That's about all I ever do."

"I played baseball once," said Kurt, grinning wickedly. "My old man took me out for a game of catch, threw the ball in my face, and gave me a black eye."

Jackie stared at Kurt, frowning, "Christ, Kurt, you're so full of shit."

"Hey," said Phil. "Kurt was just telling us how he screwed two girls this summer—at some camp."

Jackie looked over at a beaming, cocky Kurt Cummings. He couldn't believe an obnoxious prankster like Kurt had already had sex with two girls. He figured this was just another line of Kurt's bullshit but played along anyway.

"So … what was it like?" asked Phil.

Kurt's chest puffed out, expanding like an inflatable doll. He was basking in his sudden role as the almighty Sex King of Palmyra, holding court, magnanimously dispensing his secret, arcane knowledge to pathetic little virgins standing before him.

"I'll tell you, guys, it's the greatest thing on God's green earth! It feels like you're flying on a magic carpet ride—floating on a cloud of titties!"

Jackie didn't say anything. He was lost in thought, savoring the image of drifting along on his back, floating on a cloud of titties.

"Hell, them girls weren't nothin'," said Kurt. "I saw them this summer, but I'm going out for some fresh meat here in town. I'm a member of the 4-F Club—find 'em, feel 'em, fuck 'em, and forget 'em!"

Everybody laughed at Kurt's club membership, but Jackie soon learned that it was an overused, worn-out, stupid philosophy among the guys. Jackie glanced once more across the gym to see if he could locate Vera. The dance floor was teeming with sweaty, pulsating teens swishing and swaying to "Don't Be Cruel" by Elvis. He didn't see Vera in the crowd. He was about to excuse himself and roam over to the other side to look for her, but unexpectedly Dutch Lear came rushing toward them wearing worn-out dungarees and a loud paisley shirt.

"Did you tell them?" he yelled, looking straight at Phil DeMarco. "Did you tell them who won?"

Phil looked at their classmate Dutch Lear as if he was a cockroach he'd like to step on.

"Tell them what?" asked Phil.

"The contest! I won! Fair and square, right?"

"Bullshit," said Phil. "My stuff was worth more money. All you got was some cheap-ass shit."

Tommy Waters blurted, "Okay, assholes, tell me what the hell you guys are arguing about?"

Phil sighed loudly, giving Dutch a look he usually reserved for the nerds in advanced math class. His words came out strained and painful, like a person who knew he was giving a boring speech. "We had a contest last Thursday to see who was the best thief in town. We both went into Rogers News Agency at the same time to see who could steal the most stuff. Dutch thinks he won."

"Thinks?" protested Dutch. "Come on, Phil! I brought out six more items than you did!"

"Okay, fuckin' Robin Hood. You got the most stuff—but what the hell? It was junk—pencils, bubble gum … and shit."

"So what?"

"You see the stuff I got? I stole Zippo and VU lighters, fountain pens, notebooks—and fancy Cuban cigars! My stuff was way more valuable!"

"Yeah," agreed Dutch, "but … as you will remember, the contest was to see who could steal the *most* stuff."

"All right … all right …" conceded Phil. "So, you're a master thief. Go steal Eisenhower's fuckin' golf clubs—but hey, I want a rematch. This time we're not fooling around with some crappy news agency. We go big-time—to Green's Department Store or Schwerings Hardware!"

"You're on, pal," said Dutch.

As it turned out, Phil and Dutch did clash again in the second round of the Great Palmyra Steal-a-Thon. Every kid in town knew these two guys were in a thievery class all by themselves, and their shoplifting exploits were the stuff of legend. Phil won the second round decisively, pilfering a shotgun and a record player by ingeniously sewing a huge burlap pocket on the inside of his bulky trench coat. Dutch could only muster a can of Sterno and a hacksaw. Dutch was forced to concede that Phil was the best thief in town. Phil said they were really close in terms of thievery skills. In fact, Phil seriously suggested they join forces and hijack a Brink's armored truck. Dutch said he'd think it over.

Jackie listened patiently to the guys exchanging stolen merchandise stories, but he still wanted to know if Vera had come to the sock hop. He kept glancing toward the dance floor, but most of the girls were sitting in the bleachers on the other side of the gym. He could only glimpse faint, shadowy figures.

"Hey, guys," he said. "I'm going to check out the other side."

Kurt gave him a sly, knowing look. "Oh, you looking for someone special?"

"No, I just want to see one of my friends. She lives in my neighborhood."

"Good luck," said Phil. "Ask her to dance. Girls love that shit."

"See you guys later."

He started walking around the dance floor toward the stage. The deejay with the loud paisley shirt was still commanding the stage, bouncing around energetically, shuffling through a handful of 45s, raving about the records he was playing. At the moment, he was exhorting all the kids to get out on the floor and do the "Stroll," a slow dance where boys and girls formed two lines facing one another and a couple would come together and stroll down the lane of on-lookers.

The gym lights shining above were tinted with muted colors of red, yellow, and blue, and several floor lights pointed to the ceiling of the main dancing area, giving the court a dreamy atmosphere very different from the glaring lights set up for a basketball game. He spotted Vera by the punchbowl table talking to a couple of other girls. She was wearing a black satin wiggle dress with a scooped neck and holding a small cup in her hand. Her lithe, petite body was highlighted from the back by a floodlight on the floor. A pale blue glow washed over her from a light above. She lifted the cup, took a sip, tossed her head back, and smiled. The soft lighting accentuated her flawless complexion, violet eyes, and bright red lips, making her look grownup and developed beyond her years. He couldn't believe this was the same girl he had seen wearing an apron and slinging hamburgers in her parents' luncheonette.

"Hi, Vera."

Vera turned aside and saw him standing awkwardly in front of her. She smiled instantly, lighting up every dark part of his soul.

"Oh, hi!" she exclaimed enthusiastically, tossing her black, wavy hair away from her face. "I'm glad you could make it! Isn't this a great dance?"

"It sure is! I never knew so many kids were into dancing."

"It's great. But, you know … it's kinda silly, because all the girls stick together on one side and the boys stay on the other. It's like we think the other side has cooties or something."

"I think the boys are too shy. I know I am."

"Oh, that's silly too. We're easy to talk to. Boys just don't give us a chance."

Jackie was so nervous he thought he was going to throw up on her. Standing rigid and speechless, he was paralyzed by her presence, drowning in the soft glow of her eyes. He tried to sound nonchalant and cool, but the words rushed out as if he had just discovered the place was on fire.

"Would you like to dance?"

Vera calmly set her cup on the table and flipped her hair back again, batting her eyelashes.

"I thought you didn't know how to dance?"

"My sister … she's been helping me out …"

"In that case, let's go!"

In his haste, Jackie completely forgot to notice if it was a fast or slow song. He grabbed her hand, and they dashed out on the dance floor just as "Whole Lotta Shakin' Goin' On" exploded from the speakers. They started jitterbugging with him leading her, swirling her around the dance floor, their arms waving and legs moving furiously to the pounding piano rhythm. He held on to her right hand, and they swiveled their hips back and forth. Then he pulled her near him, slipping her under his arm before twirling her around like a spinning top. They danced for a couple of minutes, and then in a moment of exuberant spontaneity, Jackie tossed Vera high into the air, swinging her around in a dizzy circle before they stumbled across the dance floor, collapsing beside each other on two chairs, out of breath and laughing hysterically.

"Wow, that was fun!" cried Vera, still breathing heavily.

"What a great song!" Jackie yelled, slumping back in the chair.

"And you said you couldn't dance! You can really cut a rug!"

"My sister Donna taught me some steps. She's been on *Bandstand!* She's got the greatest collection of 45s—Jerry Lee Lewis, Elvis, Chuck Berry, all of them!"

"Well, she's a great teacher. You don't need me to teach you *anything.*"

"I don't know … We can dance some more … right? You're so easy to lead. It's like we're a natural team—like Fred Astaire and Ginger Rogers!"

Vera smiled, lighting up the room. "Oh boy, look out Fred and Ginger! You've got some competition!"

"Hey! How about some punch? I'm dying of thirst."

"Sounds good to me."

The couple walked over to the punchbowl table and drank two cups of grape punch, never taking their eyes off each other. Jackie had never felt this way before. He knew he was experiencing something totally different, and his usual level of high anxiety around girls seemed to be melting away. He was waiting for the panic attack that happened just about every time he met a girl his age. Jackie hated these attacks and felt his whole body was betraying him. His heart would start pounding as if it was going to burst out of his chest. He would break out in a cold sweat. He would lose concentration, becoming frustrated, thinking he was going to jump out of his skin. Most of the time he managed to check these attacks by keeping his interactions short and always made an excuse to leave quickly.

Nobody really knew why he was such a good baseball player. Jackie knew. He felt at home and at ease on a baseball field. On the diamond, he displayed confidence, self-assuredness, and could practically feel his self-esteem rising with every inning he played. It was like he was transported to another world when he crossed the baselines onto a field of dirt and grass. And in a sense, he was. His anxieties, fears, frustrations, and feelings of inferiority vanished as if the baseball field was his private haven, his sanctuary from the harshness and brutality of the real world.

The baseball rules were clear and simple. He knew exactly what he was supposed to do: hit the ball, throw the ball, and catch the ball. And there was no clock to watch, so the game felt like it had its own natural rhythm like the changing of the seasons. Time was measured by otherworldly things like how fast a player could get to the ball and throw another player out. Violence and aggression were controlled, and at the end of the game you either won or lost, and it was over. The same bad game never kept repeating itself, and you always thought the next game would be better, and you would play better. And the crowd would cheer you even louder. Where else were they going to cheer him? So far in his life, Jackie had been able to survive in school by seeking perfection on a baseball field and pretending to be relaxed and gregarious among his peers. But his unexpected anxiety attacks were getting worse, and he worried that someday he might explode and do something stupid like beat up someone for no reason. Jackie wished he knew the source of his attacks, but he had no idea. They seemed to be so much a part of him that he thought perhaps he had been born this way.

But Vera made him feel comfortable, and her presence at the dance reminded him how few times he felt truly comfortable in this world. He kept a stomach-full of emotions bottled up inside, fearing that once they were released he'd never be able to control himself.

But on this night, he decided to let his emotions flow and not put a check on his deep feelings and caring for someone—or loving someone. If he was going to fall head-over-heels in love with Vera, then so be it. He wouldn't hold back. Jackie knew he was feeling something special for Vera, but at the moment he didn't know quite what to call it. He *did* know one thing: he wanted to spend more time with her.

They continued getting to know each other at the punchbowl table, talking about their likes and dislikes and friends they had in common. After a while, Jackie and Vera moved to a seat on the bleachers, acting as if they were the only two people in the gym.

Jackie really wanted to tell Vera everything about his life. He wanted her to know about the hard times his family suffered. He wanted to tell her about his evil stepfather in Baltimore and how they had escaped in the middle of the night. He wanted to tell her how much he hated him and how he still possessed a terrible urge to cause him harm. He wanted to tell her how much he was embarrassed by how poor they were and how he sometimes felt he should never have been born because there was never enough food in the house. He wanted to tell her how hard it was to be a Jehovah's Witness and not celebrate holidays or pledge allegiance to the flag. He wanted to tell her how much he loved baseball and how much he admired Coach Martin and considered him the greatest man he had ever met. He wanted to tell her about all his hopes and dreams and how excited he was about meeting her.

But he didn't tell her any of these things. He was afraid to unload all this baggage on her and end up babbling for hours. Jackie figured he would sound so screwed up he would chase her right out of the gym.

They ended the evening slow-dancing with each other to a ballad called "In the Still of the Night." Jackie held her hand and led her out on the dance floor, joining other couples swaying and swooning to the song. Holding one another closely, dancing cheek-to-cheek, they moved together effortlessly. As she glided weightlessly over the dance floor, Vera was a perfect picture of elegance, grace, and style. And as the song swelled to a magnificent crescendo, Jackie gazed into her eyes as if he was going to dissolve into them.

Hold me again, with all of your might,
In the still of the night ...

He lifted his head away from her cheek just as they passed under a golden light bathing her face in soft illumination. Radiance seemed to glow from within as if her soul was reaching out to embrace him. He leaned toward her, kissing her on the lips. He hoped this magic and the mystery of it all would last forever. Jackie had once told his friends that hitting a line drive in baseball was the greatest feeling in the world. Following the night with Vera, he realized there was another sensation that was even better—the touch and warmth of a young girl, the arousing scent of femininity, someone caring for him, maybe even loving him.

7

September 1958

T HE FIRST DAY OF SCHOOL finally arrived.

Charles Street School was only a short walk across the ballpark and up a few blocks from the Riddicks' apartment. Donna took Jackie shopping, picked out his outfit, and got him up early to make sure he followed all her instructions. She was going to buy him a pair of blue jeans, but he told her that the school dress code didn't allow blue jeans in grade school.

"What!" she cried. "What kind of school is that? School for nerds? I guess they wouldn't let Brando be a student there, huh?"

Donna settled on a pair of tight-fitting khakis, a burgundy short-sleeved button-down shirt, and a shiny black patent leather belt with a silver buckle. She told him to wear the Pat Boone white bucks with black socks.

"Listen, kid," she lectured, "you're not a greaser. Greasers are as uncool as auto mechanics, so don't go putting that greasy kid's stuff in your hair—leave it dry and comb it loosely over the side of your face. I know it looks like straw and the wind blows it everywhere, but the girls will love it. You got the carefree, windblown look, dorky!"

After a final inspection for any uncool fashion faux pas, Donna sent him out the door.

He was in Mrs. Wilson's sixth-grade class. As he was walking toward the school, he saw a small group of students hanging out by the bicycle racks and approached them.

"Say, does anybody know where Mrs. Wilson's class is?"

A cute, perky girl with blonde hair and bright blue eyes turned toward him. "It's in room 210!" she gushed.

"Thanks."

Jackie looked around for someone from the Little League or pick-up games that summer, but he didn't recognize anyone in the crowd. He was early. Other students in the distance drifted leisurely across an open field toward the school. He was hoping to see Vera as soon as possible. Since the night of the Community Center dance, he had spent several afternoons at the luncheonette getting to know Vera and her parents. So far, their only date had been a Saturday-afternoon trip to the movies to see the horror film *The Blob* staring Steve McQueen. He had cautiously placed his arm around her shoulder in the theater, leaning over and kissing her on the cheek. He figured it was too early to think of Vera as his girlfriend, but he felt they were moving in the right direction— whatever that was for twelve-year-olds. She had already told him she liked him a lot, jokingly calling him her friend Tom after Tom Sawyer. He had said that was okay with him as long as she could be his Becky Thatcher. Jackie had lightheartedly suggested that they get engaged and seal it with a kiss like Tom and Becky in the book.

He continued walking down a narrow, gray-tiled hallway lined with pictures of historical figures, stopping at a picture of Benjamin Franklin next to room 210. He peered through the thick glass window and spotted about a dozen students in the room. He opened the door and glanced to the right, noticing a large round clock on the wall that read 7:50. He quietly took a seat in one of the wooden flip-top desks in the middle of the room. He stared straight ahead, occasionally looking down at the drawings and initials carved into the writing surface. Within minutes, the room filled up with students laughing, talking, joking with each other. He still didn't recognize any of his teammates from the summer, but he did notice the perky blonde with the big blue eyes sitting in the front row. The girl reminded him of Vera for some reason, and he wished she was in his class, but the school had placed her in Mrs. Chambley's class down the hall. At precisely eight o'clock, a bronze bell high in the corner rang out loudly. An elderly, dignified woman in a print dress and perfectly styled gray hair entered the room, gracing everyone with a wide, pleasant smile.

"Good morning, class!" exclaimed Mrs. Wilson.

The whole class responded with an energetic "Good morning, Mrs. Wilson!"

Before Mrs. Wilson had a chance to say anything, Kurt Cummings cracked open the door and tried to sneak in unnoticed.

"Excuse me, young man," said Mrs. Wilson, "who are you and why are you late?"

"Sorry, ma'am," Kurt replied, looking down at his shoes. "I'm Kurt Cummings. The chain on my bike broke, and I had to walk my bike all the way here."

"Well, don't let it happen again. You'll be penalized for being late. It's rude, uncivil behavior and shows a lack of respect. Do you understand?"

"Yes, ma'am," said Kurt, quietly slipping into one of the desks.

Jackie was bemused to see the loud-mouthed class clown of the All-Star team behaving so meekly, but he was glad to see a familiar face. He looked over and got Kurt's attention, giving him a wave of his hand. Kurt was immediately animated, waving back at him, putting his hands together and swinging his arms like he was hitting a baseball. Jackie smiled and turned back to Mrs. Wilson, wondering if Kurt still carried a spider in his back pocket.

Mrs. Wilson was standing in the middle of the room in front of the blackboard, commanding absolute attention. Jackie hadn't noticed it before, but there was an American flag hanging unfurled from a wooden stand in the corner.

"Now we will all stand for the Pledge of Allegiance."

Jackie froze. His mind suddenly flashed back to images of rats running out of a cellar. He felt even more panic.

He had completely forgotten about the Pledge of Allegiance. Everyone stood up, facing the flag. Jackie rose from his seat, looking down at the floor, cursing himself for not taking a seat in the back row. Now everybody would think he was an unpatriotic pinko Communist. All the students solemnly placed their hands across their chests, stared at the flag, and began to recite the pledge. He decided to fake it. Placing his hand on his stomach, he mouthed the words without speaking: "I pledge allegiance to the flag of the United States of America ..."

He was terrified that someone would notice his lame commitment to the United States of America and curse him out in front of the whole class. He thought, *God, they're going to tar and feather me and ride me out of town on a rail. I might as well be John Wilkes Booth!* But none of the students did anything. Everyone sat back down like programmed robots, waiting for class to start. Jackie figured no one had noticed today, but he had probably been lucky. He needed a new strategy to cope with this problem or he would quickly become the most despised kid in school.

Mrs. Wilson moved to the front of her desk while the students remained silent, patiently waiting for her to speak. "I'm Mrs. Wilson, as most of you know from last year. But we have a couple of new students this year, and I would like to introduce them to you and have them say a few words about themselves."

Jackie's body stiffened, battery acid suddenly bubbling up from his stomach. Tiny beads of sweat formed on his forehead. His heart abruptly began to run on overdrive. *Please, Jehovah. Not me. I just got over being John Wilkes Booth!*

Mrs. Wilson picked up a roster sheet from her desk. "Let me see ... We have three new students: Judy McCallister. Robert Purcell, and Jackie Riddick. Judy, where are you?"

Judy McCallister, a thin, cross-eyed girl with thick glasses wearing a pleated brown dress, stood up clumsily and told everyone that her family had just moved from Philadelphia and she liked drawing pictures of elephants, sewing for pleasure, and playing hopscotch. Then Robert Purcell announced that he was from upstate New York and liked riding his bike, fishing, erector sets, and building model airplanes.

Mrs. Wilson, gazed around, surveying the class, then paused.

"Jackie Riddick? Are you here today?"

Jackie stood up, grabbing the desk for support, wishing he could vaporize out the window. He hadn't gotten over the Pledge of Allegiance debacle, and now he had to make a damn speech! He was so self-conscious he could feel the tiny bones in his neck crunching together.

"Well ..." he began. "My family just moved here from Baltimore, Maryland, and I'm a big baseball fan and I really like the Orioles—even though they *really* stink right now."

A smattering of laughter gave him a much needed boost.

"... and I like to read adventure stories. The one I am reading right now is called *The Cruel Sea,* and it's a great story about ... the ocean—"

"That's cruel!" shouted Kurt Cummings, unable to contain himself.

Mrs. Wilson gave Kurt a nasty look, but before she could say anything, Jackie continued, "That's right, Kurt. It's all about swashbuckling musketeers sword fighting and dangerous hurricanes ... and terrible shipwrecks, stuff like that ... I also like rock 'n' roll music, and sometimes I sit on my back steps and sing Elvis songs to myself."

Again the class laughed. He sat back down in his seat, wondering how big a fool he had made of himself and cursing under his breath for telling the class about singing Elvis songs.

Mrs. Wilson handed out the books for the coming year and explained the class schedule. Then she held math, reading, and writing lessons, followed by a fifteen-minute break. After the break, she covered history and social studies. Following a discussion of the Civil War, the bell sounded at eleven o'clock, indicating it was time for lunch and recess. Jackie walked out of class pleased with Mrs. Wilson's personality and teaching methods. He also enjoyed the subjects they were learning, especially reading and history.

He was too nervous to eat in the cafeteria, so he walked home for lunch. Danny was also at the apartment for lunch break. He told Jackie what it was like at the high school where they taught grades eight through twelve. Danny had already made a few friends in his class and was adapting well to their new life in Palmyra. Danny was more calm and self-assured than Jackie. His easygoing, quiet manner appealed to his eighth-grade classmates. Jackie asked him about the pledge.

"Just fake it like you did—or say the damn thing. I quit that shit a long time ago. You think Donna never said the Pledge of Allegiance? She's addicted to being popular." Danny took a bite out of his bologna sandwich, gulping it down with a sip of Coke. "You know everyone is gonna think we're some kind of commie weirdos if we sit there and ignore the American flag."

"I guess you're right. I just won't tell Mom, like I did when I went to a dance."

Danny took another bite out of his sandwich and gave his brother a devious smile. "Yeah, you know what they say—what she don't know won't hurt her."

After gobbling down a peanut butter and jelly sandwich and a glass of milk, Jackie headed back to school to check out what the kids did for recess. Charles Street School was a plain, one-floor T-shaped brick building lined with rows of identical four-foot-high windows spanning the entire circumference of the school. The only hint of creativity was a half-moon red ceramic courtyard at the entrance with three marble benches that nobody ever sat on. The school was centered in the middle of a huge, grassy field surrounded by hopscotch and jump-rope areas, basketball courts, a football field, a baseball diamond, and a solid row of metal bicycle racks. Jackie naturally veered toward the diamond, but he quickly realized they were not playing baseball. No one was wearing a baseball glove. He searched all over for Vera and saw a bunch of girls in the distance skipping rope and playing on the monkey bars. Jackie quickly realized that recess was totally segregated by gender, as if they considered each other alien species to be avoided.

The boys were playing kick soccer, which was basically baseball with a soccer ball. The pitcher rolled the ball to the kicker, and he kicked it for a base hit. If someone caught it in the air or picked it up and threw to first base before you got there, it was an out. Jackie arrived just as they were picking up teams. He recognized the familiar faces of Jimmie Harlow and Louie Foreman. They were the two captains choosing up sides. Jimmie was the first one to notice him.

"Jackie Riddick! Hey, he's on my team! Hey, Jackie, come on over!"

He was elated to see his two buddies and ran up to them and shook their hands. Then Louie's team went out to play defense.

"Hey, Jackie," yelled Jimmie. "You're gonna love this game. Ever play?"

"No."

"It's easy. He rolls you the ball, kick it as hard as you can—then run the bases!"

"Okay."

"All right! Let's go, team. Jackie, you kick number three!"

The two players who kicked the ball before him made routine outs. As the ball rolled toward him, did exactly what Jimmie had told him to do. He kicked the ball deep into right field with his left foot and took off running toward first base. He was running so hard he wasn't following the flight of the ball. As he rounded second, he heard everyone screaming for him to slow down. When he reached third base, he asked the third baseman what had happened.

"You don't have to run," he said. "You just hit the longest home run I've ever seen."

Jackie's early success was short-lived. The next two times up, he struck out and grounded out weakly to first base. His team won, and Jackie enjoyed the game, but he figured he'd never be as good at soccer as he was at baseball. He returned to the afternoon school session. Mrs. Wilson spent the time going over natural science, art and music, and geography before the three o'clock bell signaled the day was over. Jackie got up from his seat and said a couple words to Kurt Cummings, finding out that he possessed a new spider named Fred Junior "to scare the hell out of the girls." He was walking down the hall when he heard the perky blonde girl from the front row call out his name.

"Hey, new kid! Jackie! Jackie Riddick!"

He spun around and faced the girl.

"Hey, I'm Dottie McDougall," she uttered breathlessly, striding up beside him.

"Hi," he muttered. "Thanks for the directions."

"Hey, no problem. You really read books?"

"Yeah, I—"

"Me too!" she interrupted, lifting up the textbooks in her hands. "I love all kinds of books—like Nancy Drew and Donna Parker! Do you *really* sing Elvis songs on your steps? That's so cool."

"Yeah ... but I make sure nobody hears me."

"Listen, I'm on the social committee this year, and we're putting on a talent show. The fifth- and sixth-grade classes put one on every year. Why don't you sing a song?"

"Me?"

"Sure, the kids would love it!"

"But I'm lousy. I didn't mean to give the impression that I could really sing."

"Come on!" she cried, clutching her books, jumping in the air like a jubilant cheerleader. "We really need people! And the guys in our class are such dorks! They don't do *anything!* You'd be a big hit!"

"Well, I'll tell you. The last time I was on stage was in fourth grade in Baltimore. The teacher asked me to play Robin Hood, and I guess I was dumb enough to say yes—"

"Hey, that's great! You've done it before!"

"Well, I sure did. At one point Friar Tuck handed me some coins, and I dropped them. I bent down and stretched to pick them up—and split my pants in the back right in front of the whole school. Talk about embarrassment! No, I think doing anything on stage is kaput for me right now."

"Wow, that sounds awful. What did you do?"

"I guess I'm the only person to play Robin Hood without the audience ever seeing the back of his pants. It was mortifying."

"Hey! But you finished the play! That's what counts!"

"You mean the show went on."

"Right! The show *must* go on! And you *must* sing us a rock 'n' roll song! Please?"

"Well, I don't know … Let me think about it. I'll let you know. When is the show?"

"It's not until October, so you have plenty of time to rehearse—on your back steps!"

"We'll see …"

Dottie looked up, saw some of her friends down the hall, and took off running, yelling back at Jackie, "Good-bye, Elvis! See you at the concert!"

IT WAS THE SECOND WEEK of classes. Jackie was sitting in class listening to a lesson about the Louisiana Purchase when an extremely loud, high-pitched siren wailed from the intercom on the ceiling. He thought an earthquake was happening.

Then Mrs. Wilson screamed, "Air raid! Duck and cover! Under your desks!"

Jackie quickly twisted around and saw everyone leaping out of their chairs and ducking under their desks, curling up in fetal positions. Like little soldiers in foxholes, they scrunched their bodies into coiled balls, covering their heads with their forearms. Jackie wondered if the Russians were dropping an atom bomb. The siren continued to screech so loud he couldn't hear the voices of the other kids. Not all the kids were screaming. From beneath his desk, he looked over and saw Kurt Cummings laughing wickedly, shoving Fred Junior in a girl's face. The guy couldn't even take a nuclear holocaust seriously.

He glared at Sally Ann Meyers, a quiet, studious girl with thick, heart-shaped glasses who definitely seemed to be taking it seriously. Sally Ann was lying prone on the floor, sobbing uncontrollably, eyes bulging wide open. Her body was shaking in short, quick spasms, twitching on the floor. Jackie thought she might be having a seizure. She stared at him with inflamed eyes and a twisted mouth, her body frozen.

Abruptly, the siren ended. An eerie silence filled the room. The students slowly crawled out from beneath their desks like jittery airplane passengers who had survived a crash landing. Amazingly, all the kids regained their composure, sat back in their seats, and silently returned to being obedient students. Mrs. Wilson did not seem disturbed at all.

"Okay, students," she said. "It's all over. Now let's get back to the Louisiana Purchase."

Jackie looked over at Sally Ann. She was calmly adjusting her sweater, taking out her notebook and pencil, wiping her glasses, waiting patiently for Mrs. Wilson to begin.

But something did happen. Didn't it?

He was going to raise his hand and ask a few questions: How did they expect these wooden desks to protect them from a nuclear holocaust? Hadn't atom bombs destroyed two Japanese cities? Shouldn't the school issue the students dog tags like soldiers in wartime? Jackie could imagine Mrs. Wilson explaining the dog tags: "Now, class. Please wear these around your neck. We will be able to identify you in case you are burned beyond recognition in a nuclear holocaust."

He wondered how they could simply return to the study of American history without discussing the possibility that they might perish any day in a world-destroying ball of fire. *Why would the Russians attack us?*

Why do they hate us so much? Are the Russians going to come over and turn us against our parents? Make us inform on them for not being loyal party members? A flood of thoughts ran through his mind, but he just sat there and took notes. Mrs. Wilson continued to tell the class how lucky the United States had been to obtain such a huge amount of land.

He thought about Sally Ann lying under her desk petrified with fear. He was growing up in a weird world—a world that seemed to have two different realities. The first one appeared to be perfectly normal, well-adjusted and stable—the above-the-desk world. But something was happening below that level of reality—the below-the-desk world. Jackie had witnessed a hidden world underneath the smooth current of life presented on nice TV shows like *Ozzie and Harriet* and *Father Knows Best*. Things seemed blandly normal at that level. But Jackie had experienced something else—an alternative, nightmarish world lurking beneath their plain wooden desks. Sally Ann was having a nervous breakdown. Then, like a robotic windup doll, she returned to the normal above-the-desk world. But did she *really* return to normal? Maybe the whole country was having a nervous breakdown beneath this calm parallel universe of the above-desk United States. Maybe somebody was keeping a big secret—a secret well hidden through regular channels of communication like stupid television. Why didn't Mrs. Wilson explain the reasons the country was living under the threat of instant, total annihilation? Jackie felt like he had made a horrible discovery; the below-desk world was real, and he had already experienced it without realizing it. His father's death was below the desk. Roy Shifflette was below the desk. Their poverty was below the desk. Mrs. Wilson and the rest of the class took cold comfort in ignoring the other reality, but Jackie felt it was just as real. It was on this day in particular that Jackie believed he lost a large part of his innocence and began a whole new worry in his life. When would the below-desk world appear again? How much of his life would be lived below the desk? Was there any way to escape the below-the-desk world?

Jackie had a lot more questions but didn't say anything. He made a mental note to talk to Coach Martin. He wasn't sure why, but he thought he would be able to give him some answers.

Jackie was blessed with instant grade-school popularity. Mr. Ryan, the athletic coach, conducted several races—the hundred-yard dash, the quarter-mile, and the mile. He was the fastest kid in school. They played games of dodgeball where the goal was to be the last player standing in a circle. His natural quickness made him the hardest player to knock out of a game. In pick-up basketball games, he was a slick ball handler with cat-like reflexes who possessed a deadly jump shot. There were track-and-field events—high jump, broad jump, relay races, pole vault, high hurdles. He excelled in all these contests. Whenever he walked across the field at recess time, he heard enthusiastic cries from guys picking teams: "We want Jackie!" "Jackie, play for our team!" "Jackie, over here!" One time a new student saw Jackie's name posted on a bulletin board as athlete of the month. The newcomer asked a student who Jackie Riddick was. The student replied, "He's skinny and runs like the wind."

At the annual awards convocation before Halloween, he received the Most Popular and Best Athlete awards along with a special announcement from the principal that he had been nominated the Huckleberry Finn of Charles Street School. Immediately following the awards, he ran to Vera, and they broke up laughing about the principal getting it all wrong: he was Tom Sawyer, not Huck Finn! Vera said she thought the principal's choice was a little weird, telling him, "Jackie, Huck Finn *hated* school, doing his chores, and would rather float down a river on a raft than be civilized."

Jackie said, "That's okay with me—when do we begin our river raft trip?!"

Vera and Jackie were on top of the caste-like social hierarchy of American grade schools. Already, young students were placing their classmates into social pigeonholes with ossifying death labels like greaser, nerd, jock, loser, brainiac, and so forth. At the top of the heap, a few exalted winners soared to the greatest heights, the lucky ones blessed with good looks, athletic ability, school smarts, coolness, and likable personalities. Jackie felt he had been inexplicably chosen by God or a divine spirit to lead a charmed life. He just knew in his bones that he was destined to do great things. Every guy wanted to be him, because he made it look so easy—and it was. For a while his anxiety attacks and lack of self-confidence abated, and he thought he was rid of them forever, forgetting that the below-desk world was always there, lurking beneath the surface, sometimes so docile and contained that you could mistakenly forget its existence.

He even thought it had something to do with being a Jehovah's Witness. After all, the religion claimed you would never die and would live on this earth forever. He believed he was a special person selected from high above and of course these feelings of being exceptional, special, popular, and living above the desk would flow on forever. Surely, that's one of the advantages of being a twelve-year-old kid: you think some things can last forever.

8

Colonial Beef Inc.
Philadelphia, Pennsylvania
October 14, 1958

B ETTY WAS SITTING IN THE lounge of the Colonial Beef Company rubbing her reddened, stinging hands, trying to induce some circulation back into her fingers. She knew her hands would sting during the break, but she couldn't handle the freezing temperatures in the meatpacking room any longer. She glanced back at her fellow workers through the dirty plate-glass windows of the lounge. They were all dressed in identical white aprons, working mechanically side-by-side in a straight line. Betty thought they might as well be androids. Thelma Morgan, one of the few friends she had at work, was lying on her back on one of the benches across the room smoking a cigarette. Thelma was a short, obese woman lounging without her apron on, exposing rolling lumps and bulges of a body currently contained by a thin leather belt cinched tightly around a plain gray cotton dress.

Lying there, Thelma reminded Betty of a large gray cushion with a noose tied around the middle of it. Betty ordinarily detested cigarettes, and Jehovah's Witnesses strongly disapproved of smoking. But today, mainly as a precaution against going out of her mind with boredom, she decided to ask Thelma for a cigarette. She wondered if she could gain some small pleasure in this habit, since at this point in her life even simple pleasures were hard to come by. She glanced back once more to her work area and noticed the stainless-steel storage room located in back of the employees. The cold room lit by harsh, florescent lights contained straight rows of grotesque cattle carcasses hanging from iron hooks. Betty thought about her working life, the cold, numb feeling of being surrounded by dead animals and blood everywhere—unbelievably everywhere, soaking the floors, staining your clothes and shoes, seeping into your pores, and sticking to your hair. The blood was always there in the morning as if red rain fell in the workplace every night.

"Say, Thelma," cried Betty. "Do you think I could borrow a cigarette?"

"Sure," yelled Thelma, assuming a sitting position. "But, Betty, you don't *borrow* cigarettes. You gonna pay this one back?" Thelma flipped one of her Old Gold's to Betty. Betty tried to catch it, but it fell to the floor. She picked it up and stared at it like it was an artifact from an unknown civilization.

"I suppose you need a light too?" asked Thelma.

"Yes, I'm sorry."

Thelma got up slowly from her bench, walked over to Betty, and tossed a pack of matches on the table.

"Want me to smoke it for you too?"

"No … No thanks. I think I can manage from here."

Thelma started to return to her seat but then hesitated, and turned back toward Betty. She reached over and grabbed the pack of matches, lifted the cover, and extracted a match. With a cigarette dangling from her lips, Thelma struck the match, leaned over, and lit Betty's cigarette; then she blew out the match and tossed it on the floor. Betty sucked in a tentative drag, but the smoke cut her throat like a rusty razor. She coughed out streams of smoke in short, jerky gasps for breath, scattering embers down the front of her apron.

"Sorry, Thelma. I'm not much of a smoker."

"No big deal. Mind if I sit down?"

"Not at all."

Thelma took a long, slow drag from her cigarette, paused, and then looked at Betty, her eyes narrowing, a furrow forming between them.

"Betty, do you mind if I ask you a personal question?"

"No."

"Why do you work so hard?"

"What do you mean?"

"I mean you hardly ever take a break, and you haven't missed a day's work since you've been here."

"I don't know," said Betty. "I guess I would feel guilty if I missed work or ... slacked off on company time."

"Company time? We're getting a buck and a quarter an hour, and you're worried about the *company's* time?"

"I know what you mean. I guess I don't know any other way to work."

"Betty, what do you do for fun, anyway?"

The question should have been easy for anyone to answer, but not for Betty. She hesitated for a second. "I suppose I get the most pleasure going to the meetings."

"The meetings?"

"Oh, I'm sorry. I'm a Jehovah's Witness. We call our church services the meetings."

"Betty—no offence—but *really,* what the hell do you do for fun? You consider going to church fun?"

"Well ..."

Suddenly, Virgil Potter, the frozen-food manager, barged into the lounge, his blood-stained white apron loosely hanging from his body. If he hadn't been short, dumpy, bald, and unshaven, he would have looked like a surgeon leaving the operating room after surgery.

"Thelma Morgan!" bellowed Virgil. "You've been in here fourteen minutes! That's four minutes over the limit! Now let's get back to work!"

Thelma gave Virgil a look that signaled in no uncertain terms that she wanted to plunge a dagger through his heart.

"Yes sir, Mr. Manager. I was just leaving. Sorry I wasted four minutes of Colonial Beef's precious time."

"That's enough sarcasm, Thelma. You know the rules."

"Yeah, I know the rules, Mr. Potter—and the rules suck!"

"I don't make the rules, Thelma. Now let's go. Betty, you have five more minutes."

Thelma left Betty alone in the room holding the cigarette. She placed it in a nearby ashtray. Betty was thinking about whether or not to smoke any more when her mind drifted to her sister Virgie. She couldn't help but think about her sister Virgie when Virgil Potter's name was mentioned. Virgie was still living back in Wise County and married to a nice man named Luther. Virgie and Luther had six kids, and they all seemed so well-behaved, and their lives seemed so well-ordered—nothing like the chaos and confusion Betty felt about her own life. Of all her sisters, Virgie was the one who was most critical of the way Betty was raising her children. Virgie and Luther were not Jehovah's Witnesses but Southern Baptists, avowed Puritans who never hesitated to punish their children for the slightest misbehavior. Virgie felt Betty let the kids get away with murder, and Betty didn't disagree with her.

But Luther was a decent husband and provider, and they had been married twelve years without any hint of drinking, violence, or abuse. Betty felt sorry for her children; she knew they had suffered more than most kids and did not want to inflict any more pain in their lives. Virgie said Betty was foolish and her lack of discipline would come back to haunt her in the end. As Betty thought about Donna's current lifestyle, she hated that her sister's words were already becoming all too true. Donna had recently dropped out of high school at sixteen. She just would not get up in the morning—mainly because she came in at all hours of the night. She knew Donna was leading a carefree, deviant, irresponsible life, but Betty seemed paralyzed to stop her. How could you make a sixteen-year-old go to school? Betty was unsure, but she knew that Virgie and Luther would never have let it happen in their household. In the past week Donna had bleached her hair platinum blonde, and she went out dancing in skimpy dresses and skin-tight slacks and sweaters, looking way too sexy for a girl her age. Betty figured Donna was already having sex, but had no idea how to approach the subject. It terrified her to think about having a conversation about sex with Donna; it terrified her even more to think about Donna's private life.

Betty once again peered through the glass into the meatpacking area. The employees were still performing their monotonous tasks, and Betty noticed there were more meatpackers standing in a line facing her as mounds of ground beef rolled down the conveyor belt. Betty stared for a few seconds, and then she flashed to an *I Love Lucy* episode in which Lucy and Ethel were hired to wrap chocolates coming out of a similar conveyor belt. Lucy's boss saw that they were doing such a good job that she sped up the machine. But each time she sped up the machine, Lucy and Ethel got further and further behind. Finally, the chocolate balls were traveling so fast that Lucy and Ethel had no choice but to stuff them in their uniforms, gobble them down, or toss them over their shoulders. Betty thought it was a hilarious scene, but there was nothing remotely amusing about her job.

She got up from the table and left the cigarette burning, untouched. She wandered over to a stack of magazines haphazardly placed on a small metal shelf. The company provided the magazines as reading material during breaks. They were torn and stained, with pages ripped out and each one at least three months old. She spotted copies of *Colliers*, *The Saturday Evening Post*, and *Reader's Digest*. She picked up a copy of *Good Housekeeping* and leafed through it. She came across an article entitled "You Too Can Be a Spotless Cleaner!" She looked around the filthy lounge, noticing the foul mildew smell, the discarded cigarette butts crushed on the floor, the greasy stains and cracked cheap linoleum covering the room. The walls and ceiling were painted a sickly pale yellow. Used soda bottles, candy wrappers, and empty crinkled bags of potato chips and pretzels were scattered throughout the lounge area. It was clear there was no spotless cleaning in Betty's working environment, and certainly not at home. She worked too many long hours and received so little help from her kids that a spotless house was just impossible. Betty was a very neat person, but somehow cleanliness was not a trait that had passed down to her kids. She envied Lucy and her husband, Desi, even though they were not real. Lucy may have had housework, but at least she had a husband who loved her and played the role of breadwinner. Betty felt like she wasn't winning anything.

Bored with the company's selection of reading material, Betty returned to her seat, noticing that the cigarette was practically out.

She tried to focus on more pleasant things, but she couldn't stop thinking about her problems. She wanted to be a good parent—strong, confident, and certain. But her secret was out; even her children were no longer fooled. She was weak, insecure, and did not possess an ounce of self-esteem. The fact that she had married Roy Shifflette seemed proof enough. She always said she lived for her children, and that much was true. But her children were not turning out to be anything like she expected, and thus she was living for lives that were totally out of touch and alien to her. She hated to think about it, but it was possible that none of her kids were going to be Jehovah's Witnesses. Lately, Betty was going through a crisis of faith that she didn't dare share with the congregation or her kids. She was beginning to question why Jehovah picked her to be inundated with more problems than non–Jehovah's Witnesses. And what was the point of being a dedicated follower of the church if your children were not in the faith? She already knew the answer from her Bible studies. Jehovah was not doing this to her—Satan was. It was Satan who ruled this world and caused all the pain, sorrow, disease, death, and every wicked evil thing. Jehovah was giving Satan a long period of time to bring down all the nonbelievers, and then Jehovah was going to destroy this earth and create a new, perfect world. If you were alive when Armageddon came, you never had to die. You wouldn't be an angel flying in heaven with wings; you'd be living in a new earthly paradise without sin, misery, or death, because Jehovah was finally going to destroy Satan. So all Betty's troubles could be traced to Satan testing her, trying to make her give up her faith and join the evildoers. She knew the drill by heart. But there was a little voice in the back of her mind that was getting louder. It bothered her that she had no fun, couldn't go out drinking and dancing, couldn't smoke a cigarette, couldn't join the company bowling team or partake in any sins of the flesh. She was getting tired of postponing the kinds of gratification that other people seemed to enjoy without any punishment; yet it was she who was leading a good Christian life and got dumped on with a pile of miseries. It didn't seem fair. Life was wearing her down, and she knew she shouldn't blame Jehovah, but that little voice reminded her that if she wasn't a Jehovah's Witness, she'd be having a lot less misery in her life and a lot more fun.

Betty emerged from her daydreaming, startled to find herself in the lounge, feeling like she had been living in another world for the last few minutes. She looked at the lounge clock. She had taken a twelve-minute break—two minutes over the allotted time. She didn't want Mr. Potter to yell at her. She stubbed the unsmoked cigarette out in the ashtray and returned to packing frozen hamburgers.

AFTER WORK, BETTY TOOK THE number 9 bus from Philadelphia to Palmyra and arrived home at six o'clock tired and hungry, her body aching and her sore muscles begging for a much-needed rest. She opened the door to the apartment and saw Donna asleep on the couch surrounded by her beloved rock 'n' roll records. She was hoping Donna had prepared dinner for the family, but she was not surprised to find her sleeping, knowing that she had already danced away all her energy. She put her purse on the coffee table and shook Donna gently, wondering why she felt a tinge of guilt for disturbing her lazy daughter. Donna opened her eyes, waved her left arm weakly in her mother's direction, and slowly managed to sit up straight.

"Are the boys in their room?" asked Betty.

"Yeah, they're sleeping. What are we having for dinner? I'm hungry."

Betty glanced toward the tiny kitchen, trying to remember exactly how much food they had in the house. She knew she had some ground beef and pinto beans, and there might be a few potatoes left.

"I'll make something," Betty muttered under her breath, too worn out to deal with Donna's chronic idleness. She went over to the bedroom to look in on the boys. They were still sleeping peacefully. Betty returned to the living room to see Donna sitting on the floor watching *The Little Rascals* on their nineteen-inch Philco.

"Can you peel me some potatoes, Donna? I think we have a few left."

Donna turned away from Spanky and Buckwheat racing in their soapboxes. "Sure, mom. I'll peel them in here."

Betty found four potatoes in the cupboard and brought them to Donna with a sharp knife and a dish towel. She returned to the kitchen to prepare the hamburger and beans. Ketchup was the only condiment in the house, but Betty was too tired to be concerned with trivial matters. For now, ketchup would have to do. She opened the refrigerator door and grabbed the leftover ground beef wrapped securely in tinfoil. She sat at the kitchen table shaping the ground beef into rounded patties. The irony was not lost on her that she was doing the same thing she did at work. She wondered how many people left for work in the pitch darkness of early morning and in the winter came home from work riding the same foul-smelling bus for an hour after the sun had already disappeared. In the winter, working five days a week, she saw little daylight except on weekends. In a few minutes, Donna came into the kitchen holding the peeled potatoes with the leftover peelings wrapped in the towel.

"Do you want me to smash them up?" asked Donna.

"Yes."

Donna bent down and secured a medium-sized pot from the beneath the oven and grabbed a fork from the silverware drawer. She found milk and butter in the refrigerator and began cutting up the potatoes into smaller pieces.

"How was work today?" Donna asked.

Betty was now hovering over a white porcelain stove flipping four patties in a frying pan. "It was okay ... but I don't like to take the breaks."

Donna paused. "What do you mean? You don't like to take a break from work?"

"Well," said Betty, who was so tired she felt as if her strained words were falling directly from her mouth to the floor, "we have a lounge where we can relax for ten minutes every two hours ... but I work in the frozen-food department."

"So?"

"Well, of course my hands freeze handling those cold patties, and when I go into the lounge, they thaw out—and sting. I'd rather keep them numb and stay out of the lounge. It's much less pain."

Donna stopped trying to whip the potatoes by hand and dropped the fork on the table. She began to cry.

"What's the matter?" asked Betty.

"You work eight hours a day, five days a week, for what? A dollar and a quarter an hour? And your hands are frozen the whole time? That's terrible! We're terrible! I should have had supper ready! The boys are sleeping! They never do *anything* around here! All they do is complain!"

Donna continued sobbing, her hands folded into the misery of her face, elbows resting on the kitchen table.

Betty reached over and placed her arms gently around her daughter's shoulders. "Donna, it's okay … really. We're much happier now, right? Believe me, I'm much happier knowing we got away from Roy—and knowing my kids are safe. That's all I care about is you kids. If you're happy then I'm happy."

Donna looked forlornly at her mother, eyes red and puffy, tears running down her cheeks. "I know we're better off."

Betty smiled. "Then everything's okay, right?"

9

Cherry Hill Lane, Cinnaminson, New Jersey
October 21, 1958

HERMAN GOLINSKI WAS LYING ON his sofa suffering from a raging, hair-burning hangover when he heard the doorbell ring.

"Jesus Christ," he said to himself. "Who the hell could that be?"

Herman was going to ignore whoever was disturbing him, but he thought perhaps his ex-wife might be paying him a visit. He rolled out of the sofa onto the floor, down on one knee, barefoot and shirtless, wearing only a pair of wrinkled, soiled khakis. As he stood up, he felt a dagger of pain shooting from his arthritic knees, his head exploding as if someone was pounding a jackhammer on his brain. He waddled to the door and opened it. Before him stood two smartly dressed young boys, one slighter taller than the other one. They were carrying magazines in their arms. Herman stared down at them through bloodshot eyes, groaning. "What the hell do you want?"

"Good morning, sir," said the taller one. He was dressed in a plain blue suit, a white shirt, and a bright red tie. "Do you believe we are living in times of great turmoil and confusion—"

"I *said* what do you little punks want from me?"

"Well," continued the boy, "we'd like to give you some valuable spiritual information for you to—"

"Jesus Christ, you guys are Jehovah's Witnesses, right?"

"Yes, sir," they both muttered.

"What is it with you people? Do you carry little hangover detectors with you?"

"Sorry, sir. I don't know what you mean," said the shorter youth, who was wearing the same outfit as the other boy except that the suit was gray and the tie bright blue.

"Forget it. You wouldn't know, would you? You people don't drink or smoke or dance or have any fun—just run around Sunday mornings bothering the hell out of unsuspecting citizens. Well, I ain't buying what you're selling, so beat it!"

Without saying anything, the two youths sheepishly turned and walked down the steps of the porch, jolted by the slamming of the front door behind them. They continued walking down the sidewalk of the residential neighborhood.

"Well, that was fun," said Danny.

"Boy was he mad!" cried Jackie.

"Jackie, this is getting … I don't know … ridiculous."

"What do you mean?"

"I mean I don't blame the guy. What are we doing disturbing all these people on a Sunday morning?"

"We're trying to sell Watchtowers and Awakes."

"Really? What for?"

"So we can save their lives."

Danny paused.

"Do you believe that?"

"I don't know. I guess."

"So someday soon, there's gonna be this big ball of fire that's going to explode and destroy all the bad people on earth except for a few Jehovah's Witnesses?"

"Mom says you don't have to be a Jehovah's Witness to make it to the New World."

"So I ask you again, what are we doing?"

"Well, I guess if they become a Jehovah's Witness they have a better chance of living forever."

"Let's sit down underneath this tree and rest awhile," said Danny.

"Fine with me."

The boys sat down on the curb beneath a multicolored poplar tree. Danny leaned back, unbuttoned his top button, yanked his tie loose, and stared up at the sky through the autumnal colored leaves of the tree.

"Jackie, I've got to tell you something," said Danny, placing his hands behind his head. "I just don't believe it."

"What?"

"I don't know. Look around. Can you imagine a big ball of fire coming over that hill and wiping out millions of people but not us?"

"Oh, I see what you mean. It doesn't seem possible because—"

"Because it's crazy!"

"It is?"

"You know those fairy tales we read as a kid? Hansel and Gretel, Little Red Riding Hood?"

"Yeah."

"Well, that's what I think the Witnesses are doing—telling a big fairy tale."

"Don't you want to live forever?"

"Hell, yes! But really, has anyone ever been resurrected—come back from the dead?"

"Well, Jesus—"

"Right. Another fairy tale. What? It happens every two thousand years?"

"Danny, what are you going to do? Give up going out in service, going to the meetings?"

"I don't know, but I can't do this much longer. I feel like shit. I felt like telling that man I was sorry for waking him up for no reason."

"But Mom would be disappointed."

"Yes, it's a complete guilt trip, but I don't care. Hell, look at Donna! Does she ever go to any meetings? Out in service? She's probably sleeping right now."

"I know, but Mom is always upset with Donna."

"And you think Donna cares if she upsets Mom?"

"No."

"Well, there you are. Now Mom is going to be zero for two. I'm gonna tell her I'm not going to church anymore. I've had it. Everybody thinks we're weird, and I'm tired of it."

Jackie rested his elbows on his knees, cupping his hands to his cheeks, looking down at the side of the road. "So that will leave just me."

"I'm afraid so, bro."

"But what if I quit?"

"Jackie, this is our *lives* we're talking about. Being a Witness is a full-time job! There's no way to just go to church on Sunday—that's not good enough. They control every aspect of your life! You can't even smoke a damn cigarette!"

"When are you going to tell Mom?"

"Today."

"Really?"

"As soon as we get home."

"Wow, she's going to be hurt."

"Jesus, Jackie, stop it! Are you going to lay a guilt trip on me?"

"No, I didn't mean—"

"Okay, forget it. Sorry. I know it's going to upset her, but I don't believe I have a choice."

"Why not?"

"Because I'm living a lie. I just don't believe the Witnesses are the chosen people of God. You want me to pretend to believe when I don't?"

"No, that would make you a phony."

"Right."

"Look, let's quit for the day. I'm worn out."

"Me too. I'm getting hungry."

"Me too."

The boys stood up, gathered their magazines, and began walking home. Cherry Hill Lane was more than a mile from their apartment in Palmyra, and they trudged along Cinnaminson Avenue toward Main Street. They arrived at the center of town, turned east down Main Street, and made a right onto Market Street. Halfway down the block, Jackie spotted Rufus Johnson sitting under a tree in the same rickety lawn chair dressed in his worn-out overalls and a red T-shirt, his battered brown fedora pulled tightly over his eyes. His carved wooden cane rested beside the chair next to an open bottle of Pabst Blue Ribbon beer. For a moment, Jackie wondered if he ever left the spot.

"Hey, there's Rufus."

"Who?"

"He's this weird old drunk I met a few months ago."

"He looks interesting."

The boys approached Rufus, who was reading the *Philadelphia Inquirer.*

"Hi, Rufus!" exclaimed Jackie.

Rufus glanced up from his paper, smiling broadly through crooked yellow teeth.

"Well, well, well, if it isn't the next Mickey Mantle! How are you, son?"

"I'm fine. This is my brother, Danny."

"Pleased to meet you, young man. Your brother here is quite a baseball player."

"I know," said Danny. "He's something else."

"What are you two boys doing on this gorgeous autumn morning?"

"Well," said Jackie, "we're Jehovah's Witnesses, and we were out in service."

"Out in service?"

"Yes. We go door-to-door trying to save people."

"From what?"

"From Armageddon."

"I see. I've heard of your religion. You put a lot of emphasis on the book of Revelation, right?"

"Yes," said Jackie. "That's right. That's the book where it talks about Armageddon. Do you know about Armageddon?"

"Of course, son. I know my Bible. Been reading the Great Book since I was knee high to a grasshopper."

"Do you think it's really going to happen?" asked Danny.

"I sure do. It's in God's plan. He's going to get real mad one of these days and start getting rid of all these unholy people doing bad things like stealing, fornicating, robbing, killing. Gonna be like the big flood in Noah's time."

"But you're not a Jehovah's Witness," said Jackie.

"No, I'm not. I'm not anything but a good Christian who reads the Bible and figured it out for hisself."

"Rufus, you are amazing," said Jackie.

Danny nudged Jackie in the shoulder, indicating he wanted to leave.

"Well, Rufus, we gotta go."

"It was nice seeing you again, Jackie. Glad to hear you are spreading the Word of the good Lord."

"Thanks, Rufus. See you later."

"Good-bye, Rufus," said Danny. "Nice to meet you."

"Nice to meet you, son. Any brother of Jackie is a friend of mine."

The boys continued walking home, Danny remaining silent until they neared the house. "That old man sure was surprising."

"What do you mean?" asked Jackie.

"He looks like a total bum, but he's real intelligent. You could see it in his eyes. He doesn't miss a thing. Does he look like the kind of guy who knows the Bible inside and out and reads the Sunday newspaper?"

"No, I guess he doesn't."

"I bet there's a real story behind that guy's life."

"I was thinking the same thing. It would be cool to find out about his past."

"I know one thing," said Danny.

"What?"

"I bet it's colorful."

THE BOYS ARRIVED AT THEIR apartment and glanced over at Mrs. Antonioni, who was, as usual, staring at the trash dump across the street. And, as usual, the boys cried out a cheerful hello and were met with stony silence.

Danny whispered, "Maybe she's dead," as they climbed the stairs and entered the apartment. No one was in the kitchen or living room.

"I guess Donna is still sleeping," said Danny. "Mom must still be out in service."

"Who did she go out with?" asked Jackie.

"I think Sister Turpen."

Jackie headed for the kitchen. "Well, I'm getting something to eat."

"What do we have?"

"I don't know. I think there's some bologna and maybe some cheese. You want me to make you a sandwich?"

"Okay, I'm going to see what's on TV."

"Sunday morning?"

"Yeah, it's pretty bleak. Nothing but church stuff and boring news programs."

Danny turned on the TV, adjusted the rabbit ears, and turned the dial, looking for a good station.

Suddenly, the door was flung open, and Betty burst into the living room screaming hysterically, "It's the demons! Great Lord Jehovah! The demons were after me! I saw them!"

Danny and Jackie rushed to their mother, yelling, "What happened? Are you all right? What's going on?"

"Hey, Mom!" hollered Danny. "Take it easy! Sit down here on the couch!"

Betty lunged for the couch as if it was food for a starving person, her body trembling, turning white except for her face, which was distorted and flushed bright red. "Oh, Danny, Jackie, you won't believe it!"

Danny grabbed Betty's shaking hands, holding them steady while smoothly stroking her arm "Okay, Mom, relax. Tell us what happened."

Betty tried to control herself, taking deep breaths while Danny rubbed her hands and Jackie massaged her shoulders.

"It all right, Mom," said Jackie. "Take your time."

Betty's breathing became more normal. She gazed into Danny's eyes as if she was pleading for him to wipe out the pain and terror with his hands. Then a gray, glassy film spread quickly over her eyes, and she gave the living room wall a thousand-yard stare.

"Hey, Mom! Snap out of it!" shouted Danny. "Everything's okay!"

"Oh, Danny—Jackie! I saw the demons!"

"Where?" asked Danny, squeezing her hands even tighter.

"Sister Turpen and I were on a gentleman's porch witnessing to him, and he seemed genuinely interested. Then, all of a sudden, I saw three of Satan's gruesome demons rising above his head, charging after me! I screamed bloody murder and fell down on the porch, praying for Jehovah to make them go away. They were going to capture me and take me away! But I closed my eyes real tight and prayed real hard to Jehovah to save me—and he did! In a few minutes, I opened my eyes and they were gone! Praise Jehovah!"

"Holy cow!" exclaimed Jackie. "What did they look like?"

"Like monsters! Fire-breathing, hideous monsters!"

"And they were after you?" asked Danny.

"Oh yes! They didn't come near the man or sister Turpen. They were after *me!*"

Danny turned his mother's head toward him. "Well, it's all right now, Mom. You're safe with us. There's no demons around here."

"That's right," said Jackie. "They wouldn't dare come around Danny and me. We'd fight them! We're not afraid of no demons!"

"Oh, Jackie, you should be. They are real! And powerful! They were going to try and make me lose my faith. It was a test from Jehovah—I know it. I didn't tell you guys that lately I have been questioning my faith in Jehovah and his great plan for mankind, and this was a test!"

"What do you mean, Mom?" asked Danny.

"You remember Job in the Bible? How Jehovah tested Job and took away everything he had to see if he would remain faithful? Well, that's what happened to me. I questioned my faith, and Jehovah tempted me by allowing the demons to corrupt me. But I prayed and prayed and told Jehovah I was sorry and I would never—ever—question my faith again. I am saved! Bless Jehovah!"

Danny and Jackie were stunned. They had never seen Betty act like this and had never even heard about Satan's demons. They had no doubt that she had seen something. Their mother was not the hysterical type.

"Gosh, Mom," said Jackie. "You're lucky. They could have taken you to hell!"

"Well, son, there is no real hell like false religions say there is. We just go to sleep when we die. But they were going to try and make me turn my back on Jehovah and worship Satan." Betty's body was on the verge of collapsing. She leaned into the back of the sofa, off balance and shaky. "Boys, I better get to bed. I need to relax and calm down."

"Yes, Mother," said Danny, picking her up and walking her to her bedroom door. "Are you going to be okay, Mom?" he asked.

"Yes, son. I'll be all right—with Jehovah's help."

Betty disappeared into the bedroom, and Danny came back to Jackie. They were silent for a moment. Then Danny said, "I guess this is not a good time to tell her I'm quitting, huh?"

Jackie only nodded.

10

November 1958

THROUGHOUT THE SCHOOL TERM, JACKIE and Vera continued to be a popular couple, spending a lot of time together. They sat by themselves in the luncheonette after school; sipping milkshakes; flirting with each other; confessing deep, dark secrets; and solving the problems of the world. They danced together cheek-to-cheek at the Community Center and rode their bikes to Palmyra Park and picnicked along the banks of Strawbridge Lake. They went to the movies downtown and made out in the balcony and spent time in Kurt Cummings's basement playing taboo kissing games like Post Office and Spin the Bottle.

They were the hottest young couple in town. Many classmates wanted to embrace them, to be a part of their world, as if their mutual intimacies and furtive whispers held clandestine, arcane meanings. Out on the playground during recess, Jackie and Vera would share lunch together, oblivious of the other kids literally circling around them. Their soft murmurs and seductive glances made the other kids think they were two extraordinary people dwelling in their own mysterious world.

Jackie was beginning to understand the enormous power of sexual attraction. At this point in his life, no one had told him very much about sex, apart from the crude stories and egoistic exaggerations of other guys in the class. He desired the closeness and warmth of Vera's body, and when they kissed for a long time in Kurt's basement, he felt an overpowering urge to feel every part of her, to press and rub her budding breasts against his chest. He was overcome with the longing to touch her breasts and smother his lips over every inch of her body. He had experienced wet dreams and knew about the basics of having sex. But unlike many young boys, Jackie associated these nocturnal emissions with his feelings for Vera. He did not know why or how it happened, but he learned to associate the physical sex drive with powerful feelings of love and affection. He was too young to know the implications—and limitations—of expressing his emotions through a primitive sex drive. For Jackie, at this time in his life, he had no idea how complicated relationships could be with the opposite sex. At the present time, the equation was simple: Vera equals affection. Sex shows affection. Have sex with Vera.

Never again would it be that simple.

During the same period, Vera was becoming acutely aware of her sexual attractiveness. She adjusted to these changes by carrying herself with elegant, decorous restraint. She knew, like most girls her age, that appearing undignified or too loose would only invite unwanted, vulgar advances from immature boys. In order to signal a modest retreat from the male gaze or crude comments, she presented her social self like a princess, an untouchable icon, a girl so fragile-looking she might break into pieces like a china doll if you shook her too much. Her desires were held in check, but the same urges that were beginning to consume Jackie were also frustrating Vera. Living in a state of coiled sexual tension, she wanted Jackie to totally possess her, to take her in his arms and caress her whole body and light the sexual fuse inside her that could detonate at any time. But the Victorian-like mores of the time placed her in an untenable world of sexual repression. She might as well have been wearing a chastity belt.

The couple handled their growing sexual passion toward each other by trying to convince themselves that sex was shameful, sullied behavior and a veritable sin unto God. Jackie wondered if there was a distant, erotic paradise on earth where two young people their age could fall in love; have delicious, delirious sex; and create a lasting relationship. In reality, there were such places in the world, but for Jackie and Vera these little pockets of paradise may as well have been beyond the Milky Way.

Jackie and Vera were hanging out in Kurt Cummings's basement. All the kids agreed that Kurt had the coolest parents in town, because they let Kurt and his friends have the basement to themselves to socialize and play games. The games were making-out games like Spin the Bottle, Seven-Minute Honeymoon, and Post Office. Vera would arrive early in the evening with her girlfriends. Boys and girls being alone together in the evenings was taboo, so they told their parents they were going to another friend's house, the movies, or the community center. At the beginning of the evening, Vera and Jackie would play games where they kissed other people, but gradually they wandered off to themselves, huddling together in one of the basement lounge chairs. Jackie would embrace Vera, holding her in his lap. They would stare into each other's eyes and kiss softly, whispering sweet nothings—the very essence of young romantic love. Kurt was crazy about the Platters and played "Twilight Time," "My Prayer," and "Smoke Gets in Your Eyes" over and over again. Some of the couples slow-danced while others disappeared behind a musty bookcase, a boiling furnace, or a stack of suitcases to explore their affections and desires.

Jackie knew it was up to him to make the sexual advances, such as feeling Vera's developing breasts or rubbing her body close to him. He never considered going any further. Getting a quick feel, for the guys, was considered tantamount to rolling in bed with Miss America. There were braggarts who claimed to have had forbidden sexual episodes, but these sexual adventures never seemed to occur in Palmyra. They all seemed to happen when the lucky guys were away during the summer or with a girl "passing through town." There was a palpable undercurrent of tension about sex; it was the elephant in the room that their parents never talked about, but it was constantly on their minds.

Vera said she really liked Jackie and said she was very curious about sex but would only have sex with someone she loved. Both Jackie and Vera thought that waiting until you were married seemed impossible. Jackie told Vera that his mother had told him to wait until he was married, which to him may as well have been fifty years. Then he exclaimed, "Vera, that's a lot of cold showers!"

Vera laughed and then asked seriously, "What the hell are we supposed to do? At least you're allowed *think* about sex."

In the darkest part of the basement, they were leaning back in an antique recliner, their arms wrapped around each other. They were barely visible to the rest of the kids. Jackie kissed Vera tenderly on the lips. She edged closer to him. She kissed him back, giving him a seductive wink, and then nestled her head on his shoulder. He moved his hand slowly around her waist, reaching under her sweater and sliding his hand to the small of her back. Her body felt deliciously warm, silky soft, and smelled like lilacs and orange blossoms. He pulled her closer to him while massaging her back, letting his fingertips glide up toward her shoulders. He separated slightly from her, allowing room to slide his hand from around her shoulder just above her breasts. Then he moved his hand down her slender neckline. Vera reached over, placing her hand on his, and then gently slid his hand down to her left breast. She pressed his hand softly over her breast, pulling him closer to her, placing another kiss on his lips. Jackie was aflame inside, caressing the contours and silky smoothness of her supple, lithe body. An intoxicating, trance-like delirium was overwhelming him.

"Vera," he whispered. "I just want to say that—"

"Oh, that's gross!" Someone screamed from the other side of the room. Vera and Jackie quickly looked up to see what was going on. Jackie saw a hazy, silhouetted figure standing in the middle of the room.

"What's going on?" Jackie yelled.

"Come here and find out, you two lovebirds," said Joanne Harrison, one of Vera's closest friends.

They got up from the recliner and walked across the room to where Joanne was standing under a dim blue light. As they approached, they spotted Kurt Cummings, Phil DeMarco, and Dutch Lear lying on a battered mattress on the floor laughing hysterically. The commotion caused a few of the other kids to materialize from their secluded spots.

"What's going on?" asked Abby Freedman.

After getting everyone's attention, Joanne pointed her finger at Kurt Cummings, who was laughing and covering his head with mock shame.

"Kurt Cummings just lit a fart with his lighter—that's what!"

"No wonder the place stinks," said Linda Smith. "Jesus, Kurt—in your own house?"

"Hey," replied Kurt, sitting up on the mattress and reaching for a cigarette. "I can't help it if I've got special talents. Can anybody else do this fabulous trick?"

"Kurt," said Joanne, "I don't think anybody here wants to learn your stupid trick—even the guys."

"Well," replied Phil DeMarco, "that's not technically true. I tried to learn Kurt's amazing skill, but I burnt my ass and had to wear a pad for a week."

"Well, Phil," remarked Joanne, "I guess that just makes you more stupid than him."

Kurt had broken the romantic mood of his own party. He didn't have a girlfriend, and Jackie figured he had done it to get attention. He probably had used it as a ploy to bring everybody out in the open.

"Come on, everybody, just relax," insisted Kurt. "Let's play a game—all of us."

"Jesus, Kurt," said Jimmie. "You think we're in third grade? You want to play Go Fish or something?"

"No, man," said Kurt. "I just want to hang out with my friends. All you people do is come over here and disappear!"

"Well," said Linda, "maybe if you didn't do shit like light farts, we might hang out in this room a little more. Besides, it's not normal."

"What do you mean it's not normal?" asked Kurt. "There are hundreds of boys all over the country lighting farts this very minute."

"Well, you just made my point," replied Linda. "There's not a normal boy our age within a thousand miles of Palmyra."

"Wait a minute!" cried Phil. "What the hell is normal, anyway? Our parents think making out and playing Spin the Bottle is not normal."

The whole gang took Kurt's fart lighting as an opportunity to take a break. Soon everyone was sitting or lying on the mattress.

"You know, Phil has a point," Jackie said. "Most of what we like to do is not called normal."

"Jesus, Jackie, you might have something there," said Jimmie. "My mother told me that listening to rock 'n' roll wasn't normal—said it was just noise that was going to destroy my ears—and my tiny brain."

"How about too much makeup and wearing tight jeans?" asked Abby. "My mother made me put on a lighter shade of lipstick before I left the house. Of course, after I left, I changed back to—"

"Hey, that's nothing!" cried Kurt. "My old man thinks reading comic books and chewing gum is not normal!"

"How about long hair greased back in a duck's ass?" asked Phil.

"How about riding your bike after dark?" asked Jimmie.

"How about doing *anything* after dark?" countered Joanne.

"I was dancing the other day in my room," said Linda, "and my mother came in and asked what kind of dance I was doing. I told her the Slop. She said that was not proper behavior for a young girl."

"Hey!" yelled Phil, "It could have been worse! It could have been the Dirty Dig!"

"Or Willie and the Hand Jive!" screamed Jimmie.

"My mother told me that flirting with boys would ruin my life—like I'd wind up crazy or a prostitute," said Linda.

"You know," said Vera, "some of the things we are *supposed* to do … well, really stink."

"Like school!" exclaimed Kurt.

"Church!" yelled Phil.

"Lawrence Welk!" blurted Joanne.

"Our gym uniforms!" screamed Abby.

The kids were all laughing, pushing each other affectionately, and sharing Cokes together. Then there was a brief moment of silence.

"Maybe that's the problem," Jackie said. "Sure, they can say Kurt is not normal for lighting farts, but they have a whole list of things that are not normal—the things we all like to do. So really, what is normal? I'll tell you. Normal seems to be a state of mind or a place where nothing ever happens—a vegetative state that parents keep hoping we will attain. When they say to be normal, it sounds to me like they're saying, 'Shut up and follow the rules—even if they make no sense.'"

"Like always tucking in your shirt," asserted Jimmie.

"Or wearing your skirt above your knees," said Allie.

"How about hiding under your desk and thinking that it will protect you from a nuclear holocaust!" Jackie shouted.

Then they heard a door open at the top of the stairs. Everyone looked up, but before Kurt's father could say anything, Kurt announced, "Okay, party's over! I want all of you below-normal people out of my house! I have to get up early and read my comic books!"

"Kurt," said Stan Cummings, standing on the top step, "it's getting late, and it's a school night."

Kurt turned around, facing his friends. "Everybody's just leaving, Dad. I'll be right up."

Everyone gathered their winter coats and filed out the cellar door and up the stairs leading to the backyard. It was a clear, frosty night. A couple kids hopped on their bikes and rode off in different directions, and a few kids, including Vera and Jackie, went walking home together. Kurt lived about a half-mile from Vera's, and they walked leisurely down Delaware Avenue toward Lincoln's Luncheonette. He was holding her hand, and they walked in silence for a few minutes, unable to speak about their newborn intimacy. Jackie was beginning to realize why grownups called it an awkward age. He was content not to talk about anything too seriously. He was afraid he might make a clumsy mistake and scare Vera away from him. He wanted her close to him but had no idea how to go about it. Maybe that was why everybody was so awkward. Parents spent all their time telling you what not to do instead of letting you know how to deal with this crazy thing called growing up. He admitted to himself he had no idea what it meant. Suddenly, Vera spoke: "Jackie, I had a wonderful time. I always do when I'm with you."

"I had a great time too. I really like going to Kurt's house. He's so funny, and I like all the kids. I like … you know … the chance for us to get to know each other."

"Me too. I like it best when we are alone and nobody else is around. You make me feel very special inside. I never felt like this before."

"Me neither. It's like we're the only two people in the world when we are alone at Kurt's."

"Say, Jackie," said Vera. "You know, Christmas is coming up, and my parents had a swell idea. They wanted me to ask you to come to our house on Christmas—for Christmas dinner. How does that sound?"

"Gosh, Vera … that sounds … terrific. We can … I can come over Christmas morning—or afternoon—and we can … have dinner—and I want to get you a real nice gift!"

"That sounds wonderful! My parents really like you. They say you're a real swell kid—and their favorite customer!"

"Did they say that? Wow, I got them fooled!"

"Okay, then it's a deal. You're spending Christmas with the Lincoln family!"

"Whoopee!" he cried, quickly grabbing Vera's hand, and they started running toward the luncheonette. They ran for a few blocks and arrived at Vera's house huffing and puffing.

"Wow, that was fun!" yelled Vera, bending over and gasping for air. "I love to run fast—but I'm not as fast as you!"

"Almost!" he cried.

Vera was still panting heavily, her hands braced on her knees. She looked to the side, glancing at her house. "Well, I guess I better be getting in. My mom's probably wondering where I am. I told them I was going to Judy's—"

"And you ran into me on the way home!"

"Yes, of course! It was fate!"

They both laughed, gazing into each other's eyes. Then Jackie quieted down, growing more serious. "Vera, before you go in, I want to tell you something."

"Okay ..."

He leaned in, acting like he was going to whisper in her ear. Instead, he turned and kissed her on the lips. "I lied—I just wanted to kiss you goodnight. Like Jackie Gleason says, 'Baby, you're the greatest!'"

"You're not so bad yourself, kiddo. Well, goodnight, sweet prince. I'll see you at school tomorrow."

"Sounds good to me. Recess—twelve o'clock!"

"Goodnight!"

She turned and sprinted to the rear of the luncheonette, waving to him the entire time.

After she disappeared behind a wrought-iron gate, Jackie continued walking home. All he could think about was the invitation to Christmas dinner and how his mother was going to react. But he already knew how she would react. She would forbid it. It was considered just about the most horrible thing a Jehovah's Witness could do—celebrate Christmas. They thought it was an evil pagan ritual dreamed up by some ancient ruler named Nebuchadnezzar. He might as well ask his mother if he could bow down and worship the golden calf. As he approached his house, he was thinking about all the strategies he might use to get his mother to allow him to join Vera and her family. None of his ideas seemed workable short of outright lying. But he just couldn't do it. He bounded up the rickety steps, but before opening the door, he gazed toward the heavens, muttering out loud, "Thanks a lot, Jehovah. Another fine mess you've gotten me into."

He walked in the door and saw his mother sitting in her favorite chair reading the King James Bible.

The living room was dark except for a solitary beam of light shining down on the Bible from a small lamp placed next to the chair. She had a concerned look on her face, and at first he thought she might be mad at him for being late. Lately, he had noticed that his mother was beginning to show unmistakable signs of premature aging. Her once lovely face seemed pallid and weary; her pale green eyes appeared more tired and sunken. The long hours of drudgery and responsibility of raising three kids was eroding her vigorous youthful persona; she was now a person who seemed defeated, exuding signs of weary resignation.

Betty's concerned look was not for Jackie; it was for Donna. She had been going out every night to different dances in Philly and South Jersey. She stayed out late every night until the wee hours and then slept until noon. She had quit school and was not even looking for a job.

"Hi, Mom," Jackie said. "Is everything okay?"

"Hi, son. Yes, everything is all right. Your sister is still out …"

"When is she coming home?"

"Lord knows."

"Mom, can I ask you something?"

"Sure, Jackie. Let's sit on the couch."

Betty closed the Bible on her lap, placed it on the table, and then walked over to the couch. She turned on the lamp next to the sofa. Jackie took off his coat, tossed it on the couch, and sat down.

"What is it, son?"

"Well, you know I have been sort of seeing this girl Vera—the one whose family owns Lincoln's Luncheonette."

"Yes. She's very pretty."

"Yes, that's her. Well, for one thing, I was going to ask her to go steady. I was going to buy her a nice ring, and maybe she would be my steady girlfriend, because I really like her, and—"

"But, Jackie, she's not in the truth."

"Yes, I know, but I'm not interested in any of the girls at the Kingdom Hall."

"Maybe you haven't met the right one. Anyway, aren't you a little young to be thinking about getting serious over someone?"

"I don't know. All I know is that I really like her, and all the kids say that ... well, they kinda expect us to go steady, because that's what kids do these days when they really like someone."

"Jackie, I was afraid of this. You are getting too involved in the world. You know what the Bible says about getting too involved in worldly activities, don't you?"

"Yes, Mother. I know the world is full of sin and corruption and it's going to be destroyed by Armageddon, and it might prevent me from being resurrected ..."

"Jackie, if you are alive when Armageddon comes, you will never have to die. You will go straight into the New World—a perfect paradise where there is no more death and disease. Don't you want to live forever?"

Jackie frowned. *How do you answer a question like that? "No, I do not want to live forever"?* Jackie knew this was not going well. The problem was that although Betty was convinced that Armageddon was coming within the next few decades, he had a hard time believing there was only one religion on earth that had the big truth about God's divine purpose. *What about the Chinese? What about the Jews? The Muslins? Were they all going to be wiped out by God because they were not Jehovah's Witnesses?* It was no use arguing. Betty was a true believer, and he knew it was useless to try and change her religious views. He felt Betty did not understand how hard it was to give up the world. For Jackie, it meant giving up Vera, his friends, dances, parties, sports, and every other activity that did not involve the Witnesses. Sooner or later there was going to be a major confrontation, but for now he was too young to be defiant. He had tried to ease into the Christmas invitation by seeing how she would react to him and Vera going steady. He considered lying to her and telling her that he was going somewhere else on Christmas.

"Jackie ..."

He heard his mother's voice floating in the air and realized he had lapsed into a trance. "Sorry, Mother. I lost track of things there for a while. Well, yes, of course I want to live forever, but is Jehovah going to punish me for liking Vera Lincoln? That doesn't seem right to me."

"It's not just Vera, Jackie. I'm sure she is a real nice girl, but you will be pulled further and further from the truth if you keep doing these worldly things."

"Mother, I hear what you are saying, and I will not get Vera a ring. We can just remain good friends. But, as you know … well, Christmas is coming, and I know we don't celebrate it—and that's okay. I really don't mind. It's all about silly people selling things and trying to make money. But Vera has asked me to come to her parents' house on Christmas for dinner … and I wanted—"

"To know if I would say it's all right," interjected Betty.

"I guess so."

Betty leaned back on the sofa, sighing deeply. She gazed at the ceiling as if expecting Jehovah himself to appear and whisper the proper guidance in her ear. "Jackie, I'm sorry, but I can't let you go. The church is very clear about the celebration of Christmas. It's a pagan ritual not even mentioned in the Bible. Don't you think if Jesus wanted us to celebrate Christmas, he would have told us?"

Jackie didn't bother answering the question. He remained silent, sitting with his mother, sharing a few quiet moments.

"Well," he said, "I guess I better get some sleep. It's a school day tomorrow."

Betty reached over and held Jackie's hand. "I'm sorry, Jackie—I really am. But I can't go against the teachings of the church. Please understand. I might think differently if it was not for the presence of those demons trying to make me lose my faith. I was very near giving up my allegiance to Jehovah's Witnesses. But Jehovah saw that I was beginning to be spiritually weak and fall into the hands of Satan and his demons. So he tested me, and I survived! With Jehovah's help I chased them out of my life. Can you imagine what our lives would be like if I abandoned Jehovah and started worshipping Satan? No, Jackie, we are all saved now, and my faith is even stronger than it was before."

Jackie leaned over and kissed his mother on the check. Betty gave Jackie a big hug and then wiped away the tears streaming down her face. A solid lump the size of a baseball lodged in his throat, causing him to choke, a series of silent hiccups emerging from his stomach. His face was downcast and empty, his entire mind and body overcome by the sadness of it all. He got up slowly from the couch and went into the bedroom. Danny was already asleep in the top bunk. He dropped down on the bed without removing his clothes and burst into tears, holding the pillow to his face, muffling the sounds of sobbing.

The last thing he remembered before slipping into dreamland was a fleeting thought he had never had before: *Maybe life isn't worth living after all.*

THE NEXT DAY JACKIE WAS walking back to school after lunch near the grassy field surrounding the school. Despite the chilly temperatures, the kids were playing outdoor games. He spotted boys running relay races, playing kick soccer, shooting baskets, and playing baseball on one of the fields. The girls were playing hopscotch, jumping rope, running races, and chatting together in small groups along the bicycle racks.

He strolled past an excitable group of boys on their knees playing marbles. They had drawn a wide circle in the dirt and were taking turns trying to knock other players' marbles out of the circle with their own marble. The marble used to knock the others' out was called a shooter, and the ones inside the circle were peewees. When he first came to school, Jackie wondered why some of the boys' pants, shirts and hands were so dirty and dusty after recess. He quickly figured out that playing in the dirt for an hour would do that to a kid. Of course, the boys didn't care; they bragged to each other about who was the dirtiest.

Jackie had just gotten a free glass cat's eye marble from a box of Post Toasties Corn Flakes, and he kept some marbles in the top drawer at home. He had not played the game at school, because he was not very good. He tried kick soccer one more time after his first game, in which he had gotten one big hit in three tries. The second game he didn't get a hit, so he stopped playing soccer. Jackie didn't want to appear mediocre at anything. He wondered where this compulsive need to be perfect at everything came from and why he was so afraid of just being average. It wasn't even good enough for him to be better than average at something. He had to be great. When he had first started playing baseball when he was eight years old, he had almost quit because he didn't get a hit every time. One of his coaches had explained to him that in baseball if you fail two out of three times, that's a .333 average, and over a lifetime in the majors, it would put you in the Hall of Fame.

He spotted Vera walking past the jump-rope area with her friend Judy. As soon as she spotted him, Vera enthusiastically waved him over. Smiling broadly, Jackie immediately started jogging and ran up to them a little out of breath and still smiling.

"Well, hello, Prince," said Vera, a twinkle glistening in her eye.

"Hi, Vera … Judy … Boy, am I getting out of shape? I can't breathe!"

"You're in fine shape as far as I can see," said Judy, glancing at Vera with a mischievous grin.

"Judy's right," said Vera, giving him a sly wink. "You run like the wind, remember?"

"Oh, yeah—but I'm skinny too!"

"I like skinny," said Vera. "My dad is fat, and he looks like a slob."

"My dad's not fat," said Judy, "but he's old."

"How old is he?" Jackie asked.

"I don't know. But he's got gray hair and reads the newspaper—that's old … Well, folks, nobody likes a third wheel. Vera, I'll see you after school."

"Okay! I'll meet you at Mac's!"

Judy turned and walked toward the school. Vera and Jackie were alone listening to the high-pitched squeals of spirited jump-rope jingles.

"Hey, Vera, can we go over to those tables?"

"Sure."

Jackie led Vera to a couple weather-beaten picnic tables. They sat down on one of them, facing each other.

"Gee, it's getting colder," said Vera, wrapping her coat tightly around her body. "Pretty soon they'll move us into the gym."

"I guess you're right. I'm afraid winter's coming on …"

"Yes."

"Vera, I want to say I am very pleased that you want me to come to your house for Christmas dinner. I really like your folks, and I think we'd have a swell time—"

"It really *is* a fun time of the year."

"Yes, it is. I think it's a great holiday where everybody can exchange gifts and celebrate together and have a great time ..."

"... and celebrate the birth of Jesus."

"Yes, well ... I need to tell you something, and I hope you won't be mad at me—"

"Mad at you? Don't be silly, Jackie. I could never be mad at you—you're too cute!"

Jackie smiled thinly. "Well, I don't know about that, but what I want to say is that my mother will not allow me to come to your house for Christmas."

"Why not?"

"Well ... it's kinda hard to explain, but my mother is a Jehovah's Witness—and I guess that makes me one—and they do not celebrate Christmas."

"Really? Why not?"

"As far as I can tell, my mother says it's not really a Christian holiday, and it's not mentioned in the Bible. I know it sounds strange, and I don't understand it all myself ..."

"Well, it really does sound strange. I never heard of Jehovah's Witnesses. Are they, like, a *real* religion?"

"I guess they are real, but there's not very many of them."

"I don't know what to say. As far as I'm concerned, it's okay with me. I think everybody should have the right to worship as they please. It's a free country, right?"

"Yes, it's a free country, but some people don't understand this religion, and they think we're some kind of cult, or heathens, or something awful."

"Jackie, that's silly. You are nowhere near being a heathen—you're too nice. Don't worry about it. We can get together with my parents another day. It's okay—really."

"Are you sure? Because, Vera, I don't want anything to mess up our ... uh ... you know ... the way we feel about each other."

Vera's bright, beautiful violent eyes focused on him, her voice dropping a bit lower. "My feelings for you are not going to change because of this. Our family is Methodist, and they are kinda strange too. If you have a beer, it's like you committed a mortal sin."

"Really?"

"See, your religion is just one of a lot of quirky religions floating around. Don't worry about it."

"You sure?"

"You already asked me that."

"Sorry, it just makes me uncomfortable, and that's one thing I have always been with you … comfortable."

"Nothing's going to change, Jackie. Now let's get out of this freezing cold and get in the classroom. Maybe we can learn some valuable knowledge."

"Like what?"

"I don't know. Maybe they'll tell us why religions are supposed to bring people together, when all they do is tear people apart."

Jackie laughed, leaned over, and gave Vera a big hug. But there was something in her voice that made him feel uneasy.

The next day was overcast, gray, and nearly freezing, with the wind blowing briskly in intermittent squalls. During recess, Jackie was on the sidelines watching the kids play kick soccer.

"Come on, Jackie !" yelled Phil DeMarco. "We could use another player!"

Jackie waved him off, wrapping his arms around his coat, jumping up and down, and mock shivering, indicating to Phil that it was too cold for him to play. Then he spotted Vera in the distance walking alone past the basketball courts.

"Vera! Hey, wait for me!"

Vera turned slightly in his direction, gave him a quick glance, and then kept walking toward a group of girls gathered at the lunch tables. He sprinted across the field and caught up to her, completely out of breath.

"Hey! Guess what? My sister just got some new records, and she said I could borrow them. We could listen to them at your house!"

Vera smiled slightly, and then her eyes shifted briefly to the girls at the tables.

"That's swell, Jackie," said Vera, gazing past him to the kick soccer field. "Those boys are having fun, huh?"

"Oh, they're just crazy—a bunch of nuts!"

Vera remained silent. She rubbed her hands together, adjusted her burgundy scarf tighter around her neck, and then twirled her hair with her index finger. She turned slightly away from him, gazing again in the distance.

"Say, Vera, why don't we go to the movies Friday night? There's a really good movie playing. It's called *High School Confidential*—and it's got Jerry Lee Lewis in it!"

Vera hesitated. "I don't know, Jackie ... I might be busy."

"Busy?"

Something wasn't right. The way her eyes flickered back and forth, not maintaining direct contact. The way her body was leaning away from him. There was something in her voice, a hint of tiredness, a lack of energy he had never sensed before.

"Is everything all right? You seem ... uh ... a little down."

"Jackie, I need to tell you something."

"What's that?"

"It's my parents ..."

"What about them?"

"They ... well—they don't want me to go out with you anymore."

"What? Why?"

"Jackie, this is hard for me. I'm confused."

"About what? Tell me."

"My parents, they think I should stop going out with you because of your religion. They say the Jehovah's Witnesses are a dangerous cult and you're going to drag me into their religion and brainwash me like the Communists."

"The Communists? You think I'm a Communist?"

"No—not a Communist! But like a cult where they turn you against your parents—and your country!"

"Do you think I'm against your parents and my country?"

"That's what my parents say. They say you don't salute the flag and you don't celebrate Christmas or serve in the military. They ... they think you are going to ruin me, or something—change me into a person who hates everything."

"Hates everything? Are you serious? Do you think I hate everything?"

"Of course not, Jackie. But it's my parents! What am I supposed to do? They won't let me see you anymore. I'm not even supposed to be talking to you right now. They're very strict! You don't know! They can make my life a living hell!"

"Well, you're doing a pretty good job right now of making *my* life a living hell."

"I'm sorry, Jackie. What am I supposed to do?"

He couldn't believe this was happening. How could her parents think he was part of some weird brainwashing cult like Communism? Was Communism a cult? Were the Jehovah's Witnesses a cult? He didn't think so, but he was beginning to understand why other people thought his religion was so outrageous. No Christmas? Not serving your country? How unpatriotic could you get? But this was the United States of America, and there was supposed to be religious freedom! Didn't that mean that you didn't hold someone's religion against them? Was it right to stop a girl from seeing her boyfriend because he had a strange religion? Weren't all religions kind of strange?

"Vera, please," he urged. "Let me talk to your parents. This is just a big misunderstanding. We are *not* a cult! I can explain—"

"I've already tried! You have no idea how much they hate your religion. It's like you're *worse* than Communists!"

"Worse?"

"I don't know … it's like they think you're invaders from outer space!"

"Outer space? Holy cow! Now I'm an alien?"

"Jackie, please. I'm not calling you an alien. It's just that I have no other choice. What am I going to do? Run away from home?"

"Yes! Let's run away—and get married!" He knew he had just said the dumbest thing in his whole life, but it came screaming out of him from an uncontrollable part of his brain.

"Jackie? Really? We're twelve. We're just kids. Maybe when we grow up …"

"Maybe what?"

"Well, maybe after I'm not under the control of my parents, we can see each other."

"You mean like in six years?"

"Possibly."

"We can't see each other for *six years?*"

"I don't know what else to do. Don't you understand?"

He did understand; that was the problem. Of course her parents hated him and his religion. The Jehovah's Witnesses were going to knock her over the head, drag her by the hair, tie her across an altar, and cut her heart out as part of a pagan sacrifice to the gods. Who could blame them for trying to keep an evil, mind-destroying religion away from their precious daughter? But still it didn't seem fair that they wouldn't give him a chance to defend himself. He could explain his religion. It was not *that* crazy; they went strictly by the Bible. It was just another interpretation—a different interpretation from theirs. Wasn't that why there were so many religions anyway? He looked closely at Vera. She was crying.

"Vera? Are you okay?"

She wiped the tears from her moist eyes. "Yes, I'll be okay. Let's just stay apart for a while. I'll talk to my parents. Maybe I can get them to change their minds. I need some time, okay? This is *very* hard for me."

He paused. Vera was right. It was hard for her. He realized the position she was in. And he was not going to win. It wasn't a baseball game. He couldn't be the hero and knock in the winning run and have everybody cheer his extraordinary athletic abilities. This was real life, and it sucked. It was *nothing* like being on a baseball field. The rules were different; it was clearly a different world. He felt comfortable and secure on a baseball diamond. As soon as he crossed the white lines, it was like entering a magical, secret place where everything was miraculous, breathtaking, and astonishing. He was the golden boy, the conquering hero. "Hit the ball to me! I'll never drop it!" And he never did. But this situation with Vera was real life, and he was a long way from comfortable and secure. Now, unlike any moment on a baseball field, he felt helpless. Suddenly, he was overcome with the strangest sensation, as if he was shrinking or maybe sinking farther into the ground. Dizziness overtook him, and he heard a whirring noise in his head followed by echoes of bombs exploding on the school grounds. He leaned back on the picnic table for support, wiping his sweaty brow. Staring up at the sky, he thought sarcastically to himself, *Well, I'll be damned. It's the below-desk world coming to get me.*

"Jackie?"

He emerged from his stupor, glanced at Vera for a second, and then lowered his head to the ground. "It's okay, Vera. Really, it's okay. Don't worry about it. Like the deejay says, 'If it was meant to be, it will be.' I'm sorry too. Believe me—I am sorry. I really like you a lot. I dream about you all the time. You're the nicest, prettiest girl I've ever known—and you make great milkshakes! I guess we live in this world, but it seems we don't make it like we please, at least when you're our age. It kinda makes it for us, one way or the other—good and bad. Either above the desk or below the desk."

"Below the desk?"

"Never mind. It's just a phrase I heard from somebody."

"Jackie, this is really bad. I never wanted this to happen, believe me."

"I believe you, Vera. You're right—there's nothing we can do."

"Maybe things will work out in time."

"Now you sound like one of our parents."

"I don't know what else to say."

"Well then, how about a kiss good-bye?"

Vera looked at him, tears welling up, managing to force a faint smile. "Of course, you silly kid."

She leaned closer and kissed him tenderly on the lips. They both closed their eyes, wondering the same thing: *Is this the last time we will ever kiss each other?*

"Jackie, I must be going. Judy is waiting."

"It's okay. I'll see you around. I'm not leaving town, you know?"

"Well, neither am I."

Then she turned and walked away. She never looked back.

11

December 1958

J ACKIE WAS SITTING IN MRS. Wilson's class shortly before Christmas break counting his calories for the week. Mrs. Wilson was in front of the room teaching the students about health, nutrition, and eating a balanced diet.

"Now, class," said Mrs. Wilson. "I want you to add up your calories for the week and divide the total by five. This way you will know how many average calories you are taking in per school week."

Jackie picked up his nutrition notebook and consulted his total for the week. It came to 6,240. After dividing by five and coming up with an average of 1,248, he put down his pencil and waited for everyone to finish. In a few minutes, Mrs. Wilson got the students' attention.

"All right now, students. Look at your averages. Sally Ann, how many did you have?"

"I had one thousand eight hundred and fifty-two."

"That's very good," said Mrs. Wilson. "You have just about the right amount for a girl your size. How about you, Kurt?"

"I had two thousand four hundred and ninety-eight."

"That's also about right. It's a little high, but you are a bit bigger than some of the other boys in the class. How about you, Barry?"

"I got two thousand two hundred and twenty-four," said Barry.

"Very Good. That's just about right."

Jackie stared at his total until his eyes hurt. *Holy shit!* he thought to himself. *I'm a loser! I'm not getting enough to eat! What if she calls on me?*

Jackie didn't have enough time to decide what to do.

"Okay, Jackie, how many did you have?"

"Uh … well, I wasn't very hungry this week."

"That's okay," said Mrs. Wilson. "Some kids don't take in as many calories as others. How many did you average?"

"Well, like I said, I was busy all week and—"

"Jackie, just tell us."

"Well, it came to one thousand two hundred and forty-eight."

Everyone in the class turned around in their seats, staring at Jackie as if he was an orphan who had just farted.

"Well, that's kind of low for a boy your age. You really should be eating more nutritious meals."

"Yes, ma'am," said Jackie, sinking farther into his seat.

"Can you see me after school, Jackie?"

"Yes, ma'am."

Mrs. Wilson was finishing up her lesson plan on health and nutrition when the 3:15 p.m. bell rang. Students began to file out of the room, no one paying any attention to Jackie, who was thinking, *They probably assume I'm a pathetic poor kid who has no food in the house.* He waited until all the students were gone and then ambled to the front of the room, facing Mrs. Wilson at her desk.

"Jackie, I'm a little concerned about your calorie count. It's very low for a growing boy your age."

"I don't know what to say, Mrs. Wilson. I guess I just don't eat very much."

"It's none of my business, but, Jackie, are you sure there is enough food for you at home?"

"Oh, yes! My mother is a great cook, and we have a hot meal every night! Hamburgers, potatoes, beans, lots of stuff!"

"Okay, Jackie. It is my business to make sure my kids are not being neglected for any reason."

"Oh, I'm not neglected, Mrs. Wilson—really. There's lots of stuff to eat in our house. I just don't have a big appetite."

"I see. Well, keep counting your calories, and let me see the average for next week. Just show the number to me after class. I want you to start eating, young man."

"Yes, ma'am."

"Okay, you can go now. See you on Monday."

"Yes, ma'am." Jackie turned to leave the room.

"Oh, Jackie, just one moment."

"Yes?"

"Your arm. What is that red mark on your arm?"

Jackie looked down at the welt forming just above his wrist. "I don't know, Mrs. Wilson. I just noticed it yesterday."

"Well, it looks like it might get worse."

"What could it be?" asked Jackie.

"I'm not sure, but keep an eye on it, okay?"

"Yes, ma'am."

Jackie left the room and walked down the hall and out the main door. The playground and field were deserted. Jackie gazed into the distance, wondering why the walk home seemed so much longer than before.

Later on, Jackie would attribute his popularity downfall to Vera breaking up with him, the misery of counting calories, and a small red welt that kept getting more grotesque. He believed in the signs. And the signs foretold the coming of the below-desk world. Of course, he didn't see it approaching, although he knew in an abstract sense that popularity was capricious, a gift bestowed on you by your peers, and preteen peers were notoriously fickle. Yes, the signs were there, but he thought he was living in a world of his own creation and had some control over his fate and a great spiritual being was looking after him, protecting him from falling into the bottom of the sixth-grade social hierarchy. He came to believe that living above the desk was his rightful, preordained destiny, and no amount of bad luck or mistakes on his part could possibly cause a sudden slide downward into the bowels of hell below the desk.

Jackie arrived home. He didn't see Danny, but Donna was sitting in front of the TV watching a cowgirl show starring Sally Starr.

"Hi, sis," said Jackie.

"Hey, Jackie. How was school?"

"It was okay."

Jackie kept walking toward his bedroom.

"Hey, little bro! Is that it? Just okay? *Nothing* interesting happened?"

Jackie stopped, hesitated. "No, not really." Then he continued walking.

"Wait a minute!" shouted Donna. "Come over here!"

Donna reached up and switched off the TV and sat on the sofa. Jackie sat down next to her, unable to hide his forlorn mood.

"All right. Let's hear it," said Donna.

"Hear what?" asked Jackie.

"You know, Jackie, you are really lousy at hiding your feelings. Even a robot could tell something is wrong. Now what is it?"

"We're poor, aren't we?" asked Jackie.

"Whoa, where did this come from?"

"We counted our calories for the week—"

"And?"

"Well, I only got about half of what the other kids got."

"Wait a minute. Back up. This was part of a classroom assignment?"

"Yes, it was part of health and nutrition week. Everybody recorded what they ate and how many calories they were consuming. I—we—don't get enough to eat. We're poor."

"Come on, Jackie! Get real. Have we ever gone hungry?"

"No ..."

"Well, what are you saying?"

"I don't know. Why am I so different from the rest of the kids?"

"Jesus, I thought you had some self-confidence. Jackie, you are better than the rest of the kids—smarter, funnier, better looking, and a great athlete—"

"But I'm not getting enough to eat! I'm not gonna grow!"

"Hold on, buddy. Let me tell you something. Okay, Mother works late hours, and we do have to fend for ourselves. I know other families all sit down and eat dinner together. We sort of ... do it by ourselves—not all the time, but sometimes. Does anybody ever tell you to eat everything on your plate?"

"No."

"Well, remember Roy, the biggest son-of-a-bitch in the world?"

"Yeah."

"Well, most parents are like him. They force their kids to eat everything on their plate, and guess what?"

"What?"

"They learn to eat when they are not hungry, and then guess what happens?"

"What?"

"They get fat! They grow up to be giant cows! You're lucky. You'll never be fat."

"So it's a good thing I'm a little different?"

"Absolutely."

"Well, what about this?"

Jackie showed his sister the red welt on his arm. Donna grabbed his arm and stared at the sore.

"What is it?" asked Jackie.

"Gosh, I don't know. Its looks different from a pimple. It's really hard and tender around the edges, and it looks like white stuff is forming in the middle."

"It's beginning to hurt—and it gets bigger every time I look at it."

"Let me get some hydrogen peroxide."

"Will that help?"

"I think so. Mom uses that stuff for everything."

Donna went into the bathroom, opened the medicine cabinet, and retrieved a bottle of hydrogen peroxide, two balls of cotton, and a Band-Aid.

As she entered the living room, she declared, "Hey, this stuff will kill any germs within three states." After pouring the solution on a cotton ball, Donna took Jackie's arm and rubbed the sore.

"Ouch!" screamed Jackie. "That burns!"

"Of course it does. You think germs are easy to kill?" Donna slit open the Band-Aid and covered the sore. "There you go. Good as new."

"Is it going to go away?" asked Jackie.

"Of course. Forget about it. It's no big deal."

"Thanks, sis."

"Don't mention it. Dr. Donna at your service any time."

AT SCHOOL THE NEXT DAY, Jackie was talking to Kurt Cummings before class. They were discussing what they were going to do over Christmas break. Another student, Wayne Guy, came over and sat down next to them.

"Hey, guys, what's going on?"

"Nothing," said Kurt. "We're trying to figure out our Christmas vacation."

Wayne looked at Jackie, eyeing him up and down like a sergeant inspecting a young recruit.

"But, Jackie, you don't celebrate Christmas, do you?"

"Well—"

"You're one of those Jehovah's Witnesses, right?"

"Yes, well, it's not—"

"And you don't salute the flag? That's really sick."

"Wayne," said Kurt, "what the fuck are you doing here?"

"I'm just curious, that's all. There's a new girl in Mrs. Chambley's class, and she's a Jehovah's Witness and everybody hates her. Christ, she didn't even wear a Halloween costume."

"Get lost, asshole," said Kurt, rising up from his chair and clenching his fists.

"All right. All right. I just wanted to know if wonder boy here was an unpatriotic atheist."

Kurt lunged at Wayne, but Wayne quickly ran over to the other side of the room.

"Fuckin' asshole," said Kurt. "I'm gonna kick his ass after school."

Jackie turned around, staring at Wayne, who was blathering nonstop to a group of students. *Well, there it goes,* thought Jackie. *My secret's out. I'm a dirty, rotten, un-American Communist freak, and now the whole school knows about it.*

Kurt glanced at Jackie, placing his hand on his shoulder. "Hey, Jackie, don't let that little bastard get to you. Everybody knows what a king-sized jerk he is."

"I know," said Jackie.

The bell suddenly rang, and Mrs. Wilson entered the class. Everyone in the class stopped talking and faced the teacher, except for Jackie, who was staring at the graffiti on the top of his desk.

12

January 1959

J ACKIE MUST HAVE HEARD A hundred songs about broken hearts. He listened to them, danced to them, and memorized the lyrics. The best songs in the world were broken-heart songs. Everybody knew that. He wondered how many fewer songs there would be in the world if all the broken-heart songs suddenly disappeared. But he had never thought about something like that happening to *him*. He figured you had to be an adult to be seriously in love. Kids just didn't suffer broken hearts. The world seemed to have collapsed on top of him, crushing him as if he was a nasty cockroach. As soon as Vera broke up with him, he somehow lost the ability to enjoy life. It was like Vera tossed a blanket of doom and gloom over him. He wondered if this was normal, because he assumed this only happened to someone whose heart had been irrevocably shattered like in the popular songs. Did you have to be in love to have your heart busted to pieces? Was he too young to be in love? If he was too young for a broken heart, then what *did* he have? Was there another word for this lousy feeling that applied to guys who were around thirteen years old? Was it the same for girls? What was he supposed to call what Vera had done to him? Was this why girls were on the planet—to set you up, smash you like a grape, and then leave you helpless and stupid like you'd been kicked in the guts?

It dawned on him that he hated being thirteen. He hated being confused, and nobody seemed to have any answers. So when did he stop being a kid? It seemed the older he got, the less the world made sense. Sometimes he was supposed to act like a man and be mature, but then most of the time he was treated like a kid with a bunch of silly rules and regulations. He wished somebody—maybe the president of the United States or somebody important—would declare a meaningful day of transition, an exact birthday that determined when you went from being a boy to being a man. Then everybody would have a big celebration (except Jehovah's Witnesses), and from that day forward, every boy would know he was a man. He would be expected to act like a man, and the adults would cut out all these stupid rules that made no sense and trust you to follow the ones that did make sense. They would also have to take you seriously—and if you said you had a broken heart, then they would have to show you how to fix it. Instead, all he heard from grownups were stupid phrases: "You're too young," "It won't matter in ten years," and "It's only puppy love."

In a confused state of mind and wanting some answers to his problems, Jackie found himself standing in front of Osa Martin's house on a cold January evening. Mr. Martin only lived a few blocks from their apartment. But Jackie had never been to his house, even though he had told him to stop by anytime. He didn't know anything about Mr. Martin's private life, whether or not he was married or had any children, or even what he did for a living. He walked up the steps and knocked on the door.

Osa Martin immediately opened the door and gave Jackie a broad smile.

"Well, look who it is! My favorite player! Come in! Come on in!"

"Hi, Mr. Martin!"

Jackie walked into a small, modestly furnished living room with plain brown paneling, immediately observing that the furniture was arranged in a cozy semicircle around a roaring, glowing fire, red and yellow flames shooting in from the gray stone fireplace at the far end of the room. He noticed a burgundy print couch, a large brown coffee table, and two matching end tables. To the side, he spotted a cloth-covered patterned recliner that looked eerily like the one he and Vera had used to make out in Kurt's basement. The only other furniture in the room was three identical oak bookcases filled with a vast collection of neatly stacked books. Jackie had never seen so many books in one room in his life. On top of one of the smaller bookcases there was a brown, rectangular record player with albums and 45s piled neatly on top of one another. One album featuring a black trumpet player on the cover was face-up, tilted against the wall, and he assumed this was the soft music playing in the background. Mr. Martin turned and faced him.

"Nice to see you, Jackie. Have a seat. What on earth brings you out on a freezing night like this? Never mind. You don't have to answer that! Would you like something to drink? How about a soda? I have some Royal Crown."

"That would be great, Mr. Martin. Thanks."

He took off his overcoat, folded it in his arms, and took a seat on the sofa, sinking into the soft fiber. He could feel the comforting heat of the blazing fire already warming his cold toes, and the unusual music was mellow and soothing. He immediately felt relaxed.

Osa walked through a narrow hallway into a small kitchen. He grabbed a bottle of Royal Crown Cola from the refrigerator and brought it to Jackie.

"Here you are, son."

"Thank you, Mr. Martin. Aren't you going to have one?"

Osa smiled slightly. He sat down on the other end of the sofa, glancing at a glass of Hennessy brandy on the coffee table. "I already have a drink, Jackie. Now tell me why you stopped by. Is it just for a visit?"

"Well, yes. I know you said I could stop by any time—"

"And you were in the neighborhood?"

"Right. I was just passing by …"

"Well, I'm glad you came. How are things going? I haven't talked to you in a while. School going okay?"

"Oh, yes! I'm doing great in school. I haven't even gotten a B yet— all As!"

"Hey! That's terrific! You're in sixth grade now, right?"

"Yes. Charles Street School. Next year I go to junior high."

Osa leaned forward, took a sip of his brandy. "You'll do fine. And next season you'll be playing in the Babe Ruth League. I'm sure you will be the first player chosen."

"Well, I hope to make a team ..."

Osa stood up and took a step toward Jackie.

"Let me take that coat. You don't have to hold it." Osa took the coat and hung it up in a closet by the door. "Jackie, I don't think you have to worry about making a team. Your only decision will be whether you want to be a pitcher or an outfielder. I would recommend you concentrate on being a regular position player. With your speed and hitting ability, you could go a long way."

"Thanks, Mr. Martin. I really value your opinion. You're the best coach in the world."

"Well, I wouldn't go that far. You know, that guy Casey Stengel for the Yankees isn't so bad."

Jackie laughed. Then he paused. "Yes, but you don't have Mickey Mantle playing for you."

"Well, you were a close second. We never would have won the All-Star game without you."

"Thanks. That game was something else ..." Jackie glanced up at a row of pictures on the mantelpiece. "Can I look at your pictures?"

"Sure."

Jackie eased off the couch, still gripping the soda. He walked over to the fireplace and surveyed a line of black-and-white photos arranged on the shelf. One of them looked like Mr. Martin when he was young; he was wearing a baseball uniform with *Crawfords* printed across the front. There were other pictures of an attractive woman and Mr. Martin laughing together, always smiling and caressing each other like a perfectly happy couple. In some of the pictures, there was a small, slender boy either wrapping his arms around Osa and the woman or alone, playing in a yard, posing, and smiling joyfully at the camera. In one photo, the boy was holding a baseball bat on his shoulders, wearing a T-shirt and a Pittsburgh Pirates cap.

"Is this your wife and your son?"

"Yes, Jackie. But I'm afraid they are no longer with us. They went to heaven."

"Oh, I'm sorry. I didn't mean to … I mean, I didn't mean to bring up bad memories."

"It's okay. Their lives ended in a car accident a long time ago. They were alone—hit head-on by a drunk driver."

"I'm so sorry. How old was your son?"

"He was ten. He was going to be a really good baseball player. He was a Pirates fan like his dad. His favorite player was Honas Wagner, a great shortstop in the twenties."

Jackie kept staring at the little boy in the picture. He wondered why no one had ever told him about Mr. Martin's personal tragedy. Maybe nobody in town knew about it. Mr. Martin was a quiet, reserved man, a real gentleman in his eyes. He reminded him of a great Civil War general like Ulysses S. Grant, who was highly intelligent and commanded great loyalty and respect from his troops. He was still staring at the photos when Mr. Martin spoke.

"Jackie, did you want to talk to me about something? It seems you have something on your mind."

He turned and faced Mr. Martin, who was relaxing on the couch, taking a sip of his brandy.

"I'm sorry about your wife and son."

"It's okay. That was a long time ago. Now tell me why you're *really* here. You didn't just drop in for a soda, did you?"

"No, I didn't. I guess I came for some advice. As you know, I don't have a father at home, and well, my mother and I have a hard time talking about certain kinds of stuff."

"Like what?"

Jackie hesitated, glancing around the room as if searching for a lost object.

"Well, like … my girlfriend just broke up with me—mainly because of religion—but it still kinda bothers me. I can't seem to concentrate on anything else. It's like somebody pulled a rug out from underneath me."

Osa rose from the couch and went over to the chair Jackie thought looked like the one in Kurt's basement. He pulled it closer to the fire. "Okay, Jackie. Sit here. I'll get another chair."

Jackie got up from the couch and moved over to the chair while

Osa went into the kitchen and seized another chair, placing it across from him.

"Jackie, have you ever heard of fireside chats?"

"Fireside chats? No, sir."

"Well, during the Great Depression and the Second World War, President Roosevelt would broadcast on the radio from the White House. He wanted to reassure the American people that things were going to be all right during these tough times. He was a very popular president, and millions of Americans would sit around their living rooms, sometimes beside a fireplace, and listen to Mr. Roosevelt's words of wisdom and encouragement on the radio. He was a great leader—a great president."

"I have heard my mother talk about President Roosevelt. I remember she said after Roosevelt was elected, she never went hungry."

"So your family was poor like mine?"

"They musta been *real* poor, 'cause my mother said they collected berries for food and ate bark off trees."

"Well, you're one up on me there, Jackie! We were poor, but we managed to avoid eating bark."

"So are we going to have a fireside chat?"

"If it's okay with you."

"It's fine with me, but where do we start?"

"Well, let's start with how you feel about your girlfriend."

"Vera."

"Yes, how you feel about Vera and losing her as a girlfriend."

"Well, I feel terrible. I don't think she really wanted to break up with me, but her parents hate my religion, and they won't let us go out together."

"What's your religion?"

"We're Jehovah's Witnesses, and it's a really weird—"

"I know all about them. My sister is a Jehovah's Witness."

"Really?"

"Yes, really."

"So I guess you know why they forbid us to date."

"I assume it's because your mother doesn't want you to have any worldly friends."

"Exactly! How did you know?"

"Well, I told you my sister is a Jehovah's Witness, and that's the way I was raised too."

"You mean you couldn't have any friends outside the church?"

"That's right."

"But, Mr. Martin, I don't understand. You must have been very popular and a great athlete—"

"Well, I think I was. You can still play sports and be in the truth. You can also have friends, but they can't get in the way of your obligations to the church."

"But you're not a Jehovah's Witness, are you?"

"No, I quit the church a long time ago."

"How did you do it? I mean, your parents must have been very upset."

"Oh yes, believe me, they were upset."

"Well … how old were you when you left the church?"

"I was seventeen."

"And what happened?"

"I decided I had reached a point in my life where I was mature enough to make my own decisions about my faith. Jackie, parents want their children to grow up a certain way. Maybe they want them to go to law school or be a doctor. Maybe they want their son to go into the priesthood. Maybe they want their daughter to marry that nice boy down the street. But here in America, for better or worse, young people have to be themselves, develop their own identity and moral values—and not attempt to be carbon copies of what their parents want them to be. I saw many of my friends trying to live up to the expectations of their parents, and they were miserable because they knew they were just different inside from the picture their parents had. It happens all the time."

"But your parents must have been terribly disappointed and hated you!"

Osa paused, took a sip of his brandy, and gazed up at the pictures on the mantle. He seemed momentarily distracted. "No, Jackie, they didn't hate me. They respected me. They respected my decision."

"Really? Boy, I can't see that happening in my family or congregation. There's so much pressure, and leaving the church is like abandoning your whole family. My sister Donna quit going last year, and then my brother Danny refused to go a month ago. I'm the only one left. My mother is really sad, and if I quit ..."

"She won't have any of her kids in the truth."

"That's right."

"Jackie, you're in a tough spot, and I would not advise you to quit right now. You are too confused, and you might make the wrong decision. It seems to me it's all about how, when, and why you make this decision. I would wait until I was really sure about my beliefs, and then I'd follow my conscience. I know kids hate it when grownups say, 'Wait until you are older,' but in this case it might be the right thing to do. Later, if it turns out you don't believe in the Jehovah's Witnesses faith, you can decide to leave. No one wants you to attend a church you don't believe in."

"Not even my mother?"

"I think your mother will keep trying to keep you in the faith no matter what decision you make."

"You're right. She might not like it, but she sure won't stop witnessing to me. If I said I wasn't going to go to church anymore, it would be a major conflict, and my mother would ... well, I don't know what she would do, but she'd be mighty disappointed and probably send me away to a reform school or something."

"I think reform school might be a little drastic."

"But how did you do it?"

"Well, first of all, I was seventeen, not thirteen like you. It helps if you pick the right age to rebel and you are clear in your values and the choices you want to make. It's easier to defend unpopular opinions the older you get. It just comes with age, and if you are a responsible kid like I was, parents see you as level-headed and are more likely to take you seriously. But, Jackie, it's a lot more than age and maturity. It's the way you handle the difficulty—the conflict with your parents—"

"So how did you do it?"

"Well, you need to pick the right time and place. You want to make sure your parents—or your mother in your case—has the time and energy to have a serious discussion. It's not a good idea to scream out, 'Mother, I'm leaving the church!' as she goes out the door to go to work. So I picked a time after dinner when everyone was present, including my sister and grandmother."

"Wow, that takes guts. Your grandmother? I bet she wasn't happy."

"No, she wasn't."

"Did you break it to them all at once?"

"Well, yes and no. I said a few words before I told them about my decision."

"Gee, I better write these down! I might need them someday!"

"You don't have to write them down. It's very easy to remember. First of all, I told my parents, sister, and grandmother that I loved them very much and how much I appreciated all the things they had done for me. I was going to tell them something they would not approve of, but it had no reflection on my love for them and the fact they were great parents. Basically, I said to them, 'I love you dearly, but I am not going to turn out exactly like you want me to.' I told them it was a difficult choice and I didn't want to hurt them, but I had to live my own life on my own terms and basically insisted that at this point in my life, I had the right to choose my own religion."

"Wow, that was gutsy."

"It wasn't easy. All around the table I could feel their disappointment, anger, and frustration. I saw their tears and heard their pleas to change my mind. But I went into it determined not to change my mind and let them talk me into a life I did not want to live."

"But why didn't you want to be a Jehovah's Witness?"

"Jackie, that's a complication question, and someday when you're older we can have that discussion. The short version is that I became a nonbeliever. I lost faith in their teachings."

"I see. I think I understand. And what about now?"

"What do you mean?"

"Your family. Are you allowed in the house?"

Osa laughed, took a sip of his brandy. "Of course! And yes, my mother hasn't given up. She still witnesses to me."

"You're lucky."

"Why do you say that?"

"I bet the other kids in school didn't make fun of you or call you a Communist for not saluting the flag."

"Did they do that to you?"

"Yes, among other things."

"What other things?"

"I got a boil."

"A boil?"

"On my arm. It was a disgusting red thing that swelled up and turned purple with white puss coming out of it. I couldn't hide it, and everyone thought I was some kind of freak from a leper colony. They thought I was dirty."

"Jackie, that's not true. Boils can result from a variety of reasons."

"I know. That's what my mother said, but all the kids started avoiding me like I had the plague or something."

"Jackie, I wouldn't worry about those kids. They weren't your friends in the first place. Not all of your friends acted that way, did they?"

"No ... there was Kurt, and Louie, and Archie ... a few others."

"Well, now you know who your real friends are. Jackie, it seems to me you're trying to be too perfect in everything."

"What do you mean?"

"I mean you want everyone to like you, to admire you. That's not going to happen in life. You want to be a perfect role model with no flaws. Well, that's not possible. Even I have flaws!"

Jackie laughed in spite of himself.

"And, Jackie, the very things that make you a terrific baseball player don't always work off the field."

"What do you mean?"

"Sometimes, all the hard work and preparation does not lead to being the best at something. Yes, you are the best baseball player in town, but you can't be that good or perfect in everything—and sometimes life is going to throw you a curveball, like being popular one month and not so popular the following month."

"But it seemed like everything crashed down at once. I never dreamed that Vera would bust up with me."

"That's how life is. Some things just don't work out. My father used to say that if a woman breaks your heart, well, it's just like missing a bus. If you wait long enough, another one will come along. I know that's a cold comfort right now, but I bet there are other girls who would like to go out with you."

"Well, there was this blonde girl named Dottie, but as soon as she found out I was a Jehovah's Witness, she avoided me like I was Adolf Hitler."

"I know it sounds very simplified, Jackie, but time really does heal all wounds—" Osa stopped abruptly, gazing momentarily at the pictures on the mantelpiece. "Well, maybe not all wounds ..." Then he continued, "But like the Bible says, 'This too shall pass.'"

"I hope so. I'm tired of being Mr. Doom and Gloom."

"Oh, you'll cheer up. Things will get better."

"You know," said Jackie. "Just a couple years ago, I couldn't figure out why God put girls on this earth. I mean, they were lousy at dodgeball, couldn't swing on the monkey bars, they all had cooties and played that stupid hopscotch game."

"So what made you change your mind?"

"I think I know the exact moment. I was at the community center, and I was slow-dancing with Vera when I got a strange feeling ... It was like something was driving me, like a force. I was suddenly yearning for her. I never felt this ... urge, this powerful force outside of me—or maybe *inside* of me—that made me want to hold her so closely—*real* closely, like I could just devour her or something. Her ... body was so tempting, so warm and inviting ... and I had no idea where it came from or what I was supposed to do about it. I felt something, you know, down ... I thought for sure my pecker was going to explode!"

Osa Martin laughed so hard he almost spilled his drink. "So! You were going to explode! Well, that's a good way to put it. I never heard a young man express it that way. But it's okay, Jackie. Actually, you just described the experience pretty well. I had almost forgotten what those first feelings were like. You probably felt like you were a revved-up engine that was going to blow up if someone didn't let up on the pedal!"

"Exactly!" he cried, practically jumping out of his chair. "Just like a revved-up engine ready to explode—or burst!"

Suddenly, Jackie kicked his own foot, thrusting his fists into the air, punching an imaginary person. Then he slumped back in the chair.

"Gosh, Mr. Martin. I'm making a fool of myself. I don't make a lick of sense."

A smile spread across Osa's face. He reached for his brandy glass, took a healthy sip, and then stared directly into Jackie's eyes. "Of course you're making sense. I must admit I never heard a kid your age say their penis was going to explode, but believe me, I know what you mean. That's normal, Jackie. You are going through what we call puberty. It happens to all boys your age at different times, and I guess at different levels …"

"Levels?"

"Well, maybe *level* isn't the right word. What I'm saying is that you are just beginning to experience a normal sex drive, and believe me, a sex drive is a very powerful force in a young man's life. Pretty soon, and maybe even right now, it's beginning to happen—"

"What's happening?"

"Well," said Osa calmly, "pretty soon you are going to be thinking about sex a lot. Actually, pretty much all the time. This is normal for young boys. It's a bit different for girls, but that's a topic for another time. Right now, this urge you're talking about will lead you to be very curious about sex and how your body works. Do you know what I mean?"

"To tell you the truth, Mr. Martin, I'm not sure. I really don't know how to do it. Kurt Cummings told me he already had sex last summer at camp. I think he's a liar and full of crap, but he told me my … you know … penis … would get hard and I would stick it into a girl's hole … down there … and I would, uh, spray her, or like he said, cum would come out of me like I was a fire hose … and it would feel really great, like eating twenty ice cream cones …"

Osa chuckled again. "Well, Jackie, I think you're right. Your buddy Kurt is probably full of crap. I mean, how much knowledge can you expect from someone who carries around a dead spider on a string?"

This time it was Jackie's turn to laugh. "Yes! Kurt's full of … *bull crap!*"

"I would say so," said Osa. "Anyway, Jackie, Kurt is probably half right. He forgot to mention a few things. First, a boy gets excited. The word is stimulated. You know what that means?"

"Yes, you feel turned on by somebody … excited."

"Right. Then, after a young man get stimulated sexually, his penis gets hard. And yes, the act of sex involves putting your penis into a girl's private parts. And after you put your penis into the girl, after a while, you do what Kurt says—"

"You cum!"

"Yes, the word is *ejaculate*."

"Does it feel like eating twenty ice cream cones?"

"Hmmm … that seems like a poor analogy. The feeling is very physical and pleasurable, but not like eating ice cream cones. Have you ever been on a roller coaster?"

"Oh, yes! Echo Glen Park in Maryland!"

"Well, it's something like when you are approaching the top and there is a slow buildup of tension as you get closer, then you go over the edge, and you get this great physical sensation all over your body like … well, like you are going to explode."

"Wow, Mr. Martin. Nobody ever explained it to me like that. I think I see what you mean. It sure makes me realize why guys are so nuts about sex. Gee, you could have many roller coaster rides and maybe roller coaster rides all the time! How about the time I was swinging on the rope at Spring Lake and splashed into the chilly water! Boy that was exhilarating!"

"I'm sure it was. But we're a long way from the end."

"The end of what?"

"Jackie, there's a lot more to sex than putting your penis in a girl and feeling good."

"Like …?"

"Well, sex should mean something, right?"

"Yes, it means you got real lucky!"

Osa smiled. "Jackie, that's only part of it—and it's not even the best part."

"I had a feeling there was more to it. I know it's got something to do with falling in love and getting married, but no one has ever told me exactly what the connection is. All the guys talk about is getting into a girl's pants. After that, it's a mystery to me."

"Well," suggested Osa, "maybe we can save that subject for another fireside chat. You probably should be getting home. It's getting late, and your mother will be worried. Did you tell her where you were going?"

"Oh, yes! She thought it was a great idea. I'm not sure she knew what we were going to talk about."

"Well, that makes us two of us. We can talk about other stuff too.

Sometimes, it helps to get a man's opinion of things. So you want to come back for another fireside chat?"

"If you don't mind ..."

"Not at all. As you can see, I live alone, and I could use some company once in a while."

"How about if I come back tomorrow night?"

"How about next Monday. Come around the same time—right after dinner."

"Thanks, Mr. Martin. I really appreciate the advice."

"No problem, Jackie. I'm not sure many people, girl or boy, would want to go back to being thirteen again. It's a tough age."

"So I'm not alone by feeling so screwed up?"

"Not by a long shot. See you on Monday."

Mr. Martin led Jackie to the front door. He grabbed his coat from the closet and opened the door for him. A blast of wintry wind immediately surged through the opening. Jackie turned up his collar, wrapped his coat around him, and bounded down the stairs. As he hit the bottom, he turned abruptly and yelled back to Mr. Martin, "Oh, Mr. Martin! Can I ask you a dumb question?"

"Sure, Jackie."

"Do black people do sex differently than white people?"

Osa grinned, shaking his head. "No, Jackie. It's pretty much done the same way by all different races and nationalities—but remember, individually, people vary a great deal."

Jackie took off running down the street toward home, hollering behind him, "See you later, Mr. Martin!"

Osa Martin watched Jackie disappear into the night, closed the door, and walked over to the coffee table to take a sip of his drink. He couldn't help glancing at the row of pictures on the mantelpiece. His eyes slowly scanned the row and then froze in place when he came to the picture of his son wearing the baseball cap. He sighed deeply, quickly polished off the last swig of brandy, and calmly walked back to his easy chair. He picked up a book and continued reading where he had left off.

WHEN JACKIE ARRIVED BACK AT the house, he saw Donna sitting quietly on the couch reading *Silver Screen* magazine. He peered into the kitchen to see if Betty was washing dishes or cleaning up after dinner, but she wasn't there. He walked over and took a seat next to Donna.

"Hi, sis. How's it going?"

"Great. I was just reading about this hot actor named Tab Hunter. He's cute, and I bet he's gonna be a big star."

"I never heard of him. Where's Mom? Is Danny here?"

Donna glanced up from her movie magazine. "Well, believe it or not, Mother is out on a date, and Danny is studying in the bedroom as usual."

"Wait a minute! Mom is out on a date, and you're home reading a magazine? Am I in the right house?"

"Of course you are, birdbrain. You think I go out every night?"

"Yes."

"Look, smarty pants, I'll have you know I do more things than go out to clubs and dances."

"Oh really? Like what? Job hunting?"

"Hey! Since when did you become a cynical little bastard? I thought you were my best buddy?"

"I'm only kidding—but really, why are you not out?"

"Okay, so I got stood up—but don't tell anybody. I was supposed to go out with this big-time basketball player from Palmyra High, and he hasn't shown up. I hope he's got a good excuse, like a car accident or something."

"Donna, please. Don't wish a car accident on anybody."

"Sorry, but he pisses me off."

"Who's the guy?"

"Paul Larson."

"Paul Larson? The Gooch?"

"Who?"

"That's what people call him. It's a nickname. Donna, he's the biggest jerk in school. Everybody hates him."

"Why?"

"Because he's a stupid egomaniac. All he talks about is how great he is. Even the kids at my school know he's a jerk."

"Well, he's certainly a jerk if he's standing *me* up. I could be going out with anybody at that school—and half the guys in Philly."

"On second thought, maybe you two are made for each other."

"Very funny. You know, I don't think I like this new Jackie. He's a sarcastic, creepy kid with no manners. What's the matter? You been reading *Catcher in the Rye?* Think you're the next Holden Caulfield?"

"Okay, sis, I declare a truce. Sorry for being a bit holier-than-thou. Hey, wait a minute! Did you say Mom is out on a *date?*"

"Boy, are you slow! I thought you'd never ask! Yes, our own hardworking, never-goes-anywhere, never-has-any-fun mother is having dinner with a man she met at the Kingdom Hall—and he's not ugly!"

"You saw him?"

"Well, yes and no. After spending an eternity in front of her dressing table, she came out and waited by the door—just sitting there like she was in church or something. Honest to God, she got all dolled up, even borrowed my makeup and brand-new red lipstick. You wouldn't have recognized her. She was wearing a dress I've never even seen before. I thought all her dresses were hand-me-downs from the old maid's section of the Salvation Army. But I tell you, Jackie, she came out of her room dressed in this sexy black satin pleated dress with a matching wide belt. She also wore a white nylon cardigan over the dress. Black shoes, hose—the whole Hollywood makeover. Very classy. Of course, she was a nervous wreck, mussing with her hair every two seconds, acting like a school girl, taking her compact out of her purse, primping herself, putting it back. She was acting like you before *your* first date. Well, around six thirty someone knocks on the door, and she quickly opens it, says hello to a tall, good-looking man, and runs out the door—didn't even say good-bye to me. Strange, huh?"

"I wonder why she's keeping it so hush-hush?"

"Who knows? After that bastard stepfather of ours, she's probably being a bit … you know, overly cautious. Can't say I blame her."

"Yeah, but how many Roy Shifflettes are in the world?"

Donna tossed the magazine down hard on the seat cushion, her eyes receding into tiny, foggy gray pinholes. "One too many, as far as I'm concerned."

"Well," said Jackie, "I'm going in to see what Danny's up to. I might even do some homework—"

At that moment, Betty walked in the door followed by a tall, thin man in his early forties wearing an unbuttoned Bogart-type trench coat. He was smartly dressed in a pair of pressed tan slacks and a thick wool navy sweater over a white shirt with a button-down collar. His wavy, dark brown hair was parted and combed neatly to the side. He had an angular, sharply chiseled face featuring a prominent nose, sleepy gray eyes, and perfectly formed white teeth. Donna immediately thought he looked like a dentist or a pharmacist.

Betty and the man walked directly toward Donna and Jackie. She looked nervous, but the man behind her had the look of someone confident and at ease in social situations. He became more alert and animated, smiling at Donna and Jackie before Betty spoke.

"Donna, Jackie. I'd like you to meet Richard Longstreet. He's one of the brothers at the Cinnaminson Kingdom Hall."

Donna and Jackie leaped up together and shook hands with Mr. Longstreet.

"Nice to meet you both," said Mr. Longstreet. "Betty has told me all about you. And there is Danny too, right?"

"Oh, yes!" yelled Donna. "Let me get him!" Donna sprinted to the bedroom, and within seconds Danny emerged walking slowly like he had just woken up.

"Danny," said Betty, "this is Mr. Longstreet."

Mr. Longstreet and Danny shook hands.

"Pleased to meet you," said Danny.

"My pleasure," responded Mr. Longstreet. An awkward pause followed, interrupted by Mr. Longstreet's exclamation, "Oh, I forgot something! I'll be right back!"

Mr. Longstreet was gone for a few minutes and then returned with a gallon of Breyers chocolate ice cream. The kids knew Breyers was very expensive ice cream, and they had never tasted the brand.

"Here's some ice cream for you kids," said Mr. Longstreet, taking the container out of a large paper bag. "Your mother said you all liked chocolate."

"Gee, thanks!" Jackie yelled.

"Wow!" cried Donna.

"Gosh, thanks," muttered Danny.

"I'll put it in the freezer for now," said Betty, who took the ice cream from Mr. Longstreet and walked toward the kitchen.

"So," said Mr. Longstreet, "I hear you kids really like rock 'n' roll music."

"We sure do!" Jackie cried. "Donna's been on *Bandstand!*"

"Hey, that's a great show. Dick Clark is a cool deejay." Another pause. Betty returned to the living room. Mr. Longstreet reached into his trench coat and produced three 45 rpm records. "Well, it just so happens that I have three rock 'n' roll records in my possession. Imagine that! Let me see ... here's one by Chuck Berry called *Roll Over, Beethoven.* I believe this one has Danny's name on it. And this one ... is called *That'll be the Day* by Buddy Holly. I believe this one's for Jackie. And what do we have here? Hmmm ... looks like *Rockin' Pneumonia* by Huey Smith and the Clowns. Donna, I guess this one's for you."

The kids were stunned. They were not used to anyone, especially a kindly man, giving them gifts. As Jehovah's Witnesses, they hardly ever received presents. Betty was on the verge of tears. She couldn't remember the last time she had seen all three of her kids so happy at the same time. Donna wanted to give Mr. Longstreet a big hug. It reminded Betty of how little her children received in terms of material possessions.

"Well, children," said Betty, "Mr. Longstreet has a long day ahead of him tomorrow, and you all have to get your rest."

Danny and Jackie said good-bye and proceeded to go to their room. Donna was going to do the same, but her enthusiasm got the best of her. She blurted out, "Oh, Mr. Longstreet! Do you work in Palmyra?"

"No, Donna. I work across the river in Philadelphia. I'm a lawyer— just one defense lawyer among many in a large firm."

"Wow," said Danny. "That's what I want to be—just like Perry Mason!"

"I'm afraid it's not that exciting, Danny."

"Okay, children," insisted Betty. "Off you go."

She waved her hands toward the bedrooms, and the children obediently scuttled out of the living room. Then Betty walked Mr. Longstreet to the door.

"Betty, I had a great time. Your kids are wonderful."

"Well, sometimes ..."

"How about this coming Friday? Would you like to go to a show in Philadelphia? We can have dinner first."

"I'd love to."

"Then I'll call you on Wednesday and—like lawyers say—finalize the deal."

Mr. Longstreet turned to leave. Betty watched him descend the wobbly stairs and walk toward his car. She quietly closed the door and then leaned back on it with her hands folded behind her. She sighed, letting the air slowly out of her lungs, feeling as if an enormous burden had been lifted off her shoulders. Then she gazed toward the ceiling, calling forth the heavens, uttering a solemn prayer to Jehovah, thanking him for bringing these precious moments of happiness into her life.

13

January 1959

T HE FOLLOWING MONDAY EVENING, JACKIE was on his way to Mr.
Martin's house. It was pitch dark, and a steady, light snow was
beginning to powder the sidewalks with a thin layer, the wind swirling
all around him, blowing bits of frozen ice in his face. He lowered his
wool toboggan hat down over his forehead, leaving just enough room to
see the sidewalk in front of him. He pulled his overcoat tighter around
his body, crossing his arms, bending forward, plodding along with his
eyes glued to the ground below. Tiny specks of ice were already sticking
to the front of his hat, and his hands were stiffening from the cold. As
he was shivering past one of the maple trees lining the street, he heard
an alarming voice bellow out, "That you, Jackie Riddick?"

He instinctively jumped two feet away, losing his balance and
staggering to the other side of the sidewalk. From a crouching position,
he peered over at the tree, unable to see anything. *Did a phantom person
say my name?* He began to slowly slink away.

"Wait, Jackie!" the voice cried. "Don't be scared! It's only me—ole
Rufus! You remember me! I saw you last October when we talked about
the Bible!" Jackie took a few steps toward the tree. He knew there was
something familiar about the man's voice. Then he remembered his
encounters with Rufus Johnson. He was a hard person to forget. He

was that old drunk he had first met last summer sitting on a lawn chair, and then later with Danny selling *Watchtower* magazines. *What is he doing out in this weather? And how on earth did he recognize me?* Jackie's curiosity got the best of him. He cautiously approached the ghostly figure huddled under a tree. Gradually, he was able to make out the dim figure of Rufus, and sure enough, he was sitting in the same broken-down lawn chair. As Jackie inched closer, he realized he was dressed exactly the same in tattered overalls and a beat-up fedora full of holes. Not surprisingly, a bottle of Pabst Blue Ribbon was leaning against the side of the chair. His only other protection from the elements was a wool blanket wrapped around him, but this too was full of holes.

"Rufus?"

"You bet it's ole Rufus! Come here, Jackie! I hear you're just about the best darn young baseball player in the state of New Jersey! Bats left, throws left, pitches like Warren Spahn, got a batting eye like an eagle, and runs like Willie Mays himself. Come here, Jackie, and say hello to ole Rufus!"

Jackie approached Rufus, took off his toboggan hat, and dusted off the ice and snow, slapping it repeatedly against his left leg like it was baseball cap.

"Hi, Rufus. Isn't it kinda cold and snowy for you to be out here?"

"Don't you worry about ole Rufus, Jackie. This weather ain't nothin'. You shoulda seen the winter of '48. Damn blizzard every day, and no shelter anywhere for Rufus. I lived in a cardboard box for three freezing months. Hell, this ain't nothin', I tell ya."

Jackie had wondered if Rufus was homeless, and now he knew for sure. He had probably not enjoyed the security and pleasures of a real home in a long time. In spite of it all, Jackie couldn't help but like the old guy. If nothing else, he had an engaging personality and Jackie had the feeling there had been plenty of fascinating episodes in this man's life. He seemed like wizened philosopher who had gained wisdom from the hobo jungle. He had certainly been around—where, Jackie didn't know, but the old-timer looked like he'd traveled many a hard road and seen many things that Jackie could only imagine.

"Well, Rufus, it's still very cold out here, and it might get worse. Don't you want to go inside someplace?"

"Hell, no! You go inside someplace and right away they wanna start puttin' rules on you, tryin' to civilize you, makin' you hide your liquor, make your bed—treat you like you was a kid or somethin'. Better off here. Nobody tells ole Rufus what to do."

"Okay, I was just suggesting—"

"Wanna sip of my drink?"

"Uh, no thanks. I'm not much of a drinker."

"Well, I am!" screamed Rufus, instantly tilting the bottle to his lips, taking a long gulp, and then lowering the bottle and wiping his mouth with his tattered sleeve.

Jackie laughed. "I can see that, Rufus. You sure enjoy your beer."

"Damn right. Now, where you goin' anyway? Too damn cold out here for young-uns."

"I'm going to Mr. Martin's house. You remember, he's my Little League coach."

"Oh, yes! The Mighty Man hisself. Best damn coach in the state. I heard about that All-Star game—and that stupid Dunberry. He kept Nate Green in_way too long. I know'd Osa wanted to pull him and put you in, but that Dunberry's stubborn as a broke down mule. He almost blew the game for you kids. Good thing you had ole Mighty Man Martin to talk some sense into him."

Jackie had forgotten about Rufus referring to Mr. Martin as Mighty Man. At the time, he had just assumed it was the ramblings of an old drunk.

"Didn't you say he played professional ball someplace?"

"Jackie, I know you ain't dumb. You look kinda dumb to me, but you's a smart youngster. I already told you about Osa Martin being one of the finest Negro League players I ever saw—and I seen 'em *all*. Satchel Paige, Smokey Joe Williams, Buck O'Neil—all of 'em."

Jackie remembered the odd names of the players. He had thought Rufus was making them up, but now, for some reason, he believed Rufus. Then suddenly it hit him. The picture on the mantelpiece! There was a picture of Mr. Martin in a baseball uniform with a team name printed across the front. He couldn't remember the team name, but it was definitely a young Mr. Martin, and he certainly looked like a professional ballplayer.

"Rufus, tell me again. Who did Mr. Martin play for?"

"I told you, son. The Pittsburgh Crawfords!"

"Right! The Crawfords! I remember now!"

"Maybe you ain't so dumb," muttered Rufus.

"You said he was great, but he stopped playing, right?"

"Yes, that's what I said—and I told you not to tell anybody. You never told anybody, did you?"

"No, sir. I never told a soul."

"Well, you keep it between you and me."

"But I don't understand, Rufus. Why can't I say something? I think it's great that he was a terrific player and all. People in town should know about it."

"Now, Jackie. You is a good kid. I like you. But there are some things that need keeping quiet, you understand me?"

"Yes, sir."

"Did you say you were headed for Mr. Martin's house right now?"

"Yes, sir."

"You been to his house before?"

"Yes, sir."

"He ever mention the Pittsburgh Craws?"

"No, sir."

"Why you going over there?"

"Well, I've been having some problems, and Mr. Martin is giving me some real good advice. I don't have a father at home and, well, he's been helping me out."

"Couldn't find a better man. Osa Martin is one of the finest men I ever met. Maybe you're a smart kid after all."

"Do you think I could ask him about his baseball career? It's only the two of us, and I'd like to hear it from him. You said he quit playing after just a couple years?"

"That's right."

"But you're not going to tell me why he quit, are you?"

"No, I'm not. If Osa wants to tell you, he will. If he don't, he won't. Simple as that."

"Do you think it would be okay for me to ask him?"

Rufus thought for a second, placing his hand on his chin. "I don't think he would mind you asking, Jackie. Osa is a very private man, but if he likes you and trusts you, he might open up to you. Might do him some good. It's not a good thing to keep everything bottled up inside of you. Turns your guts sour. Might do some good. Never know in this world. You say Osa Martin is helping you out with some problems?"

"Yes, sir."

"Might work the other way, son."

"What do you mean, Rufus?"

"Maybe you can help him out with some of his."

Now Jackie was even more intrigued by Mr. Martin's past. He decided to play it by ear and not bring up the subject unless it felt right and he could sense that Mr. Martin wanted to tell him about his baseball career. He would not press the issue but would do the right thing and protect his privacy, if that was what he wanted.

"Well, Rufus, I better get going. It's getting late, and the snow seems to be picking up. I don't want to come home in a blizzard."

"Can't blame you there, son. Sure you don't want a sip? Warm your bones!"

"No thanks. I hope to see you again sometime."

"Well, son, you never can tell. One thing about life. You never can tell. You take care, now—and keep playing baseball for as long as you can. There ain't nothin' better in a boy's life—or a man's life either, for that matter."

Jackie waved good-bye, twisting around one more time to see Rufus taking another swig from his bottle and brushing the snow away from his face.

After several minutes trudging through the thickening snow, Jackie finally arrived back at Mr. Martin's house. Once again, he walked up the steps and knocked on the door. Coach Martin opened the door, immediately expressing delight in seeing him. "Well, look who it is! The next player to hit .400 in the majors!"

"Hi, Mr. Martin. Is it okay to come in?"

"Of course! I was expecting you! Come in! Come in!"

Before stepping into the house, he removed his overcoat, shook off the snow, and then went through the door, handing it to Mr. Martin.

Osa took the coat, hung it up in the closet, and walked energetically toward the fireplace.

"Come on over by the fire, son. It's a lot warmer over here!"

Jackie walked over and resumed his place in the same chair that reminded him of Kurt's basement. He was silent, gazing into the fireplace. Osa walked into the kitchen and retrieved a Royal Crown Cola. He came back, handing it to his guest.

"You're a Royal Crown man, right?"

"Yes, sir!"

"So how's it going?" asked Osa, taking a seat.

"Oh, fine. My mother is going out with a new man."

"That sounds wonderful. What's he like? Do you like him?"

"Oh, he's a real swell guy! He's a lawyer in Philadelphia, and he brought us some ice cream and some rock 'n' roll records! He's also a Jehovah's Witness, and my mom is *really* glad about that."

"That *is* good news. I'm sure your mother is very pleased."

"She's like a changed person. She even smiles sometimes."

Osa laughed good-naturedly. "Well, that's certainly good to hear."

"My mom sure could use a man to treat her nice. She hasn't had much luck in the men department."

"Well, maybe this will work out for her. I know it must be tough on her, trying to raise three kids all by herself."

"It sure is. I heard a song on the radio the other day—something about 'It's so nice to have a man around the house,' and it made me think of our home situation. We don't have a man around the house, and when we did, it was just terrible …"

Jackie faced the flickering fire, staring at the lively, jumping flames as if answers to his problems could be found smoldering in the burning embers.

"So how do you feel about that?" asked Osa.

"What?"

"I said how do you feel about that?"

"About?"

"Not having a father in your life."

"To tell you the truth, Mr. Martin, I feel like I'm not learning a bunch of stuff that the other kids at school are learning."

"Like what?"

"It just seems like the other boys talk about hunting and fishing and building model airplanes, and making go-carts, and reading compasses, and building tree houses—a whole bunch of stuff they must have learned from their fathers. I can't even hammer a nail in a board."

"Maybe they're in the Boy Scouts."

"Right. I guess so. But I wouldn't even know how to join the Boy Scouts—and the other boys are already way ahead of me."

"Jackie, I wouldn't worry about it too much. You certainly have other skills. You're an excellent student and the best young athlete in Palmyra."

"But, Mr. Martin, I'm weird."

"Really? How's that?"

I have this urge—this powerful need—to be perfect, or the best at everything I do, and if I'm not, I quit—like marbles and kick soccer."

"So how do you feel about that?"

"I feel, like, terrible … stupid."

"Why?"

"Because I know in my heart it's not possible, but I try anyway, and I get just … paralyzed."

"Paralyzed?"

"Well, maybe that's not the right word. I get tense all over, and my mother calls them panic attacks."

"You get nervous."

"Right. I feel very uncomfortable, and I want to jump out of my skin."

Osa got up from his chair and went over to a small cherry cabinet with glass doors and took out his bottle of Hennessy brandy. He grabbed a glass from the shelf and poured himself a drink. Jackie glanced around the room. His eyes came to rest on the album he had seen before, the one with the black man playing the trumpet on the cover. It was a shadowy, black and silver picture of a man who looked like he was thrusting the trumpet in your face.

"Say, Mr. Martin, what is that album over there? The one propped up next to the record player on top of that bookcase."

Osa returned in his chair, took a sip of brandy, and then looked at the album. "That's a classic record by a jazz musician named Miles

Davis. He plays the trumpet, and he has a great band backing him up. The album is called *Birth of the Cool.*"

"Wow. That's a cool title."

"It's a cool album. You know, Jackie, I think learning about jazz can help you with some of your problems."

"Really?"

"Well, jazz is all about free form and flowing and changing the tempo according to your mood and the mood of the audience. For the most part, it's not written down like classical music. In other words, it's almost the opposite of trying to be perfect and play the same song the same way every time. It's about mood changes and improvisation."

"Wow, that sounds so cool!"

"It is. It's really cool. And you can borrow it if you want to."

"I can?"

"Sure. You can take it with you tonight."

"Gee, Mr. Martin, thanks. I promise to take real good care of it."

"No problem, Jackie."

There was a pause. Jackie took a sip of soda. Osa took the opportunity to go over and stoke the fire. He grabbed a poker from beside the fireplace.

"Mr. Martin, do you remember what we were taking about last time, about Vera and how boys are different from girls—that stuff?"

"Sure," said Osa, poking logs on the fire.

"Well, I'm not sure what happens afterward."

Osa stopped prodding the fire, turned toward Jackie. "Afterward?"

Jackie leaned forward, placing his hands on his knees. "You remember about the twenty ice cream cones ..."

"Oh, yes! I said something about a roller coaster."

"Right! We were talking about the physical things that happen ..."

"Yes ..."

"Well, how does it feel afterward?"

"Oh! I see!" exclaimed Osa, placing the poker back on the rack and returning quickly to his seat. He raised his right hand, pointing to the ceiling. "That's a good question!" Then he sat back in his chair and took another sip of brandy. "Let me see ... afterward, it feels like a great sense of satisfaction, sort of like crossing home plate after you hit a home run and looking up in the stands and experiencing a kind of glowing contentment all over. Also, maybe like you feel after a great meal like Thanksgiving dinner … a feeling of warm satisfaction."

"We don't have Thanksgiving dinner."

"Oh, I forgot. Bad analogy. But you know how you feel after a wholesome meal, right?"

"Sure."

Osa turned more serious. "But, Jackie, that's really not the important thing."

"What?"

"That great sensation you get before, during, and after."

"What is important?"

"Well, sex for boys is about approaching manhood, and sex means you can make babies—be a father. Sex lets you make a baby, but being a real man means taking responsibility for your wife and kids. It means you cannot be constantly thinking about yourself. You can't be selfish and be a good parent."

"But, Mr. Martin, I only just turned thirteen. So I shouldn't have sex until I'm married and like … old?"

"You mean old like … say, twenty-five?"

"Yes, that old."

"I see. Well, I am not saying you have to wait twelve years to have sex—that's a long time for anybody. So you are probably going to have sex with girls—and it seems it's not very far away, considering your popularity. But you must be careful not to get a girl pregnant. Do you know what a condom is?"

"Yes—rubbers, right?"

"Right."

"I see them all the time washed up along the Delaware River. Looks like a lot of white balloons fell from the sky."

"I'm not surprised. What I'm saying is that you should never have sex without a condom. It prevents pregnancy. And don't ever force yourself on a girl—always show respect. If she tells you to stop, then you stop. No questions asked."

Jackie rotated his body away from Osa, gazed intently into the fire, and slumped back in his chair.

"I wanted to have sex with Vera, but now we are never going to have the chance."

"Why? Because you have strong feelings for her?"

"Yes, that—and she's beautiful, and sexy, and I have a strong feeling that she already knows it."

"She probably does."

"So girls are kinda ahead of boys, huh?"

"In many ways."

"I guess girls are learning stuff when they talk to each other, like on the playground. It seems like they are *always* talking to each other. And us boys, we just run around playing games and sports. We just keep bumping into one another while they're getting way ahead of us."

"That's an interesting way to put it. The boys should talk more to each other about the things that really count."

"Like what?"

"Well, for one thing you need to show confidence with girls. Girls like a boy who is secure and confident in his feelings and actions—and how he presents himself."

"But what if you *are* insecure around girls?"

"Fake it."

"Fake it?"

"Let me explain. I don't mean to be insincere, but sometimes just pretending you are confident will *create* feelings of confidence."

"Really? Even if you don't have it?"

"Well, it has to come from *some* place. And if you pretend long enough, it might begin to feel natural. Do you remember what I said about jazz? How do you create new forms of music? After you practice for many hours and learn from the masters, you begin to experiment with your own sound, your own feelings about how you want to express yourself. Sometimes you don't know yourself what it will sound like, but at a certain point it begins to feel natural, and you have created a sound all your own."

"Wow, Mr. Martin, I never thought of it like that. Instead of creating my own sound with a trumpet, I experiment with feelings of confidence and then eventually I might actually feel confident—naturally."

"That's right, Jackie. You're at a difficult age, and to tell you the truth, you are going to be frustrated in many ways—particularly when it comes to girls. But you need to control your emotions, and I don't mean it the way most adults tell you. I know adults are always telling young kids to control their emotions, but that's wrong. We call people like that uptight. You're going to have powerful emotions, and you need to express them but in appropriate ways."

"I'm not sure I understand, Mr. Martin. Am I supposed to express my emotions or not?"

"I'm saying that you should definitely express your emotions, but let me be clear about this. Let's use anger as an example. Look, anybody can be angry, right?"

"Right."

"Well, that's the easy part. But to show the right amount of anger to the right person at the right time—that's not so easy."

"I guess you're saying if I get frustrated not to go off the handle and punch somebody or act stupid."

"Right. But unfortunately, many adults never figure it out."

"My stepfather ..."

"Your stepfather?"

"He would beat everybody—anybody—over the dumbest things, like not eating the peas on your plate."

"That's a perfect example. It's cowardly to pick on women and children who are weaker than you. That sounds like a man who got no respect outside the home and acted like a tyrant inside the home."

"Tyrant? Is that the same thing as a bully?"

"Yes."

"But, Mr. Martin., I still feel a lot of anger toward my stepfather. I want to stick a knife in his guts—"

"Jackie! What are you saying?"

"I'm sorry, but that's the way I feel. He beat up my mother, sister, and brother. I hate him."

"Jackie, you need to understand one thing. The proper response to hating your stepfather is *not* to put a knife in him. Why do you think there are so many men in jail? They could not control their emotions and channel them properly. They acted on impulse and did not have what I said earlier—"

"What?"

"They didn't show the right amount of anger to the right person at the right time."

"Oh, I see. Just because I hate my stepfather and want to stick a knife in him doesn't mean I should do it. He's the wrong person, and it's not the right time."

"Well, not exactly. First of all, hate is a very self-defeating, negative emotion, and we should try not to hate people."

"But I do hate him."

"I believe you. But the right reaction is to get over your hatred and realize nothing was your fault, and that part of your life is over. It's not good to carry feelings of hatred within yourself. It only causes bitterness in your soul. It will wear you down."

"So I should forgive him?"

"I didn't say that. You need to *forget* him. If everyone who hated someone went out and stabbed them, it would be a pretty horrible world, wouldn't it? That's why we have laws against violence. You may feel like doing violence, but the prisons are full of people who acted on impulsive emotions and did things that are not permissible in our society. Do you understand?"

"Yes, sir. I need to get over what he did to us. It's not good to carry hatred around in your heart. It … messes you up."

"Right. It messes you up."

"But …"

"But what?"

"Well, I still have nightmares."

"About what?"

"It's pretty much the same bad dream. I'm being chased by demons who want to harm me because I didn't stick that knife in my stepfather's guts. They want to punish me for not protecting my family."

"Jackie, you were ten years old."

"But I just sat in the corner and watched him beat up my mother and sister."

"So you have feelings of inadequacy."

"What?"

"It seems you're not just angry at your stepfather. You're angry with yourself."

"I don't understand."

"Let's get back to this idea of you trying to be perfect, like quitting soccer and marbles because you were not great at either one."

"Yes…"

"Well, you obviously don't want to be inadequate at these things—"

"Wait a minute! Are you saying I don't play soccer and marbles because I am angry with myself?"

"In a way, yes. Your nightmares and your avoidance of doing anything where you would appear inadequate or average are probably connected to your feelings of being a failure at … what did you say? Protecting your family? There's not a ten-year-old boy alive who is capable of defeating a man like your stepfather. But you turned that anger inward, directed it at yourself, and you are punishing yourself for no reason. I don't know, but some of this could also be part of the reason for your panic attacks."

"Gosh, Mr. Martin. How did you get so smart?"

"I've been around young men a lot, Jackie. And don't forget I was young once myself. Let me throw on a couple more logs. We don't want this fire to give out on us, especially tonight. It's bitter cold out there."

"I'll say. I think the snow is picking up." Osa grabbed a few logs, threw them on the fire, and then prodded the logs with a black poker. He returned to his chair and took a sip of his drink.

"So what am I supposed to do, Mr. Martin? How do I make these bad feelings go away?"

"That's a very good question. I'm not your personal therapist, and it will probably take some time to work out your negative feelings toward yourself and your stepfather. But I believe that doing something will change your attitudes, not sitting around waiting for them to go away."

"I don't get it."

"I think a psychiatrist would put it this way: it's behavior that changes attitudes, not the other way around. So instead of waiting around to feel adequate about playing soccer, you go out and play. And you're not so good. So what? You're out there to have fun, not show the world how great you are. Then, by playing soccer—maybe not so well—you realize that it's okay to be not so good. Or as I said, you lose these feelings of inadequacy, because you realize that being average at soccer is not connected to who you are as a person."

"I'm not perfect."

Osa laughed. "Jackie, nobody's perfect—not even me!"

It was Jackie's turn to laugh. "Gee, Mr. Martin, you coulda fooled me!" Jackie sat back in his chair, relaxing for the first time, and glanced over at the bookshelf.

"Mr. Martin, can I hear your record? The one about the beginning of cool?"

"Sure, Jackie. It's called *Birth of the Cool* by Miles Davis."

Osa walked over to the top shelf of the bookcase and placed the album on the turntable. He hit a switch, and the arm swung over, dropping the needle down on the record.

Jackie heard a strange, captivating sound he had never heard before. He only knew rock 'n' roll and a little country music. He had never heard jazz and only a spattering of classical music, but the sound reminded him of powerful classical music, only it was made by a small number of musicians. He imagined himself sitting in a black nightclub in a city somewhere late at night, musical notes evoking soulful, heavenly vibrations from a trumpet player on stage creating the sound of magic on earth. He lay back in his chair, mesmerized by the beauty of the melody, almost too powerful and beautiful, as if it was emanating from another universe, timeless and profound. He tried to figure out what other instruments were playing, but he was not used to listening to music this closely. Rock 'n' roll blasted you in the face; this music was more subtle, and the instruments blended together. He thought he heard a saxophone solo, and there was definitely a piano and drums. Osa and Jackie listened to one side of the album in complete silence.

When the music ended, Jackie sat up and looked at Mr. Martin. "Gee, Mr. Martin. I never heard anything so beautiful in my life. It's like he's playing from a place I never knew existed—like someplace where great spirits are celebrating life."

"That's a good way to put it, Jackie. Jazz is the music of soul. It's like the breath of spirits creating an atmosphere for harmony and splendor to come together."

Jackie leaned back in the recliner. He was anxious for Mr. Martin to play the other side of the record. Listening to the music made him feel closer to Mr. Martin, and he wanted to know more about his life. He thought this might be a good time to ask him about his baseball career. Jackie hoped Mr. Martin wouldn't get angry and kick him out of his house. He had no idea what to expect. He didn't want to do anything to cause him any pain or bring back bad memories, whatever they might be. Osa reached for his drink.

"Mr. Martin, do you know an old man named Rufus in town? I think he's probably homeless, but I have run into him a couple times."

Osa paused before taking another sip of brandy. "Yes, Jackie. I have known Rufus for a long time. He was a scout for the old Negro Leagues a long time ago. He's a very odd person, but he's remarkably intelligent and knows the game of baseball inside and out. He discovered many excellent prospects in the old days, including me. I see him occasionally, but we don't keep in contact anymore."

"Well, I don't know how to say this, but Rufus told me you were a great baseball player and you had a funny nickname—Might Man. Is that true? Do you want to tell me about it? And please don't think I'm prying into your life! You don't have to tell me anything—really, Mr. Martin!"

"It's okay, Jackie. I don't mind telling you, but it's a rather long story. Are you sure you want to hear a long story?"

"Yes, sir."

"Well, feel free to close your eyes and relax in the warmth of the fire. I'm going to tell you the whole story. And by the way, I have never told this story to anyone—ever."

Jackie closed his eyes. Osa began to speak:

"I was playing for the Pittsburgh Crawfords in 1934. The fans called us the Craws. We had just won the most games of any team in the Negro Leagues and fielded a great team composed of some of the greatest players in the Negro Leagues. We felt we were good enough to beat any of the white major-league teams, but of course we never got the chance. I played right field, because I had a strong arm and could make that long throw from right field to third base. Later on, Satchel told me that I played just like Roberto Clemente—only better. I was in my second year. I batted .325 the first year and .376 in 1934. That was when I got the nickname 'Mighty Man.' A really good pitcher named 'Cannonball' Willis gave me that name after I hit two home runs in a game in St. Louis. I hit twelve home runs my first year, and then in 1934 I hit fifteen—just one shy of Josh Gibson. So my career was really taking off, and after the season was over, the owner, Gus Greenlee, took me to the Crawford Grill, one of Pittsburgh's favorite night spots, and we listened to a young singer named Lena Horn that night. That woman could sing like an angel ... Anyway, Mr. Greenlee told me that I was going to get a nice, fat contract for the coming year, and he said, in a joking manner, to go out and get me a fancy Packard automobile.

"After the season was over, we went barnstorming across the country in a cramped, sweltering hot bus, playing other touring teams or local teams they would put together. In those days, even the big white stars like Babe Ruth, Dizzy Dean, and Bob Feller would barnstorm in the off season to keep in shape or make some extra money. One time we played a white team in Mississippi, and Babe Ruth was in right field. Obviously, I had heard about Ruth, but seeing him in person was something else. He was what you call bigger than life. I think he hit two home runs, and boy, one of them was the longest home run I ever saw. He was quite a guy too. He was one of the few white players who would socialize with us, and he even came to some of our clubs at night. That Babe sure loved his cigars, women, and booze ...

"Anyway, back then us ballplayers—and every black person, really— lived in a black parallel universe. We didn't have any entries into the white world. There were segregation laws all over the South called Jim Crow laws, and everything was separate; and believe me, they were definitely not equal. A lot of times we slept on the bus, went hungry 'cause restaurants wouldn't serve us, so we'd go to the black section of town. Sometimes, we'd pull over and pick fruit from a field, and one time in Alabama, we ate sardines out of a Bell Fruit jar from a kettle fired up in someone's backyard. Since we couldn't congregate in the white world, black folks built their own social networks. We had our own churches, restaurants, schools—everything a community needs, although we were much more destitute. Also, we came across a lot of mean people who just hated us simply because of the color of our skin. But they loved to watch us play because we were so good, and we also entertained the crowds. We played a different brand of baseball—much flashier, bolder, and much more exciting than in the majors. We ran the bases like our uniforms were on fire. And the pitchers would throw any kind of pitch they wanted, like spitters, shine balls, cut balls, balls soaked with tobacco juice—anything. Everything and anything was legal—even spiking players with your sharpened cleats! And they'd throw at your head as soon as look at you—just to announce their arrival. Satchel was, by far, the best entertainer. Sometimes, he'd clown around and pitch from his knees. One time he made the catcher sit in a rocker chair, his control was so good. Other times, he ran to third base instead of first. Another time, he pitched from second base—and still struck out batters! He was something else. I used to say that if Satchel was white, he'd be a millionaire. I want to be clear about this, Jackie. Sure, we entertained white people, but we never compromised our manhood, our dignity, or acted like an Uncle Tom. If we thought they were just laughing at us and not with us, then we'd get serious and beat them by twenty-five runs. We also made fun of them, using code names for words like *cracker* and *redneck*.

"Now, besides the usual community places, we also went to what we would call 'the other side of the tracks.' Well, Jackie, I can't be too specific, but there are certain kinds of illicit pleasures that young men do that are not very nice but very tempting … Remember, there were a lot of lynchings of black people down in the South; it was a very dangerous place, especially at night in an unknown town.

"Well, I was barnstorming with the Craws in late November. We played a tough Negro League team called the Alabama Black Barons. I think Willie Mays played for this team later on. Well, we won the game, and later that night we all went across the tracks to what they called a juke house or juke joint. These were small clapboard houses along the side of the road that served beer and whiskey, and they usually had a blues player singing on the premises. There was also gambling, mostly dice games like craps or card games like bid whist. We were in the tiny town of Chickasaw, Alabama, just a few miles north of Mobile. It was Josh Gibson's idea to check out Posey's Juke House just on the outskirts of town. All of us were a little apprehensive about this place, because we didn't know anyone and these places can be very rough, if you know what I mean. It wasn't just white folks killing black folks. We also killed plenty of each other. I'll tell you how rough they were. They only served beer in paper cups, and you could only drink whiskey out of the bottle. They couldn't use any ceramic mugs or beer glasses, because the men would tear each other up, cutting and stabbing and blood flyin' all over the place …

"It was me, Satchel, Josh Gibson, Rap Dixon, and a player named Wee Willie Johnson who went into Posey's about midnight. Things were just getting started. It was a dark place. Very simple furniture. A couple of small pine tables and chairs and just a plain wooden bar with some whiskey bottles behind the counter. When I first came in I heard a blues singer who was practically hidden in the corner sitting on a cane-bottomed chair. I had never heard a voice like that before. It was very emotional and heartbreaking—a very powerful wailing, like he was some kind of tortured soul. No one was paying much attention to him. He just had an acoustic guitar and a bottle of whiskey by his side. We grabbed a table in the middle of the room, and a fine-looking waitress came over to take our order. We all ordered beer and a bottle of whisky to share. Well, it turned out we had nothing to fear, because one of the patrons who was in a corner shooting craps looked up at us and screamed, 'There's Satchel!' Well, the whole place just exploded with good vibes. Everybody loved Satchel, and then they started buying us drinks, and the blues player caught the spirit and started playing more upbeat dancing songs. I remember one of them sounded like an old ragtime jump song about hot tamales being red hot. The guy was just mesmerizing.

"So the people started getting more excited, shouting and dancing, and then all of a sudden the blues singer stood up like a rock 'n' roll singer—like Elvis—and he began to sing and shake and whirl around the whole place. We were having a great time, and then this cute girl in a plain cotton dress came up to me. She was a white girl—the only one in the place. Someone told me later that she was the farm owner's daughter, but she couldn't have been more than twenty-one years old. She was well built, with reddish hair and a charming smile that could make your heart melt. Anyway, she seemed interested in me, and we had a few drinks. Then, after a while, she asked me to go back to her place.

By this time I was—well, Jackie, truthfully, I was blind drunk. I said yes, and we left the house and went to her car—a beautiful, brand-new Ford coup. She got in and drove for a while. I don't remember how long, but I remember looking out the car window and seeing steel girding, and I realized we were on a bridge, but I still didn't know where she was taking me. We crossed the bridge and traveled a few miles, and I saw a sign that said Pascagoula River State Wildlife Area. Apparently, we were in a national park surrounded by woods and fields. I never did see a river. Anyway, the girl pulled over and said something like, 'This looks like a good spot.' We were what you kids call making out when I looked up from the seat and the harsh beam from a flashlight blinded my eyes. It was a cop, and he was none too happy. He made us get out of the car and asked us a bunch of questions, like who we were and where we were going, and he particularly wanted to know how old the girl was and where she was from. The girl told him she was twenty years old, but I don't think he believed her. After interrogating us for about a half hour, he told the girl to get in her car and go home. He told me to get in the back of the police car. We rode for a few miles, and I asked him what I was being arrested for. He said, 'The Mann Act,' as if I would know what that was. I said I never heard of a Mann Act, and he said, 'Too bad for you.' When we got to the police station, it was the first time I realized I wasn't in the state of Alabama. I was in Mississippi, and we had crossed the Mississippi River. I had no idea, but I was in big trouble. The Mann Act makes it a crime to take a woman across state lines for 'immoral proposes,' and if she's under age or a prostitute, you're in real trouble. Well, to make a long story longer, I was sent to jail for five years—Parchment Farm in Mississippi, the worst prison on the face of the earth. I can't tell you how brutal the guards were. I saw many men injured and killed by either the guards or fellow prisoners. I picked cotton for ten hours a day, six days a week, and the guards constantly lashed my back with a thick leather strap called Black Annie. I still have the red marks to this day.

"My boss, Mr. Greenlee, was outraged and hired a big-time lawyer from New York to take my case and work on getting me released. Well, the lawyer was successful, but it took three years, and by then I was worn out from the back-breaking work, lack of sleep, and terrible food. Mr.

Greenlee gave me another tryout, but it seemed my body had suffered too much abuse. So that was when I hung up my spikes. After that, I wanted to get far away from the South and Midwest, so I came to Palmyra.

"So that's what Rufus was talking about when he told you I was nicknamed Mighty Man. And also why I suddenly disappeared from the world of baseball. But I have no regrets. There were many other players who never got the chance to play in the majors because of the color of their skin, the war, or unexpected injuries. You need talent to make it as a professional player, but a little luck doesn't hurt either. I guess my luck wasn't so good, but I don't blame anyone but myself. I should have never gone to that juke joint and certainly never left with that strange girl. Those were dangerous times and I was young, naïve, and pretty stupid. So, Jackie, don't make any similar mistakes. Some of these temptations like drinking, gambling, and women can be a pretty powerful draw on a young person, but you must keep your eyes on the prize, and the prize is not just becoming the best baseball player you can but also becoming the best person. You can't let these other things distract you from your future goals, whatever they may be."

Osa paused. Jackie still had his eyes closed. He wondered if he had put the boy to sleep. Then Jackie opened his eyes.

"Mr. Martin, that was the best—and saddest—story I ever heard. I couldn't imagine spending three years in a horrible jail, getting whipped with a black belt. And you missed out on a chance to be a major leaguer. Golly, I guess you wish you coulda done things differently ..."

"I don't know, Jackie. From where I'm sitting right now, I wouldn't change a thing."

"You mean you're not bitter about the way you were treated?"

Osa paused, glancing at the mantelpiece. "Well, in life, you really have no choice. You need to take the good with the bad and count your blessings every day."

"Gosh, I never realized how hard it was for black players in those days. I never even heard about the Negro Leagues. That seems strange to me. All I ever heard about was Jackie Robinson and how great it was, letting black players in the majors. But now I know there were so many great players before him who never got the chance to play—and just because of the color of their skin. And boy, I *never* want to go to Alabama or Mississippi. They sound like awful places."

"Well," said Osa, patiently, "they might not be so bad if you're white, but it's a whole lotta trouble for black folks down there."

"I'll say."

"Jackie, it's time for you to get back home. It's late, and it's snowing harder outside. Do you want me to drive you home?"

"Oh no, Mr. Martin! I love to walk in the snow—and I've got a lot to think about! I'm so glad you told me about what happened during your baseball career—even if there were a lot of bad people in your life. It's fascinating—and I won't tell anybody!"

"It's okay, Jackie. You can tell people. You can't run from your past. I just prefer to keep it to myself. It's no big secret."

"Well, I think you had the most wonderful, exciting experiences, and I wish I could have seen you play! Could you really throw harder than Roberto Clemente?"

"Well, that's what Rufus says."

"And Rufus is never wrong!"

"Right," said Osa, smiling. "Now, you get along. I'll see you next week, if you want to come by."

"Can I? I'm not being a pest, am I?"

"Not at all, Jackie. I'll see you next Monday, same time."

"Sounds great!"

"Oh, Jackie! Hold on! You forgot something."

"What?"

Osa went over to the record player, grabbed the album, came back, and handed it to Jackie. "Here you are, Jackie. Enjoy."

"Thanks, Mr. Martin. I'll take real good care of it."

"No problem. Watch your step going home." Then Osa went to the closet and retrieved Jackie's coat and hat. Jackie put on his coat and stretched the hat down over his head. He opened the door and was greeted by a swirling gust of wind and snow. Briskly trotting down the steps, Jackie started walking home.

Osa watched him until he disappeared into the darkness of the night. He closed the door, walked over to the coffee table, and picked up his glass of brandy. He stood in front of the fireplace, his head bowed, watching the flames burning intensely. Osa's eyes drifted slowly upward to the pictures on the mantelpiece. He looked at them for a moment before lifting his glass in front of one of the pictures.

"To you, Helen and Josh. I still love you." Osa lowered his glass, gazed into the fire, and then polished off the last of his drink.

14

The Riddicks' apartment
January 20, 1959

I T WAS CLOSE TO SIX o'clock on the Friday evening following Jackie's visit to Mr. Martin's house. His mother was sitting at her dressing table in front of the mirror putting on her makeup, getting ready for her dinner date with Mr. Longstreet. Donna was stretched out across her bed on the other side of the room writing a passage in her diary about her latest boyfriend, Troy Ashburn. She was going to put in an entry about the night they had sex in his car but glanced over at Betty and decided it might be too risky. Betty would die if she ever read Donna's diary. Betty had told her she would never touch her diary, but Donna wasn't taking any chances. Instead, she wrote, "Troy works in his father's clothing store in Philadelphia, drives a cool red Cadillac, and looks cuter and dresses sharper than Tab Hunter! I've got the meanest crush on him!"

It was quiet in the small apartment except for the low drone of muted voices coming from the television. Danny was alone in the living room drinking a Coke and watching an old Roy Rogers western. Jackie was in the bedroom lying in the lower bunk, reading Mark Twain's *Life on the Mississippi*.

They heard a knock on the door. Danny turned away from the

television and glanced at the clock in the kitchen. He yelled out, "Are we expecting anybody this early? I thought Mr. Longstreet was coming at seven."

Betty cracked open the bedroom door, still wearing a slip and her makeup still unfinished. "Danny! Get the door! It can't be Mr. Longstreet!"

Donna stopped writing and stared at her mother, who had instantly become a nervous wreck, haphazardly slapping powder all over her face as if she was keeping Eisenhower waiting in the other room. Betty was afraid it really was Mr. Longstreet and she had somehow misunderstood the time of the date.

"Who could that be?" asked Donna.

"I don't know!" screamed Betty. "Go see who it is!"

"Okay, okay. Relax, Mom. Mr. Longstreet's not due for another hour!"

"Just get the door, Donna!"

Donna tucked her diary under the mattress, climbed out of bed, and strolled into the living room. Jackie emerged from the bedroom just as Danny was opening the door.

Mr. Martin was standing on the tiny porch. The coach was sharply dressed in a dark gray double-breasted pinstripe suit, a white shirt, and a printed tie. He draped a folded black overcoat across his arm and held a black fedora in his hand. In spite of his surprise, Danny quickly composed himself and offered Mr. Martin a warm greeting.

"Oh hi, Mr. Martin. Please come in. It's really nice to see you."

Osa hesitated in the doorway. "I'm sorry to interrupt your evening, but I'd like to have a moment with Jackie, if it's okay with your mother."

"Sure, Mr. Martin. Jackie's right here. I'll get my mother."

Osa walked into the apartment and stood motionless near the doorway. Donna thought something terrible must have happened, given the serious look on his face. A few seconds passed. Abruptly, Danny spoke up. "Please, Mr. Martin, have a seat." He motioned Osa to the couch. The coach nodded and walked to the couch, passing by Jackie on the way and giving him a wink.

After hurriedly throwing on a dress and wiping off most of her makeup, Betty materialized from the bedroom. She saw Mr. Martin sitting on the couch. Her three kids were stone-faced, standing like statues in the middle of the room.

"Oh, Mr. Martin! It's so nice to see you! Can I get you something to drink? We have Coca Cola and some orange juice, and I think there's some Kool-Aid in the refrigerator."

"No thank you. I just wanted to talk to Jackie for a few minutes."

"Oh, no problem! Would you like to be alone?"

Mr. Martin shook his head slightly. "No, that isn't necessary. It's not something that is confidential."

"Well," said Betty. "Why don't we leave you two alone just the same. I'm sure we'd just get in the way."

Betty turned around to go back to the bedroom while motioning with a nod for Donna and Danny to do the same. After everyone left the room, Jackie joined Osa on the couch.

"Jackie, I know this is unusual, but I thought it would be best to see you in person. I have some important news to tell you."

"Yes?"

Osa took a deep breath, placing his coat and hat next to him on the couch. He looked directly at Jackie. "There has been a very big change in my life—a much unexpected change. And I wanted to let you know right away, in person, what it was."

"All right …"

Osa's voice was low, deep, and solemn. "You see, I have a sister in North Carolina—"

"The Jehovah's Witness?"

"That's right. She's married to the owner of a minor league team in the Carolina League in Winston-Salem. They're called the Red Birds. Well, it seems they're looking for a new manager for the team, and Lucille—that's my sister—suggested to her husband that I might be a good candidate for the job. Apparently, Mr. Gibbs, her husband, did some fact-finding on me, and to make a long story short, he offered me a job for the upcoming season."

"Gee, Mr. Martin, that sounds like a great opportunity for you. You're the best coach I've ever known, and you're much too good to be coaching kids—you should be managing professional players like yourself!"

"Well, Jackie, it is a good opportunity. I think you know from the story I told you the other night some of the reasons why I have not been given many offers. I wouldn't have gotten this one if it wasn't for my sister—and the fact that they finished in last place this year."

"So I guess you are going to take the job, right?"

"Yes, I am—"

"And will you be leaving soon?"

"Very soon. Within a week. I have to go down and go over the roster and learn the system and give them advice about trades. There are lots of things for me to do, and they want me right way."

"Wow, that's big news, Mr. Martin. You can't pass it up. That would be, like, crazy."

"It's probably my last chance, realistically."

"What about your job here? I mean, you *do* have a job, don't you?"

Osa laughed. "Yes, Jackie. I'm the manager of a post office in Philadelphia. It's a decent job, but it's obviously not what I really want to do with my life. I have already given them my notice. I really want to get back into professional baseball."

"And you should! You'd make a great manager!"

"I don't know about that, but I'm certainly going to miss coaching the Kiwanis club and especially watching you develop in the Babe Ruth League. And of course, I am going to miss our fireside chats. We were just getting started."

"Mr. Martin, that's okay! I'm very happy for you. I can come and visit, and you can show me what a real professional ballpark looks like!"

"I was hoping you'd understand, Jackie. It wasn't easy for me. Sometimes, in order to go someplace, you have to leave some things you really care about behind. That's the way I feel about you. I hope you don't think I am abandoning you."

"Not at all! I want you to go down there and win a championship—the very first year!"

"Well, I don't know about that ..." Osa paused, his voice fading to a soft murmur. A watery layer of film glazed over his eyes.

Jackie asked, "Would you like something to drink, Mr. Martin? We don't have any brandy, but there's some Coke in the kitchen."

"No thanks, Jackie. Not everybody keeps brandy around the house. Really, I must be going. Please tell your mother I apologize for busting in on you like this. But I figured I didn't have much time, and like I said, I wanted to talk to you in person."

"It's okay. I understand. I really appreciate you taking the time to come here and let me know. It's a lot better than learning it some other way, like showing up Monday night and seeing an empty house. That woulda been strange!"

Osa grinned expansively. "Yes, indeed! I couldn't let that happen." Osa grabbed his coat and hat and stood up from the couch. He walked pensively across the room. "Again," said Osa, "tell your mother I said thanks for putting up with the intrusion. Also, be sure to tell her she's got a son who's the best young ballplayer I have ever seen—and he's a great kid too! Tell her how lucky she is!"

"Thanks, Mr. Martin. I'm going to miss you."

Osa moved closer to the door and opened it halfway. "I am going to miss you too, Jackie. But I'll write you and send you my address, and maybe someday you can come down and see a game."

"Wow! That would be swell!"

"Well, good-bye, son. Take care, and keep doing the best you can in everything—and I don't mean just baseball."

"I'll remember. I'll remember everything you taught me."

"Good-bye, son."

"Goodbye, Mr. Martin—wait!"

"Yes?"

"Your album! *Birth of the Cool!* Let me get it!"

"Oh no, Jackie! That's for you. It's my going-away present."

"Thanks, Mr. Martin! You sure?"

"Yes, I'm sure."

"Wow, it's like the best gift ever."

Osa opened the door and trotted briskly down the steps, Jackie following him the whole way. Just before he got into his car, Osa turned around and waved to Jackie. Then he drove off, Jackie watching the car until it disappeared into the shadows of the narrow street. He closed the door and went into the bedroom. Danny was lying on the top bunk.

"What did he say?" asked Danny.

Jackie collapsed on the bed crying. Danny was about to say something else but decided against it. It was a long time before Jackie stopped crying.

15

February 3, 1959

BUDDY HOLLY DIED IN A tragic plane crash along with Ritchie Valens and the Big Bopper. When Jackie heard the news, he immediately left the house without telling anyone. He walked down by the railroad tracks with no particular destination in mind. He simply wanted to be by himself, as if being alone could provide answers he couldn't find anywhere else. It was a cloud-covered, raw, chill-to-the-bone day, and a relentless freezing rain pelted his face with swarms of prickly icicles. He plodded along a muddy dirt path parallel to the tracks, his body bent, his arms folded, and his uncovered head tucked into his chest, like a soldier steadfastly marching in a driving rain. He felt he was running away from something, or maybe toward something, or going to a place he had never been before. It occurred to him that the future was going to be very different. And he was not sure he liked the feeling. Mr. Martin had left Palmyra, and he somehow knew that he would never return. His coach had left a gaping hole in Jackie's life, as if he had lost a piece of his soul.

And now Buddy Holly was dead. Of course, he hadn't known Buddy, but he sensed something meaningful had been lost not just for himself but for the whole country. It was as if someone had come up to him and told him there were not going to be any more cheeseburgers in America.

It seemed that when Buddy was alive, everything made sense. Now, nothing did.

The freezing rain continued its assault. He had left the house wearing only a cotton-padded jacket over his jeans and shirt. He thought about going back to get his Orioles cap but decided to trudge on without it. He could feel the icy rain beginning to seep into his body but kept moving along, struggling mightily against the wind and the rain.

Then, in a flash, he started to run full speed along the path with reckless abandon, cold, muddy water splashing at his heels. There were not many people out in this weather and only a few cars moving on the streets. The only person who noticed him was Sarah Parker, the owner of Parker's Flower Shop, who glanced out her store's front window and spotted an unlikely youngster running wildly along the railroad tracks.

Now, he was running and crying, tears mixing with chilly torrents of sleet splattering in his face. He thought about what they said about him at school: he was the skinny kid who ran like the wind. And then the wind changed direction, pushing him from behind. The wind seemed to be his best friend, urging him to run faster and faster down the muddy path as if together they could outrun insensible, deadening illusions and confusion.

The howling wind propelled him past the houses and stores along Main Street as the sky darkened and the clouds rolled undulating in ominous billows. He ran and ran with no sense of where he was going or how far he had gone. All of a sudden, he slapped himself in the face and stopped crying. He lifted his head up, jutted out his jaw, and dared the torrential rain to stop him. At this moment, he felt invincible, but he also hated everything in life. Nothing was fair. Nothing ever lasted. Nothing was what it was supposed to be. Nothing was ever going to be the same again.

Then, out of nowhere, a mangy, rain-soaked mutt came trotting up alongside him. He peeked down at the dog through squinted, burning eyes, wondering who was crazier, him or the dog. The dog seemed totally unnerved by the storm, appearing perfectly content to take a brisk jaunt with a small boy on a cold, rainy February day. Jackie stared down at the dog once again and swore he saw a spark of curiosity, as if the dog just wanted to know where he was going. He lost track of time and distance but kept running close to the railroad tracks for some directional support, trying to maintain a fragile semblance of security. After a while, he was unsure who was leading this wretched twosome, him or the dog. Although the dog looked like a drowned rat, Jackie had never seen a happier, friskier dog in his life. He wondered if he had a home.

Unexpectedly, they came upon a railroad crossing with a large Riverton Memorial Park sign on the other side of the tracks. They had run nearly three miles. The dog immediately sprinted across the tracks, heading toward the baseball fields. They ran up Juniper Street past the basketball courts and the Babe Ruth field and turned into the Little League field. Jackie was sopping wet, exhausted, chilled, and shaking from exposure. The dog ran out to the middle of center field and then stopped and plopped down, panting profusely. The dog looked proud and confident, like his duty had been performed. Jackie wanted to tell him that he played in Palmyra Park, not Riverton, but obviously it didn't make any difference to the dog. Jackie didn't feel the need to be near his old playing field. Maybe the dog knew that too.

Still breathing heavily, Jackie collapsed on the near-frozen field; he lay on his back, assuming the snow-angel position with the dog sitting obediently by his side. The bitter rain continued hammering his face. He closed his eyes, oblivious to the cold overtaking his body and the tiny spikes of ice pricking his face.

Within seconds, he felt himself drifting upward, suspended in midair, floating toward the heavens, unsure if he was hallucinating or dying. He kept his eyes closed, not wanting this sensation to end. For the first time in a long time, he was completely at ease and gave in without a struggle to this otherworldly experience. Feeling light-headed and disoriented, he kept rising into the cosmos, floating along weightlessly.

As he soared into space, Jackie had the strangest feeling that he was leaving something meaningful behind. Maybe it was his childhood—now almost certainly a thing of the past. But as he traveled upward, he couldn't visualize any more years unfolding before him. Everything was eternal blackness. Then in an instant he realized why he was crying. The tears were not just for Buddy but for himself. Osa was gone. He had lost Vera. He had lost his religion, finally admitting to himself that he was never going to be a dedicated Jehovah's Witness. And that meant he had lost a part of his mother; they would never share the same sacred religious experience together. And surely he would never play a more perfect baseball game. As he drifted along, another sense of loss weighed him down emotionally: even rock 'n roll would never be the same. He began to think that there really was no above-the-desk world—not for him, anyway. The dream of living above the desk was just an illusion. Perhaps it was achievable for some people, but Jackie felt condemned, terrified that he was going to live the rest of his life below the desk.

He was shrouded in blackness, drifting above the town. He couldn't sense anything and wondered if he had already frozen to death. If his life was over, then that was okay with him; his greatest moments were already frozen.

His tranquility was disrupted when he experienced a flush of unexpected warmth over his chest as if someone was spreading a blanket over him. He opened his eyes. The freezing rain had stopped. He was back on solid ground, staring at the darkening clouds in the distance as they moved swiftly toward him. Then he saw the clouds split open as if a knife had sliced through them, and a luminous liquid brilliance burst through the incision, sweeping along the sky, moving rapidly past the flagpole, lighting up the entire field, and blinding him with a radiant beam of yellow light. He closed his eyes again and floated up over the town until it was practically out of sight. He opened his eyes one more time. Down below, he spotted miraculous bright colors of red, white, and blue glittering like the sun shining on a lake of precious stones.

Then the clouds quickly closed together again, spreading shadows over the land, leaving him calm and peaceful, his body lying motionless next to the dog.

THE NEXT MORNING FRANK BERMAN was driving down Juniper Street on his way to work at Merrifield Landscaping and Gardening. As he passed the Little League field, he heard a dog barking loudly. He looked over and saw a youngster lying in the middle of the field with a small terrier sitting beside him. He slammed on the brakes and ran to the boy and the dog, wondering if that little boy had frozen to death.

PART FOUR

Maybe this world is another planet's Hell.

—Aldous Huxley

16

Park Tavern
Palmyra, New Jersey
Summer 1967

J ACKIE RIDDICK ENTERED THE PARK Tavern from a side door and at first glance couldn't see anything in the dimly lit tavern. It seemed darker than the night. Gradually, his eyes adjusted, and he looked to his left toward a long, ornately carved mahogany bar that resembled a prop from a western movie, a blackened, boot-heeled brass rail rimming the bottom. A straight row of popular-brand liquor bottles lined the back of the mirrored bar, and an assortment of glasses and pitchers were bunched together beside the wooden-handled labels advertising Old Milwaukee, Schlitz, Budweiser, and Miller High Life. A cracked and faded yellow sign that said Espresso Yourself hung on the wall, and a Miss St. Pauli Girl calendar incorrectly identified the month as September. Jackie spotted Jimmie Harlow sitting alone at the bar. When Jimmie saw Jackie coming toward him, his eyes lit up, and he jumped out of his stool, running up to his old buddy.

"Well, I'll be damned! It's Jackie Riddick, back from the dead! How you doin'?"

"Hey, Jimmie. I'm just fine. How's it going?"

"You won't believe it! I got a real job! I'm slinging liquor for Roger Wilco in town. I was salesman of the month in June! Come on—sit down and have a drink! Hey, Jake!"

Jake Thompson, the owner, was perched on a stool down the other end reading a newspaper. He slowly glanced up at Jimmie, eyes at half-mast, as if irritated that someone was interrupting his reading time.

"Jake!" yelled Jimmie once more. Are you glued to that seat?"

Jake smiled sardonically, dropped his newspaper, and came over to the two men. "Hi Jackie, it's good to see you again. Are you playing any ball?"

"Not right now. I
gave it up for awhile."

"Well, if you make it to the big leagues, be sure to send me some tickets."

"No problem," said Jackie.

Jake looked at Jimmie. "I assume you want another Budweiser, Mr. Harlow. How about you, Jackie?"

"Make it two."

"Coming right up."

"Two Budweisers, coming right up!"

Jake went to get the beers. Jackie and Jimmie grabbed two stools at the bar, alone except for three regulars at the end of the bar wearing plaid flannel shirts and bib overalls silently sipping draft beers.

"Looks like we beat the crowd," said Jimmie.

Jackie turned around and surveyed the rest of the bar. "Yeah, it's a slow night in Palmyra."

"Isn't every night slow?" asked Jimmie.

Jackie smiled and rotated around the stool, facing Jimmie. "As far as I know."

"So how long are you in town?" asked Jimmie.

"Not too long. A couple days. A week, maybe."

"Where you headed from here?"

"I got in touch with Archie Steele. I'm going to his place in Virginia."

"Just for a visit?"

"Yeah, just a visit."

"What's he doing?"

"I only talked to him once. As far as I know he's working in a frozen-food factory."

"Jesus, that's sounds rough."

"He's on the graveyard shift."

"That's *really* rough. So, slugger, what are you doing? Why are you in town? And don't tell me your long-term goal is visiting Archie Steele, the frozen-food magnate."

"I got kicked out of school."

"You're kidding. What for?"

"You ready for this?"

"Sure."

"Grilling stolen steaks."

Jake returned with the beers, placing two mugs in front of Jackie and Jimmie. "Here you are, boys. Drink up!"

"Thanks, Jake," muttered Jackie.

"Hey, Jake!" cried Jimmie. "Don't go too far away. I'm really thirsty!"

Jake turned and smiled at Jimmie. "Jimmie, you're *always* thirsty."

Jimmie returned the smile, hoisting his glass high in the air. "Here's to the best bartender in the world!" Then Jimmie gulped down half his beer, set the mug on the bar, and looked over at Jackie. "Okay, my brother, you got some explaining to do. What's this about stolen steaks?"

"Well," began Jackie, "we were all in the dorm, just hanging out—bored, actually. Someone was complaining about the food, as usual, and said they were still hungry from the lousy dinner. I said I could get us all some steaks, already grilled. Well, that got everybody's' attention. They said it was impossible because it was one o'clock in the morning and every store in town was closed, and we didn't have any freezers in the dorms. So they started betting on whether or not I could produce the steaks. I think my odds were about fifteen to one."

"So, you stole some steaks? Where from?"

"Well, the cafeteria, of course. I left after the betting ended and pried opened a window in the cafeteria. I went in the back and got about twelve steaks and warmed up the grill."

"Wait a minute! What about security?"

"I knew their schedule. They weren't too bright. They made their rounds the same time every night. I knew I had forty-eight minutes to complete the job."

"So you calmly grilled twelve steaks—"

"Mostly medium rare."

"You took orders?"

"Yeah, I was playing this caper right up to the hilt."

"So how'd you get busted?"

"I came back with the steaks and I thought I was safe, but someone—I think our RA—ratted me out."

"And they kicked you out."

"They gave me an hour to clean out my room."

"During baseball season?"

"Right in the middle. I was hitting .432."

"Wow, that's a tough break."

"Yes, but it's all my fault. How stupid can you get?"

Jimmie took a big gulp of his beer, polished it off, and then set it down hard on the bar. He turned and stared directly at Jackie, sighing. "Well, it's no more stupid than my cocaine habit."

"I heard about that."

"Jackie, I was really a mess. That white shit—and alcohol—almost ruined my life."

"Are you okay now?"

"I'm totally clean. Like I said, I got a good job at Roger Wilco and a fantastic new wife who comes with me to AA meetings. You've gotta meet her. She's a jewel."

Jackie absentmindedly doodled a baseball and a bat in the condensation on the bar. "I'd like to," he said.

"Hey, Jake!" Jimmie suddenly yelled. "How about two more! You sleeping over there?" Jimmie turned and faced Jackie. "You'll never guess who got me the job."

"Who?"

"Phil DeMarco."

"Get out."

"No kidding. He's an up-and-coming politician around here. Got a job in the mayor's office. The guy knows everybody. Anyway, he went down to the man himself, Roger Wilco, and put in the good word for me. He said if I screwed up, he would contribute a great deal of money to his favorite charity—which for Roger Wilco would be himself."

"So the great winner of the Palmyra Steal-a-Thon is headed for a career in politics."

"Hey, it's perfect. He'll fit right in with the rest of the thieves. Hey, where are you staying?"

"Danny's got a little cottage on his property. It's my hideout away from it all."

"I heard Danny is doing real well. He bought the old Morgenstern Estate, right?"

"He sure did. Can you imagine a combination high-school teacher and trader on Wall Street? He teaches at Lenape High School and buys a lot of stocks. The guy's a genius at making money."

"Unlike us."

"Right. Unlike us."

Jake returned with two more beers. "Here you are, gents, on the house."

"Hey, thanks," said Jackie.

"You're a prince," uttered Jimmie.

Jake smiled broadly. "Let's get one thing straight, Jimmie. Around here, I'm the *king.*"

Jimmie laughed cheerfully and raised his mug again. "Here's to the king! All hail king Jake!"

Jackie lifted his beer along with a couple regulars at the end of the bar. Jake shook his head, smiled, and went back to reading his paper.

"So," said Jimmie, clicking his mug with Jackie's, "you never told me where the hell you're going after Archie's. Try out for the Orioles?"

"No, I'm taking a break from baseball. Jimmie, I know this may sound funny, but I want to know what all the players are doing now."

"What players?"

"The players on our all-star team."

"Why?"

"I knew you were going to ask me that."

"And?"

"I'm not sure. Maybe I'm just curious—"

"About some guys you played with in Little League?"

Jackie paused and stared up at a Buy or Bye-Bye sign hanging on the wall. "It wasn't just some guys. You know that. It was a pretty special team."

Jimmie nodded, taking another sip of his beer. "Probably the best Little League team ever put together. I can't argue with that. You writing a book or something?"

"No, I'm not trying to live in the past or anything. I thought since I'm at loose ends, I'd travel a bit, and this seems like a good way to do it. At least it gives me a direction."

"No direction home?"

"Like a complete unknown?"

"Like a rolling stone ... Christ! We're starting to finish song lyrics together!"

Jackie grinned, shrugging his shoulders. "I guess we've known each other too long."

Jimmie stared solemnly at Jackie, a furrow forming between his eyebrows. "Jackie, let me get this straight. You're going to visit every player on that team?"

"No, just the starting nine—eight. I've already visited myself. And I'm not going to visit Phil, because I know what he is doing. I know Nate is on the Palmyra police force, and I think Louie is in Vietnam—"

"He is. I saw an article in the paper. He's moving up fast in the ranks already."

"No surprise there. I need to find out where Louie is at."

"What for?"

"I'm going to write him a letter. I need to tell him a few things in case he—"

"Doesn't make it?"

"Yeah ... before it's too late."

"Well, you don't have to visit me, do you?"

"No, I don't."

"So," asked Jimmie, "who does that leave?"

"Well," said Jackie, draining his beer, "Archie's covered. I don't know what happened to Ritchie or Dave, and I'm going out to see Kurt Cummings after I see Archie."

"I heard Dave has turned into a weirdo."

"What do you mean?"

"I heard he's still in town, staying at his parents' house."

"What's so weird about that?"

"I heard he never goes out."

Jackie raised his glass, silently motioning to Jake for another two beers. "You mean Dave is a recluse?"

Jimmie shrugged. "I don't know. It's just what I heard, but I never see him anywhere."

"That is strange."

"The guy was always a bit strange, if you ask me—also a lousy right fielder. What's Kurt doing?"

"He's living in the Haight-Ashbury district of San Francisco. His hair is down to his shoulders, and he smokes a lot of dope and drops a lot of acid."

A look of incredulity spread over Jimmie face. "He's a hippie?"

"I guess so, but I don't think he likes being labeled anything. He has a little shop. Makes turquoise jewels, trinkets, arts and crafts, stuff like that."

Jake came up to the guys, two beers in his hand. "Sorry, fellas, this one's not on the house."

"Geez, what a cheapskate!" cried Jimmie.

Jake placed the beers on the counter. "Jimmie, it's a good thing you're here with Jackie; otherwise I'd flag your ass."

"Flag your best customer? Jake, you can't be serious!"

Jake turned, took a few steps, and then turned back. "Like I said before, if you're my best customer, I'm really in trouble."

Both guys laughed. Jimmie yelled, "Jake, you're always in trouble!"

Then there was a moment of silence. The two friends quietly sipped their beers, listening to a Rolling Stones song playing in the background.

"Well," said Jimmie, interrupting the stillness, "I guess you've got them all covered except for Ritchie and Dave. But Jackie, I don't see the point."

"What point?"

"Learning about these guys' lives. I mean, so what? We played a stupid game nine years ago. You think we have something in common now?"

Jackie glanced thoughtfully at Jimmie. "I don't know. Do we?"

Jimmie seemed to ponder the question. He took a slow sip of beer, gazing into it as if looking for the right answer. "Jesus, Jackie, I don't know. To tell you the truth, I never thought about it. If we have something in common, what is it besides playing on a winning team together?"

"Maybe that's it."

"What?"

"How many winning teams have you played on?" asked Jackie.

"One."

"How many do you think the rest of us have played on?"

"One."

Jimmie looked up from his beer, and stared at Jackie. "Do you really think that game had some important influence on us?"

"I don't know, Jimmie, but I know it had an effect on me, and certainly Osa Martin had an influence on me, so it's just something I want to do. Like I said, I'm at loose ends."

Jimmie didn't say anything for a few minutes. He kept staring at the Expresso Yourself sign. Finally, he muttered, "We really were a great team, weren't we?"

"The best," said Jackie.

Jimmie suddenly came to life as if a wire had sprung out from his stool. "Okay, no more talk of nostalgia," he said, gulping down the rest of his beer. "Let's go challenge those losers over there."

Jackie followed Jimmie's gesture to where two players were shooting pool on one of the three tables in the Park Tavern. They looked like a couple of young college kids with short hair dressed in nearly identical Dockers pants and flannel shirts. One of them was quite a bit taller than the other one; except for that, Jackie figured they might as well have been twins.

Jackie was about to decline the offer, but Jimmie suddenly jumped off his stool, practically sprinting toward the players. "Wanna play partners?"

"Sure," said the taller college kid as he lined up an easy side-pocket shot. "After this game."

Jimmie motioned to Jackie that the game was on, and he left the booth, taking a seat next to Jimmie near the pool table. They grabbed sticks from the rack and sat on stools, drinking beer and patiently chalking their cues. The taller player was currently on a six-ball run, beating the other player handily. After several minutes, the two players finished up and motioned for Jimmie and Jackie to come over and rack the balls. Jimmie grabbed the rack from underneath the table and started setting up the balls for the match. He squeezed the rack tightly, pressing in with his fingers, and then gently lifted the rack over the balls without any contact.

"Play for a buck and a beer?" asked Jimmie.

"Sure," said the shorter player.

The pool table was located in a little alcove away from the main section of the tavern near a few tables and chairs, a pinball machine, and a large-screen TV. The tables were empty except for a young woman in her early twenties sitting alone, passively watching TV and sipping a Coke. She was a petite, round-faced, attractive young woman with lively bright blue eyes, a shapely figure, and a smooth, magazine-cover complexion. She was wearing tight-fitting jeans, a black V-neck pullover, and a navy-blue beret tilted jauntily to the side of her face. Strands of short-cropped hair the color of golden wheat fell loosely on her forehead. The beret almost covered her left eye, and she occasionally checked out the customers in the tavern with one seductive, dazzling blue eye. A thin necklace bearing a silver cross hung around her neck, and on her sweater she wore a silver-dollar-sized button that sported a picture of a cocker spaniel.

The taller guy came over to Jackie and shook his hand. "Hi. I'm James."

"Hey, I'm Jackie. This is Jimmie."

Jimmie shook James's hand. The shorter player came over to join the group.

"I'm Chuck."

The guys all shook hands. James went to the end of the table, grabbed the white cue ball, lined up his shot, and with a sudden, powerful slam from his right arm, broke the balls, exploding them in all directions like they were bowling pins. The six ball and three ball fell directly into pockets. James ran two more balls before missing a tough shot on the two ball. It was Jackie's turn to make some high balls. As he was sinking the twelve ball, Jimmie approached the table where the girl was sitting.

"Okay if I sit my beer here?"

"Sure," said the girl.

Jimmie left his beer and came back to the pool table. Jackie just missed an easy shot at the fourteen ball.

"Damn," Jackie muttered under his breath. But the taller college guy could not make a shot. It was Jimmie's turn. He made a thirteen-fifteen combination and then missed a shot at the eleven.

Jimmie came back to get his beer. He noticed the button pinned to the girl's chest. "Okay, I'll bite. Why do you have a picture of a cocker spaniel on your shirt?"

"I'm a vegan," she said, "a vegetarian and an animal-rights advocate."

"Are cocker spaniels endangered or something?"

The girl laughed. "No, I just love them. They're my favorite dogs."

Chuck, who had been eavesdropping on their conversation, seized an opening. "I got the best dog."

"What kind of dog do you have?" asked the girl.

"Pit bull. Mean as a son of a bitch."

"You have a mean dog?" asked the girl.

"You bet your sweet ass. Dog will attack anybody who comes near him. Got loose one day on my old man's farm and almost killed my sister. If I say, 'Sic 'em,' he'll go for your throat!"

"I wouldn't want to have a dog like that," said the girl.

Chuck threw his hands in the air. "He's a great dog! He's the best dog a man can have! He's loyal, brave, and will do *anything* to protect me!"

Jimmie left the two of them to take his turn. Jackie came to the table, joining Chuck and the girl. He had overheard their exchange.

"Hello. I'm Jackie," he said to the girl.

"Ginger. Nice to meet you."

"So," Jackie said, turning to face Chuck, "you got a killer dog?"

"Yup."

"I'm just curious. Why would you want to have a dog like that?"

"Are you kidding? To protect me from the rednecks."

"Sorry, pal, but you don't have a dog—you have a robot. That dog doesn't even have a mind. All that dog can do is what you programmed him to do—be an asshole like you! He can't even think without you giving orders, like a Nazi storm trooper! You're a bully. I hate fuckin' bullies!"

Chuck's face reddened with rage. He quickly grabbed Jackie's stick, twisting it from his hands, and then shoved him mightily against the opposite wall, forcing the stick against his throat. Chuck pressed the cue stick higher into Jackie's face, a blue spot from the tip smudging his cheek.

"Listen, you creep," snarled Chuck, "you don't know a goddamn thing about dogs!"

The cue stick bore down on Jackie's neck like a steel bar choking him to death. His words sputtered out in short, gasping spasms as if he was having a seizure. "That's right! I don't know ... anything about dogs! I like mutts who are members of the family ... who chew carpets, bite furniture, dry ... hump everybody, who live in the house—but people have dogs ... and live with them because they *like* each other, and they come—come ... and go as they please! And nobody has to worry about ... getting killed!"

Jimmie and James moved behind Chuck and Jackie, standing side by side. Jackie thought Jimmie was going to pummel Chuck with his own stick. But then Chuck let up slightly on Jackie's throat, turning toward Jimmie and James as if he'd had enough. "Gee, guys," said Chuck, "sorry about that."

Then, swiftly, Chuck reared back, swinging the stick at Jackie's head. Ducking to his right, Jackie avoided the blow, the stick whizzing over his head like a baseball bat. From a crouched position, Jackie came up swinging, landing a solid punch to Chuck's chin, driving him backward. Chuck crashed into the table, shattering glasses and sending the girl scrambling for cover. James ran toward Jackie, but Jimmie tackled him from behind, pinning him to the floor, landing a barrage of punches to his face. Chuck got up from the floor, preparing to annihilate Jackie. He took a few steps forward before Jake came charging up from behind the bar.

"Hey! That's enough! Break it up! Where do you think you are? There's no goddamn fighting in here!"

The four youths calmed down and straightened themselves up,

wiping the beer from their pants. Jake glared at the two college guys. "Okay, you two. Get the hell out and don't come back."

"What about those guys?" screamed Chuck. "They started it!"

"Look, you assholes. This is Jackie Riddick, and that's Jimmie Harlow. You are two fuckin' assholes I've never seen before—so get the fuck out!"

Jake ushered the two guys out the door. Jimmie and Jackie returned to the table, wiped it down, and put back the ashtrays and napkin holder. Ginger emerged from the corner where she had been hiding and took her place back at the table.

"Gosh, I'm sorry about that," she said.

"It's not your fault," said Jimmie. "Those guys were jerks."

"Do you believe that guy?" Jackie asked. "He's got himself a killer dog, and he's calling *someone else* a redneck. Unbelievable. He's the biggest redneck on the planet."

"I'll get us some beers," said Jimmie. "Ginger, what'll you have?"

"Just a Coke for me, thanks."

"Coming right up!"

"You don't drink?" Jackie asked.

"No, I don't think it's good for you."

"Yeah, I guess you're right. But right now is as good as you're going to feel all day."

Jackie took a seat next to her. "So, what do you eat?"

"What do you mean?"

"You told Jimmie you were a vegan."

"Oh, I see. Well, anything that doesn't come from an animal. I don't eat meat, cheese, milk … lots of stuff … honey."

"Honey?"

"Bees."

"Bees are an animal?"

"They're alive."

"I thought bees were an insect."

"It doesn't matter. We don't eat anything that comes from something that's alive. It causes too much pain for the animal."

"You know, plants cry when you kill them too. You just don't hear them scream."

"I think plants are different from animals. Animals have a face. I just couldn't eat something that has a face."

They sat in silence for a few seconds listening to "Hey Jude" by the Beatles. Jackie was waiting for her to make up an excuse to leave. Instead, she surprised him by clasping her hands together, leaning over the table, staring directly into his eyes.

"What did that guy mean when he said, 'that guy is Jackie Riddick'? Are you some kind of rock star?"

Jackie laughed. "No, I'm no rock star—that's for sure."

"Well, you must be somebody. He sounded like he screwed up, like picking a fight with the president."

"I don't know ... I don't know who those guys are."

"Well, apparently they know you. Are you from Palmyra?"

"Yes, but I'm only passing through. I'm just here for a little while."

"So you went to school here?"

"Yes."

Jimmie returned from the bar, set the drinks on the table. He sat next to Jackie, facing Ginger. A brief pause. Then Jimmie broke the silence. "I just ran into Burt Louderman at the bar, and he told me the funniest story."

"Does that mean we have to hear it?" Jackie asked.

"Yes."

"Okay, but remember there's a lady present."

"Hey, this is actually a clean story. Burt tells me his friend Fred just came back from Tijuana. Fred was traveling down in Mexico for months. Anyway, Fred takes his pet pig into a bar down there—you know, one of those nasty little dives with banditos in ponchos and sombreros slugging down shots of tequila. So Fred orders a couple beers for him and his pig—"

"The pig is drinking?" Ginger asked.

"Oh, yeah. Pigs drink. In fact, the pig was Fred's best drinking buddy."

"And this is a true story?" Jackie asked.

"Would I lie?"

"Yes. And you'd better not be setting us up for one of your stupid jokes."

"No way. I just heard it from Burt. He's an honest dude."

"Okay. Go on."

"So the pig's getting drunker and drunker, and so's Fred. Then Fred decides to meet one of his buddies at the train station, and he leaves the pig tied up at the bar and tells the bartender he'll be back in an hour. Well, the train is late—after all, it *is* Mexico—and he doesn't get back for three hours. Finally, he walks into the bar with his friend, anxious for his buddy to meet his really cool pig. They walk in, but there's nobody around—and no pig. The whole place is empty except for this one drunk slumped in the corner. Fred goes up to him and asks where everybody is. The drunk screams, 'Out back! Out back!' In Spanish, of course, but Fred gets the message. Fred and his buddy go out back, and he runs into this Mexican dude who says to him, 'You want some pig?' And Fred says, 'No, I don't want *some* pig. I want *my* pig. Now where is he?' The Mexican dude shrugs his shoulders and points to a barbecue pit. Fred practically shits his pants, because he sees his pet pig roasting over a fire, burnt to a crisp. Man, they took his best friend, his only pet, and made him into a Mexican fiesta. Is that a sad tale, or what?"

Jackie glanced at Ginger, rolled his eyes, and leaned back in his chair. "Do you expect us to believe that story? That dude Burt was bullshitting you."

"No, he wasn't!" exclaimed Jimmie. "And I'm going to write a song about the whole episode. Do you know what I'm going to call it?"

"No."

"'Tequila Pig!' You know—to kill a pig!"

"Jesus, you got me again."

Ginger looked at the two men, perplexed. "You mean you made up that whole story?"

"I sure did," said Jimmie.

"You're a regular comedian," Jackie said. "Take it on the road, funny man."

"Actually, I am taking it on the road. I gotta get up early tomorrow. Somebody has to hustle the booze."

"Where do you work?" asked Ginger.

"I'm a salesman for a liquor company. Do you want any free samples?"

"No, thanks."

"I don't blame you. Stuff almost ruined me. See you guys later. Jackie, don't forget to get in touch before you leave."

"I'll call you!"

"Great. Adios!"

Jimmie got up from the table and left the bar. Once again, Jackie thought Ginger would make an excuse to leave as he gazed into his beer, swirling the mug, making beer waves. "So, Ginger, what do you do besides stay away from meat?"

"I go to school—Penn State."

"Oh, so one of those dudes is your boyfriend?"

"No way. Do you think they look like my type?"

"No. In fact, you don't even look like you're from Penn State."

"You mean I don't look like a sorority girl," she said, taking off her beret, shaking her hair loose, and flipping her bangs back over her forehead. She stuffed the beret into her handbag and then looked at Jackie, expecting an answer.

"Sorry," he muttered. "I didn't mean it like an insult or anything. I hate being stereotyped myself."

Ginger took another sip of her Coke and then slowly stirred the drink with a straw. "It's okay. I just don't like the thought of someone thinking I'm like everybody else."

"No, I really am sorry. That's probably one of the worst things you can say to someone— 'Gee, you're a typical person, just like everyone else!'"

"Hey, it's okay—really. I'm not from New Jersey. My parents live here now, but I was born in Canada—British Columbia. Then we moved to a farm in upstate Oregon. They didn't send me to a regular school. I was home schooled."

"Really? How was that different?"

Ginger paused, stopped stirring her straw, and looked directly into Jackie's eyes. "I didn't learn to hate school, and I learned about a lot of different things."

"Like?"

"Well, like some of the things hippies are into now ... Zen Buddhism, rock 'n' roll, cool jazz and poetry, expanding your consciousness, stuff like that."

"Kerouac is into Zen," said Jackie.

"Jack Kerouac? The Beat writer?"

"He volunteered to be a lookout in a fire tower on a mountain range for three months. All he did was gaze into the forest, pray, and meditate all day. Are you into poetry?"

"Yes. I love poetry."

"I write poetry all the time."

"What kind?" she asked, flipping her hair again, the palm of her hand resting on her chin.

"I don't know … the bohemian kind, I guess. Hey, just a minute!" Jackie fumbled in his pants and shirt pockets, pulling out a ring of keys, a bottle opener, some coins, and scraps of paper crumbled into balls. "I think I got one here."

"What are those pieces of paper?"

"Well, they're all poems. I just don't have them organized."

"I'll say."

"Here's one I wrote last night. Jackie handed Ginger a wrinkled supermarket receipt with a handwritten poem scrawled on the back. She read the poem out loud:

> *The lost butterflies, the flowerless grass,*
> *stirred by a whirlwind of furious fire.*
> *The velvet whiteness of the woman's body*
> *possesses diamonds of affection,*
> *glittering from her breast.*
> *Yet, devoured long ago.*
> *Where the sleep of the dead intoxicate …*
> *… an ancient, celestial love.*
> *She lies still, weeps in vestal waiting …*
> *trembling in forbidden catacombs.*

Jackie said, "You've got a nice voice. You read very well."

"I like your poem. You've got others?"

"They're all over the place. My pockets are full of them. Hey, I have an idea. I'm staying at my brother's cottage for a couple days. Would you like to go back there? I have some more poems there, and I've got some great records."

"Sounds like fun."

Jackie went to the bar, paid the tab, and then returned to the table. "We can take my car. It's right outside."

They left the Park Tavern. Jackie walked Ginger to the parking lot and toward his 1957 bright red and white Chevy Impala convertible with a continental kit on the back.

"Nice car," she said as he opened the door for her.

"It's a classic. I keep it in my brother's garage most of the time."

Jackie went around to the other side of the car, got in the driver's seat, started the engine, and pulled out of the tavern. They rode together for a few moments. Ginger looked at a picture of a shaggy terrier taped on the dashboard next to the radio.

"That's such a cute dog. Yours?"

"He used to be."

"You mean he died?"

"Yes, just last year. I still miss him. You know—man's best friend ..."

"What was his name?"

"Holly."

"That's a strange name for a boy dog."

"Well, he's named after Buddy Holly, but the name Buddy just seemed too generic."

"I see what you mean. You must be a big Buddy Holly fan."

"Yes, a big fan. He found me on the day Buddy Holly died. He was with me for eight years."

"Did you say he found you?"

"Did I say that?"

"Yes."

"Well, I suppose it's true. I was the one who was lost at the time."

"Do you want to tell me about it?"

"It's a long story."

"I've got time."

Jackie turned, gazing into her eyes to see if there was a hint of sarcasm, wondering if she really wanted to hear his story. She looked at Jackie, giving him a nod and a wink.

"Okay, I was twelve years old and a little mixed up, like a lot of kids. I didn't have a father at home, and my mother took care of my older sister, my brother, and me. Anyway, things were going great at school. I had a girlfriend, and I was a really good athlete. I also had a great coach who helped me through some tough times, giving me really good advice."

"So what happened?"

"I don't know. Things just fell apart on me. I went from being real popular to being just a nobody. I lost my girlfriend and my coach at about the same time."

"How did you lose your girlfriend?"

"Have you ever heard of Jehovah's Witnesses?"

"Yes, they're weird."

"Right. Well, my mother was one of those, and my girlfriend's parents wouldn't let us date—"

"Because you were a Jehovah's Witness?"

"Yes."

"That's not fair."

"That's what I thought."

"And your coach?"

"He went to North Carolina to become a minor league manager, and I never saw him again."

"Why not?"

"Well, he did come back a few times, and I knew he was asking about me, but I didn't want to see him."

"Why?"

"I felt he would be disappointed in me. I respected him so much, I hated for him to think I didn't turn out ... I don't know. I guess he expected big things from me."

"So you got a dog?"

"Oh, no. Holly spotted me running down the railroad tracks the day Buddy Holly died. It was a really cold, rainy day, and I kept running for miles."

"And the dog followed you?"

"Yeah, the whole time. Then I passed out."

"Passed out?"

"I ran to a baseball field and collapsed on the ground. It was freezing, and I just lost consciousness."

"Wow, you could have died."

"I almost did. A man came and rescued us."

"Us?"

"Yes, the dog stayed right with me. Isn't that strange?"

"And you never saw the dog before that day?"

"No. It was funny. I was in the hospital for a week recovering, and my mother brought the dog in to surprise me. I just had to name him Holly. See? I told you it was a long story."

"And you recovered okay?"

"Yes. I lost a little feeling in my fingers and toes, but I survived all right. I was lucky."

"So you ran until you collapsed and almost died?"

"Yes."

"Because the world seemed to be crushing you."

"Yes, that's a good way to put it."

"Are you still a Jehovah's Witness?"

"No, I'm afraid I'm a nothing. I don't belong to any organized church. I would say I'm an agnostic or a Buddhist. I'm not sure which one. It just came down to the fact that I couldn't believe the teachings of the Jehovah's Witnesses, and I quit. That's another person I disappointed—my mother."

"She was upset when you left the church."

"Yes, but she understood. I told her I loved her very much, but I couldn't go to a church I didn't believe in. She's a very special person. We laugh about it now, and she still tries to preach the Bible to me once in a while, hoping I might change my mind. She ought to be a saint, or something ... well, here we are."

Jackie pulled the Chevy into Danny's driveway, drove past the house, and followed a single-lane dirt road down to a red brick cottage surrounded by tall Leland cypress trees. It was almost hidden from the house. Just before he opened the door, he leaned over and almost whispered, "I should warn you, I live a pretty Spartan existence."

"That's okay. So do I."

Jackie and Ginger entered the cottage. Jackie switched on a lamp, illuminating a plain, brown-paneled living room furnished with a dusty black couch, a stained wooden coffee table, and assorted musical equipment. Stacks of paperbacks and wads of balled-up paper were scattered around the coffee table. Several pictures from magazines were duct-taped to otherwise barren walls—torn, discolored photos of James Dean, Jimi Hendrix, and Walt Whitman. In the rear of the room, near a bathroom door, a classic Gibson electric guitar rested against a dust-covered fifty-watt Marshall amp. A Pioneer receiver and turntable with Advent speakers rested on a couple of orange crates below the window. Beside the stereo, a stack of record albums leaned against the crates.

Jackie said, "Have a seat," motioning Ginger to the couch.

"Thanks," said Ginger, pushing away a couple books while sliding onto the couch.

"How about some music?" asked Jackie.

"Sure."

"What kind do you like?"

"Oh, anything. Blues. Jazz. Rock. You name it."

"I thought vegan people listened to real loud music that nobody else can stand."

"They do—most of them. But I'm not typical. I don't like to follow trends."

Jackie went over to the stereo, turned on the receiver, and lifted an album out of a cover, placing it on the turntable. As the needle dropped down, a soft, acoustic song drifted from the speakers.

"Who's that?" asked Ginger. "Sounds real nice. Folk singer?"

"Yes, it's Phil Ochs."

"Oh, I know him. Didn't he write 'There but for Fortune'?"

"Yes, it's on this album. This song is called 'Changes.'"

"It's beautiful."

"I know. He's really underrated. I love the line, 'Like petals in the wind, we're puppets to the silver strings of souls, of changes.'"

"Do you write songs?"

"No. It's strange, but my words come out as poetry. I can't seem to put the words in my head into songs."

"Well, then you need someone who writes music—you're a Lennon; now you need a McCartney."

"Yes, I'll be the next John Lennon. I thought you were a sane person? How about a beer?"

"No thanks. I don't drink, remember?"

"Sorry. Let me see what I have in the fridge." Jackie went over to the refrigerator, knowing we didn't have anything else to drink. He opened the door, looked at the pitiful contents. He spotted a six-pack of Old Milwaukee, an opened pack of hot dogs, a bottle of ketchup, and a day-old container of sweet-and-sour pork.

"Sorry, I don't have anything besides beer—just water."

"That's fine. Water's fine."

Jackie ambled over to the sink, poured a glass of water from the tap, and returned to the couch, handing the glass to Ginger.

"Thanks," she said.

He sat down next to her.

"There's no munchies or anything. Maybe we could order a pizza. Jake makes a great pizza."

"I don't eat pizza, remember?"

"Oh, right. It's the cheese, I guess."

"Right."

"You're gonna live to be a hundred."

"I have my weaknesses."

"Oh? Like what?"

"I'm into unusual people. Sometimes I fall for guys who are somewhat … unstable. I have a weakness for people with weaknesses."

Jackie smiled broadly. "Well, you certainly came to the right place! Welcome to the home of the grossly unstable and certifiably weak—in spirit and character!"

"I'll drink to that," said Ginger, hoisting her glass, winking and taking a sip.

Jackie grinned sheepishly at her. "Do you also have a weakness for marijuana?"

"As a matter of fact, I do."

Reaching underneath the couch, Jackie produced a small tin container of marijuana and papers. He began to roll a joint. Ginger moved closer to him on the couch, gazing at him as if she'd never seen anyone roll a joint before. Jackie finished rolling, lit it with a Bic lighter, and took a deep toke before sending a lazy plume of smoke drifting toward the ceiling. He handed her the joint. She puffed on it, held her breath, released a billowing lungful of smoke. Soon they both slumped back into the couch, content to be speechless. After they finished the joint, Ginger glanced at the clumps of paper scattered on the floor.

"Let me see some of your poems."

"Sure."

He rifled through loose wads of paper before settling on a poem scratched in pencil on the back of an envelope from a loan company. "Here's one I like."

He handed it to her, and she read,

> She closed her red lips with an obsessive love,
> forgetting that her sinuous flesh was pure harmony
> in the preternatural dawn ...
> as her astral tears fell from violet eyes.
> Gazing at her now, aching, burning appetites,
> rays of blue moonlight striking like a golden sword.
> Amazing! A beatific lady child, rustling white trees with
> tender roots,
> vanishing from my sight.
> A sudden blink, starlight visage,
> she departs forever ... teardrops melting into indigo pearls.

"It's very beautiful, Jackie."

"I wrote it while thinking about an old girlfriend."

"I love the line, 'as her astral tears fell from violet eyes.'"

Ginger placed the poem on the coffee table, inching still closer to Jackie. She was relaxed and comfortable, while Jackie's body stiffened when he felt her knee touching his. Jackie nervously rubbed his pants legs with both hands, attempting to dry off sweaty palms. He glanced at her, staring into her luminous, alluring, perfectly round blue eyes. She reminded him of the girl with the violet eyes. Thin wisps of golden brown bangs almost covered her eyes.

"He has a gentle voice, doesn't he?" she said, motioning toward the record player.

"Yes, it's a quiet sound—like you would hear in a coffeehouse late at night."

She edged closer to him, placing her hand on his thigh. He instantly tightened up; then he caught himself and took a deep breath before reaching over, placing his arm around her, and slowly inching his way toward her. They were very close, bodies touching. He kissed her on the lips; she closed her eyes, kissing him back. He leaned toward her until the weight of his body created a slow-motion descent, his arms wrapping around her, creating two entwined bodies on the couch. He propped a pillow under her head, kissed her again, and then gently traced the soft line of her cheek down to the slope of her neck with his hand. She wrapped her arms around him, pulling him closer.

He leaned away from her. "Wait one second."

Jackie slid off the couch and went over and switched off the light. As the light went out, he could barely see, but in a few seconds his eyes adjusted and he could make out the outline of her body lying on the couch. A beam of light from a lamppost outside was shining through tiny cracks in the venetian blinds, creating tiny splinters of shadows on the wall. He saw her rise up from the couch and remove her clothes. He took off his pants and shirt. His nervousness was quickly giving way to excitable, heated anticipation. He walked over to the window and closed the blinds all the way, completing the darkness in the room. He came to her side, snuggling next to her. She leaned over and whispered in his ear, "You're not going to tell me very much about yourself, are you?"

"Well, I—"

"It's okay. We're going to make love anyway. And afterward …"

"Yes?"

"I want you to read me some more of your poems."

A WEEK LATER, JACKIE AND Ginger were lying naked together on his rumpled bed, silent in the afterglow of making love. Ginger's cheeks were flushed like two pink rose buds as she turned her body over on her side. She moved closer to Jackie, wrapping her arms around him. Responding in kind, he inched his way toward her, easing gently into her arms. The bedroom was almost completely dark, lighted only by a blue candle on the nightstand flickering nervously, and casting shimmering images on the walls. Gazing in the soft light, Ginger couldn't get over how cute Jackie looked as the luminosity from the candle softened his features. She understood why they thought he looked like Huck Finn when he was a kid. She could still see traces of freckles dotting his face, and his sandy hair always seemed loose and floppy, as if he just came in from a windstorm. She looked at him closely, marveling at the flashes of tiny golden stars twinkling in the microscopic universe of his eggshell-blue eyes. She ran her fingers down his back. His skin was soft to the touch. He was thin, but his angular body felt taut and muscular, and she could tell he was a great athlete by the graceful, fluid way he carried himself across a room.

From outside the cottage a dump truck loaded down with car parts rattled along the road, rudely breaking the quiet intimacy of the moment. Jackie lifted his head in the direction of the window, pausing until the clattering faded into the night.

Smooth, melodic sounds, scarcely audible, whispered from the radio beside the bed. She stroked his collar-length hair, twirling the ends with her fingers. Ginger thought that he looked more like a youthful adolescent than a full grown man, with his all-American good looks, finely chiseled jaw, and lonesome blue eyes. She felt the warm glow of his not-yet-cooled body as his hands moved from behind her back and traveled slowly to her breasts. Jackie clutched them both and then gently kissed her, resting his head on her shoulder. A tingling sensation shot through her body like a current of erotic electricity from a libidinous generator. He released a low, sensuous murmur of pleasure as he sank between her breasts. Ginger moved her head from side to side, creating shifting shadows on the wall. Leaning slightly away from him, she strained to hear the song coming out of the radio. It sounded familiar. She reached over and turned up the volume, immediately recognizing one of the Beatles' heartfelt ballads.

"Jackie," she said, "they're playing 'Here, There, Everywhere.'"

"Probably one of the most beautiful songs ever written," he said. "I love the line, 'changing my life with a wave of her hand.'"

Ginger pressed her body against Jackie, gazed up at him, and waved her hand in front of his face.

"I think you have," he said.

"Have what?"

"I think you know. My life hasn't been the same for a week."

"Has it changed for the better?"

"Ginger, right now all I can say is that you are the most wonderful thing that has happened to me in a long time. How about you?"

"Jackie, I feel … overwhelmed."

"What do you mean?"

"This has never happened to me before. I've had boyfriends, you know, but this is something different, don't you think?"

"Yes, it's very different."

"We haven't been apart for over a week. How many times have we left this cottage?"

"Wow, not too often. If there was a restaurant in here, we'd never leave."

"Do you think it's too much too fast?"

Jackie glanced at the shadows dancing on the walls, the flickering blue candle on the nightstand illuminating Ginger's features. "No," he said, "it feels just right … perfect."

"Is it possible to fall in love this fast?" she asked.

"It's more than possible. I love you, Ginger. I feel as if I've known you for years."

"I love you too, Jackie. I really do. Now I can't image us ever being apart. Do you feel the same way?"

"Yes, even more so. It's like I never want you out of my space. Hey! I might keep you prisoner here for a long time!"

"Fine with me. Prisoner of love?"

"Is there a better way?"

Ginger rolled over on her back and placed her hands behind her head, staring at the ceiling. "Jackie, can I be serious for a minute?"

"Sure."

"I know most guys hate this question, and I know we've only known each other a short time, but I need to ask you something."

"What?"

"Where are we going from here? You know—what are we going to do? I'm not putting any pressure on you, but I have to go back to school, and well, I don't know where I fit into your plans. Gee, I don't even know what your plans are."

Jackie laughed, smiling at Ginger while giving her a big hug. "I just said I loved you, right?"

"Yes."

"Well, I don't throw that word around very often. I mean it, Ginger. I am deeply in love with you, and right now, honestly, I want to spend the rest of my life with you."

"I feel the same way, Jackie, but how are we going to work this out? I can't see you hanging around the Penn State campus until I graduate."

"Well, it so happens I do have a plan. It's brilliant, of course."

"Of course."

"I told you about my crazy idea to see the guys on the all-star team. I still want to do that, but it won't take long. I need to find Dave Carmichael and Ritchie Edwards and visit Archie Steele and Kurt Cummings. I've got some leads on Dave and Ritchie, and then I'm going to visit Archie and Kurt. The whole deal should take less than a month."

"I'll be in school by that time."

"I know. I know my grades aren't good enough to get into Penn State, but I applied to Dickinson College. It's not that far from College Park. I had my baseball coach in Tennessee talk to their coach, and after talking to him, he's going to give me a full baseball scholarship—if I get in."

"Oh, Jackie! That's wonderful!"

"Well, I haven't gotten in yet."

"Of course they'll let you in! You're a genius!"

"Okay, Ginger, back to earth. My scholastic record is not exactly impeccable, and there is that minor incident in the cafeteria."

"Oh, bullshit! That's a great plan!"

"So you think you can wait for me for about a month?"

"Don't be silly."

17

July 1967

J ACKIE DROVE HIS CHEVY TO Dave Carmichael's house. Dave's parents owned a fancy seventeenth-century Scottish mansion located on a high embankment overlooking the Delaware River. It was an imposing L-shaped brownstone residence featuring several crow-stepped gables with deep-set windows on the second floor. He parked his car in the horseshoe-shaped driveway, which was flanked by a four-foot stone wall. As he walked up to the house, he spotted three large chimneys rising above the endpoints of the house. Jackie had never seen a house with three chimneys or been in a house that looked like a medieval castle. All it needed was a moat.

He knocked on a gigantic teakwood door decorated with a set of wrought-iron bars resembling a tic-tac-toe design. After a moment, Mrs. Carmichael creaked opened the door. Instantly, she offered him a wide, beaming smile, flashing her beautiful iridescent green eyes. Her deep auburn hair was styled in the crisp bouffant made popular by Jackie Kennedy. Jackie had forgotten forgot how beautiful she was. She placed one hand on her hip, flinging the other one in the air as if striking a pose for the paparazzi. She was wearing just the right amount of understated makeup and impeccably dressed in a burgundy satin cocktail dress with a string of pearls around her neck. Jackie thought he might be interrupting a formal dinner engagement. Before he could speak, Mrs. Carmichael greeted him warmly.

"Oh! Hi, Jackie! It's so good to see you! Come in, please."

"Hi, Mrs. Carmichael. I just came by to say hello to Dave. Is he home?"

"Yes, of course. Come on in. He's in his room."

Jackie obediently followed her to an elaborate, garish Egyptian-style foyer. A gargantuan crystal chandelier hung from a cathedral ceiling, casting slivers of golden light throughout the room. Suddenly, he felt like a tourist in an Egyptian museum. The walls were covered with paintings of the great pyramids, Ben-Hur style chariots, and drawings from the tombs of the ancient pharaohs. He spotted a golden statuette of King Tut in back of the chandelier next to a framed discolored papyrus with obscure markings. A set of winding, hand-carved wooden stairs led upstairs to a marble balcony, forming a half-circle around the chandelier. In the middle of the balcony, a silver bust of Queen Nefertiti was placed on a pedestal, staring down at him like he was one of her peasant subjects. In one corner there was a poster of Elizabeth Taylor wearing a golden headdress from the movie *Cleopatra*. The whole room made him dizzy.

As he walked across the foyer, Jackie thought it was odd that Mrs. Carmichael did not ask him anything about his life, but it dawned on him that it would probably start a conversation about what Dave had been doing. He had the feeling Mrs. Carmichael would be the last person in town to admit there was a problem with her youngest son. Her oldest son, Jerry, was currently in a correctional facility for vandalizing an elementary school and then taking a piss through a police car window. Mrs. Carmichael told everybody that Jerry was on a Fulbright.

"Dave's room is upstairs. The first one on the right—just go on up."

"Thanks, Mrs. Carmichael."

Jackie climbed the stairs, found the room, and knocked on the door. Dave immediately said, "Come in."

He was lying on his bed reading a book, surrounded by a room full of sports posters, mostly from Boston's professional teams. Dave was currently lying under a large poster of Bill Russell blocking one of Wilt Chamberlain's shots.

"Hey, Dave, how you doing?"

"Jackie … it's good to see you. How's it going?"

"Good. I'm just in town for a few—"

"Hey, that's cool."

Dave gave Jackie a blank, faraway look and then continued reading. Jackie walked over to a chair by the bed and quietly sat down, suddenly feeling like a fool for coming in the first place. Dave was obviously having some problems.

"Hey, what are you reading?"

Dave did not look up. "*Darkness at Noon.*"

Jackie thought this was a strange book to read, since *Darkness at Noon* was a depressing book about Stalin's reign of terror before the Second World War. He glanced down on the table next to the bed. There was a four-by-six-inch stamped card with the *Sports Illustrated* logo printed in the left-hand corner. It was an order form to subscribe to the magazine. Dave had filled it out and was going to mail it. The card read:

Name: Dave Carmichael

Street: 22 West River Lane

State: Confusion

Dave finally looked up from his reading. "Is Dif down there?"

"Uh, no. I didn't see him."

Dif was Dave and Jerry's nickname for their father, who was a rear-admiral in the Navy, Jackie's family doctor, and a survivor of Pearl Harbor. They were a well-respected family in town, but his nickname stood for "Dick face." They called their mother "Sud," which stood for "Suck dick." Jackie had never figured out why they showed such disrespect for their parents, but they ridiculed them all the time.

"Wanna hear some Baby Ray?" asked Dave.

The question surprised Jackie. The last year of high school, they had spent many hours listening to Ray Charles, staying up all night drinking beer and playing cards. At that time, everybody else had been listening to British invasion groups or Motown. Dave played old stuff like "Lonely Avenue," "Smack Dab in the Middle," and "I'm Gonna Move to the Outskirts of Town." Dave knew all about jazz and blues.

He listened to Jimmie Reed, Etta James, Sonny Boy Williamson, and other obscure great singers and musicians. Dave knew them all, plus the record labels and producers. In those high-school days, he would talk about Jerry Wexler at Atlantic, the Chess Brothers at Chess, and even Elvis's producer, Sam Phillips, at Sun Records. Dave would comment on them all, saying irreverent things like, "Elvis's plane should have crashed going over to Germany. He'd be a fuckin' God now instead of a B-movie joke looking for his balls."

Dave dropped his book, got up from the bed, walked over to his record player. There were stacks of albums leaning against a cabinet. He pulled one from the pile and placed it on the turntable. The needle lifted, swung right, and then dropped on the album. Soon, the man himself was singing mournfully about gambling his money away on the game of blackjack.

Dave and Jackie lay back on the bed, grooving to the music. When the record was over, Jackie thought Dave would flip it to the other side. Instead, he asked Jackie if he wanted to go to the Park Tavern for a couple beers.

"You want to go out?"

"Sure, I haven't been out in a while."

"Okay, sounds good to me."

Dave was mostly quiet during the short drive to the bar, but he muttered, "Jesus H. Christ," several times.

As soon as Dave and Jackie entered the bar, Dave's demeanor changed—and changed very quickly. He turned into a hyperactive, out-of-control maniac. He immediately ran up to random people, shaking their hands, introducing himself, gibbering bullshit a mile a minute like he was running for mayor. Then he spotted Mike Barnes, the pitcher for the Sacred Heart Yankees, sitting quietly at the end of the bar drinking a beer.

"Mike Barnes!" screamed Dave, slapping him on the back so hard that Mike spit out some of his beer.

"Jesus Christ!" blurted Mike, swirling around on his bar stool, ready to explode. Instead of punching someone out, he saw a goofy-looking Dave Carmichael smiling dumbly in his face. "Fuckin' Carmichael! Where'd you get your manners—in a fuckin' jail?"

"Sorry, Barnesy. Didn't mean to scare the shit out of you. How you been?"

Mike saw Jackie standing awkwardly behind Dave. "Hey, Jackie—Dave. What are you guys up to?"

Jackie was dumbfounded. Dave had always been cynical and critical of "people of a lesser mind," but he had never been intentionally cruel and had the decency to criticize his peers behind their backs. A simple car ride had somehow tipped the scale to the other side of sanity. The old Dave had at least been bearable for short periods. The new Dave was absolutely intolerable, spewing forth a constant barrage of obnoxious, boorish, rude, egotistical ranting.

Jackie was anxious to catch up on what Mike was doing, but Dave never gave him a chance. He continued his verbal assault, launching into a long, convoluted monologue about how great he had been in school and why he was the smartest kid in class, the best looking, had the best personality, was the best athlete, and on and on until everyone's ears were bleeding.

Barnes tried his best to have a conversation with Jackie, but Dave was so loud and insufferable that he made another conversation impossible. Finally, Mike gave Jackie a weary what-can-I-do look of groaning discontent, polished off his beer, and headed for the door. As he was leaving, he turned to Jackie and said, "Good luck, Jackie. See you in Yankee Stadium, slugger."

JACKIE LATER LEARNED THAT DAVE's behavior became even more manic and irrational until his parents committed him to a mental hospital in Ancora, New Jersey. He began writing a book called *The Real Catcher in the Rye*. Someone told him that Dave had essentially become Holden Caulfield. Now the phrase "Jesus H. Christ" made sense to Jackie; that was exactly what Holden said all the time. Before Jackie had a chance to visit him at Ancora, he hanged himself in the bathroom of the hospital. He left a short note, which read, "Sorry about the mess."

18

Palmyra Country Club
Palmyra, New Jersey
August 18, 1967

F OUR BLACK MEN PLAYING CARDS in the Palmyra Country Club caddy shack were in the middle of a spirited game of knock rummy. A raucous chorus of shouts, curses, and complaints echoed from the walls of the makeshift holding pen for caddies:

> "Seat open!"
> "Raise the stakes!"
> "Quarter and a half?"
> "Half and a bean!"
> "Curtis pulled ass!"
> "Motherfucker can't play no cards."
> "Shut up and deal."

Several other men, both black and white, were watching or listening to the game, waiting to carry bags, talking among themselves, smoking cigarettes, drinking quarts of Colt 45 malt liquor, or scanning today's racing form, looking for some winners. The caddies were a ragtag crew of working-class black men, white high-school dropouts, drifters and hoboes, card sharks, petty thieves, drug dealers, horse racing gamblers, numbers runners, and chronic alcoholics.

It was so hot that more than a few of the men had already decided they were not going out for a loop, even if Byron, the caddy master, called their names, begging them to go.

"I don't care if fuckin' Arnold Palmer himself shows up and asks for me personally," said caddy Clyde Roberts. "You ain't gettin' me out there today."

Hardly anyone noticed when a skinny young man with orange hair and freckles entered the caddy shack. He was wearing clean, pressed khaki pants and a green polo shirt and carrying a notepad and pencil. He looked more like a member's son than someone who might be interested in caddying. He hung around for a while and then drifted over to the card game. Dickie King had just plucked rummy in the blind, pissing off the other three players.

"Rummy dummies!" he screamed.

"Jesus Christ! You lucky bastard!" yelled Johnnie Johnson, throwing his hand into the pile.

"You believe that shit?" muttered Kapon. "A seven of diamonds— right in the gut!"

Bobby Stanford threw his cards on the bench, grabbing his Colt 45 and taking a huge gulp. "Hey, Kapon! Shut the fuck up! It's history—tell it to your history teacher! Deal the fuckin' cards."

Kapon picked up the deck, started shuffling the cards, singing a song that sounded like a Motown hit:

> Lady, lady, lady why do you holler
> When nobody's seen your Johnny Dollar.
> I can't get no sleep ... in this noisy street.
> I got to move ... I got to find me a quiet place ...

"Okay, David Ruffin," said Johnnie Johnson, smiling as he lit a cigarette. "Deal the cards."

The other players picked up their cards as Kapon quickly dealt seven to each of the other players, who organized them according to suits.

"It's on you," said Johnnie, nodding to Bobby Stanford.

Bobby plucked a card from the deck, put it in his hand, and then discarded the six of hearts.

"Don't you ever throw anything?" asked Dickie King, picking up the top card from the deck while discarding the three of spades.

The young man in the polo shirt stood over Dickie, looking at his cards.

Dickie turned around, hissing at him, "The fuck you looking at?"

"Sorry," said the young man, backing away and turning toward a white teenager with a pimply face who was wearing a T-shirt bearing a picture of a Stihl chainsaw.

"Excuse, me," said the young man, "do you know anything about the incident at Mac's soda fountain four nights ago?"

The boy shrugged, offering a blank, quizzical look. "Huh?"

"The racial incident—"

"The fuck are you?" interrupted Bobby Stanford.

"I'm Jason Whittier. I'm a reporter for the *Palmyra Banner*. I'm trying to do a story about what happened at Mac's—and Gene Washington's house."

Bobby tossed the queen of diamonds on the pile and then half-turned to face the reporter. "Oh, we got a regular Clark Kent among us, fellas. He wants to know about those white motherfuckin' devils downtown."

"I want to cover both sides," said Jason. "Can you tell me what happened? I know Ritchie Edwards was involved, and I heard I could find him here."

"You mean Cush X," said Johnnie Johnson.

"Cush X? I thought it was Ritchie Ed—"

"Same thing," snapped Johnnie, cutting him short. "He changed his name. Where you been, boy?"

"I just moved to town a few months ago—from Indiana."

"And you wanna know about race relations in Palmyra?" asked Kapon.

"Well," said Jason, "I know there was a fight at Mac's and Ritch— Cush X and his friends were pretty upset—"

"Upset?" snarled Kapon, taking a card, slamming it into the pile. "Would you be upset if you sat in a restaurant for a half-hour without being served? That ever happen to you, Mr. Polo Shirt?"

"No," said Jason. "But that's what I want to report. I want to know if Mac's is discriminating against black people."

"Son," said Johnnie, his voice dropping lower, "the whole damn country is discriminating. Why don't you print *that* in your little newspaper?"

The kid with the Stihl T-shirt was listening intently to the conversation. "Hey, I heard about Mac's, but who the hell is Gene Washington?"

"Guess you don't know about the Set," muttered Dickie King.

"The Set?"

Dickie King ignored him. "Some white rednecks threw a bunch of rocks through his front window. Almost hit one of his girls."

"Why would they pick on Mr. Washington?"

"That don't concern you, Chainsaw," said Johnnie. "The man's house was terrorized because he was black."

At that moment, a brand-new coffee-colored Cadillac pulled into the adjacent parking lot designated for visitors and caddies. The man who emerged from the car bore little resemblance to the flamboyant, emotionally charged Little Leaguer who hit two of the most famous home runs in the history of Palmyra Park. He had grown tall, broad shouldered, well-tailored, and resplendent in a Latin-style white suit with wide lapels, a bold green paisley shirt, and bright yellow shoes with red laces. Ritchie had grown into a handsome young man who still exuded the confidence and poise of his early years, but now he dominated the space around him like a charismatic film star. He walked up slowly to the caddy shack, carrying a small black leather case and dressed like he was entering the Copacabana on Saturday night. As he entered the open archway, several players and hangers-on took out slips of paper from their pockets and started circulating a pencil. Several caddies wrote three-digit numbers on bits of paper while Ritchie unzipped his leather case, collecting the slips while writing in his notebook. He took a seat next to Kapon, who was singing another verse:

Oh, there's a man upstairs with a radio,
and he plays it all through the night.
There's a couple in the apartment above my head,

and all they do is ... fuck and fight.
I can't get no sleep in this noisy street ...
I got to move ... I got to find me a quiet place ...

Ritchie pulled out a Kool cigarette and lit it with a VU lighter, inhaling deeply while listening to Kapon's smooth, velvety voice. "Kapon, you sound better than ever ... cigarette?"

"Thanks, Cush."

"How the cards running?" asked Ritchie, handing Kapon one of his Kools.

"Man, not so great. Fuckin' Hoyle couldn't win with these cards."

Bobby Stanford nodded to Ritchie without speaking and then laid his open hand down on the bench. "Eighteen," said Bobby.

"Shit," muttered Kapon, tossing his cards on the discard pile.

"Beats me," said Dickie King. "I'm stuck with a fuckin' million."

"I got thirteen," said Johnnie, showing Bobby his cards.

"Fuckin' A!" cried Bobby, flipping his cards into the pile. "Sandbagged again!"

Each of the players handed Johnnie fifty cents. Bobby paid a dollar. Caddies were still drifting over to Ritchie to play their number for the day. One of them, Dolphe Simmons, asked Ritchie for a racing tip.

"I like Tango Red in the sixth at Garden State. He's got Kelso's bloodline in him, and he's dropping down in class."

"Good enough for me," said Dolphe.

Out of nowhere, Dickie King began to sing totally off-key, imitating Kapon:

Oh, there's a man inside the caddy shack
And like Johnny Dollar, he knows how to sing.
So let me tell you, brothers ...
In the land of the blind, the one-eyed-man is king,
But in the caddy shack ... Dickie's King!

The caddies laughed uproariously. Kapon rushed over and gently jabbed Dickie with a few mock punches, like they were in a boxing match. "Kapon gonna float like a butterfly, and sting—the Dickie King!"

Dickie King grinned at Kapon, gave him a couple of light jabs, and then turned toward Ritchie Edwards. "Kid thinks he's fuckin' Muhammad Ali, Cush."

"Yeah, he thinks he's Sam Cooke too."

"Well, I'm gonna cook—and fry—his ass on the next hand!"

"Come on, you jokers," said Johnnie Johnson. "Let's play some cards."

The players returned to the game, forming the original group. Bobby Stanford began dealing.

Jason Whittier had been standing by the entrance, waiting for a chance to talk to Ritchie. He approached him like a nervous nephew wanting to ask the Godfather for a favor. "Excuse, me, Mr. Cush. I'm Jason Whittier from the *Palmyra Banner*. Can I ask you a couple questions about the other day at Mac's soda fountain?"

Ritchie glanced up at the young man and then looked over at the four card players. "This kid legit?" he asked.

"Seems to be," said Dickie, "except for that polo shirt."

Ritchie smiled. "I didn't know they had reporters who looked like Howdy Doody," said Ritchie. "Come here and sit down. What do you want to know?"

Jason sat down next to Ritchie, who was jotting down numbers on his notepad.

"Smoke?"

"No thanks," said Jason. "I just want to know what happened at Mac's last Tuesday. I've heard conflicting stories, and I want to get it right."

"Conflicting stories, huh? Well, there's nothing conflicting about what happened—nothing conflicting at all. There's only one story, and that's the one where me and three of my friends went into Mac's and waited over half an hour to get waited on. Finally, my buddy Wilson went over the old lady who runs the place and asked her for some service. She said she was busy—she'd get around to it soon. Wilson told her that three tables had already been served ahead of us—"

"And what did she say?"

"She said, 'Oh, really? I wasn't aware of that.' Wilson told her she was full of shit and took a sugar container and dumped it on the counter.

That's when six rednecks came over from two other tables and started giving Wilson a hard time, telling him to clean up the sugar. Then Wilson took a napkin holder and bashed in one of these asshole's faces. Then all hell broke loose. There was like ten of us punching, swinging, and stomping all over the place—chairs flyin', dishes breaking over their hard heads, ashtrays flyin' in the air. Wilson threw one of those rednecks into the jukebox—cutting his ass, glass shattering all over the place. Well, someone musta called the cops, because three or four of them came in right in the middle of this mêlée—which those white boys were losing, by the way. The four of us turned around when the cops came in and we thought, oh shit, more trouble, like getting clubbed over the head and taken to the joint. We were standing our ground waiting to see what they would do when one of them says, 'Ritchie, what the hell are you doing? You think you're the fuckin' mayor or somebody?' Then I looked closer and it was Nate Green!"

"Nate Green?"

"A buddy of mine from Little League and high school. And by the way, he's black. I said to Nate, 'No, I'm just waiting to get served in this fine establishment, but I don't think they like us poor black folks very much. In fact, I am thinking about running for mayor and tar-and-featherin' these crackers out of town on a rail.'

"Well, the other cops started moving toward us with their clubs raised, but Nate raised up his arms like he was Moses partin' the Red Sea and told them cops to get the fuck out. Those white boys didn't know what to think. They were hovering in a corner shitting themselves, thinking Nate just might shoot their white asses. Nate was as calm as a man holding four aces in Vegas. He asked me and my buddies to step outside and told those white assholes to clean up the mess. We walked right past those other cops, who didn't know whether to shit or go blind. We strolled on down to the park bench by the bus stop, and Nate told us to just go on home and forget the whole thing. One of my buddies, Michael, asked if we were going to be arrested or anything. Nate said if anybody was going to be arrested it was that old racist fleabag of a woman and those white boys. Apparently it wasn't the first time people of color have had a hard time getting served in that place. Nate said he was gonna find some reason to shut it down, or he was gonna bring in his whole family, pitch a tent, and just live there for a few weeks. That Nate is something else—hell of an athlete too."

"Did he shut it down?"

"Didn't have to. They changed their policy soon as they realized we would just keep comin' and comin' like we were marching with the Reverend King on the city of Washington, DC. There ain't no stopping us now."

"Can you tell me what happened at Gene Washington's house?"

"Not really. Everyone knows it was a couple of them white boys from Mac's. Don't know why they picked on Gene. They wouldn't have won a single damn football game in '56 if he wasn't on the team."

"Do you think it's over?"

"What's over?"

"You know—the racial tension."

"Son, it's just beginning."

19

Bien Hoa Province,
South Vietnam
August 1967

L OUIE'S NERVES WERE RATTLED, TORN, and frayed and his body
  exhausted after marching all day in the relentless torrential rain,
leading his tired squad slogging over the water-soaked ground and
sucking muck of the deep, gloomy jungle. It seemed like days since he
had seen the full blazing sun; since then he had caught only occasional
slivers of sunlight streaking down through the tops of wide-leafed trees
and spiraling vegetation. With Louie on point, the twelve men behind
him marched with their heads down, trudging slowly through the deep
brush, snarling vines, and thick trees, grunting and groaning, swinging
their machetes and KA-BARs. As the darkening sky signaled the coming
of night, Louie thought the jungle was actually getting thicker and
denser as his men stomped, slid, sweated, cursed, and hacked their way
through the unending masses of tangled thickets and banyan trees.
The men's hands were raw and blistered, and their bodies were fighting
insects, leeches, fatigue, and muscle pain, trying to forge a narrow path
through the heavy jungle. The temperature rose steadily above a hundred
degrees during the day, followed by unexpected bursts of rainfall that

would drop temperatures to lower than thirty degrees at night. The men marched methodically without speaking, looking more like prisoners on a chain-gang than men at war. Louie had never understood the phrase "blanket of humidity" until he went to Vietnam. The blanket weighed down every ounce of their equipment, dehydrated them, and made the marching slow and tortuous, like trying to walk through a valley of Jell-O. Some of the men took off their jackets and shirts completely to avoid overheating and make it easier to locate leeches.

Louie regularly rotated each fire team, because after a couple hours, their psyches were frazzled by the constant nervous tension of being on point. The bleeding blisters on his feet stung like they were caught in a bees' nest every time he lifted his boots out of the sucking mud. He estimated that they had traveled maybe a hundred meters in the last two hours, and if they didn't find some kind of natural shelter, they would have to spend another night huddled under their nylon ponchos in the drenching rain.

Louie glanced behind him and saw Franconia from fire team two flailing away at a swarm of mosquitoes swirling around his helmet. "Jesus Christ!" Franconia screamed. "These fuckin' mosquitoes are the size of Buicks!" The young Marine stopped in his tracks, flung his KA-BAR on the ground, and reached into his rucksack. "Corporal!" cried Franconia, hollering up the column to Louie. "I need to get some more bug juice!"

Louie turned around and faced his men, who now looked like bent, shadowy silhouettes on the brink of collapsing. "No problem, Franconia," said Louie. "I think we could all use a break. Let's set up in this area for the night. Maybe the rain will let up tomorrow."

The rain continued its steady downpour as the men cleared a small area and strung their green ponchos together with wire between two large trees. They happily dropped their rucksacks, canvas tarps, shovels, M-16s, machetes, and KA-BARs to the ground and then removed their helmets, shirts, and boots. PFC Anderson flung his heavy M-60 machine gun into the mud like he was lifting a refrigerator off his back. Everyone grabbed their canteens, gulping water voraciously while reaching for insect repellent, anxious to rid their bodies of sickening leeches that literally fell on them from the trees. A few of the men reached for a combat rations or lit cigarettes, not even caring if the tips might be seen by any Vietcong in the area. Bravo One had told them there was no enemy in the vicinity, and an ambush was very unlikely at this point in the mission. This was hardly consoling, since most of the enlisted Marines thought the top brass were rich, spoiled college kids who came over as second lieutenants right out of basic school in Quantico. They didn't want any part of leading a rifle platoon, and the ones who did were usually glory hunters and ended up being fragged by their own men. The officers and lifers were the guys who opted out to be commanders of weapons platoons, holed up safely at a company command post, trying to be successful at deciphering maps, locating enemy ammunition dumps, or planning effective strategies for victory. This was one reason they respected Corporal Foreman. He was a fighter who wanted to kill the enemy, not spend the day sticking pushpins in a map or sitting at a typewriter sending Marines to their deaths.

But it didn't matter. If they were ambushed right now, they'd be dead anyway. They didn't have enough fire power or the strength to fight, and there was no immediate backup.

Louie squatted in the mud, pulled a Lucky Strike out of his shirt pocket, lit it, and held it between his teeth as he removed his boots. The blisters were red, purple, and pulsating, the size of fifty-cent pieces. He rolled up his fatigues and was not surprised to spot three bloody red leeches attached to his legs. Louie pulled the leeches off his legs and burned them with his cigarette lighter. He made a mental note to ask one of the men to check his back for any others. He wondered why he could not feel them sucking his blood like vampire worms and why God would permit such a creature to exist on earth, since he could not think of a reason for their existence. He was rubbing his toes, thinking about oiling his M-16, when Private Gonzalez from fire team three came up to him, soaking wet, his helmet tilted back on his head. "Corporal?"

"Yes, Gonzalez. What is it?"

"It's Private Dempsey. I think you should have a look."

Louie put his boots back on, strained to get up, and grabbed his helmet out of habit. He followed Private Gonzalez, sloshing through the line of ponchos in his rolled up fatigues.

Louie and Gonzalez arrived at fire team three's lean-to and saw two men hunched over another Marine.

"What's the problem?" asked Louie.

One of the men whispered, "It's Dempsey, Corporal. Look at his feet."

Louie took out his flashlight and shined it down on the young Marine, who was propped against a tree with his pants up to his knees, his socks off and his feet exposed.

Louie peered through the red beam of light and almost gagged. He fought the urge to throw up, swallowing hard, trying not to look too concerned. Dempsey's feet were dark blue, swollen twice their size, and covered with open sores and ugly ulcers. His toes looked like they were rotting off.

"Jesus Christ!" barked Louie. "He's got jungle rot!"

"Jungle rot?" asked one of the men.

"He's got immersion foot—old-timers call it trench foot," explained Louie. "It's from the marching ... in the sweat, cold, and damp."

Dempsey looked up at Louie, squinting in the quickening darkness. "I'm sorry, Corporal. They're pretty bad, huh?"

"Dempsey, what the hell were you thinking?" demanded Louie, bending down to examine Dempsey's feet. Louie saw white pus oozing from the ulcers and fungal infections already spreading upward beyond his ankles. "How on earth have you made it this far? Why didn't you say something?"

"I don't know," replied Dempsey. "I didn't want to complain ... I didn't want to slow us down."

Louie turned to Gonzalez. "Get me Jackson right away. Tell him to meet me at team one's position—pronto."

Louie stood up and switched off his flashlight. "Dempsey, you hang loose, you hear? Rogers, get some clean bandages or anything else that might help from the medical kits."

"Aye, aye, Corporal," said Rogers, running down the line, imploring the men to dig into their rucksacks for any clean bandages or disinfectant of any kind.

Louie returned to his hooch, followed closely by Jackson, who ran up to him with his bulky PRC-25 strapped to his back, scratchy sounds emanating from the handset. Louie sat down in the mud and leaned back against a tree, the rain poring over the lip of the poncho just beyond his feet. He switched on his flashlight and pulled a map out of his flak jacket pocket. "Get me the CO of Bravo One actual. His code name is Rolls Royce." ordered Louie.

Jackson flipped a switch on the handset. "Bravo One, this is Red Dog DiMaggio. Come in. Repeat. Come in, Bravo One. Red Dog DiMaggio."

"Come in, Red Dog. We hear you."

"Bravo One. Character Chevy Two actual needs to speak with Character Rolls Royce actual. Over."

"Roger that, Red Dog. Is this an emergency?"

"Roger that, Bravo Two. Over."

"Hold on, Red Dog. Out."

Louie waited a few minutes before he recognized the voice of Second-Lieutenant James Edwardson, the platoon commander.

"This is Character Rolls Royce actual. What's the trouble?"

Louie grabbed the handset. "Character Rolls Royce, this is Character Chevy Two. We have a bad situation here. One man down with jungle rot on both feet, gangrene setting in quickly. Over."

"Is he going to make it? Over."

"No, sir. We need a medivac chopper and a corpsman on the double. Over."

"Shit, Chevy Two. Our fuckin' birds are all up and down the D Zone right now in the middle of a major shit storm. They're bringing in dozens of wounded and casualties—a lot worse than feet amputation. Over."

Louie gritted his teeth and tried to sound rational. "Sir, we need more than medical help. We've been humping our asses off all day, and we need food, water, medical supplies, power sources for radios, bug juice—we're running out of everything. Over."

"Roger that, Chevy Two. What are your coordinates?"

"From Pepsi, up two-point-four and right three-point-one. Over."

"Wait one second, Chevy Two. Over."

Louie waited a few minutes. Then the platoon commander's scratchy voice returned "Chevy Two actual, come in."

"Chevy Two actual here."

"We got a CH-46 due to unload at 1900 hours, if he makes it here. He'll need an LZ. You're in the thick of it. Over."

"Roger that, Rolls Royce. Let me check the map for a clear zone. Will get back with you. Over."

Louie handed the handset to Jackson and unfolded his map. The paper map was a confusing series of contour lines indicating longitude, latitude, uneven terrain, and small villages, but some of the lines did not even join with each other. Even the damn mapmakers didn't know the whole country. Louie knew the squad was currently located in a valley heading for the high country, but the really steep mountains were still farther north. The chopper would be taking a chance by coming in over high ground, but if the sky was clear, Louie felt they could get one of the birds over the crest of one of the smaller mountains. The problem was building a landing zone for the helicopter. The jungle was too thick, and his men were too tired to clear trees and bushes. They needed to find a meadow or farmland with elephant grass as their worst enemy. Louie noticed the map showed a level contour in between two lines that did not join about 450 meters due east. With any luck, the blank spaces would mean a rice paddy or meadow. Louie figured this was Dempsey's only chance to save his feet. If they could reach the landing zone area and clear it by morning, he would have a good chance of going back home, starting a new life, and taking dancing lessons.

"Jackson, get me Character Rolls Royce actual back on."

Within a few seconds, the CO responded. "Character Rolls Royce here."

"Character Rolls Royce, this is Chevy Two. We found a good place for an LZ at Coca-Cola up five-point-seven, left nine-point-one. Over."

"That's near Binh Gia. We bombed the shit out of that area. That whole place is loaded with water-filled bomb craters from B-52 strikes. Nothing but farmland and the remains of a village—should be abandoned by locals, but you never know."

"Roger on that. We'll be on the lookout. Over."

"We can't get there before 2200 hours. Over."

"No problem. We'll be waiting. Over."

"Chevy One, we can't delay your mission any longer than this. Charlie Company is putting the fuckin' squeeze on me. Over."

"Roger that, Rolls Royce. We're committed to the mission. We still have time. Over."

"Let's hope so. Good luck, Chevy Two. Over and out."

Louie handed the handset to Jackson and put the map back in his jacket pocket. He realized his squad would have to do some serious humping through the jungle to get to the drop area by morning. His men were already exhausted, and he wasn't sure how they would react to diverting a mission and marching all night for the sake of one Marine. He called out to Jackson, "Jackson, tell the men to meet in fire team one's hooch in fifteen minutes. No delays."

"Yes, Corporal," replied Jackson.

Fifteen minutes later, Corporal Foreman was standing before his squad, who were huddled tightly together, still soaking wet and looking like a cluster of tired seals. With the coming of night the temperature had dropped, and some of the men were shivering, their arms folded together tightly. A few were smoking cigarettes. Two guys were sharing a can of combat rations. None of them looked like they were in the mood to march all night.

"Listen, men. All of you have seen Dempsey's condition. It's a bad case of immersion foot—the worst I've ever seen. If we don't get him medivacked in eight hours, the gangrene will do him in. I contacted Bravo One, and they can get us a chopper here around 2200 hours."

"Did you say *here?*" asked Atkins, one of the members of fire team two.

"No," said Foreman, "there's no way to clear an LZ near here. I checked the map. There's a clearing about five hundred meters due east."

"So," said Private Sanders, tossing a cigarette into the ground, "we need to hump all night."

"That's right," said Louie.

There was a brief moment of silence.

"Well," said Sanders, "what the fuck are we waiting for?"

"Nothing, Sanders. Everybody get their gear. We move out in ten minutes."

Corporal Foreman's squad resumed hacking and cutting their way through the thick brush. It was normally pitch black, but the trees had thinned out, and a full yellow moon was casting enough light on Louie and his men for them to see a couple feet in front of them.

Louie turned his head around and spoke to Private Williams, who was marching right behind him.

"Hey, Private Williams! You ever hear of a song called, 'There's a Moon out Tonight' by the Capris? It came out around 1958 or so."

"Yes," said Williams. "It was a make-out song, wasn't it?"

"You bet it was."

Louie turned back around and continued plodding through the thicket. After a few minutes, Williams called out to his squad leader, "Why did you ask me that, Corporal?"

Louie turned around again. "You ever go to the sock hops when you were a kid?" he asked.

"Yeah," said Williams. "They were great."

"We had ours at a community center, and they had this really cool deejay. He played the best records—"

"And you remember dancing with a cutie to 'There's a Moon out Tonight'?"

"Yeah, it's that damn moon ... reminds me of stuff I need to forget about right now. Takes you to the wrong place ..."

Louie turned away from Williams and resumed his steady chopping with his machete. Williams was about to mention his own cutie from junior high but remained silent, sensing that reminding Corporal Foreman of beautiful memories right now might not be such a good idea.

As the late-night march wore on, the jungle remained spookily silent except for a chorus of exotic birds making high-pitched, eerie sounds like a dissonant symphony from sirens in Greek mythology. After fifty meters, Dempsey was unable to walk even with one of his fellow Marines holding him up. Finally, the men took turns carrying Dempsey piggyback while another Marine cleared the path in front of them.

As he was tramping through the bush in a kind of self-induced coma, Louie was thinking about all the different ways you could die in Vietnam. Sure, the gooks could wipe you out with rifles, machine guns, grenades, bombs, and mortars, but that was only part of the equation. He was terrified he might piss off a venomous snake every time he took a step. He had been told last week about a Marine who died after being sprayed in the eyes with venom from a king cobra. Louie knew about king cobras, but sprayed in the eyes six feet away? It was a good thing the Marines didn't have to tell the next-of-kin exactly how a Marine died. There were numerous other horror stories of men being eaten alive by tigers or crocodiles or succumbing to poisonous bites from an endless variety of reptiles, scorpions, lizards, and even some types of tree frogs. You could also step on one of the hundreds of land mines or unexploded bombs waiting for your false step in the valleys and farmlands. Men also died from malaria, pneumonia, friendly fire, fragging, eating bad fish, or drowning in bombed-out craters. The ways to die seemed as infinite as the jungle itself. Louie knew a complete waste of humanity when he saw it, and for the life of him, he couldn't understand how the hell these random, stupid deaths had anything to do with containing Communism. But after all, like the poem said, his was not to reason why; his was but to do or die. Trying to reason things out only made you crazier.

After about 350 meters, the jungle thickets became less dense, the brush thinned out, and the trees became smaller. Louie could sense that they were nearing the perimeter of the jungle. Around daybreak, the beaten squad finally reached a clearing of tall grass and masses of matted bamboo stretching over fifty meters. It was tall grass, but it wasn't elephant grass, and Louie was relieved that the men could hack away without getting stinging cuts on their bodies. In the distance, Louie could see what the second lieutenant had told him about. There were several acres of farmland destroyed by giant round craters filled with dirty rain water. In the middle of the craters, he spotted a row of burned-out straw huts and the charred remnants of a stone building. Louie saw a broken cross tilted to its side on top of the building. *Jesus,* he thought, *what the hell is a Christian church doing out here in the middle of nowhere?*

The men worked their sore bodies as hard as they could to clear an area for the helicopter to land. They slowly opened a patch of crumpled, twisted vegetation in the valley floor surrounded by dark green mountains towering above them on all sides. After two hours, Louie told them to put down their machetes and KA-BARs, lie down, close their eyes, and pretend they were on R&R, getting laid in Hawaii. It wasn't much, but this space would have to do. As the men were relaxing,

Louie was lying on his back in the grass, staring into the sky. He sat up, reached in his pocket, and produced a wrinkled, unopened letter. He slit open the envelope with his knife, removed the letter, and began to read:

Dear Louie (number 24, Kiwanis Tigers '58),

I hope this letter finds you safe and out of harm's way, but from what we hear back home you're in some mighty dangerous territory. I also hear that you are already a corporal and moving up the ranks fast! We all knew you had great leadership skills, besides being the best Little League catcher in the world!

I just wanted you to know that I'm always thinking about you and how we made such a fantastic pitcher-catcher combination. I have great memories of being successful on the mound with you behind the plate, calling out the right signals and giving me much needed encouragement when things didn't go so well. I know we were only kids and it was a long time ago, and of course very few people even remember our team or the fabulous All-Star game. But I remember and cherish the great glory days on the field when we were young and innocent and we were all going to be famous Big League players. I wanted to let you know that you may not be famous, but you are in the real Big Leagues, and I know glory on the battlefield is a lot more important than glory on the playing field.

You have probably heard that there are a lot of protests against the war here at home. I was raised as a conscientious objector, and I don't believe that this war, in particular, is worth one American life. But don't believe what you hear about the protestors. The government is trying to demonize the citizens opposed to the war, calling them unpatriotic and un-American for not supporting the troops. Louie, they couldn't be more wrong. All the protesters I have met are very concerned about the loss of life over there, and if anything they are more supportive because they want the war to end right now and have you come home in one piece. I keep hearing the phrase, "Declare victory and leave." I hope they find a way to do this quickly, although I have my doubts. Anyway, brother, I miss you and envy your strength of character, courage, and leadership that make you a special person and a great friend.

Make sure you keep your head down and come home safe. All the guys are asking about you, and everyone is anxious to buy you a bunch of drinks at the Park Tavern—on the house!

Take care, buddy.
As ever, Jackie (number 10, Kiwanis Tigers '58)

Louie carefully folded the letter, put it back in his jacket pocket, lay back down in the grass, and covered his eyes to avoid the blinding sun.

WITHIN AN HOUR, THE SQUAD heard the whirring blades of the chopper in the distance looming over the crest of one of the smaller mountains. A roaring sound came booming through the valley like a rocket ship. The canyon was not very large, but it still blocked some of the transmissions from the PCR-25. Jackson was talking feverishly on the radio, giving the coordinates, tinny voices barking out from the handset. Louie overheard something scratchy that sounded like, "Your best approach is from the south. Zone's secure. Over."

The chopper came in fast, turned, and made its approach, setting down gently. The blades of the chopper lashed the puddles of water beneath it, sending splashes of dirty water over the men. The rear jaws of the chopper opened. Two Marines in the helicopter ran out quickly with a stretcher and placed Dempsey on it, giving the squad an enthusiastic thumbs-up. Two other Marines began throwing supplies out the open door, laughing and trying to make jokes above the din of the swirling blades. Louie's men grabbed the packages, and the tailgate immediately closed. They waved to pilot and crew as the chopper lifted quickly into the air, disappearing within seconds.

Louie tried to gather his men together, but they were laughing, joking, opening packages, and joyfully passing around cans of warm beer. Louie decided to wait a while until the men felt ready to return to their mission trail. Private Sanders wandered over toward the wasted village, carefully walking around several craters, peeking in to see if there were any bodies floating in the water. As he neared the village, he stood in front of the church, turned halfway around, and shouted back to his squad, "Hey, guys, I'm going to church!" Sanders looked up at the cross, dropped his rifle, placed his hands in prayer position, and kneeled down "Please, father, send me down a Thailand babe with big tits and a pile of money!" The other Marines laughed at Sanders, shouting back at him, making fun of him.

Private Rogers screamed, "God doesn't listen to stupid Marines—he keeps those babes for himself!"

Sanders turned to walk into the church, and a bullet from a VC's AK-47 blew a hole in his heart. Sanders looked down at his chest, but before his eyes found the hole, he was dead, falling to the ground with a dreadful thud.

The other Marines quickly grabbed their rifles and scrambled for cover. Louie immediately hollered for everyone to charge toward a nearby three-foot dike built up behind a rice paddy. Several other shots rang out, bullets whizzing by their heads. The frenetic squad all seemed to dive into the muddy dike at the same time, splashing muddy water high into the air. Louie collapsed on his chest at the end of the line, raising his rifle on his shoulder. He was lying next to Private Elms.

"How many do you think there are?" asked Elms.

"I don't know. I could only make out scattered shots of AK-47s coming from three directions—but I know one thing."

"What's that?"

"We can't stay here and let them pick us off one by one. There's no cover for a retreat. We've got to clean them out!"

"Okay, listen up, men!" yelled Louie down the line at the leaders of each fire team. "Fire team two, you take the left flank! Circle around!

Use the craters for cover, but find those motherfuckers! Fire team three! Take the right flank! Keep pushing ahead! I don't think there's too many of them. Don't be heroes! Just one crater at a time. Got it? Team one will head straight in."

Louie gathered his team around him.

"Okay, we're gonna be patient. Just one crater to the next—as fast as we can. Got it?"

The men nodded.

"Okay, follow me!"

Louie lunged out of the dike, heading for a crater about ten meters away. His three fellow Marines followed close behind. The other units moved forward, drawing fire, bullets cracking overhead as the M-16s, on full automatic, answered back with bursts of gunfire before the men leaped into an open wet crater. Louie continued firing rounds into the huts; they were still too far away for grenades. One VC was gunned down by Private Atkins as he tried to move from one bunker to another. Fire team three, dodging bullets all the way, managed to slip behind the enemy in back of the village, quickly opening fire. The VC were now in a crossfire, a firestorm of bullets hissing through the air. In the middle of the chaos, Private Elms, who was still lying beside Louie, yelled over at him, "Look at that!"

Louie looked over to the front of the church and saw a young peasant woman scrambling for cover, a baby wrapped in her arms. She was totally confused, running in one direction, then darting in another, looking desperately for a safe place to hide, caught between two enemies in mortal combat.

"Christ," mumbled Louie.

"Look at that fuckin' idiot!" screamed Elms. "Is that funny, or what?"

Louie looked again and understood what Elms was saying. She did look rather comical, like something you might see in one of those silent films with quick, jerky movements by the actors.

"Yeah," agreed Louie as he aimed his rifle at one of the bunkers. "It's fuckin' hilarious."

"No shit," said Elms.

Elms aimed his rifle at the woman, shot her in the head, and then fired again, splitting the baby in half.

"Well, she's okay now! She's found a home! Right in front of a church!"

The woman and child lay lifeless and bloodied in the street.

Louie smiled broadly. "She sure has. That kid won't be killing any Americans—that's for sure!"

The fire teams quickly closed in and surrounded the snipers. They shot two enemies in one bunker and then three more in another. Two others were gunned down trying to escape into the jungle.

Suddenly everything went quiet.

The men hunched down on their knees, rifles in hand, eyes darting swiftly from one spot in the jungle to another. They listened and watched carefully for any sound or movement, any hint of possible danger in front of them. After a few anxious minutes, Louie signaled for his men to regroup and check out the wounded.

They were lucky. Private Armstrong had suffered a bullet wound to his arm, and PFC Erickson had had a bullet go right through his side. Both would be able to make it back to the mission site. Louie instructed Jackson to radio Bravo One to pick up Sanders. In the aftermath, the Marines were sitting quietly on the broken steps of the church in front of blanket-covered Sanders and the gruesome, exposed dead woman and child.

"How the fuck did that happen?" asked Private Anderson as his arm was being wrapped.

"She obviously got hit by friendly fire, you idiot," said Elms, laughing out loud while swinging a burlap sack of eyeballs back and forth. "Besides, can't you see that AK-47 lying beside her? She was armed and dangerous!" Elms held up the sack for everyone to see. "I got six more today, brothers!"

"Right," said Anderson.

But he wasn't laughing. None of the men were laughing except Elms.

Louie stared at Elms and then looked at the woman and child. "Hey, Elms," commanded Louie. "Shut the fuck up. I'm gonna write your ass up—it's not funny."

"But you—"

"I said shut the fuck up, Private!"

"Yes, Corporal!"

Louie turned away from his unit and gazed down the long, low, yellow valley toward the dark green mountains. He had never felt more alone in his life. And for a few minutes, he was lost. It was one of the few times in his life when he was numb and speechless. He did not know how long he stared into the vacant distance, but finally someone whispered in his ear.

"Corporal, are you all right?"

Louie felt like he was a hundred years old. He turned and glanced up at a kid who looked about fourteen. "Of course, Private," he replied. "Let's pull out."

20

Crozet, Virginia
August 1967

A RCHIE STEELE WAS A LONG way from Palmyra and even farther from a life in the major leagues or being a rock 'n' roll star. He was currently driving a forklift, loading boxes of chicken products for a frozen-food company in Crozet, Virginia. With every crummy dead-end job he had over the years, he swore it was only a temporary setback until he became successful in the music business. His dream of playing second base for the Cleveland Indians had evaporated in high school, where he made the varsity but hit a paltry .245 before losing his starting job to a hot-shot sophomore. He still believed he wouldn't be at the factory for a long time. Soon he would be traveling on the road with his band, singing and playing in front of screaming fans, or recording a great album in a studio.

He could not stand the thought of being a local loser—which, he knew, was how most people thought of him. Lyrics from his favorite rock anthems haunted his days and nights. Lines like, "We gotta get out while we're young, 'cause tramps like us, baby, we were born to run!" were just painful reminders of his situation. He dreaded winding up one of those old farts at Zipper's bar telling boring stories, bitching about how nothing ever changed in this good-for-nothing small town. Archie was keeping his idealism and hopes for the future alive, but his optimism was getting harder to maintain, especially hot, suffocating nights at the Crozet plant. Archie was a dreamer, but no amount of faith in the future could erase the harsh reality of factory work, the mind-numbing boredom of everyday life.

He slid off the forklift, ambling over to the packing area to check the machines. He noticed that one of the machines was only loading half the potpies as they glided down the conveyor belt.

"This machine is screwed up," complained the girl at the packing station, who was wearing a "Die Yuppie Scum" T-shirt.

"Do you know what?" Archie asked.

"What?"

"It's four o'clock in the morning."

"I know. I'm dead tired."

"Yeah, me too. You know what else?"

"What?"

"Everybody in their right mind is sleeping."

"I know. This job bores me to death."

"It's borgeous, all right."

Archie looked at her more closely, noticing she was an attractive, small-framed brunette with hazel eyes that twinkled in the glaring lights shining down on the factory floor. Her hair was pulled back in a ponytail to protect it from getting caught in the machine. For some reason, the girl reminded him of his mother.

Archie switched off the machine, reached into his tool kit, and produced a screwdriver. He thought about his mother again. He wondered where she was. The only thing he knew for sure was that she had run off with an insurance salesman from Philadelphia ten years ago.

"Hey, jerk weed! You with the forklift! Get that goddamn machine over here! You're on company time, remember?" It was the plant foreman screaming in his ear.

"Hey!" cried Archie, emerging from his stupor. "Chill the fuck out, okay? That truck will go out on time."

The foreman turned away, hissing, "Just get it loaded, okay?"

Archie located a loose screw and quickly tightened a lever on the girl's machine. He hopped back on the forklift and drove around to the loading dock.

Sure enough, he concluded, *everybody in their right mind is sleeping.*

After work, Archie was sitting alone in his one-room apartment located on top of a garage next to a funeral home. He was sitting on his battered brown sofa drinking a beer and reading an old copy of Spiderman. He was also sinking lower into the depths of depression, feeling like his whole life was just one long bloody waste of time. The phrase "local loser" kept jamming up his thoughts like a repetitive demonic voice from a broken record. He felt constant low-degree gaseousness burning in his stomach, which he blamed on a steady diet of beer, junk food, and amphetamines. But he knew it was more than that. His body was trying to tell him something—something unpleasant. In fact, he couldn't remember a good, warm feeling; his life was becoming one long, drawn-out hangover. His skin was beginning to look old and withered, corroded with irremovable dirt and worn calluses. He murmured out loud, "I could easily die here."

The room was very dark. He could barely see into the tiny kitchen area, where crumpled boxes of Domino's pizzas nearly reached the ceiling, forming a red and white pyramid. Crushed Budweiser beer cans were piled in the corner, forming a four-foot mound of aluminum disposal.

Archie gazed around the room, drifting into a trance, examining his living conditions. A stack of dirty, food-stained dishes stacked grotesquely on top of one another spilled over into the rusty sink. An opened box of a half-eaten chicken potpie lay rotting on the stove, a grim reminder of his horrific job. *Nice benefit,* he thought. *Five chicken potpies a week.* No wonder his stomach burned. A faded, greasy Pep Boys calendar hung crookedly over the stove, frozen in time on December 1970. He could not detect a speck of sunlight or life in his apartment. Everything around him smelled like something decaying. A paper-thin, bleached-out, yellow window shade covered the only window, eliminating the sun, creating a gray catacomb of vacancy and despair. Layers of dust had settled on the windowsill, flakes of dull brown snow forming a blanket. Billy walked over and ran his finger through the dust, creating a tiny dogsled trail down the middle of the windowsill. He wiped his finger on his shirt.

Smells of abject poverty wafted from every crevice and rat hole. The room was entombed in permanent odors: burnt grease, cat shit left by a mangy stray, stale beer, two day-old Big Macs, the faint stench of Black Flag Roach Killer, dank mildew oozing from musty newspapers. All together, the room smelled like a combination of rotting food and kerosene.

The walls were bare, crumbing gray cinder blocks littered with obscene drawings left by a former tenant. Pencil penises and crayon vaginas. A lone forty-watt bulb dangled over the couch. He had seen cozier jail cells. The water pipes clamored like an army of hammers when the toilet flushed. Everything was dead here. The Milwaukee's Best clock on the wall was long-since broken. There were no curtains, no flowers, no rugs. There was one picture pinned next to the clock. It was a faded photograph of him and Jimmie Harlow as kids in their baseball uniforms, arms wrapped around each other, smiling widely into the camera. He had not heard from Jimmie in a long time but had been told by someone from Jersey that he was having gambling and drug problems out west somewhere.

Archie wondered about the word *minimalist* and whether it applied to him. Somehow he thought the word would not apply to him, although it seemed a good word for his surroundings. *After all,* he thought, *I'd like to see the poor son of a bitch living more minimal than this.* Perhaps only the stiffs next door had him beat on that one.

He knew he was stripped to the bone with little hope for the future. He tried to console himself by thinking about all the other artists and rock stars that paid their dues, living like bums to preserve their freedom to create great music. Dylan claimed at one point he had been making a dollar a day in Greenwich Village. Eric Clapton had lived alone in one room for a year, cultivating his heroin habit. Springsteen came from some dreary factory town just north of Palmyra. All four of the Beatles had lived in a one-room flat in Hamburg for over a year. It may have been some comfort for Archie, but it was a cold comfort at best. In his heart, he knew he was no Dylan or Clapton, but he could not face the terrifying prospect of being a nobody, another loser who never escaped a small town.

He turned away from the window, dragging his body over to the other side of the room. He picked up his acoustic guitar, began strumming a few chords. He sang softly to himself, his voice barely audible:

They say there's one thing about being poor,
You reach a place where you can't go lower.
Well, way, way down is where I dwell,
Come see me knockin' on the gates of hell.

Losing interest, he dropped the guitar and leaned back on the couch. He thought about an old gangster movie he had seen on TV late one night when he was barely conscious. He was halfway paying attention, ready to nod off, when he saw two guys walk into a motel room to gun down this dude and the guy just stared at the killers, didn't even flinch. He just stood up like he was in church and waited for the men to blow him away. They shot him dead and fled the scene. Archie had watched, fascinated by that scene. Why didn't the guy make a move to save himself? Say something? He just stood there like he wanted to die. Archie was convinced that the man had welcomed the bullets. Actually, he thought a lot about that scene. What would it take in your life to make you want to stand in front of death and not give a shit about the outcome? What if two assassins came into his apartment right now?

Suddenly, he heard a rustling sound outside. *Christ,* he thought, *maybe there* are *two guys out to get me.* Archie turned out the light, pulled the shade aside, and peered down at the driveway next door. He spotted a red 1957 Chevy convertible pulling up beside the garage. Moments later, he heard footsteps on the stairs, then a knock on the door. Archie sat quietly on his couch, staring at the picture of him and Jimmie Harlow. He heard another knock. Then another, louder. Then another, even louder. Finally, he heard footsteps descending the stairs followed by the crunching sounds of gravel in the driveway. When he heard the Chevy's engine fire up, he peeked out the window to see the car backing slowly out of the driveway.

21

Haight-Ashbury District
San Francisco, California
September 1967

J ACKIE TRIED TO GET IN touch with Archie a few more times but then
gave up and headed out to California to visit Kurt Cummings. He
made the trip in four days, staying in cheap motels along the way. The
Chevy cruised smoothly down the two-lane highways, and occasionally
Jackie would let the top down, allowing warm southern breezes to blow
in his face and soaking in the exhilarating sense of freedom that only
the open road can provide. He arrived in San Francisco and easily
located the Haight-Ashbury district. As he maneuvered the Chevy down
the street, he felt like he had suddenly been plopped into the middle
of a gypsy music festival with carefree, long-haired flower children
skipping merrily down the street, live acid rock music blasting from
the windows of the massive, ornate Victorian homes, street musicians
playing guitars and saxophones, occasional quarters flipped into their
instrument cases by passers-by. It was true what the song said about
wearing flowers in your hair. Along with flowers, the women sported
brightly colored skirts, blouses, and T-shirts. He spotted one lovely
girl with long, golden-yellow hair traipsing down the street wearing a

tangerine dream maxi shirt, a "Free Your Mind" tie-dyed T-shirt, and a flower power headband.

As he cruised along Ashbury Street, he saw an assortment of improvised kiosks and head shops selling turquoise jewelry; colorful beads and necklaces; peace and love bracelets; original watercolors; home-made pottery and ceramics; drug paraphernalia; and hippie clothes like bright scarves, leather sandals, Mexican ponchos, leather and denim vests, brown suede hats and jackets, and long, gypsy-style skirts. Groups of hippies were hanging out on the large porches smoking weed, dancing like snake charmers, and singing songs with acoustic guitar accompaniment. A shit-eating, stoned-out grin was frozen on everyone's lips as if they were playing in a magic garden, marveling at the bucolic, sensuous beauty of being alive in the sunshine of their life. One guy sitting in a jewelry kiosk wearing a T-shirt with a slice of lemon pie on the front noticed Jackie's car and gave him a big thumbs-up and screamed out, "Nice ride!"

Jackie realized this was the most religious, communal, Aquarian vibe he had ever experienced. Everyone seemed so high and satisfied, as if they didn't have a care in the world—and they probably didn't. He couldn't help but wonder what would happen to them when the real world—the below-the-desk world—invaded their lives and they had to deal with the harsh realities of someday growing up. These were the flower children, a whole community of Peter Pans who valued good highs over good jobs. Jackie understood their independent, bohemian ways. But he wasn't optimistic about their future. Eventually, money, marriage, mortgages, bills, ill health, and just plain adulthood would probably erase the beauty and innocence of this movement. For Jackie, the new Aquarian Age was a brief, glorious moment in the sun before the evil forces of the Combine, the fog machine, Moloch, Big Brother, the Military-Industrial-Complex, and the iron cages of bureaucracy ground them down and kept them stuck in the cogs of the petrified, impersonal wheels of society.

Jackie turned left off Ashbury Street onto Schrader Street and drove down it until he came to number 132. He parked the car in front of one of the many painted ladies Edwardian homes in the district. He walked up the steps and noticed a row of mailboxes on the side of the entrance.

The old, classic homes were being converted into apartments, and he spotted Kurt Cummings's name as the occupant of apartment number 2. He walked up the stairs and knocked on the door. After a moment, Kurt answered with a joint in his hand wearing a Grateful Dead T-shirt, tan shorts, and sandals. As he spoke, a large plume of smoke hit Jackie in the face.

"Jackie Riddick! You've come at last! Come in! Come in! Here! Take a hit!"

Jackie took the joint from Kurt, sucked in a big hit, and then handed it back to him as he entered the apartment. He came into a large living room sparsely furnished with a plain brown sofa, two beanbag chairs, a cloth-covered wingback chair, and a wagon-wheel coffee table.

"Boy, am I glad to see you," cried Kurt. "Guess what?"

"What?" asked Jackie.

"We're going to Acapulco!"

"You mean right now?" asked Jackie.

"Yeah. Right now."

"Why?"

"I have a connection down there—Yancey D."

"Yancey D?"

"Yeah, he's the real deal. We're gonna score some high-grade dynamite Acapulco Gold—in Acapulco! Wait here!"

Suddenly, Kurt bolted into his bedroom, grabbed his money belt, marijuana stash, and a weather-beaten rucksack. He quickly stuffed a few wrinkled clothes, a toothbrush, soap, rolling papers, tarot cards, and a couple paperbacks into the rucksack. He hurriedly returned to the living room, grabbing a six-pack of Budweiser from the refrigerator. "Hey! I know you may be a bit tired from the trip, but I'll do most of the driving. I've got a brand-new car from my old man. Did you see it downstairs?"

"No … what is it?"

"It's a blue Malibu Sport Coup just waiting to cruise south of the border down Mexico way!"

Jackie was slightly stunned. "Uh, are you sure about this? Acapulco is a long way off."

"You bet, Jackie. We're going on the road!"

"What about my car?"

"You drive the Chevy?"

"Yeah."

"We'll park it in my friend's garage. It'll be safe—don't worry."

"You ready?"

"I guess so."

"Well then let's blow this joint."

Jackie parked his car a couple blocks away, and before Jackie could think twice, they were on their way to Mexico. Kurt drove nonstop for two days. They popped pills and dropped a tab of acid until their brains were wired, their bloodshot eyeballs grotesquely shocked open like horror-movie zombies. In the early morning of the third day, the two weary, wasted travelers finally reached the border town of Santa Ursala. They were immediately searched by two surly customs security officers who assumed they were long-haired hippie radical drug dealers, but somehow the border police missed the bag of dope stashed in the wheel of the spare tire.

"What the fuck?" Jackie asked. "Did they think we were going to smuggle dope *into* Mexico?"

Having cleared customs, Kurt and Jackie began the long, arduous journey across the arid, red clay plains, climbing steadily toward the mountainous desert plateaus of Mexico. They drove the same narrow, two-lane road for miles, spotting only a few American cars and a couple rickety farm trucks loaded with produce. The landscape was bleak and barren, a vast world of endless sand, dry brush, and brown scrub that seemed to go on forever. Gradually, they could discern the faint outline of the snow-covered Sierra Madre Oriental Mountains rising in the distance beyond a thin line of live oak.

THEY CAME UPON A CLUSTER of ancient salmon-colored mud-brick houses and ramshackle chicken coops and slowed down to check out the odd assortment of local inhabitants. In the hazy, dust-cloud distance, they noticed a few aged peasant men, their faces hidden beneath wide sombreros and rainbow-colored ponchos, lying in lotus positions in the shade like a roadside collection of large ceramic souvenirs. They also spotted back-bent, sweaty farmers wrestling with tired horses and rusty plows, turning over rows of parched land with matronly señoras yelling out and being ignored by *los niños* kicking a battered soccer ball in a field of dirt and weeds. On a side street leading to a cluster of tiny huts, they caught sight of a lovely, long-haired señorita in a flimsy cotton dress swaying her hips gently back and forth as she carried a pail of water, looking sexy as a movie star swinging her purse down the red carpet. She turned around, glancing seductively at the strange-looking hippie Americans gliding slowly past her in the fancy blue car, checking her out like cops on patrol.

"I think I just fell in love," said Kurt, turning and staring back at the girl and continuing to push the Malibu steadily uphill into the desolate mountains.

After a few aching, thirst-filled hours, they stopped in an isolated adobe café beside the road near the city of San Luis Potosi. Kurt parked the car outside, and the two men walked into the mud-brick hut, their grimy clothes clinging to them, drenched with sweat. The hut was nearly empty. They grabbed a small round table in the middle of the room. Kurt looked over to his left and spotted four teenage girls giggling in a booth, shooting furtive glances their way. One of them hollered over in a high-pitched voice, "Oh, Los Beatles!"

Kurt looked at Jackie. "Do we look like the Beatles?"

"I guess any American dude with long hair qualifies," said Jackie.

From a side kitchen, a craggy-faced old woman with wild, frizzy gray hair came waddling over to take their order.

Kurt looked up, thinking the old woman must have been dipped in vinegar. "*Hola,*" he said. "Uh … *seis tacos y cervezas.*"

Despite Kurt's broken Spanish, the waitress understood the order and left. A few minutes later, the old woman brought their food and drink, offering no sign of a good-natured remark for her foreign customers.

The hungry travelers devoured their tacos, washing them down with several beers in less than an hour. The girls in the booth stared at them the whole time. Kurt wanted to go over and say hello, but Jackie reminded him he couldn't speak Spanish and they still had a long way to go. The surly waitress came back and placed the check on the table.

"How much is it?" asked Kurt.

"A hundred and twelve pesos."

"Wow. How much is that in dollars?"

Jackie said, "It's a little over a dollar."

"You're kidding."

Kurt smiled and then pulled some bills out of his pocket. "I think I'll be real generous and leave a 20 percent tip."

"Why?" asked Jackie. "For the polite service?"

Kurt shrugged. "So she hates Americans. Probably has some good reasons. Let's get out of here."

They got up to leave. Kurt smiled, waving good-bye to the pretty young girls. As they left the café, one of them screamed, *"Via con Dios, Los Beatles!"*

They returned to the Malibu and continued their journey, ascending higher and higher until finally reaching the last great plateau. In the distance, they spotted thick, grassy forests lined with banana trees gleaming in the sun. The blue Malibu choked and struggled in the blistering heat, the temperature gauge hovering dangerously close to red-line alert. After driving steadily upward for four hours, they decided it was time to give the Malibu and themselves a much-needed rest. Kurt pulled the car over to the side of the road, stopping near a grove of mango trees near a salmon-colored mission with a brown wooden cross centered high above its entrance. Three ancient, shoulder-bent sheepherders wearing ankle-length robes and clutching long, carved staffs were herding sheep in a grassy meadow beyond the grove.

"Jesus," said Kurt. "We're in the Old Testament."

"I'd say Jesus was the operative word," said Jackie.

The two men rested their aching, stiff bodies for an hour in the tall grass and then continued on their journey. They also continued smoking joints, dropped another tab of acid, and swallowed Black Beauties like they were a bag of M&Ms. Kurt began to drive like a demon, feverish and in the throes of an intense, burbling, nonstop monologue, imitating Kerouac's soul brother Neal Cassady, reciting passages from *On the Road*. He raved on like a lunatic about how much money they were going to make with the Yancey D connection, how great the acid was— but not as good as Tim Leary's LSD-25—how he missed his pals from Palmyra, and how he thought his mother really didn't love him. On and on he rambled, pushing the drained Malibu deeper and deeper into the infinite, lonely Mexican wilderness.

Jackie remained mostly silent, unable to get a word in. At one point, staring out the car window, surrounded by interminable bleakness, Jackie experienced a Zen-like epiphany: They were sweating like the whores of Indonesia and smelled like escaped convicts tunneling out of a New York City sewer.

ON INTO THE THIRD MEXICAN night the two stoned-out friends pushed the lumbering Malibu, veering westward over the desert, the howling winds and wailing coyotes creating eerie, ghostly sounds in the desolate, ink-black darkness of night. Fueled by speedballs, surviving on borrowed adrenaline from their bodies, Jackie and Kurt, weary as dustbowl refugees, ascended a high desert mound, the Malibu sputtering and coughing desperately until they reached the crest. Then they began the descent, the Malibu cooling off, gliding with ease down the mountain.

Within two hours, Kurt spotted the glittering lights of the famous tourist resort. He practically leaped out the car with excitement, pointing his finger at a red painted sign posted on the side of the road: Welcome to Acapulco.

Kurt wasted no time searching for Yancey D. Reading from a set of directions scratched on notebook paper, Kurt drove to a small cottage on the edge of town, away from the tourists' sites and expensive hotels. Kurt parked the car and knocked on the door. A wiry, stick-figure thirty-something man with a gaunt face, a pointed nose, and a wispy beard opened the door. He was dressed like a Hollywood cowboy in a pair of Wrangler jeans, a buckskin coat with tassels on the sleeves, leather boots, and a wide-brimmed John Wayne hat.

Jackie had no idea how Kurt knew Yancey D. The two men never spoke of how they knew each other or where they had met in the first place. They got right down to business.

"Okay," said Yancey D. "Here's the deal. The dope is in the mountains outside of town, up beyond the Red Zone. You follow this map until you come to a small grass hut with a peace sign carved into a tree next to it. Just yell for Roy when you get there. He'll come out and make the deal. Remember, no guns—only dollars—and no bargaining."

Yancey D handed the map to Kurt. Then he brought out his private stash and a Turkish bong loaded with Acapulco Gold.

ARMED WITH THE MAP, A canteen of water, a few oranges, and a full tank of gas, Jackie and Kurt drove up the Red Zone, which turned out to be the prostitution district. They rode past pretty, scantily-clad senoritas outside tiny houses waving their arms, beckoning them to come and pay them a visit. Kurt leaned out the window, gesturing to the women, screaming, "We'll be back!" as if they understood what he was saying. They followed a rutted dirt road littered with sharp-edged rocks and fallen tree branches up the mountainside, their bodies jostling up and down, like they were riding a bucking bronco. After an hour, they reached the top of a steep precipice, a patch of weedy dirt barren except for a couple huge boulders, a spattering of conifer and oak trees, and a small clustering of greenish-yellow cacti. They saw no animal life except for an ugly green iguana crossing the road in front of them and a lazy rattlesnake sunning himself on a rock. There seemed to be nowhere else to go, but Kurt turned the Malibu to the left, advancing cautiously down a narrow road covered with overhanging brush. Jackie felt like they were entering a dark cave. At the end of the road, they came upon a grass-covered hut and an oak tree with a peace sign carved into its trunk.

"Well, obviously this is the place," said Kurt.

Jackie looked around. "Couldn't be two places like this."

"Hey Roy!" yelled Kurt.

A moment later, a burly, beer-bellied man with no shirt on and smoking a big cigar emerged from the hut. He carried a long-barreled pistol holstered on a leather belt slung around his waist.

"You friends of Yancey D?" he asked.

"Yes," said Kurt.

"Come on in."

Jackie and Kurt got out of the Malibu, stretching their tired, sore muscles. As they entered the hut, Roy motioned them to sit on one of the four beanbag chairs in a dark, shadowy living room. A lone candle flickered near a kitchen area a few yards away.

"How much you want?" asked Roy.

"Well, we have two hundred dollars," said Kurt. "How much will that get us?"

"It's twenty dollars a kilo. So that's ten kilos—according to my math."

"Sounds good to me," said Kurt.

"Stay here," demanded Roy.

Later, Roy came back from the kitchen with ten tightly packed bricks of marijuana. "I don't have a scale. It might be less—it might be more. Who the fuck cares?"

"Not us," replied Kurt.

Kurt gave Roy the money. The two men got up to leave.

"Good luck going back," said Roy. "Don't stop for anybody."

"Is there anybody up here?" Kurt asked.

"Well, just some crazy guerillas. You guys armed?"

"Yancey D told us not to carry any weapons," said Jackie.

"That's a bit strange … but don't worry. If you come across anyone, just keep going. You'll be okay."

The boys returned to the Malibu. Kurt hid the stash under the backseat, and they turned around, heading cautiously back down the mountain.

About halfway down, Kurt suddenly screamed, "Jesus Christ! Fuckin' bandits!"

Jackie peered down the mountain, spotting a band of well-armed, ugly desperados wearing big sombreros, ponchos, and bandoleers of bullets strapped across their chests waiting to rob them.

"Hang on!" cried Kurt, quickly jerking the Malibu off the road, veering sharply into the rocky terrain. The Malibu lurched forward, shaking up and down, banging into rocks and boulders, zigzagging crazily down the mountain away from the banditos charging after them. Jackie and Kurt hung on for their lives. Kurt turned around, saw a hoard of bloodthirsty throat-slitters raising guns in the air, preparing to shoot them. Then crackling sounds of gunfire, bullets whizzing past them.

"I'm shot!" cried Kurt.

Kurt collapsed on the inside door panel. Jackie grabbed the wheel, quickly shoving Kurt aside, steering the car to avoid hitting a boulder. Jackie ducked his head low, feeling the Malibu crashing and banging its way down the rocky terrain. Jackie strained mightily to keep the car from overturning or sailing off a cliff. The banditos kept firing but missed their target. The Malibu slid awkwardly but rapidly down the mountain, moving faster than the outlaws storming after them.

The car miraculously made it to the bottom, skidding to a halt and stalling beside a tiny house in the Red Zone. Jackie reached over and pulled Kurt to his side. He was unconscious, bleeding from his shoulder. Jackie desperately looked around for help. A young girl ran out of a hut screaming words in Spanish that made no sense. The girl quickly helped Jackie drag Kurt into the house. She immediately placed him on a cotton mat on the floor and began to examine and treat his wounds as if she was an expert bullet-wound specialist in a hospital. Jackie managed to find out from her through sign language that Kurt was lucky; the bullet had passed right through him. He also found out her name was Teresa. She put some ointment on the wound and bandaged him up like a professional.

Kurt slept for two days.

Kurt rewarded the Teresa for her amazing medical skills. She also rewarded Kurt in her own special way.

AFTER KURT'S WOUNDS HEALED, JACKIE drove the battered, wrecked Malibu back to the Haight-Ashbury district, exhausted, burned-out, and wired—but glad to be alive. Kurt wound up selling all the Mexican marijuana in four days after breaking it down into smaller units of pounds and lids. Kurt sold one pound to Jerry Garcia, a famous musician who lived next door.

Jerry would tell everyone for the next twenty years that it was the best weed he ever smoked.

PART FIVE

But if you weren't mad, you wouldn't be here.

—the Mad Hatter

22

Brewerytown Section
Philadelphia, Pennsylvania
August 1985

D ONNA ALLENSON WAS SITTING IN a battered, moth-eaten wingback chair in the throes of a bad heroin situation. She was also in a bad mood because one of the wiry ends of a broken spring in the chair was poking her in the ass. Ordinarily, on the nod, she didn't give a flying fuck about that stupid wire, but her grim, junkie misery amplified every incidental irritation in her life. Her face contorted spasmodically as if a mouse was crawling around in her mouth, and her head jerked side to side as she thought, *This little bastard wire is penetrating me like a gigantic hypodermic needle, piercing my ass six inches, seven inches deep! Christ, I'm squirming in my seat like I've been stuck in church too long. Goddamn wire is alive! Stalking me! I'm gonna sit on the floor. Where else? Oops! Too many fleas on floor. Fleas or wire—wire or fleas—fleas on floor—wire in ass—need a blast ...*

Donna desperately needed a fix, but her usual connections had dried up along with her skin, which was beginning to feel desiccated and bleached out, like a parchment scorching in the desert. Flicking a few loose flakes of dry skin off her elbow, she noticed a new gruesome purple abscess on the inside of her left forearm. She frowned, pinching it between her fingers as if it was a pimple, nonchalantly watching green puss squirt from the sore. She wiped the sticky mess on the sleeve of her oversized blue men's dress shirt and then looked, skittery-eyed, at her live-in boyfriend, Byron Manchester, to see if anything had changed in the last two minutes.

Nothing had. Byron was still sitting straight up, leaning to his left in a three-legged brown cloth La-Z-Boy, and fretfully gnawing the rubber end of a pencil. Staring fixedly at the floor, his sagging, heavy-lidded eyes affected a state of near coma. Donna forgot about the wire and focused her attention on Byron, wondering what the hell had happened to him, finding it hard to believe he had once been her dashing Prince Charming. Gazing across the room, the sight of Byron now repulsed her; his gloomy face seemed shrunken by junk-craving agitation to the size of a potato.

Donna and Byron were the only inhabitants of a run-down, dilapidated Philadelphia row house in the North Philly section of Brewerytown. The name was ironic, since the neighborhood had long since yielded its substance abuse identity to crack, cocaine, and heroin. They lived alone, sharing their wretchedness with battalions of fleas, bugs, and frog-sized cockroaches. The couple lived downstairs in three rooms, including a kitchen that was never used except to get a glass of water from the sink to mix the heroin. Without any dope for four days, the V-shaped sands in the hourglass of junk time were sliding down to a few precious grains.

"Did you call Sal?" asked Bryon.

"You asked me that five minutes ago."

"And?"

"Christ, Byron! I told you he doesn't have any fuckin' dope! Nobody in this fuckin' town has any dope! For all I know, the world just ran out of all the fuckin' heroin in the fuckin' world!"

"Okay … chill. What about the Prophet?"

"Oh *great*, Byron. Yeah, call the Prophet. I'm sure the guards at Rahway would let you into his cell to score some Peruvian White."

"He's in jail?"

"Just thirty years."

"Shit. We're screwed."

Donna could feel the snake coiling inside her, hungry for a blast, reminding her every second that he was going to get real nasty. She could feel the early signs of low-grade flu symptoms and knew she was headed for horrific convulsions, a miserable physical and mental meltdown. *Shit, I'm not gonna have a monkey on my back; it's gonna be a fuckin' gorilla. King motherfucking Kong is gonna come pounding down my door any minute. I need a fix!*

She looked at Byron again. He was still agitated Mr. Potato Head, staring at the shredded split ends of a pencil missing a rubber eraser, his face squeezed tight, eyes bulging, lips pursed, eyebrows narrowing to a thin black line. He looked like a hobo who had just lost a dollar in a Coke machine.

Donna knew the odds of Byron doing anything practical like getting a real job, making a meal, or cleaning the apartment were beyond the scope of any known arithmetic calculation. He was useless; but then again, so was she. Isolated, staring at one another, they were like two sick prisoners sharing the same cell. Donna gazed around the living room, trying to find something more stimulating than watching Byron chew up a pencil. The living room was sparsely furnished with Salvation Army rejects, with no pictures, curtains, or flowers to brighten their surroundings. One window built in the center of the front of the house was shut tight despite the oppressive heat. A gray plastic shade was pulled down all the way, with only a few splinters of light penetrating the edges to tell whether it was day or night. Donna oscillated between suffocating from extreme heat and shivering from the cold sweats of withdrawal. At the moment, the room was like an oven. She wanted to smash her head through the window just to get some air.

"Donna."

"What?"

"We're out of cigarettes."

"No shit, Byron. We're out of everything."

"Any big butts in that ashtray?"

"No."

"Maybe it's a good time to quit."

"Byron, it's not a good time to quit anything."

Donna saw him turn on a harsh floor lamp, spotlighting the sharp, austere lines on his face as if he was sculpted in granite, gray and inanimate, a miniature Mt. Rushmore figure.

Then, suddenly, to her amazement, she saw him pull out a dime bag of China Brown from his pants pocket, grab his works, and walk toward her, ready to load her up with a dynamite blast.

Then she blinked.

Fuck. Bryon had not moved. Another stupid junkie hallucination. Right now, she needed a plan. She needed to call her brother Danny. He would know what to do. Danny would keep the snake asleep and King Kong away from her door.

Donna got up from the chair, grabbed her pocketbook, and walked past Byron, who was looking serious and calmly writing in his notebook.

"I'll be back. I'm gonna make a call."

"You got a connection?"

"No, I'm calling my brother."

"He doesn't have any dope."

"He's got as much as you have."

Donna left the house and walked to the corner phone booth that looked like the last structure standing in a war zone. Most of the glass was busted out and shattered, random patches held together by spidery webs of chicken wire. The folding door was rusted shut, so Donna had to squeeze her body through the small opening. The phonebook had long since been ripped out, and the phone itself was a marvel of modern urban art, with crude carvings of nude women, obscenities, and scratchy phone numbers. The phone would have been destroyed a long time ago, but the drug dealers needed it for their business. Donna lifted the receiver, dropped a quarter in the slot, and dialed Danny's number in Palmyra, New Jersey.

Danny's wife, Karen, answered the phone. "Hello."

"Oh hi, Karen. This is Donna. Is Danny home?"

"Sure. Just one minute."

Danny came to the phone.

"Danny, this is Donna—Hey! I need you to come and get me! Byron is beating me up and trying to pimp me out! I need to get out of here *now!*"

Danny sighed, rolled his eyes toward the ceiling. "Where are you? Who's Byron?"

"Byron Manchester! He's my worthless junkie boyfriend! You don't know him?"

"Are you kidding? Tell me again how many boyfriends you've had— besides, the only time you ever call is when you need something."

"That's not true! Look, Danny, I'm in North Philly. You've got to help me! He's dangerous!"

"Christ, Donna, it's one o'clock in the morning. I've got like … a wife … two kids … stuff like that."

"He's crazy! He's got a knife!"

Danny pulled the receiver away from his ear, paused, and stared at the phone. He looked over at Karen, tilted the phone in her direction, and shrugged. "Okay, what's the address?"

"234 Parish Street. Hurry! I'm afraid to go inside, so I'll be waiting on the steps."

"I'll be there within the hour. Don't go inside."

Danny got dressed and apologized to Karen once again for having to interrupt their lives for one of Donna's endless dramas. Karen told him not to worry about her or the boys. "Danny, what would we do for excitement around here if it wasn't for Donna?"

"I guess you're right. It's better than you or me sticking needles in our arms every day."

"Don't worry about us. We'll be all right."

"Yeah, but what about me? What if she drives me crazy?"

"You mean *crazier*."

"Okay, you got a point. If I'm not back in three months, call the police."

DANNY LEFT HIS HOUSE ON Highland Avenue and took the Tecony-Palmyra Bridge across the Delaware River to Parish Street in Philly. As he neared the row house, he spotted Donna on top of the steps screaming at Byron, who was standing in the open doorway.

"You cowardly bastard! Hitting a defenseless woman! I'm getting the hell out of here and never coming back!"

"What the hell are you talking abo—"

"Danny! Thank God! Get me out of here!"

Donna turned and ran for the car, jumping in the front seat as Danny slammed down on the accelerator, racing down the street as if they were bank robbers in a getaway car.

"Are you okay?" asked Danny.

"Thank God you came when you did! He was going to kill me!"

"Really? He didn't look like he was going to kill anybody."

"Don't let that fool you. He beat me plenty of times."

"So, Donna, where we going?"

"Can I stay at your place tonight? Just for one night? I can sleep on the couch. I won't bother anybody."

Danny had known this was coming. If it was up to Donna, she would move in, take over the whole house, and nag him to death about why he was married, had kids, and went to work every day. His lifestyle was unimaginable to her. She considered it slightly more favorable than busting rocks in the hot sun.

"Donna, where are you going to live?"

"Listen, Danny, you need to help me! I need some money real bad! I'm withdrawing, and I need a fix—real bad! You have no idea how sick I am!"

"So this is what it's all about—you scoring dope."

"No, I swear! I'm going on a methadone program tomorrow—but I need a fix tonight!"

"No way, Donna. You're coming to my house. You can make it through the night. I've got some Xanax at my place. I'll get you to a detox center tomorrow morning."

"You don't understand! I'm sick! I need something right now!"

"Sorry, but I'm not driving around these neighborhoods looking for a bag of dope. You'll get us killed."

"Do you have any money?"

"Jesus Christ! No, I do not have any money for your stupid heroin habit. Now just shut the fuck up! You're getting on my nerves."

Donna gave up, leaned back in the seat, not saying anything until they neared Danny's house. Donna made one last effort. "Listen, Danny, I know a guy right around here. He's cool! Just let me see if he's holding, okay?"

"No, Donna. Christ, it's after two in the morning."

"Okay, but you got Xanax, right?"

"Just a couple, but you can have them—then you're going to bed."

IN THE MORNING DANNY CHECKED on Donna, and she was still in her room. He helped Karen get the kids off to school and then left for work at eight o'clock. He returned at five thirty. This time Donna was not in the bedroom. He checked with Karen and the boys. They had not seen her all day. Danny had no idea where she might be, since she had no fixed address or telephone number. He picked up the phone and called Jackie at the cottage.

"Hey, Jackie. Donna's missing again."

"You saw her? Where'd she go this time?"

"She was in Philly with some scumbag. I brought her home last night. I woke up and she was gone. She could be anywhere."

There was silence for a moment. Then Jackie said, "She has no car, no money, no dope, and no job, right?"

"That's about it."

"Pick me up in a half-hour."

"You got an idea?"

"Well, let's narrow it down. She's either in jail, at the hospital, or at the Center, right?"

"I guess that about covers it."

"So let's go to the most obvious."

"Right. See you in a few."

THE CENTER WAS THE SLEAZIEST part of Camden, New Jersey, just across the Delaware River from Philadelphia. No one was sure how it had gotten its name, but these days it was the center of crime, drug dealing, prostitution, X-rated video stores, and every conceivable form of hustling in this netherworld of hookers, dealers, runners, stick-up artists, sneaker dealers, methheads, potheads, pipeheads, and junkies. Danny and Jackie slowly cruised several blocks, gazing at the broken-down row houses; abandoned boarded-up businesses; bullet-proof liquor stores selling lottery tickets; and a minimart run by two bearded Yemeni brothers selling goods from behind bars with a .357 hidden on a shelf nearby. A steady stream of barking doormen dressed in cheap suits and loud ties exhorted them to come in and sample their topless dancers while high-heeled, grease-painted streetwalkers hollered out to the guys, offering the best time of their lives and the promise of never-before-experienced sexual bliss. Fancily dressed pimps in wide-brimmed hats cruised along the avenue, passing Danny and Jackie in sleek, tinted black sedans, searching endlessly for the suckers, the horny, the fiends, the wretched, the easy marks, and the desperate.

They stopped at a red light. Out of nowhere, a brazen hooker ran up to the car wearing cartoonish, clown-inspired makeup and decked out in a black leotard, purple high heels, canary yellow shorts, and a scraggly Dolly Parton wig. She propped her elbows on the car and leaned in toward Jackie, her carnival face taking up the whole passenger-side window. Jackie, staring pie-eyed, jerked back as if he had stepped on a snake.

"Hey, sweeties! You guys looking for a real good time?"

"No," Jackie stammered, "we're … uh … just looking!"

"Come on," she moaned. "Blow job for fifty—and that's a real bargain."

The light changed. Danny quickly jammed the accelerator, sending the prostitute reeling backward, her arms waving frantically as she struggled to keep her balance. Jackie turned around and saw her giving them a murderous look and the finger.

The Center was a huge, chaotic sales event sponsored by a new wave of reckless youth in a great wide-open drug emporium, accompanied by its own unrelenting soundtrack, as hip-hop beats and rap rhythms blasted out of tenement windows 24/7/365. On the sidelines, a few souls remembered a different kind of drug life. They remembered King Heroin. These were the ancient veterans, survivors, and prophets of the inner-city, hanging out, dispensing streetwise knowledge and urban folklore in between sips from their ubiquitous paper-bagged 40's. Even these old school, jaded heroin addicts left over from the jazz culture of the 1950's were disgusted by the over-amped, random violence, and the startling number of women and children slavering up to the crack, crank, heroin and cocaine watering holes.

"Look at them," said Spencer Jones, one of the oldest junkies on the corner watching the scene unfold, "They're all running around like cranked-up spiders on a hot oven." Old friends and fiends on the corner nodded in solemn agreement, acknowledging the wisdom in his words, as they witnessed the neighborhood dissolve before their very eyes.

Other cars and SUVs constantly circled the boulevard loaded with drunken hillbillies and college kids from the suburbs craving the crack, the ready rock, the bomb, the cock, the pussy, the crank, the crystal, the red tops or whatever blast was the flavor of the week. Young black touts, barely out of childhood perched on concrete bus stop benches hawking the latest good time shit screaming, "Five-0!" when the cops came tearing around the corner.

Danny and Jackie slowed for a red light. A skinny black kid rushed up to them sporting a Chicago White Sox baseball cap and a billowing white T-shirt. He banged on Jackie's window. "Hey, guys, whaddaya want? Coke? Pot? Pussy? Crank?"

"Let's get out of this hellhole," said Jackie, rolling down the window a few inches. "No, pal, we're just looking. Thanks anyway."

"You don't want no pussy, man?"

The light changed. Danny gunned the engine and raced down the street.

"It's her element," said Danny.

"Right. Her element."

Donna was fond of saying after she had been settled for a while— sometimes in a safe neighborhood with no crime or drugs—that it was not her element. Then she would pack up and leave for a more degenerate part of town.

THE TWO BROTHERS FINALLY SAW her staggering out of a dive bar on Broadway. She looked haggard, wasted, completely lost, her eyeballs oscillating wildly back and forth.

"Jesus," said Jackie. "She looks like the bride of Frankenstein on meth."

Danny pulled up beside her. "Hey, Donna! Get the fuck in here!"

"Danny? Jackie? What are you guys doing here? Did you bring me anything? I'm dying!"

"No, Donna," said Danny, "we didn't bring you anything. We're taking you to a hospital. Get in."

Donna, totally devoid of any motivation to move in any other direction, slid into the backseat. She had not scored any dope; her face revealed everything—she was the epitome of pure misery, contorting and twisting her face as if she was locked in a colonial pillory. She was sweating profusely, and her once-gorgeous strawberry-blonde hair was a mass of wet gnarls and tangles, partially bleached platinum blonde, strawberry roots exposed, sticking to the sides of her face. She was losing some of her teeth, and her once-sparkling emerald eyes were opaque and foggy, peering out of sunken, hollowed-out black holes. Donna's entire body was shivering, both hands gripping the backseat, knuckles turning white from the lack of blood. Her mouth was nervously twitching as if a mouse was crawling down her throat.

"Guys, I'm really sick."

Danny glared back at her. "I know. That's why we're taking you to a hospital."

They drove her to the only decent hospital they knew in Haddonfield. Following an interminable filing of forms, she was finally admitted, and her brothers left her to the care of the hospital.

A week later, Donna was languishing in the hospital bed, convulsing in the horrific throes of heroin withdrawal. She felt like an army of tiny crabs were crawling under her skin, trying to claw their way out. A bipolar woman with greasy hair and rolls of fat bulging out of her gown was lying in the next bed vacillating between bouts of comatose inaction and relentless, nervous palpitations. In her manic state, she could talk for hours. During one of her interminable blathering sessions, she discovered that Donna had gone out with the legendary Joey Korkinian. The woman was obviously impressed, gushing like a school girl, burning Donna's ears about how utterly cool Joey Korkinian was, and "Did you know he was the absolute prince of South Philly? Oh! Yes! Kid Kory? You know that dynamite superstar playboy knew everybody who was, like, anybody? Hey, the guy even hung out with a famous Italian boxer named Graziamo or Granziato and went to the horse races with Marilyn Monroe's husband, some ballplayer named Joe DeMuchie or something or other …" and on and on.

The woman finally took a breath, glared repulsively at Donna, and rolled over like a sick walrus, mumbling to herself that this psycho

Donna bitch must be full of shit. She refused to believe this lying-ass, ninety-pound wasted junkie puking all over herself actually had dated the great Joey Korkinian. She leaned back toward Donna, eyeing her suspiciously. "You *really* went out with Kid Kory? Definitely the hippest guy ever ... Did you know he was the first one in Philadelphia to wear sandals?"

Donna turned sideways, her back to the woman, staring blankly at the adjacent wall, hoping she would shut the fuck up before Donna put a gun to her head—or her own. She folded her arms over her head, squeezed the pillow into her face, and closed her eyes. In spite of the woman's nonstop twaddle and her own gnawing anguish, Donna floated briefly into a languorous daydream. She was trying to picture in her mind if Joey Korkinian had worn sandals the night they went dancing at the Chez Vous ballroom.

A FEW MONTHS HAD PASSED. Jackie was waiting to see Donna at the Ancora Psychiatric Hospital in Ancora, New Jersey. He was sitting in the dayroom across from a young female patient in her late teens with scraggly brown hair and deep-set dark gray eyes. She was thin and frail, no makeup, wearing a plain cotton brown dress. She was staring at him intently. "Who are you?" she asked.

"I'm Jackie—Donna Allenson's brother. What's your name?"

"Jill."

"Nice to meet you."

"Donna's lucky," said Jill. "If I had a brother, I wish he would be just like you."

Without giving Jackie a chance to respond, Jill got up from her chair and drifted to a large bay window overlooking the expansive grounds of the hospital. She continued observing the activities outside the window, never looking back at Jackie. In a few minutes, Mrs. Santini, the head nurse, emerged from a long corridor, Donna trailing behind her.

"Here she is!" cried Mrs. Santini.

"Oh, hi! How are you?"

"I'm fine," said Mrs. Santini, quickly turning to leave. "Now, you and Donna have a nice visit."

"Thanks."

Danny looked at Donna, but she was frowning, glaring at Mrs. Santini as she walked down the hall.

"That bitch doesn't even know my name. Cunt!"

"Whoa, Donna! Slow down! She's a nice lady!"

"The fuck she is. I told her I wasn't Donna anymore."

"Oh yeah? Who are you?"

"Christ, Jackie, are you getting stupid too? I'm the sad-eyed lady."

"The who?"

"The sad-eyed lady, silly. See, I've got hollow cheeks."

"Sorry, Donna, you lost me. Who's the sad-eyed lady?"

Donna placed her hands on her hips in an exaggerated display of exasperation. "From Bob—the sad-eyed lady of the lowlands!"

"Oh, the song!" exclaimed Jackie. Jackie knew the Dylan song, but it was certainly not one of his popular tunes. He thought it was on the *Blonde on Blonde* album, but he wasn't sure.

"I've got basement clothes and a hollow face, just like in the song. That's me—the sad-eyed lady. See my cheeks?"

Jackie noticed Donna had lost a lot of weight. Her face was thin, and she looked emaciated. He figured she was down to about ninety pounds. "Donna, I really don't think you're a character in a song. You're taking this Dylan thing a bit too far."

"Nonsense. He wrote it with me in mind. It's obvious—and don't call me Donna."

"Are you taking your medication?"

"Yes. It's working fine—and for God's sake, stop patronizing me. You sound like one of these retarded doctors. Now, little bro, look at my eyes."

"What about them?"

"Eyes like smoke, right?"

"Eyes like … green, you mean?"

"Feel my arm."

"Why?"

"Go on, feel it."

"Okay." Jackie reached over and touched Donna's arm.

"Feels like silk, right?"

"Not really. Feels like you could use a meal or two. Don't they feed you around here?"

Donna looked beyond Jackie to Jill, who was still staring fixedly out the window. "The sad-eyed prophet says that no man comes ... That girl Jill tried to off herself with razor blades. Did you see her wrists?"

"No. Is that from the song? It sounds familiar."

"What?"

"That line about a sad-eyed prophet coming."

"Ah, Jackie, you and your ghost-like soul. I just love you. I guess you heard I'm taking Bible classes."

"Not really. How are they going?"

"Great. I mean, why not? I wrote the first four books of the Bible. Man, that was a hassle ... Me and Bob and ... uh, the Kings of Tyrus."

Abruptly, Jackie left Donna and walked directly to the receptionist's desk in the lobby. The lobby was painted the usual pale green color that reminded Jackie of vomit and furnished like a cheap motel with a few mismatched maple chairs and a stained printed loveseat. At first Jackie had trouble spotting the receptionist. She was hidden from view behind a tiny cubicle, sunk way down low as if trying to avoid any contact with visitors or clients. As he peered down, a large, unkempt woman with a big nose and thick, messy black hair glanced up from a *People* magazine. He immediately thought she looked more like a patient than an employee.

"Can I speak to Donna Allenson's doctor?"

"I believe that would be Dr. Swartz."

"Can you page him, please?"

"I'll see what I can do."

The receptionist reached over, picked up a phone, and punched a few buttons. "Is Dr. Swartz still here? Okay. All right. Please tell him someone wants to speak to him in the lobby."

Several minutes passed before a tall, thin man in his midthirties with an angular face, horn-rimmed glasses, and short-cropped black hair came through a door marked Staff Only. He was dressed in a long white lab coat and carrying a clipboard. Jackie thought he looked like a research assistant in a low-budget horror movie.

"Dr. Swartz?" Jackie asked.

"Yes. What can I do for you?"

"You're Donna Allenson's doctor, right?"

"One of them. Who are you?"

"I'm Jackie Riddick, her brother."

"Nice to meet you."

"Can you tell me what's wrong with her?"

"Yes, your sister is manic depressive. She has very broad, erratic mood swings, probably due to drug abuse in the past—but we're not sure. We are still evaluating her."

"Manic depressive?"

"Is something wrong?"

"Well, are you aware that she thinks she wrote parts of the Bible?"

"Yes, she told me that."

"Then it seems to me she's not merely having mood swings, is she? I mean, doesn't that make her psychotic—schizophrenic, out of touch with reality—which is, as far as I know, a lot more serious than up and down mood cycles."

"Yes, well, technically you are right—"

"Well, *technically*, what kind of medication are you giving her?"

"Right now. Lithium and Klonopin."

"I think you better come up with something stronger. She also thinks she's a character in a Bob Dylan song."

"I didn't know that one."

"Maybe it's time you learned."

Jackie turned and walked away from the doctor, returning to Donna, who was standing next to Jill by the window. They were both looking at a skinny man with a wispy goatee dancing by himself inside a gazebo in front of the main building. He was moving gracefully, wearing a top hat, and tapping a wooden cane, performing a refined dance routine.

"It's Fred," noted Jill.

Jackie looked at him. "Is he one of the patients?"

"Oh, he's a lifer," said Jill. "He's been doing that stupid dance for ten years. You would think he would realize Ginger's not coming."

"Ginger?"

"He thinks he's Fred Astaire, and he dances every day, expecting Ginger Rogers to cruise up in a limo and take him away to Hollywood— and they think *I'm* nuts."

"It's kinda cool though, huh?" said Donna. "Maybe I'll go over and dance with him someday. He might like the sad-eyed lady over that bimbo Ginger Rogers."

Jackie nodded. He watched Donna and Jill stare out the window for a few minutes. Jackie was reminded that time in a mental hospital didn't mean very much. Nobody knew what day or month it was, and time was regulated by when the patients ate and went to bed. The days were mind-numbingly boring, routine, and without any significant events. Donna and Jill could have watched Fred for a minute or an hour; it wouldn't have made the slightest difference. They were on their own time, in their own hospital state of mind. Jackie wondered if it was the boredom alone that made them crazy or at least kept them from becoming sane. He decided to get Donna out of this hospital. They were either understaffed or incompetent—or both.

"Donna, I've got to go."

"Oh, Jackie, don't leave! You just got here!"

"No, really—I've got to go. Nice to meet you, Jill."

Jill remained glued to Fred's dancing performance.

"Donna, Listen to me," said Jackie. "I'm going to get you out of here. They're not doing you any good—really."

"Yes, Jackie! Please do that! This place is terrible—and the food sucks!"

"Don't worry. I'll be back soon and take you someplace else. I've got to go now. Take care of yourself. I love you."

Jackie hugged Donna good-bye. He walked out of the dayroom. As he was leaving, he glanced at the receptionist's cubicle and saw nothing but tufts of scraggly black hair sprouting up behind the counter.

Jill turned and looked at Donna. "Gee," she said. "I wish I had a brother like that."

23

Baltimore, Maryland
September 1986

JACKIE HAD NO TROUBLE FINDING Roy Shifflette. He still lived in the same shabby brick row house that Betty had bought more than twenty-five years before. She had felt the safety of her children was more important than any financial gain. Besides, Roy was one of those people that made you feel better just by not being around.

Jackie had been watching Roy's movements—or lack of them—for two days, staking out the house from a rented room across the street. The Chevy Impala was parked around the corner in a public parking lot. Jackie was taking no chances. Roy might become suspicious of a new car in the neighborhood.

As Jackie would soon learn, Roy spent most his time sitting in his tattered, broken easy chair, which had only three legs and was propped up on one side by an empty wooden case of beer. In addition to the beat-up chair, the house held other demolished remnants of Roy's insane rampages, such as a badly dented, leaning refrigerator, pieces of shattered picture frames and shards of glass still lying on the floor. Ripped seat cushions in one wingback chair still exposed coiled, rusted metal springs. An upside-down coffee table with three legs sticking up was leaning against the wall. In his uncontrollable fury, Roy forgot that

304

he didn't have any money to replace the items he destroyed. He had managed to replace the busted TV and had bought a used couch from the Salvation Army.

Now his days were spent watching TV, eating junk food, and drinking cheap beer and whiskey until he passed out. Empty cans of National Bohemian beer, bottles of Wild Turkey, and leftover containers of potato chips, peanuts, Cheez Whiz, and Spam were strewn around the chair, forming Roy's own personal trash dump. When he wasn't passed out, Roy would glare at the TV, cursing the actors in the show, his former bosses at Bethlehem Steel, those fuckin' Yankees everywhere, and especially his wife Betty and her pieces-of-shit kids.

The two decades of Roy's life after we escaped had not been kind to him. Those years were marked with an unfathomable series of drunken acts of stupidity, hare-brained decisions, and random acts of violence, child abuse, and miniature disasters that all added up to a big zero—or maybe less. Roy had long since been fired from his job at Bethlehem Steel for hitting one of his fellow workers in the back of the head with a board when he wasn't looking. Occasionally, he would ride around the city hoping to run into Betty, but he had no idea where she was or how to find her. He was still thinking about all the ways he was going to punish her and the kids for abandoning him in the middle of the night. Roy stayed in the house on Calvert Street despite hating his black neighbors. He fought with them constantly and called them names, and everybody wondered why he didn't move to another neighborhood—a much whiter neighborhood. But Roy took a perverse pleasure in taunting the other residents and somehow maintained the illusion that he was superior to his black neighbors based on the simple fact that he was white and they were not. Roy enjoyed beating up defenseless women and children, and whenever he got the chance, he would grab a local youngster and slap him around and then lie to the child's parents when questioned about the incident.

Roy had not had a full-time job in twenty years. He had gotten by with part-time employment in machine shops, doing odd jobs, and a number of petty thefts, scams, and capers. Betty had paid for the house, so Roy was content to make enough money to keep the lights, heat, and water turned on and continue his supply of TV dinners, booze, and cigarettes.

At night, Roy would cruise along Eastern Avenue, checking out the prostitutes and stopping to get drunk at one of the numerous sleazy shot-and-a-beer bars. When he had a little extra money, Roy loved to hang out at the Block, the notorious home of Baltimore's version of aristocratic French society. The Block had been at one time a fairly respectable, high-class downtown burlesque district. In the old days, the area had exuded a certain kind of gilded-age charm and had been a noted stopover for famous exotic dancers and strippers including Blaze Starr.

The atmosphere in the clubs resembled the high-class bordellos of Europe, complete with large, elegant foyers with crystal chandeliers suspended from the ceilings and walls lined with deep burgundy velvet drapes. An ornate sitting area provided the customers with a visual sampling of the merchandise. Lounging in finely upholstered French love seats, the fancily dressed prostitutes struck refined poses like mechanical dolls caked with enough makeup to last a circus for a year. A house madam would greet the customers at the entrance as if they were respectable businessmen. She was always soft-spoken, impeccably dressed in a long flowing gown, and looked like she could be the lead soprano in an Italian opera. Melodic sounds of cool blues and jazz from artists like Miles Davis, Billie Holiday, and Chet Baker wafted in the air. This show of refinement was designed to create the illusion that this was a classy place instead of what it was—a whorehouse. But those days were gone.

Now the Block was reduced to seedy sex shops selling erotic toys, sadomasochistic leather gear, and gaudy neon strip clubs with big-haired women in florescent bikinis exhorting passers-by to come in and gaze at a parade of big tits and heart-shaped asses snaking seductively around stripper poles. Other forms of entertainment included transvestite musicals, dance performances, and peep shows where—for a price—you could ogle naked women unveiled behind drawn curtains.

Roy spent as much time on the Block as he could, but he rarely had enough money to stay very long. He found himself spending more and more of his nights cruising the gay bars and clubs in the city. Roy hated homosexuals almost as much as black people. But he thought he had discovered an ingenious way to keep himself in booze and cigarette money. He called it "rolling queers for fun and profit, as simple as dialing for dollars." He would pretend he was gay and sucker guys at the bar into meeting him later that night in one of the darkened parking lots of the Inner Harbor. Roy made sure nobody at the bar ever saw him leave with another man, and they always took separate cars. Even though he did not consider himself gay, Roy would allow the man to give him a blowjob before Roy punched him out and took his money.

On the third night, Jackie saw Roy leave the house and followed him to one of the local bars. He sat discreetly in the back for more than an hour, watching Roy chatting up one of the men at the bar. Then Roy made a clumsy attempt to hide the fact that he was leaving the bar to meet the man, a skinny, nervous-looking guy with dark circles under his eyes. They left separately, minutes apart. Jackie stayed in the bar for a couple hours; neither man returned.

On the fourth night, Roy left for another bar. This time Jackie decided to tail him in his car after he left the bar to find out where they made the hookup.

Roy drove down to Pete's Bar in Fells Point, a hipster hangout noted for its ragtag barfly clientele. Pete's was home to an odd assortment of unemployed locals, struggling artists, lost poets, drug addicts, winos, male prostitutes, street-corner philosophers, and half the newspapermen at the *Baltimore Sun*. It was a small bar with a single row of bar stools upholstered in worn prison gray with cotton balls squeezing out the seams like puss from a pimple. A few card tables and folding chairs lined the perimeter of the bar. The bartender, Pete Garrett, was a heavyset ex-Marine with a grizzly gray beard and a Black Sabbath T-shirt. He was decorated with dozens of colorful tattoos, but he said the lettering on his left bicep was his favorite: Eat Shit and Die. Pete said he liked most of his customers, except "that asshole Roy Shifflette."

At the moment, the asshole was talking to a balding, short, fat, sweaty man with a round face and a pink complexion who looked like he had just finished his first tanning session. Jackie thought he was a dead ringer for Porky Pig's father. They had a few drinks together, and after an hour, the pink fellow got up and left the bar, nodding to Roy with shifty eyes like he was a double agent on a secret mission. In a couple minutes Roy left the bar and walked to his discolored brown 1972 Dodge

Coronet. Jackie followed him, sat in his car, and waited for him to pull out of the parking lot. He headed out of Fell's Point straight toward the Inner Harbor. On South Broadway, he made a left on Pratt Street, pulling into the parking lot of the National Aquarium. He drove around to the back of the building and parked next to another car.

Jackie parked the Chevy on Pratt Street, reached for his camera sitting beside him, and walked along the cobbled pathway of Pier 4 directly across from the aquarium. He found a deserted spot behind a wooden billboard advertising Maryland crabs. A misty shroud of fog was rolling in from the harbor. He could barely see the two cars, one of which was Roy's and the other presumably Roy's love connection for the evening. He heard a car door open and close. Seconds later, another car door opened and closed. Jackie figured one of the men had gotten in the other's car. About ten minutes later, he spotted the pink fellow stumbling out of the shadows; he clutched his side before collapsing in the parking lot. Jackie quickly grabbed his camera and got shots of the pink fellow lying on the ground. Roy appeared out of the shadows, running awkwardly from side to side like he was blind drunk, and then grabbed his victim by the shoulders, dragging him toward his car. Jackie kept clicking the camera until the two men were lost in the fog. Jackie knew something had gone wrong. Perhaps Roy had been too drunk to make his assault and the pink fellow had tried to make an escape.

Jackie ran back to the Chevy and waited for Roy to leave. Almost immediately, Roy wheeled his rust-bucket Dodge onto Pratt Street. Jackie continued following him. Roy drove along Pratt Street, made several turns, and then headed straight for the corner of North Fulton and West Fayette. He turned down Fulton and drove a few blocks before stopping beside an empty field adjacent to an abandoned warehouse.

Jackie couldn't imagine what Roy might be doing in the black part of town, parking his car in the middle of nowhere. Turning down a side street, Jackie pulled into the driveway of a boarded-up house. He looked around for signs of life, but everything seemed desolate and silent. He left his car, snuck up behind a dilapidated building, and peeked around the corner. Jackie saw the faint outline of Roy bending down and removing the back license plate from his car; then he turned around and quickly removed the one in front. Then Roy started walking directly toward Jackie with the plates tucked under his arm. Ducking back from the building, Jackie ran and jumped in his car just as Roy turned the corner, passed him on the other side of the street without noticing him. Jackie waited ten minutes and then sped away.

The next afternoon Jackie went into Millie's All-Nite Diner on the corner down the street. He grabbed a copy of the *Baltimore Sun* and sat on a stool next to a burly, toothless construction worker in denim overalls. A short, stumpy lady with stringy gray hair wrapped tightly in a bun plodded down the aisle as if trudging through a pool of molasses. She stood impatiently in front of him, holding a yellow pad while reaching for a pencil sticking out of her hair.

"Whaddayahave?" slurred the waitress.

"Just coffee and a piece of apple pie."

"That's it?"

"Yeah, that's it."

The surly waitress stuck the pencil behind her head, gave Jackie a disgusted look like she had expected him to order the smoked salmon. Then she turned and waddled back to the cook's station.

As he was waiting for his order, Jackie casually glanced at the front page of the paper. Suddenly, his eyes focused on a news story in the lower right-hand corner:

Man Stabbed to Death in Car at Inner Harbor

Baltimore police are investigating the discovery of the body of an unidentified man found slumped in the front seat of a car in the parking lot of the National Aquarium in the Inner Harbor. Aquarium security officer William Dennings discovered the body early this morning when he arrived to work. Investigating officer Sergeant Percy Grimes said the man was stabbed numerous times, and no weapon was found on the scene. So far, the police have no suspects or motive for the killing. Sergeant Grimes is asking anyone with any information about the killing to contact the Baltimore Police Department.

Jackie tried to hide his astonishment by jerking the paper close to his face, startling the construction worker. He carefully read every word. As he was reading, the bad-tempered waitress returned and placed his order on the counter. Jackie quickly withdrew three dollars from his pocket, tossed them on the counter, and rushed out of the diner like he had spotted a spider crawling on top of his pie.

He walked back to his room, planning his next move. Just before he reached the front of his building, a bizarre headline popped into his head: Who Killed Porky Pig's Father?

It was a crazy thought, but Roy Shifflette could have that kind of impact on a person. Jackie decided his first stop would be the A&P Supermarket two blocks down the street.

The next night Jackie found Roy sitting alone in Pete's bar. Roy had arrived after paying an erotic dancer at the Two-Timers' Club fifty dollars for fifteen minutes' worth of insincere conversation and a cheap bottle of watered-down champagne. The bouncers threw him out when he couldn't come up with another fifty dollars.

Roy was nursing a Pabst Blue Ribbon when Jackie sidled up to him at the bar. Roy turned and looked, spotting a man about thirty-five-years old with sandy blond hair and a scruffy reddish beard.

"Mind if I sit down?" Jackie asked.

"Seat's open," said Roy.

Pete came over, and Jackie ordered a Budweiser.

"Hey, I'm Paul. I'm new in town. Just here for a few nights."

"Really ..." muttered Roy. It was neither a question nor an invitation for further conversation.

"You from around here?"

"Yeah—but not originally."

"Oh, really? Where are you from?"

"Clarksburg, West Virginia."

"Hey, great town. I'm from Toledo in Ohio."

"Yeah, I heard of it."

"Look," Jackie said. "I only have a short time. I was wondering if you'd like to go for a ride with me."

Roy couldn't believe his luck. Normally, it took some time and a lot of bullshit to get these fags out of the bar. "Sure—after you pay for these beers. You're buying, right?"

Before he could answer, Pete came back and set a Bud in front of Jackie.

"Oh. Yeah, no problem," said Jackie, tossing Pete a five-dollar bill.

"Listen," said Roy, "we can go after these beers, but we have to go in your car. You got a car, right?"

"Yes, it's parked in the parking lot."

"Well, I'm not meeting you there. I'll be waiting down the corner—in front of Murphy's bar."

"Sounds good to me."

The men polished off their beers and then left separately. Jackie drove down the block and picked up Roy.

"Nice car," said Roy.

"It's a beaut," Jackie said.

"My car's in the shop."

"No problem."

Jackie drove Roy to a secluded area by the Inner Harbor. The streets were almost completely dark; the only light came from shimmering rays reflecting off the water from the ships out in the harbor. Jackie pulled off the road and eased the Chevy into the back lot of a flour company.

He shut off the engine. Roy remained silent. Jackie knew he wanted a quick blowjob and then to grab his money and get the hell out of there.

"Look," said Roy, "can we get this over with? How about sucking my cock?"

"Sure, Roy."

Roy was opening his fly when a look of alarm spread across his face. "Wait a minute! How did you know my name?"

"You weren't that hard to find, Roy—you wife-beating son of a bitch."

"What the—"

The knife was an inch away from Roy's throat before he could finish. "Look at me, motherfucker! You know, without the beard!"

"I don't know you—"

"Look at me! You do know who I am!"

Roy stared into Jackie's murderous eyes. "Oh shit. Fuckin' Jackie."

"Put your hands behind your back." Jackie tied Roy's arms with a piece of thick rope and then propped him up in the passenger seat. "So you remember that little kid you used to kick around like he was your own personal punching bag?"

"What are you going to do?"

Jackie reached back, slugged Roy senseless with his left fist, and then got out of the car and came around to the other side. He opened the door, grabbed Roy's shirt, and hurled a savage left hook to his face. Roy's nose was gushing blood by the time he fell out of the car, landing with a thud on the asphalt. Jackie bound his feet together and gagged him with duct tape. Roy was defenseless, curled in a fetal position, jerking his hands and feet, desperately trying to get free. Jackie could barely hear his muffled screams. It didn't matter. No one was around to hear him anyway. Jackie opened the car door, seized two heavy plastic bags from the backseat, and dragged them over to Roy. Roy's eyes ballooned to the size of fifty-cent pieces. Jackie towered over Roy, feeling the metallic burn of outrage in the back of his throat. Jackie wanted to cut his heart out and throw it in the harbor. Instead, he went to the back of the car, reached into the trunk, and picked up a crowbar. He calmly walked back to Roy, who was writhing on the ground, rolling in the dirt, squirming like a wet dog on his back.

"First of all, Roy, I want to tell you how lucky you are. I want you to know that I really want to plunge this knife into that empty shell of a heart you have. But I am not going to do it. But don't thank me. You can thank a really great man who taught me a valuable lesson a long time ago. You see, Roy, a real man knows about anger—knows when to show it and how much to show it. And—more importantly for you—who to show it to. You're not a real man, so I don't expect you to understand. You're a pathetic, ignorant, coward who beats up women and children. So I'm going to let you live, because sticking a knife into you is not the proper way to channel my feelings of anger. Hey, Roy, I'm sure you'll agree that we need to live in a civilized society. I'll let other people in authority give you the proper punishment. But really now, I don't think the cops are going to think kindly of you stabbing that poor man to death down here the other night. So let me see … what should be the proper way to express my anger?"

With the crowbar still in his hand, Jackie reared back and brutally crushed one of Roy's kneecaps. Oddly enough, it sounded just like the shattering of a baseball bat, but it was really the noise of a nasty cracking of bones echoing clear out to the boats in the harbor. Roy doubled up in agony, rolled over on his stomach, eyes bulging grotesquely out of his head.

"Say, Roy. That felt pretty good." Jackie gazed up at the starlit sky. "Thanks, Mr. Martin, for the advice. What's that, Mr. Martin? You mean it's okay to express my anger even more? Are you sure? Okay. Yes, sir!"

Once more Jackie lifted the crowbar above his head and slammed it down on Roy's other kneecap, sending him spiraling into convulsions of pain. He tossed the crowbar in the trunk. "That should about do it, Roy. I'm finished with you for good. "

Then Jackie bent down and picked up the two plastic bags. He opened them, turned them upside down, and dumped the contents on top of Roy. "Goodnight, Roy. Make sure you finish eating all your peas."

Murder Suspect Found Covered in Peas

In a bizarre twist in the murder investigation of Charles Wainwright, Baltimore resident Roy Shifflette was found this morning bound and gagged in the back lot of Penninton's Flour Company in the Inner Harbor district covered with gallons of canned peas.

Charles Wainwright of Arbutus, Maryland, was stabbed to death last Thursday night in his car behind the National Aquarium. Operating on an anonymous tip, Baltimore police Sergeant Percy Grimes said they were told that Shifflette murdered Wainwright and where he could be found. Shifflette was found lying in the parking lot with his hands and feet bound and tape covering his mouth. He also had two broken kneecaps.

Police said they had received more information that Wainwright was stabbed to death in Wainwright's car and that Shifflette abandoned his bloody car near the corner of N. Fulton and W. Fayette Streets. Sergeant Grimes said the department followed the lead and found a 1972 Dodge Coronet believed to belong to Shifflette. The front seat of the car had numerous blood stains. Police also found numerous photos of Shifflette assaulting Wainwright in the parking lot. In addition, police found a concealed knife in Shifflette's pants, which is believed to be the murder weapon.

Sergeant Grimes was asked if he had any idea who the informant was or why Shifflette was drenched in buckets of peas.

"I have no idea," said Grimes. "You work here long enough and you think you've seen everything, and then something like this comes along. We believe we got our man, and that's the main thing."

24

Trenton, New Jersey
October 1986

JACKIE DROVE THE CHEVY THROUGH the open wrought-iron gates of
the hospital in Trenton, slowly maneuvering the car along a narrow,
tree-lined driveway, and parked in a gravel parking lot beside three
identical brown cars with government license plates. He walked along
the well-worn, cracked cement walkway to the entrance of the historical
red brick hospital. An ornate bronze sign on the front of the building
revealed that the hospital had been built in 1918. The main building
was located in the center of an expansive complex of nearly identical
rectangular boxes joined together by spoke-like corridors with opaque,
glass-covered canopies. Every window in every structure was exactly
the same size, placed in exactly the same location. He wondered how
many times the word *cookie-cutter* had been used to describe the forlorn
monotony of the architecture. Not one window was open despite the
warm spring day. There was a ten-foot chain-link fence surrounding the
grounds; only circular bales of barbed wire rolled on top were needed
to make it look officially like a prison.

Jackie saw a few patients wandering around the grounds dressed
in plain white cotton gowns, slouching aimlessly, obviously with no
place to go. He noticed a discolored, chipped wooden gazebo leaning

awkwardly under a giant Leyland Cypress and wondered why mental hospitals felt it necessary to provide an obligatory gazebo on the front lawn, as if it was a required regulation in the architectural manual. Perhaps the builders did it to provide a place for the patients to relax, or maybe it was just for ornamentation. Jackie thought if he was a patient, he might mistake it for a rocket ready to launch.

As he entered the building, Jackie looked to his left, spotting a group of patients lounging in a dayroom watching television, playing checkers, staring into space, and smoking cigarettes. There were actually two televisions at each end of the room, blaring loudly as if competing with each other to see which one could be more irritating. One of them was currently blasting *The Newlywed Game*. The room exuded as much aesthetic beauty and charm as a waiting room in a government welfare office—drab hospital green. The walls, curtains, ceiling, furniture, rugs—even the patients—all seemed to be painted the same drab color. The hospital was a living testament to an institution's ability to eliminate any possibility of liveliness, spontaneity, or playfulness. He wondered why anyone would pick this particular color. Maybe a government bureaucrat came across a terrific sale in 1910 and bought a century worth of paint.

Jackie continued walking straight ahead toward a pretty young woman in a dark blue dress with long auburn hair wearing bright red lipstick. She was sitting behind a gray metal desk filing her nails, apparently as bored as the patients.

As he approached, she looked up, continuing to file her nails. "Can I help you?"

"Yes, I'm here to see Donna Allenson."

"Please," the young woman responded, "have a seat."

Jackie went over to a nearby brown padded chair and sat down. He saw her reach for a telephone. From this angle he could see about half the dayroom. One of the patients was currently walking backward, arms outstretched, like a zombie trying to retrace his steps.

In a few minutes, a woman in a stiff, starched white uniform entered the lobby from a door marked Private adjacent to the receptionist's desk. She immediately came up to Jackie, walking stiffly as her uniform.

"Yes, may I help you?"

"I'm Jackie Riddick—Donna Allenson's brother."

"I see. I'm Dr. Swanson. Pleased to meet you."

"I'm just here to take Donna out for a short time. It's all been cleared, hasn't it?"

"Yes, of course, Mr. Riddick. There's no problem."

"All right."

"Come with me, please." Dr. Swanson led Jackie through a doorway and down a narrow, half-lit hallway until they arrived at her office. She opened the door, motioning him to enter, then closed the door and disappeared down the hallway. Jackie sat in a deep burgundy leather chair facing her desk. It contained a neat pile of papers, an up-to-date computer, a printer, and two small vases filled with artificial flowers. In back of the desk there was a push-pin corkboard with photographs of what he assumed were her husband, three children, and a black Labrador retriever. Her diplomas from several colleges and universities were hung in precise rows along the sides of the corkboard.

Minutes later, Dr. Swanson returned with Donna trailing behind her, taking small, shuffling steps and looking downcast. Donna trudged into the office and, noticing Jackie, instantly became more animated, her eyes brightening like a car's high beams switched on.

"Jackie!" yelled Donna. "Are we going out?" Donna turned quickly toward Dr. Swanson. "We can go out, can't we?"

"Yes, for a little while."

"Jackie, do you have any cigarettes?"

"Not on me. But we'll get some."

"Come on! Let's get out of here! This place sucks!"

They turned to leave. Dr. Swanson adjusted a picture on her desk that did not need adjusting. "Please return in two hours."

The couple walked down the hallway, through the lobby, and out the front door. Jackie led Donna to the car and opened the door for her.

"Cool car, bro! Can we get cigarettes now?"

"Sure."

"You still smoke?"

"No, I quit. So how's the hospital?"

"It's creepy. They got me on Haldol, but I really need Navane. This one psychiatrist was giving me thirty milligrams a day. Then they cut it back to ten because I was having side effects."

"Like what?"

"I don't know … couldn't think right."

Jackie pulled out of the hospital, heading toward downtown Trenton. "There's a convenience store down the street. We can get you some cigarettes. Is there any place you want to go?"

"Palmyra. Let's go to Palmyra."

"Okay. No problem."

"Can we go by Palmyra Park too?"

"Sure."

Jackie pulled into the convenience store, purchased a pack of Marlboro Lights, and then returned to the car. He got back behind the wheel, started the car, and drove toward Palmyra.

As they traveled along, Donna smoked one cigarette after another, smiling and laughing to herself. One minute she seemed like the happiest person alive; then suddenly she would utter a dark, ominous phrase like "other people are solitary eyes of fire." Jackie stopped at a red light.

"Donna, you think that hospital is helping you?"

"Helping me what?"

"You know—get better …"

"That place couldn't help Bob Dylan sing a folk song."

Jackie nodded. "It doesn't matter. Nobody listens to folk songs anymore. Hey, Danny is coming up next week! He's going to take you out of there!"

"To where?"

"He added an apartment to that mansion of his. He wants you to live with him and Karen and the boys."

"Really? He would do that for me?"

"What can I say? The guy's a saint. Anyway, these hospitals aren't working. They are the disease for which they pretend to be the cure."

"You can say that again."

Jackie continued driving south, Donna apparently content to enjoy the ride and chain-smoke cigarettes. He heard occasional murmurs of conversation and assumed she was talking to Bob or somebody else in her own world.

After half an hour, he made a left turn on Route 130 and drove down Cinnaminson Avenue in Palmyra. Donna seemed oblivious, mumbling incoherently while making awkward hand gestures in the air. They arrived at Morgan Cemetery and Jackie turned right on a gravelly, unpaved road that curved snake-like around the grounds. He drove about fifty yards and then stopped the car. Donna suddenly sprang to life. She looked around, confused, like she had just woken up.

"Are we in a cemetery, Jackie? I hate cemeteries!"

"It's okay, Donna. I'll only be a minute. You stay here." He opened the car door.

"Wait!"

"What?"

"Are you going to see that girl?"

"What girl?"

"You know—the one who died on that motorcycle."

"You mean Ginger?"

"Yes! That's her name! Ginger! Are you going to visit her grave?"

"No, I'm going to visit someone else. Ginger is not buried here. She wasn't from around here."

"But you loved her, didn't you? You were going to get married, and then she was riding that motorcycle in the desert, and—is that right?"

"She wasn't in the desert, Donna. She was in Pennsylvania. She hit an oil slick in the middle of a curve. I probably would have married her. I loved her very much. I didn't think you would remember her. At the time, you were—"

"Of course, Jackie! How could I forget? She was short and cute and had blonde hair and always had a picture of a cocker spaniel on her shirt! And she didn't eat meat!"

"Donna, you amaze me. Sometimes, I think you remember more things than I do."

"I only remember what I want to remember, Jackie. It's the only way ..."

"I'll be right back, okay?"

"Sure, Jackie."

He got out of the car and walked down a bumpy cobblestone path, passing several large gray stone crypts and a few smaller granite monuments. The cemetery was deserted as he walked over a dry patch of unmowed grass before arriving at three identical, medium-sized headstones. The one on the right bore the name Josh Roosevelt Martin; the one in the middle was inscribed with the name Helen Louise Martin. He looked down at the one on the far left. It read:

Osa Gerome Martin
December 12, 1913–March 4, 1977
Rest in Peace

Osa had lived in North Carolina but wanted to be buried next to his wife and son. Jackie bowed his head in silent prayer and stood beside the grave for a few minutes. Then he pretended to pick up an imaginary baseball bat, taking a few practice swings before stepping into the batter's box. He looked straight ahead, keenly staring down the phantom pitcher. The pitcher wound up and delivered the pitch. Jackie saw it coming all the way, took a mighty swing, and blasted the ball deep into the woods beyond the cemetery.

"Hey, Coach," he murmured softly. "Maybe that one cleared the duck pond." Forcing a thin smile, Jackie glanced at the three headstones one more time and walked slowly back to the car. When he got there, Donna was laughing at something, but she stopped when she saw tears in his eyes.

"Jackie, are you okay? Did you visit somebody you knew?"

"Yes, my old coach, his wife and little boy."

"They're all gone?"

"His wife and son were killed in a car accident a long time ago. My coach died of cancer a few years ago"

"I'm sorry. He was the one who coached you in the big game, right?"

"Yes, but he moved away. I never saw him again."

"Why not?"

Jackie gazed back at the gravesite, his eyes still watering. "I don't know, Donna. I just don't know."

Donna stared into the woods. Jackie turned and faced her, realizing she was absorbed in something because her head always tilted a funny way when she was deep in thought.

"Donna? Are you okay?"

"Sure, Jackie. But I was just thinking ..."

"About what?"

"About that girl."

"Ginger?"

"Yes, Ginger."

"What about her?"

"You wrote poems for her, didn't you?"

"Yes, but that was a long time ago—"

"You wrote one for her, didn't you?"

"What do you mean?"

"After she died. You wrote a poem about her, didn't you?"

He was amazed at Donna's recollections of the most random things. She had no idea what her grandchildren looked like or even how many she had, but she knew that he would have written a poem about a girl he knew more than ten years before.

"Yes, Donna, I may have written a poem about her."

"Show it to me."

"What?"

"Come on, Jackie. Who do you think you're fooling? I know you carry it with you."

He shook his head. "Donna, you're something else. Okay, I confess. I do have it with me."

"I want to hear it."

"Donna, please ..."

"Jackie, this is important! I want to hear it. Please!"

"Okay, but I'm not going to read it."

"You don't have to! Just let me read it!"

Jackie dug into his back pocket and grabbed his wallet. He opened it, squeezing out a folded piece of paper buried inside a thin slit in the leather. He unfolded the paper, revealing a handwritten poem on the back of a flyer advertising a special on pizza at the Park Tavern in Palmyra. "All right, Miss Persistent, here you go."

Donna took the flyer, glanced at the back, but didn't say anything. She began to read:

In Gingerlude
Pinballs, pool halls, dodging killer dog,
tables turned, tempers flared.
Was it tequila pig or mockingbird?
But then you laughed like springtime in Big Sur.
Comin' here 'round midnight
like the birth of cool.
Whispering in the dark ...
Let's make love
like stoned bohemians
in high red mountains ...
'neath a pale pink moon.
Gimme a ticket to ride
In raging blood calamity machines,
stick-shifting, sweeping, two-lane blacktops.
The slickness black of oil twisting wire wheels—
crashing into walls—
crushing into parts unknown—
An eternity passed me by.
I wanted to pack my aching heart with gunpowder
and blow it up
when astral tears
fell
from dead blue eyes.

Donna dropped the piece of paper in her lap. "I guess you loved her very much."

"Yes."

"Can we go to Palmyra Park now? You know, Jackie, cemeteries really give me the creeps."

"Sure thing. Next stop on Donna's grand tour—Palmyra, New Jersey!"

Fifteen minutes later, Jackie pulled into the park, stopping at the basketball courts. "How's this?" he asked.

"Let's go up to the Little League field."

"Okay."

Jackie drove up the street and parked next to the field. It had not changed very much in all these years.

"I know where we are," said Donna.

"Where are we?"

"This is where you played the game."

"Do you remember?"

"Of course, silly. It was the Fourth of July."

"Yes, it was."

"Tell me the story, Jackie."

"Donna, you've heard that story a hundred times."

"I know! Tell it again, Jackie! Tell me again! It was the Fourth of July!"

"I don't know ..."

"Come on! It was the Fourth of July!"

"Donna, really ..."

"Jackie, please! It was the Fourth of July! The sun was shining down ... like on a lake of precious stones! Vera Lincoln was in the stands!"

"Okay, but this is the last time."

"Sure, Jackie."

Donna smiled, leaned back in the seat, and closed her eyes. Jackie glanced at her, fighting back tears; he felt so sorry for her. Sobbing softly, he wiped his eyes with his sleeve and was about to begin when Donna interrupted him.

"You know, Jackie, my life hasn't been so great either."

He looked at her again. Her eyes were still closed. Donna thought he was crying for himself. Then he realized she was right. He wanted desperately not to feel sorry for himself, but at that moment he couldn't help it. He was crying because Donna had mentioned Vera Lincoln, and it had created a rush of long-submerged memories. His thoughts flashed back to a small frame house on Front Street where a young baseball player and a great baseball coach held fireside chats to help a confused twelve-year-old kid learn a few truths about life. Jackie drifted further back, to the very beginning: his father lying in a casket in their living room when he was four years old. He knew what everybody knows: you can't go home again and find lost romance or regain the innocence of youth. He wondered why his memories of Palmyra were so deeply embedded in his consciousness, still so much a part of him. Maybe it was magic. Maybe it was the enchantment of unspoiled youth, a sparkling world of sweet victories, glory days on the field, breathtaking music, and the mystery of a radiant, luminous beauty.

Magic and loss. A strange combination, but he felt his life so far has been haunted by these two experiences, which seem so different and yet inextricably interwoven into the web of his personal biography. One is surreal, loaded with mystery and illusion; the other is much too real, filled with pain and regret. And now, gazing out at the baseball field, pain and regret were weighing upon him like the ghosts of his dead ancestors.

Donna was the lucky one, living in her own fantasy where she could escape the terrible abuses inflicted upon her. She chose to remember only a few memories, and her favorite one was the day her brother played a perfect game on a perfect day. Donna only preserved memories that reminded her of an unsullied world without abuse, harm, or despair. No one ever cried in her world.

It occurred to Jackie that he was part of a world that composed and decomposed itself in an endless process of rebirth and mortality. And sometimes, in the darkest moments, you can only think about and remember the passing away of it all.

He stopped crying. He reminded himself that self-pity was a truly unforgivable sin. Besides, it was Donna who had suffered all the pain and lost her mind. Once more he glanced over at her. She was still lying back in the seat and appeared to be asleep. He turned the ignition to leave, but Donna shouted, "Jackie, wait! Remember—it was the Fourth of July!"

And so Jackie told Donna the story of the greatest day of his life. Donna, as usual, insisted that he not leave out a single detail. He began, as always, by describing the way the blazing sun looked as if it was shining down on a lake of precious stones and continued all the way to the end of the story when Mike Barnes gave him a warm hug and whispered: "See you in Yankee Stadium, slugger."

When he finished, Donna was smiling. "You played a perfect game on a perfect day."

Jackie looked over at the ballpark, taking one last look at the right field fence where he hit the home run. Then he started the car and drove Donna back to the hospital. He walked her into the lobby, and soon an attendant was taking her to her room. Before she disappeared behind a door, Donna turned, uttering a hard whisper: "Jackie, go find your element!"

Epilogue

J ACKIE WALKED DOWN THE STAIRS of the hospital into the parking lot, slid into the Chevy, started the car, and eased out of the driveway. He felt like he had just left a funeral. It might as well have been. The sister he knew as a kid was gone forever, and she wasn't coming back. That's the thing about mental illness. It's not funny. It's not like somebody being wild and crazy. It steals the person's heart, soul, personality—everything. All that's left is the big empty going to the big nowhere. So he tried to forget. As he drove down the darkening streets, Jackie focused on the pair of cone-shaped headlights flashing down a two-lane blacktop. The steady, monotonous glow of the beams helped calm his nerves. He wondered where the road might lead him, as if he had no choice in the matter. As the miles wore on and the desolation of the night surrounded him, he decided to head out west. Maybe there was still a wild frontier out there for him; maybe he needed a riotous, disorderly place to raise some more hell. Or maybe it was time to settle down and try a well-behaved, disciplined life for a change. He knew that one way or the other he would try to wake from this chronic deadness in the material world and search for any mystic truths that lay beyond it all.

Jackie was driving out of Palmyra for the last time and glanced down at the picture of Holly pasted on the dashboard. As always, Holly's head was tilted to one side, grinning mischievously like the Cheshire cat as if he knew the riddle of the universe, the meaning of it all, or maybe trying to tell him nothing was ever that serious to begin with. He realized his most cherished memories were of a world that had completely vanished. For a long time, Jackie had tried desperately to hold on to the ragged remnants of childhood; then, just as desperately, he had tried to deny it. He had finally discovered he could deny his past, but he couldn't eliminate it. It was part of him whether he liked it or not. And that's what gave his life such a sad, melancholy undertone—the realization that he could not obliterate his youth even though it had disappeared forever.

Then everything in his vision grew thick and uniform as if the car itself was leading him into another dimension. A dense, otherworldly fog rolled in, creating undulating, cool vapors, which, for a moment, made him feel like he was on a phantom ship lost at sea. Outside, he could see occasional gray patches in the murky void formed by the intermittent swishing of the windshield wipers. He looked out and noticed that he was following the line of railroad tracks leading out of town, and then suddenly the tracks dimmed from his view, traces quickly erased by moments past. He reflected on a passage from Kerouac—something about leaving nothing behind yet searching for everything ahead of him as ever on the wide-open road, speeding furiously in the white fire of action, dreaming in the immensity of it all. His pulse quickened at the thought of the possibilities lying ahead in a mysterious, unknown future.

Jackie decided to keep driving until the fog burned away and revealed a new path forward.